The Golden Rose of Valenul

The Dhemon Wars Book 1

Enna Hawthorn

ISBN: 979-8-9886765-0-8

First paperback edition August 2023

Edited by Charlie Knight
Cover art by Sam Enlow
Layout by Nicole Nightshade

Enna Hawthorn
www.ennahawthorn.com
enna.hawthorn@gmail.com

CONTENT WARNING

Please note that this book contains reference to the following themes:

Self harm
Gore, physical violence
Emotional/mental abuse
Explicit scenes
Suicide and suicide attempts
Sexual violence (referenced, not on page)

If you or someone you know is contemplating suicide, please call the **National Suicide Prevention Lifeline** at 1-800-273-TALK (8255) to go online to https://suicidepreve ntionlifeline.org.

If you are a survivor and need assistance or support, please contact the **National Sexual Assault Hotline** at 1-800-656-HOPE (4673) or go online to https://hotline.rain n.org.

Please do not struggle alone, for you are not alone and people care for you. Your friends, family, and I care for you. Reach out. We want to help.

PRONUNCIATION GUIDE

Algorath: AL-gore-ath
Alek Nightingale: AL-ehk NIYT-en-gayl
Anwen: ANN-wen
Ariadne Harlow: arr-ee-AWD-nee HARR-low
Auhla: AW-luh
Azriel Tenebra: AZ-ree-el ten-EH-bruh
Brutis: BROO-tis
Camilla Dodd: cam-ILL-uh dawd
Darien Gard: DARE-ee-en garrd
Dhemon: DEE-mon
Dhomin: DOME-in
Ehrun: AYR-un
Emillie Harlow: EM-ill-ee HARR-low
Gracen Fir: GRAY-sen fer
Izara: ih-ZAR-uh
Kall: cawl
Keon: KEE-on
Keonis: kee-ON-is
Kyra: KEER-uh
Laeton: LAY-ton
Lhev: leev
Loren Gard: LORE-en garrd
Madan Antaire: MAD-en an-TAYR
Markus Harlow: MARK-us HARR-low

Mhorn: morn
Mikhal: mick-AYL
Monsumbra: mawn-SUM-bruh
Petre: PEE-tree
Pietro Niil: pee-EH-troh neel
Princeps: PRIHN-seps
Razer: RAYZ-er
Sephone: SEF-oh-nee
Sora: SORE-uh
Sul Mattson: sool MAT-sun
Thom: tawm
Trev Wintre: trehv WIN-tree
Udlow: UDD-low
Valenul: val-en-OOL
Waer: wayr
Whelan: WEE-len

To the original dragon riders in the Lands of Flame without whom I never would have begun this journey.

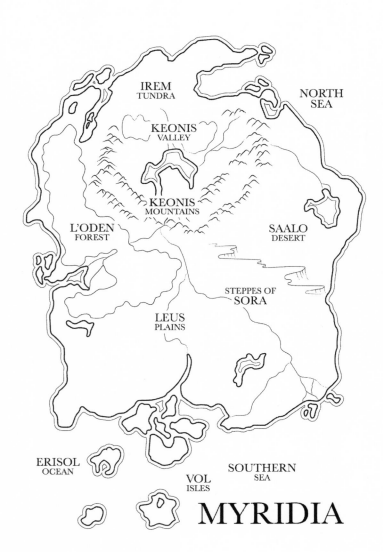

IREM
TUNDRA

NORTH
SEA

KEONIS
VALLEY

KEONIS
MOUNTAINS

L'ODEN
FOREST

SAALO
DESERT

STEPPES OF
SORA

LEUS
PLAINS

ERISOL
OCEAN

SOUTHERN
SEA

VOL
ISLES

MYRIDIA

NORTHERN MYRIDIA

ERISOL
OCEAN

IREM
TUNDRA

NORTH
SEA

NOTTEN
PROVINCE

• NORTHECROSSE

WAER
PROVINCE

THE DHEMON
KEEP

MONSUMBRA

• ARMINGTON

LAKE
CYPHER

EASTWOOD
PROVINCE

LAETON •

EASTERN
PASSAGE

• UDLOW

KEONIS MOUNTAINS

• THE HUB

KEONIS MOUNTAINS

L'ODEN
FOREST

SAALO
DESERT

N

W — E

S

CHAPTER 1

I t had been two years since Ariadne's first debut. Vampires of the aristocracy never debuted twice—to do so was unheard of in their rigid Society.

As if disappearing into the mountains and returning an entirely different person did not make her enough of an anomaly.

Ten...

Ariadne paused at the Temple doors and shut her eyes tight, inhaling deeply.

Run. She needed to put distance between herself and the throng congregating inside those doors. Succumbing to the overwhelming urge, however, would be unacceptable to her father. The highest sitting Councilman, the one who had insisted she return for the courting Season as a debutante, could not bear the shame. Not again.

Nine...

Exhale long and slow. Once upon a time, she had not required such breathing exercises. In fact, when she stood before the High Priestess the first time, she had been an eager participant.

Then the abduction happened.

Eight...

She learned the iniquity of the Society, the truth whispered to her by monsters as they wrote it into her skin and soul. Now, she wanted no part of it. She much preferred the idea of living a life as a spinster on the outskirts of the wicked aristocracy, like the friend who had sewn her a new dress for the Reveal.

Seven...

Like all aristocratic vampire women, however, she had no choice. Despite begging to be left behind, the words had fallen on deaf ears. So she had donned her black dress on her too-thin body, pinned up her midnight curls, and made up her blue eyes with a fine liner.

But to dress up was one thing. To walk the same path as she had two years before as though nothing haunted her now was something entirely different.

Six...

A hand slipped into hers and squeezed gently. Relief rushed through her at the motion. Her younger sister, Emillie, had taken to doing it as a silent sign of camaraderie. Ariadne squeezed back once without opening her eyes.

Five...

She exhaled hard and laid her free hand on the Temple door to steady herself. Voices drifted from the obsidian hall beyond, onlookers preparing to witness who Keon would deem as the Season's most desirable.

As if the god, hidden away in the Underworld, wished to evaluate vampires before he collected their souls. Ridiculous.

Four...

Ariadne opened her eyes, and her sister's pristine face, with her matching freckles and oceanic irises, swam into view. Thin, blue veins stretched up her throat from the neckline of her red gown to frame her face—the mark of a pure-blooded vampire, a Caersan.

Though Emillie's brows pinched with concern, Ariadne offered a pleasant, reassuring smile. It did not fool her sister. It never did.

Three...

She could do it all again. She had to. Another Season of scrutiny and social survival. No number of vampires, no matter how shrewd, could scare off the daughter of the Princeps, Lord Markus Harlow. She had endured worse.

Two...

Another deep inhale, and Ariadne took a wobbly step into the Temple where the other Caersan women stood, awaiting the High Priestess. Most wore red like Emillie, a sign of their eligibility for yet another year. Only a handful wore black like Ariadne, and all their mouths pursed with indignation at the sight of her debuting a second time.

If they wanted to gossip, as Caersans were wont to do, she would give them something to gossip about.

One...

Ariadne Harlow loosed the final breath, twisted her fingers into her skirts, and lifted her head high. This Season would be different. This Season, she had a plan. This Season would be *hers*.

If marriage was her only option, she would pursue the only Caersan man she desired, the one she knew would keep her happy and safe—and she would do so without remorse.

String music drifted up the staircase from the quartet below. It swept around Ariadne with gentle precision, stroking her very soul. For a moment, she reveled in it. Each note plucked at the breath in her lungs and swelled with purpose so when she exhaled in a rush, she swayed from lightheadedness.

From her vantage point, her family's ballroom gleamed. Three massive chandeliers hung from the ceiling of the long room, refracting the flickering candlelight, and sconces glowed high on the cream colored walls. The floor of dark pine could hardly be seen through the dense crowd of Caersan guests for the first ball of the Season. Heavy powder-blue drapes framed the tall windows on either end of the hall while three towering doors stood open along the length of the room, night blooming in the gardens beyond.

Resting a hand on the wood railing, Ariadne took her first descending step. If she kept her eyes forward, she would not see the heads turning her way. She could ignore the world and be happier for it.

At the bottom of the staircase stood her father, the single most powerful vampire in Valenul. Though she did not look at him, she knew he analyzed each wobbling step, as always. And though she silently prayed he would avert his attention, he did no such thing.

She slipped her arm into her father's with a false smile. Not even the presence of her only living parent provided comfort.

"Good evening, Daughter," he said, sweeping her around the edge of the ballroom where guests watched the dancers at its center with polite interest. Those who noticed her appearance whispered as they passed.

She did not reply. Why bother? He did not seek her approval for anything.

Her father's brown hair was swept back from his handsome, chiseled face, haloed by the thin blue veins like lightning across his skin. The fine suit he wore—black trousers and white undershirt layered by a black and gold brocade vest and plain black jacket—mimicked the current fashions amongst

Caersan vampires of the High Society. It had not changed in decades.

Slow to age, slow to change.

What stood out the most, however, were the faintest lines of age creeping in from the corners of his sharp amber eyes. Those eyes had seen nearly a millennia of life, and yet, they now shot from one vampire to the next, calculating each guest as a prospective suitor for his daughter.

Only the best would do, of course. He had made that known many times over, despite her pleas. Political strength meant everything to him and nothing to Ariadne.

Fortunately for him, every important Society vampire stood in their ballroom. The spring equinox celebration, Vertium, was in full swing now that the debutantes had attended the Reveal the night before. The Season lasted until the Autumnal equinox, Noctium, and filled their nights with balls, parties, dinners, and Ariadne's least favorite bit: courting.

"General Loren Gard has asked for you already," her father said in his low, smooth voice. "You are to accept a dance from him, though any other Caersan who requests would be suitable as of right now."

That was what she wanted to hear.

Ariadne eased a polite smile over her lips. "Yes, Father."

Loren Gard, the Valenul General and elder brother of her late fiancé, Darien. She had seen him many times over the last year while he interrogated her for information on the monsters who had kidnapped her. It was not until he understood she had nothing of use for the war efforts that he gave up and spoke to her of his brother instead.

The change in topic had not been much better at first. Darien's funeral included an empty pyre, his body never retrieved from the mountain keep where he had died. As time went on, however, Loren softened, and Ariadne saw the same pleasant aspects she'd loved in his brother in him.

Yet to her dismay, it was not the general who appeared before her first when the dance ended. Many Caersan vampires searching for a wife stepped forward. Sons of Councilmen, wealthy merchants, and landowning lords lined up. One by one, they bowed and, in turn, Ariadne curtsied. They spoke briefly, then signed the dance card dangling from her wrist, filling it with the names of suitors.

Ariadne smiled and prayed to the gods she hid the panic welling in her chest. Some of the men she knew from the last Season she attended, Caersans of the capital city she lived in, Laeton. Others were new faces from the other provinces. Whether they had been too young the last time she danced or had no interest in her until now, she did not know. Nor did she care.

Ariadne did not attend for them. She was there only for the one who made her breath catch.

So when the General finally stepped forward, his silver hair slicked back and tied with a thin, crimson ribbon, Ariadne could not help the flutter that kicked up in her stomach. Loren's perfectly angular jaw, webbed with Caersan blue veins, caught the light just right as he bowed and pressed his lips to her fingers. His sapphire eyes swept to hers, and he smiled, the tips of his fangs flashing while he straightened.

He was the most handsome man Ariadne had ever seen.

"Miss Harlow," he said, his voice as rich as melted chocolate. "The Golden Rose. A delight."

The Golden Rose—Keon's chosen and the High Priestess's most desirable of the Season. To have been overlooked her first time through the Temple just to be chosen after everything she had endured felt like the wizened old vampire's attempt at a mockery.

Though no one knew what had truly transpired, she remained the laughing stock of the Society. Except to Loren. Never to him.

Ariadne curtsied. "General Gard. A pleasure."

Loren turned to her father and the two clasped forearms in greeting as he said, "My Lord Princeps. A fabulous ball to begin the Season, as always. Your generosity and accommodations are unparalleled in the Society."

"My pleasure," her father said. "I am glad you are enjoying yourself."

"I would be honored," Loren said with a glance to Ariadne, "if you would grant me a dance with your beautiful daughter."

Another lurch of her heart. As if her father would deny the most powerful military figure in Valenul. To her delight, he did not hide his smirk. "Of course, though I am afraid she has many names ahead of yours on her card."

The general pulled a pen from a pocket lining the inside of his jacket. "A pity, but I am a patient man for that which is worth the wait."

If she could have melted into the floor at that moment, she would have. A spinster life be damned. With the nerves of the Reveal behind her, she could focus on her quarry for the Season.

And his name was General Loren Gard.

Ariadne extended her hand and the dance card dangling from her wrist. Loren brushed his fingertips along the inside of her arm as he opened the card and jotted down not his name, but his title. A single word—*General*—scrawled across the line in elegant script. Anyone else who signed up to dance with her would now know who the competition was.

As if it were a competition at all.

Loren excused himself with another bow and kiss of her hand, his brilliant eyes never leaving hers. Then he turned and disappeared into the crowd, leaving Ariadne's heart racing. It was a blessing to have someone like him around, particularly in the early days of her return. He had mourned Darien as she had, and together, under the careful supervision of her father, they healed.

"My Lord," a light, familiar voice spoke urgently behind her. Ariadne whipped around, her smile brimming at the sight of her family's personal guard, Madan Antaire. Since he rescued her from the mountain keep, he had become nothing short of the brother she had never had. He flicked a smile and bow in her direction, then turned back to her father. "I increased patrols near the manor as requested."

His shoulder-length dark brown hair framed his Caersan face. Though he worked as a guard, his strong line of pure-blood vampires stood out. His finely crafted features, stunning with his green and gold marbled eyes, spoke almost as loudly as the web of veins on his face.

Although Ariadne considered him beautiful, his professionalism and position outside Society slid him firmly into the *never going to happen* category.

"Very good," her father replied, clasping his forearm. "Your cousin joins us tonight to begin his duties as personal guard, yes? My daughters will each need chaperones."

Chaperones. Chaperones meant visits from suitors, and visits meant entertaining men she did not care for. Between herself and Emillie, who had debuted several years early to deflect attention from Ariadne's absence, her father would be unable to chaperone them both.

Nonetheless, Ariadne resented not knowing of her father's plan for a second guard as she would have cautioned him against it. The very idea of a new guard looking after her made her stomach churn.

"Yes, my Lord," Madan said and turned, gesturing to the far side of the room. "Azriel Tenebra, who overlooked the Caldwell Estate with me."

Through the crowd moved an imposing figure at least a head taller than most men in the room. His long black hair, pulled into a thick knot at the top of his head, put ears with rounded points on display. The thin lines of a Caersan, though faint, ran up his muscular neck. His expressionless face bore the same fine bone structure as his cousin's, and his sharp, mossy green eyes tore through her like razors.

Ariadne shrank back and swallowed hard. Though he was not unattractive, his stony countenance made her uneasy. Any greeting she may have given died on her tongue.

Unlike the guard she'd come to know and love, Azriel did not blend into the ballroom. Instead of trousers and a finely-tailored shirt, he wore thick leather pants and boots, a dark tunic tucked into his waistband, and a massive sword strapped across his back. Most Caersan soldiers and guards, like Loren and Madan, kept their blades at their hip.

"My Lord," Azriel said, voice deep and gravelly. He put a fist above his heart and bent at the waist, the traditional salute of a soldier. "I'm honored to be here."

Even his voice felt wrong. It raked on her ears, and something about it put her on high alert. Compared to Madan's dulcet tones, she could not find something positive about it.

Her mind made up, Ariadne looked for her father's opinion. Perhaps he would deem Madan's cousin too unrefined for the position. She could only hope, for speaking against him would be considered impudent.

"Welcome," her father said without hesitation. He lifted his chin a bit as though to make himself more imperious beside the towering guard. "Mister Antaire has regaled me with tales of the aid you provided him in the past. I assume that means you have been given your assignment."

"Yes, sir."

"Very good." Her father laid a hand on her upper back, and she stiffened, shifting out from under his touch. "This is my elder daughter, Miss Ariadne Harlow."

Azriel swung his pale gaze to her. For a long moment, it tugged at her in the most disconcerting fashion. It took all her self control not to squirm away. After a beat, he bowed to her and said, "Miss Harlow."

"Father!" A bell-like voice shot through the crowd behind them just before Emillie wove through, her brunette hair piled high on her head. The pale blue dress she wore swept out behind her as she reeled to a halt. Flushed freckled cheeks grew more rosy at the sight of them all, her aqua eyes widening as they swung from Madan to Azriel. "Pardon my tardiness."

Relief tangled with discomfort as Ariadne shifted aside to let her sister through.

"Daughter," their father said and turned to urge her forward. "May I introduce the newest addition to your guard, Azriel Tenebra. Mister Tenebra, this is my younger daughter, Miss Emillie Harlow."

Emillie curtsied as Azriel repeated his bow and greeting to her. The tension only thickened when Madan laid a hand on his cousin's shoulder and gave him a stiff nod. A silent command. Azriel inclined his head to the Princeps, then again to the sisters, his gaze tripping over Ariadne's face. Cold dripped down her spine. His mouth twitched, and then he was gone, weaving through the ballroom to the far corner.

"You will ensure he upholds my expectations at all times," her father said to Madan.

The guard nodded. "He's a bit rough around the edges, but I assure you, a finer swordsman you won't find."

"Very good." His most well-liked phrase of the evening. "I trust you, Mister Antaire."

"Thank you, my Lord," Madan said with a final bow. "Enjoy your evening."

With that, he was gone, following Azriel's wake and leaving Ariadne feeling exposed.

"Now." Her father turned to Emillie, his lips forming a thin line. "You have yet to fill out your dance card."

"Apologies," Emillie said with a sidelong glance at Ariadne before refocusing on him.

He turned to Ariadne. "You should find your first dance." Then to Emillie, he said, "Come."

Her sister cast her a pleading look behind their father's back. Ariadne shot back a pained smile and motioned for her to follow. If she did not dance with anyone at their own ball, their father would have a fit.

Alone, Ariadne turned toward the dance floor. Caersan vampires twirled and twisted in a wild display of colors. Dresses flared and jackets whipped out on wickedly fast turns, reducing them all into blurs of movement.

She had never been an elegant dancer. Her awkward footing always put her father to shame, and she depended on her partners to elevate her lackluster skills. Darien had done just that during their courting. He had never once let her trip or make a fool of herself. The suitors on her dance card, however, would not be so gracious.

Such as Lord Pax Tetterington. The first name on her list.

Ariadne spotted the lord on the far side of the dance floor, his tuft of red hair sprinkled with white. The vampire had seen nearly two thousand years. His first wife had died in childbirth along with their babe almost six centuries ago. Now, he searched for the next bride after a string of mistresses left him satiated and ready to sire an heir.

And she would not be that broodmare.

Thankfully, a single dance with a suitor did not promise engagement. She would endure the turn about the dance floor, then avoid him for the rest of the evening.

Pax raised his glass to her from across the room before depositing it on a passing servant's tray. When the song came to an end and the dancers departed, the next set stepped forward with bows and curtsies. Ariadne followed suit, facing off with the Caersan Lord.

"You look exquisite," Pax crooned, sweeping her into the first steps of the waltz. His centuries of experience at balls had made him an excellent dancer, though rather than preventing her from tripping over her own feet, he dragged her through the motions. At least her dress's length hid her stumbling.

"You are too kind, Lord Tetterington," Ariadne replied as they spun into the next set of steps. Diplomatic as ever. "I hope you are enjoying your Vertium."

He smirked down at her, the tips of his fangs flashing. "Quite. And yourself?"

"I chose lavender this year," she said, referring to the seeds Caersan women planted on the Spring Equinox. Each plant had different meanings and accompanied certain desired outcomes.

Pax raised a brow. "Lavender. A unique choice for the Golden Rose."

She forced out a giggle. "I sewed the seeds prior to the Reveal."

"Ah, I see," he said, then twirled her at the song's crescendo. "Purity is an excellent virtue nonetheless."

Ariadne's stomach soured. She smiled up at him, praying to Keon she had obscured her discomfort behind a mask of pleasantries.

Flashes of rough, blue hands pinning her wrists to the floor and the scent of dirt and sweat were pushed to the forefront of her mind. She swallowed hard, shoving the memory away. The gods knew that of all she had endured at the hands of those beasts, that had been the worst of them all. Purity had not been the meaning she intended.

Serenity, however, seemed to escape her as well.

"Indeed it is," she said quietly after ensuring that opening her mouth would not result in spewing vomit. "I look forward to finding a partner with similar interests."

The lord quietened after the subtle jab. Good. He was far from pure, nor would he wish to be seen in any other light. Too often, he had loudly announced his latest exploits at dinner tables, much to the delight of the men.

When the dance ended, Ariadne curtsied, then made her exit. She needed air but did not make it far before the next name on her list appeared before her, his hooded onyx eyes gleaming with wicked interest. She could not recall seeing the Governor of the Waer Province to the west in the throng of vampires she had greeted, but his name remained a black mark on her wrist.

"Ariadne," the Caersan said, bowing at the waist and planting a firm kiss on her fingers. His black hair gleamed in the candlelight.

"Lord Governor Nightingale," Ariadne replied, plunging into a curtsy and pulling her hand away far too quickly. His eyes flashed. "I am honored."

The governor simpered. "Now...after all we have been through, should you not call me Alek?"

"My Lord," she said as he steered her back to the dance floor. The quartet started up the next song. "It would be impudent of me to speak with such familiarity."

Alek pulled her closer than was proper and said in his low, dulcet tones, "Would you say we are not on familiar terms?"

Ariadne avoided his searching, greedy gaze and replied, "No, my Lord, I would not."

Sure, she knew Alek well and had practically grown up with the vampire. They had played together as children, kept one another's secrets, and teased each other relentlessly. He taught her to pick locks, ride a horse astride, and run almost silently through the woods. He had even been the first vampire she had kissed in secret.

Then he made the transition from boy to man and left her behind to govern the province bequeathed to him by his late father. Since then, and in the eyes of the Society, they could never again be friends. It would be seen as improper and suggestive to say the least.

"A pity," he murmured in her ear and stepped his hips against hers, "for I truly believed us to be closer than that."

"My Lord," she said, voice warbling as the pressure of his body against her sent her mind reeling into the past, "you would do well to remember who and where you are. We are not those children anymore."

He shifted away and spun her out, then back into his arms. "You are quite different from what I remember, *Miss Harlow*."

True. During her first Season, she had been reckless. If it were not for Darien's interest, she would have ended up like her best friend, Camilla. Though she loved her friend dearly, Camilla was known for her risque behavior, and Ariadne had been on the same path—with Alek, nonetheless—until Darien arrived.

"Much has changed," she said with as strong a tone as she could muster.

Alek hummed in response, eyeing her with his oily gaze. The rumors that swirled around him over recent years were even less savory than Pax Tetterington—yet another Caersan she did not care to match with and would be working to distance herself from. Any fondness she had once held for him dispersed at the thought of what rumors claimed he did to his less-powerful Rusan servants.

"All I ask," he said after several silent turns on the dance floor during which Ariadne avoided his gaze, "is that you remember our time together as you entertain suitors in the weeks to come."

She curled the corners of her lips and batted her lashes in a mockery of who she'd once been. "How could I forget?"

The song faded and put an end to her misery. Alek bowed, brushing his lips over her knuckles before slipping into the crowd.

This time, Ariadne followed suit, foregoing the dance card dangling from her wrist. She looked forward to only one other dance for the evening, and he would not expect it to happen yet. If she made herself scarce for a while, she could avoid any more suitors she did not care for.

As she wove through the throng of guests, eyes swung her way, and whispers followed. Discomfort in her own home was the new normal for her, it would seem.

"The Golden Rose? Her?"

"She disappeared last year and her fiancé died. Does that not sound suspicious?"

"Her father paid off the High Priestess."

"She will kill the next one, guaranteed."

"She stopped speaking with everyone out of nowhere."

Ariadne's cheeks warmed. No one knew what had happened to her last year. Her father and Loren kept it secret to preserve her reputation, but the damage was done. She blamed herself for not socializing as she once did, even if keeping to her close knit friends kept her content.

Last year's Season had been a nightmare, mere weeks after Darien's death and her rescue by Madan. Her vacancy pushed Emillie into the spotlight years earlier than planned as their father scrambled to hide her absence. Emillie's debut had been his smokescreen, and it had failed.

Air. She needed air. The entire stifling ballroom seemed to press in on her without someone she could depend on. If she could find Emillie or one of her friends, she may just be able to make it through the event.

She slipped away from the crowd to where other women milled about the sitting room. In the center of it all sat Camilla, her pale blonde hair cascading down the low-cut back of her emerald dress. She spoke animatedly with her hands and a big smile on her beautiful face. She laid a hand on another Caersan woman's inner thigh, gripping lightly. The object of her affections leaned into the touch, eyes sparkling.

"Ari!" Camilla called and motioned for her to join them. Her dark, russet eyes glittered like gems as Ariadne approached. "How are you doing, doll?"

Sitting on the far side of Camilla from the woman she still held, Ariadne kept her back straight and twisted her hands in her lap. She chewed her lower lip and tried to focus on anything but the pockets of Caersan forming to speak in hushed tones. The soft giggles and eye rolls cut deeper than she cared to admit, and she suddenly regretted leaving her room entirely.

"It has been an interesting night."

"Have you danced?"

"Twice."

Camilla's gaze flared. "With who?"

"Lord Tetterington and Lord Governor Nightingale." The very thought of either vampire so close made her skin crawl.

"Intriguing," Camilla murmured and turned to her companion to whisper something in her ear. The Caersan blushed, nodded, and slid from the couch and out of the room. Camilla returned her attention to Ariadne and stood, holding out a hand. "Let us take a turn about the room, doll, and speak plainly since others believe it acceptable to whisper behind their hands."

The room quietened, the other guests snapping their lips closed at Camilla's sharp words. Several slipped out the door, casting wicked glares over their shoulders.

In their wake, a weight lifted from Ariadne. She had always enjoyed Camilla's unabashed approach to any situation. In that moment, she was especially thankful for her friend's directness.

She stood and looped her arm through Camilla's.

"Now, doll," she said, louder than necessary as they moved around the sitting room so those who remained could hear them, "who else do you have on your dance card?"

Ariadne raised the wrist bearing the small, folded card and waved it about. "No one else of note, except..."

"Except?" Camilla lifted an elegant brow. "And who is the Caersan who caught your eye?"

She cast her friend a meaningful look as if to say, *You know exactly who*. Nonetheless, Camilla watched her with interest. This was a purposeful tactic to expose her intentions to others. Those remaining in the room listened closely.

"General Gard." Ariadne tried to ignore the collective intake of breath and remain focused on the woman leading her around the back of the couch where they began.

Camilla, satisfied by this answer, asked, "And do you believe he shares your interest?"

"I do not like to speculate."

"Doll," she said, exasperated. "That is precisely what we are here to do."

A long moment passed in which the other women pretended to engage in conversation while turning an ear toward them to listen. No doubt Camilla wanted each of them to spread the word that Ariadne Harlow was sought after by the highest-ranking military officer—the brother of her late fiancé, nonetheless. The position, second only to the Princeps, put Loren in the running to replace her father when he retired.

"I believe he does," Ariadne admitted. At least she hoped he did. Of all the Caersan, the general understood her best. Their shared loss and his care after she had been rescued from the mountains highlighted their connection.

Camilla patted her hand and stopped at the door. "Then why not find him now and dance?"

No Caersan vampire appealed to Loren Gard except Ariadne Harlow. He had danced with the beauties of the Vertium ball, her sister included, and found each of them wanting. Their vapid personalities and incessant giggling irked him.

He stood on the outskirts of the ballroom, scanning each dancer's face for the Princeps's elder daughter, yet could not find her after Alek Nightingale. The Lord Governor of Waer was, perhaps, his biggest rival in the competition for her affections. Their long-standing history provided a foundation of trust and commonalities. The lord's dark exploits, while only rumored, may not have been enough to break the two apart.

Loren, however, planned to do just that.

So when the quartet let the last note of the song die and everyone bowed at the end of the dance, he set his glass of wine on the nearest surface and set off on a mission. He had worked too hard over the last year to build a connection with Ariadne to let it go to waste. Several Caersan women curtsied as he swept by, hoping he'd take notice of them, but he kept his focus ahead, ignoring the distractions around him.

And there she was, slipping out of the sitting room with Camilla Dodd on her heels. A light sparked in Ariadne's eyes when their gazes connected, and something primal curled in his chest. He would have her, and no one could stop him.

"General Gard." Her voice, like an angel's, washed through him, stoking the possessiveness within him. She curtsied low.

"Miss Harlow." He swept into a bow and kissed her fingertips. "May I have the next dance?"

Ariadne seemed to glow at the question, and Camilla knocked into her with a shoulder. Her cheeks flushed, and those perfect lips parted. What he would give to feel them caressing his body.

"It would be my honor," she said and took his offered arm. Behind her, Camilla smirked and winked at him, then turned away. On a typical night, he would not approve of Ariadne consorting with a woman like Camilla Dodd, but tonight, he would be grateful for the brazen influence. Anything to put him in better standing.

He led her to the center of the ballroom as the strings began their next song. He bowed and she curtsied, then he swept her into his arms.

The quadrille pulled her away from him almost instantly, allowing him to study her figure from a better vantage point. She moved with grace even when she watched her own feet to keep herself steady. If anything, her uncertainty only made her that more attractive. Not a glimmer of prudishness.

As they came back together, she smiled up at him, and it was not only the yearning in his chest which throbbed at her delight. He had yet to see her look at any other Caersan the way she did him. Not even Alek.

He turned, releasing her hands again, and found a sea of eyes on them. Even the hulking guard in the corner seemed to watch from his station at the far side of the room. His chest swelled with pride. She would be his.

"You are stunning," Loren said when she returned to him. "I admit, I am quite taken with you."

Ariadne bit her lower lip. "You are too kind."

Another turn, another perfect angle to watch her move with the music. He could get used to this. With the Golden Rose on his arm, he would be the envy of Valenul. Not only was she the daughter of the Princeps and most beautiful Caersan across all provinces, she had escaped from monsters very few of his own soldiers could survive: dhemons from the Underworld.

CHAPTER 2

The first time Azriel Tenebra had seen Ariadne, she'd been no farther from him than when she danced with Alek Nightingale. His entire world changed in an instant. But the soul-deep fae bond could never be acted upon. After all, despite bearing the blue veins of a Caersan, he would never be a part of the Society. His bastard lineage kept him from transcending to the aristocratic heights of his mother.

So when Madan first approached him to become a personal guard for the Harlow family, Azriel had laughed in the vampire's face and said no. The very notion of being put in close proximity with Ariadne Harlow made every sense in his body go on high alert. To physically stand before her would destroy him.

Madan, however, won out. The Harlows needed another guard to chaperone for the Season, and he trusted no one else by his side. For Azriel, family always came first.

Walking into the Harlow Estate that evening turned Azriel's bones to flame. Unlike those who descended from the god-born fae lines, vampires didn't create soul bonds. They were once mages, cursed by rival clans to walk the night, feed off each other's blood, and disconnect from their magic. Therefore Madan could never understand the depth of white-hot pain it caused to be close to, yet kept from, a mate. Azriel's fae father—the man who'd sullied his mother outside of marriage—gave him the ability to bond.

Thanks, Pop.

A small group of young Caersan eligibles passed by for what he counted as the fourth time. Their wide eyes slid to him with interest as though they had never seen a half-breed before.

"He is quite handsome," one said, her cheeks reddening.

Another giggled behind her hand. "I wonder if all of him is that big."

"Priscilla!" The third smacked her friend's arm, yet her own gaze slid down his body with a curious glint.

He stilled under the examination. It wasn't the first time he'd been analyzed in such a manner. Traveling to the mage capital of Algorath often brought similar remarks. His size, like most fae lines aside from the petite avians, was unmatched in the human and mage world. The only beings larger than him, he'd discovered in the worst way, were dhemons, the descendants of Keon, who stood at least half a head taller than other fae.

"Do you think he'd let me compare our hands?" The second Caersan eyed him.

They spoke as though he couldn't hear them. Were all vampires of the Society so daft, or were these women just that bold?

Sighing, Azriel pivoted in their direction and, placing a hand over his heart, bowed to them. "Pardon me, ladies, but I believe such things would be inappropriate. Please enjoy your Vertium."

All three gaped at him, wide-eyed for a long moment. Then the first grabbed the wrists of the other two and pulled them away, her eyes glittering as she looked back at him. A few paces away, they giggled before continuing their analysis of his figure.

Azriel crossed his arms, elbows tight to his sides, and pivoted away again. They would not distract him or get him into trouble. Were a guard such as him to touch any Caersan outside his protective duties, he was as good as dead.

Refocused on the dance floor, his heart plummeted. The general had returned, this time sweeping Ariadne into his arms. It was the third dance of hers that he'd endured as an onlooker. The first two had been excruciating to witness. Pax, the old hack, was in well over his head if any of the stories were true; it was obvious she'd accepted out of etiquette alone. Alek, however, was a sadistic bastard who refused to pick up any of her physical cues. That he even let the Lord Governor walk away was a miracle unto itself.

With Loren, Ariadne appeared at ease. She trusted him, and even though Azriel didn't, he could convince himself she was well-off with the General. For now.

Then Ariadne shifted back from Loren, keeping distance between them and forcing his hand off her back. The subtle movement, unnoticed or ignored by the Caersan, burned into his mind. A similar adjustment had occurred when her father touched her shoulder. At first, it appeared to be a quirk. Now he knew it meant something more. A nervous habit? Or a revulsion?

He didn't want to know if it was the latter.

Azriel swallowed hard and turned to look out the window. Watching her dance in the arms of another man only made his heart ache, and he hated her for it.

Part of him blamed Madan. His darling cousin had only gotten the job as the Harlows' guard because he'd snuck Ariadne out of the dhemon keep. Yet no one knew Madan couldn't have succeeded without Azriel's help. If the fight against those monsters had gone the way Madan had planned, it would've been Azriel carrying Ariadne back to the capital instead.

As it were, Madan returned to Laeton the hero while Azriel hid in Algorath with their mage friend, Phulan, to be healed from the wounds he'd sustained. The entire ordeal had been awful. Though relations between vampires and mages had improved over the last millennium, one mage in particular had it out for him. If he'd been discovered by Melia, there would've been no escaping her wrath. Worse had been Azriel not knowing whether Madan made it back to Laeton unscathed with Ariadne in tow. Even the line of communication through their telepathic friends, Razer and Brutis, had gone silent due to distance.

But Madan had meant well. He didn't understand the pain Azriel endured to pin down his most basic instincts demanding he be with the very woman they were hired to protect. As Madan had put it, he'd thought Azriel would be the perfect candidate *because* of the wretched fae bond.

The quartet started up another song, and Azriel's gaze snapped to the dance floor. Ariadne twirled through the steps of another dance, her smile brimming. From the corner of his eye, though, he tracked as Madan slid around the perimeter of the room, closing the distance between them. With mere paces between them, Azriel's jaw tightened, and he averted his gaze again.

"Oy." Madan sidled up beside him and put a fist on the vampire's shoulder. "Focus."

Azriel slid his gaze to the vampire and scanned his face. "I am."

Madan snorted, shook his head, and shifted to watch the guests as he spoke in low undertones. Of course. No one needed to hear what he had to say. "You look ready to murder everyone in here."

"Maybe I want to."

"Gods damn it, Az."

"You suggested it."

"But you can't."

"And who would stop me?" Azriel let his arms fall to his sides, and he cocked his head to study the other guard.

Madan ground his teeth. "*She* would stop you."

Absolute stillness settled over Azriel. An icy grip dragged his thoughts back to her and a flood of warmth washed over him as he swiveled his head back to the dancers. Madan followed his line of sight. Ariadne smiled up at the General at the same moment Loren looked up and met his gaze.

"Easy." Madan's low, steady tone grated on him.

"I'm not a rabid animal."

Another snort. Madan shook his head. "Keep telling yourself that."

"Is this why you came over here?" Azriel pivoted to put his back to the dance floor. "To put me on a leash?"

"If necessary."

"I swear to the fucking gods—"

"Joking!" Madan threw up his hands, a wide grin brimming. "I'm joking. In all seriousness, I haven't had the chance to speak with you at all tonight."

Azriel rolled his shoulders, easing the tension away. "Oh?"

"I heard from Whelan about—"

"I told you not to respond." Azriel's nostrils flared and he turned to face him fully. His request–no, his order–for Madan to leave well-enough alone had gone unheard.

"You don't get to tell me what to do when it comes to this."

"I am your elder."

Madan clicked his tongue. "Now don't you sound like the Caersan?"

That stayed his tongue but did nothing to bank his temper. Azriel's pulse picked up its pace, the fiery rage coursing through him. "So what did he have to say this time?"

"He's dying." Madan studied Azriel's face as though searching for any sign of acknowledgment. Any break to the stone-like façade. Azriel wouldn't give him the satisfaction. Not tonight. "No one knows why. The Council doesn't know yet."

Azriel growled in frustration. "That doesn't help you."

"Us." Madan gestured between them. "This impacts you more than me since you're my *elder*."

"Fuck."

"Garth already wrote and signed his Will when we were there," Madan said carefully. "Everything is in motion."

Azriel pressed his fists to his eyes. This was not what he needed to hear tonight. He had enough on his mind with caging the fae bond. He sucked in a long, deep breath, and when he exhaled, his hands dropped so he could stare at the ceiling. "I don't want it."

"You don't have a choice."

"I agreed to do this," Azriel jabbed a finger at the floor, "for the Season, and then you said I could leave. If he dies and I become... *Fuck*! I'll never escape her."

Madan's brows pinched with sorrow. The vampire's eyes flickered to whatever happened behind him as the quartet went silent. A bow and curtsy between the Golden Rose and her general, no doubt. He couldn't stomach any of it. Shouldering a dying Caersan's burden was the least of his concerns.

"You still have time to figure it out," Madan said quietly after a moment. "*We* will figure this out."

Azriel blinked long and hard. "I need some air."

"Check the stations while you're out there."

He grunted in affirmation, unable to voice any words that wouldn't do more harm. He turned and hurried through the open doors. Caersans shuffled out of his path, eyeing him with mixtures of surprise and distaste. The faint blue veins on his throat and pointed ears were enough of a beacon to the members of the Society. Half-breed bastard.

No matter the title Azriel inherited, that would be all they saw.

Ariadne did not escape the rest of the Caersan listed on her dance card. One by one, they approached her, and before long, her feet ached from stumbling through the steps of the cotillion and minuet on top of more quadrilles and waltzes. Despite her quick healing as a vampire, everything hurt.

By the time the last dance on her card ended, Ariadne was more than ready to be done. She staggered away from the dance floor, snatched a wine glass from a passing servant bearing a fresh tray, and hid behind a gaggle of giggling Caersan debutantes not a moment too soon. Loren appeared a breath later, and she snaked away.

For each group dance, Loren partnered with another woman and positioned himself close enough for them to take a turn together. Ariadne returned his smiles and relished the rush she felt each time his fingers brushed hers. To feel wanted by someone she liked so much was a thrill unto itself.

Yet she could not bring herself to dance with him again. Not only did the pain drive her from the floor, the guilt did as well. She had danced and drank and flirted with her dead fiancé's brother. And she enjoyed it too much. Particularly when she blamed herself for Darien's death.

If she had not called for him that night, maybe he would not have followed.

Ariadne shook the image of his empty gaze from her head. No. She could not think of him that way. Not when there was still so much he would have wanted her to do—for them both. If it meant marrying another, even his brother, he would support her.

He had always supported her.

She emptied the glass in one large gulp. The rich wine settled in her gut like a warm pool, heating her from the inside. She placed it on the closest table before pivoting and weaving between the guests until the brisk air of the Spring equinox swept across her hot cheeks.

The upper gardens, complete with a massive lawn rolling from the doors to the forest's edge and dense bushes bursting with the first night-blooming flowers of the year, smelled fantastic. As one of Ariadne's favorite places to loiter, she always felt comfortable amid the greenery. A fountain sloshed at the center of a walking path, cutting the lawn in half and drowning out the incessant sound of strings.

Ariadne sighed in relief. Many Caersans milled about outside. Married vampires and engaged—chaperoned—couples made their way through the upper gardens. Yet despite the number of bodies, it did not compare to the ballroom. Out here, she could breathe.

Breathe and be free of groping hands. It was as if all men were trained to dance by ensuring they held a woman in the most awkward of places. Were it not for the crowd watching on, she was certain someone would have grabbed her breast.

Animals, all of them.

Keeping in sight of the doors, as all unmarried Caersan women are advised when alone, Ariadne settled onto a stone bench. She leaned over and yanked the heeled shoes from her feet with a groan. They throbbed and ached when she dug her thumb into her arch. For a brief moment, her mind went blank, forgetting where she was.

"Elevation."

Ariadne choked back a yelp and sat up, swinging her gaze to the nearby shadows. From them stepped the new guard.

"What?"

He tilted his head. "Prop them up on a pillow when you go to bed."

"Dawn is hours away."

"Then prop them up now."

She narrowed her eyes. "I must apologize. What was your name again?"

"Azriel Tenebra, miss."

"Right." Ariadne rotated her feet. "Why are you out here?"

The guard shifted further into the light, eyeing the doors behind her. "Checking in with the grounds guards."

"Then pray tell," she said, switching directions for a better stretch, "why you are lurking in the dark."

"Miss Harlow—"

"That is my name, yes."

"—it's night time." Azriel gestured around them. "It's dark everywhere."

Taken by surprise, Ariadne choked on her laughter. She tilted her head back and let the sound loose in a way she had not in what felt like ages. When she finished, she wiped the mirth from her eyes and shook her head. "Fair enough."

Ariadne leaned back on her hands, kicking her feet out in front of her, and studied him for a long moment. Perhaps it was the wine making her head fuzzy, but she found herself lamenting her first impression of the man. His sheer size and stony face painted him as intimidating. It seemed her judgment had been incorrect.

"From where do you hail, Mister Tenebra?"

He closed his eyes for a long moment as though relishing the thought of his home. "Asterbury."

"Eastwood Province."

"Have you been?"

"Not for many years." She paused, considering the route from Laeton to the eastern range of Keonis Mountains. She had passed through the area more recently than she would admit to a guard she did not know. "The first time I met the Lord Governor, actually."

Azriel grunted by way of response. Odd.

"Have you met him?" Ariadne let her feet settle against the cold stone path, soaking in the iciness on her sore pads. "Lord Caldwell, I mean."

"Yes."

Short and to the point. She pursed her lips. "How did you come to us, Mister Tenebra?"

"Madan is my cousin."

"And you followed him here?"

"He asked me to join him for the Season."

So he would not remain with them beyond the Autumnal equinox. All the more reason not to divulge too much. Madan, she knew and trusted. This man was a stranger, and before long, he would become one again.

"Where did you train to fight?"

"Quiet." Azriel's nostrils flared, and he shifted, boots sliding over the stone tiles with a hiss.

"Excuse me—"

"Silence!"

Ariadne stiffened at the sharp command in his tone. His hand drifted up and over his shoulder, gripping the handle of his sword. Her pulse picked up its pace at the implication. She had not seen or heard anything alarming, but she knew well that her failed senses meant nothing.

She had not seen, heard, or smelled anything off the night a dhemon clambered onto her bedroom veranda and dragged her into the forest, either.

Just as she opened her mouth to ask why he had silenced her, a bolt the diameter of her thumb stuck into the flowerbed a foot away. A second clattered to the stones at her feet in pieces, cut in two by a swing of Azriel's blade. Her scream stuck in her throat, and for the next few heartbeats, everything went silent.

Then absolute pandemonium erupted.

Shrieks echoed across the lawn. A Caersan running pell mell toward the manor fell to the stones mere feet away, another bolt lodged between his shoulder blades. It struck him in the heart; not even a fast-healing vampire could survive that. When she tore her gaze from the blood sliding toward her bare toes, she saw them.

Like wraiths through the shadows, the dhemons of her nightmares stalked forward. A dozen massive forms blended into the darkness with their midnight blue skin and black clothes. More shifted behind them, glints of silver from their blades reflecting the light as they butchered the guards on patrol. Red eyes of every shade burned into her soul. From their brows spiraled huge black horns; they curled like a ram's at the side of their faces before ending in a vicious point at their cheekbones. Long, pointed ears jutted from their silky black hair—the only sign of their fae heritage.

Every fiber of her being demanded she run. They had returned to finish what they had started a year ago. She had to run. Fast. Disappear and go anywhere but there.

"Ariadne!" The shout cut through the screaming in her head, and she looked up. Azriel stood low in front of her, sword drawn. He did not take his eyes off the dhemons. "Get inside."

A small noise escaped her. She knew what she needed to do, yet her body refused to respond. Running meant pain. Running meant fire or knives or worse.

"Fuck," Azriel breathed when she did not move.

The dhemons were so close, and so many vampires were screaming. She watched in horror as Azriel engaged the first. He would die. No one survived them. Even Madan had gotten out through stealth, not brawn, and without him, that keep would have been her crypt.

But the dhemon fell, the wound in his chest soaking the ground with blood. Ariadne gaped at it, mind blank with numb horror.

No time to celebrate. The next charged forward, pushing Azriel back. He stumbled and reached a hand behind him. His fingers brushed her upper arm, then latched on. One arm swung his sword, and the other hauled Ariadne to her feet to push her toward the door. She tripped on the step, falling to the floor just inside the threshold.

Azriel hissed and clutched his side. Fear spiked through her. This was it. The beginning of the end.

Madan appeared beside her. "On your feet, Miss Harlow."

With the support of her trusted guard's steady hands, Ariadne clambered upright just as the next dhemon fell at Azriel's feet. For the first time since the fight began, he looked back at her, eyes wide and brows drawn in concern.

"I've got her," Madan called over the mad rush of guests exiting the ballroom and scattering throughout the manor and grounds.

"Ariadne!" Emillie's scream over the din jolted through her, and she twisted to find her sister struggling against the crowd. "Come on!"

Her baby sister. She could not let her see this, could not let her get hurt. Mind snapping into focus, Ariadne lurched toward Emillie.

In a blink, Loren appeared. Crimson streaked his silvery hair, and his sword dripped with blood. He pulled Ariadne to him, then whipped around in time to parry a blow from a dhemon breaching the doors. Two now lay at Azriel's feet, and within moments, Loren had dispatched another.

Ariadne reached out for her sister, but Loren turned back to her and hauled her away from the carnage. "Your father's study. Now."

Then Emillie was there, too, dragging her away. "Ari, please!"

Ariadne followed Emillie down the corridor. From the heavy breathing behind her, she knew Loren was on their heels to ensure the path remained clear.

After what felt like an eternity, they slammed into the locked door and pounded their fists upon the wood. In seconds, it opened, and they stumbled inside to join several Councilmen, including their father. Ariadne turned to Loren.

"Lock the door behind me," he said and shut them all within.

Emillie fumbled with the lock as Ariadne stared at the closed door. Nothing made sense. Why were the dhemons back? What had she done to incite their wrath again?

The deaths outside that door were on her hands.

CHAPTER 3

E millie took an alternate path to the breakfast den the
following evening. While she typically went down the
corridor along the upper landing of the ballroom, she did not
want to see the crimson streaks on the floor. Even if it had
been cleaned up, she knew what seeped between the boards.

As a Caersan vampire, she was not squeamish. Delicious,
metallic blood kept her alive and healthy. But to see it ripped
from someone screaming for help...

Emillie paused, one hand against the wall and the other
pressed to her chest. Sucking in a long, deep breath, she
calmed the spike of adrenaline threatening to overwhelm her.
Once composed, she continued on, her slippered feet making
almost no sound on the long, thin runner of the hallway.

She did not often miss daylight, but times such as these
always made her skin itch for the sun. While her sister found
comfort in the night gardens, she found it in a noon swim
through the estate lake.

The transition for Caersan vampires affected them all in
different ways. Some grew stronger or more agile. Others

became enamored with the darkness. Still more flourished in beauty.

Then some, like Emillie, lamented the life they lost. Sixty years spent exploring the world's beauties snatched away in a single event.

And nothing that happened to vampires was fast. Sixty years dragged as their bodies grew at half the rate of a human's before coming to almost a complete standstill. The transition took days, for some more than a week. Emillie watched her midday swims disappear over the course of six agonizing days as her body readjusted itself to the curse woven into her blood.

Damn mages. Though vampires and mages had long since put their differences aside, she held a personal vendetta against the magic-wielders from the Mage Wars who punished her for something she had no hand in.

Despite the decades since her transition, Emillie still found herself looking out windows to the lake, yearning for its cool relief from the sun. She passed by such a window with the perfect angle to see the shore she had once laid out on and paused, fingertips on the pane. Never again would she bask in the rays streaming through the leaves of the sycamore.

If she could trade her long life for a mortal one filled with days, not nights, she would.

"You went this way as well."

Emillie jumped at Ariadne's voice. It was an observation, not a question. She turned and nodded, her heart sinking at the sight of her sister in a diaphanous white robe that enhanced her frail, ghost-like figure. Had she eaten at all last night? Emillie could not recall.

The night Madan brought Ariadne home, she had been a wreck in more ways than one. Thin, in desperate need of a meal and Caersan blood, and wholly untrusting of anyone. She cowered from them all like a wounded animal, refusing food and making almost no sound at all.

Emillie had been heartbroken and confused. Madan reminded her, though, that Ariadne did not, in fact, hate her. She was scared and hurt and needed love more than ever.

Looking at Ariadne's ghostly face in that hallway now took Emillie right back to that night. Dark circles rimmed her sister's eyes, a clear indication she had not slept throughout the day. Ariadne had never regained the elegant curves she once flaunted, so her hollowed cheeks stood out more than usual in the low candlelight. A ghost of her former self. No less beautiful, but far from who she had been.

"I did not want to see the ballroom," Emillie said and held out a hand.

Ariadne took it. "I understand."

Indeed, her sister had moved rooms upon her return, unable to stomach the sight of the suite she had once considered a safe haven.

"How do you fare?" Emillie squeezed her sister's hand lightly. A silent *I see you, I love you, I am here.*

The response was slow to come, and Emillie did not push it. She walked alongside Ariadne in quiet companionship as her sister sorted out her thoughts and feelings. Despite her patience, Emillie wished she would truly speak to her—stop filtering her words and give her the raw truth of her thoughts.

"Not well," Ariadne admitted when they turned into the empty breakfast den where the evening's meal sat waiting for them.

The table, much smaller than that of the formal dining room with only six chairs, sat before a bay of windows overlooking the lower gardens. Neither of them spent time looking out at the walking paths and flowering bushes. In fact, they both chose chairs facing away from the distant forest looming at the edge of the estate property.

"Would you like to talk about it?" Emillie pulled the serving bowl of yogurt to her and spooned some into her bowl before passing it over.

Ariadne copied the motion and said, "Yes."

The granola scattered onto Emillie's lap as she tried to add it to her bowl. Her heart stumbled. It was a rare occurrence for Ariadne to wish to speak about what had happened to her.

"I am listening," she said, sweeping the spilled grains into a napkin and setting it aside.

Another lull in the conversation. She filled it by topping off her bowl with strawberries. Though the yogurt and grains were easily accessible in Valenul, the fruit was a special treat even for Caersan. By the end of winter, they relied solely on trade with the southern half of the continent—with what remained of the mages across the Leus Plains where Caersans had first been created. If it had been a poor harvest, such as the last year, supplies ran low quickly. Emillie loved fruit too much to let it go, though, even in the winter.

"That was my first time seeing them since coming back." Ariadne's eyes focused on something much farther away than the spoon she stared at. "I thought they had returned to take me again."

Emillie bit her lip without speaking.

"I just sat there." Her voice was small and pained. "The guard kept telling me to run. I kept telling *myself* to run. But I just *sat* there."

"It was terribly frightening."

Ariadne's ocean eyes, brimmed with silver like waves on a beach, turned to her. "I tried to run once."

Breath hitching, Emillie could not look away. Shadows crept into her sister's gaze, and for a long moment, it was as though she could see straight into Emillie's soul. She opened her mouth, uncertain what to say.

"I learned very quickly *not* to run."

"Then you did what you knew was best." Emillie laid her hand out on the table, palm up. The first rule of her sister: never touch her without permission.

But Ariadne slipped her fingers into Emillie's hand nonetheless. "I never wanted you to see them."

Emillie nodded. She had seen dhemons before, of course. Terrible and monstrous though they were, they were still fae who communed with their patron god, Keon. That meant they could be found all along the Keonis Mountains, and traveling with their father required them to enter the ranges. She had seen them in passing and nothing more. Never like what she had witnessed last night.

"Did you recognize any of them?" The question left Emillie before she weighed it properly. She sucked in a breath and added, "Sorry. You do not have to answer that."

Ariadne, however, did not flinch. "A couple, yes."

Feeling braver now, Emillie pressed on. "Were any of them the ones who hurt you?"

"No." Ariadne picked up her spoon and pushed her granola into the yogurt. "They watched, though, and did not stop him."

Him. Emillie already knew the name of that particular dhemon: Ehrun. It had taken her father and Loren weeks to glean that information from her. Once uncovered, they had been able to trace the name back to the leader of the clan and the one who had likely ordered the kidnapping. To no one's surprise, it was none other than the most infamous dhemon known to the Caersan. The Crowe.

The Crowe led dhemons all along the Keonis, choosing Rusan vampire villages to raid and raze. There were rarely any survivors.

Yet the attack on the Harlow family, she had overheard her father tell his closest confidant, Lord Orlyn, one night, was not random. It had been the Crowe who murdered his first family.

Emillie had been surprised to hear her father had been married before her mother. He never spoke of them, and everyone pretended they had never existed. But it seemed the dhemon king had returned to torment him once again by stealing Ariadne.

Emillie pulled herself from the spiral of thoughts and squeezed her sister's hand. The returned squeeze was enough to tell her the conversation was over. Ariadne released her grip and turned to her yogurt.

They ate in silence for several minutes before a handful of servants stepped into the room, vases of flowers in hand. The closest Rusan vampire, made evident by her lack of blue veins webbing up her throat, curtsied and said, "These have all arrived, my Ladies, for you both."

They set the vases before each of them. Two for Emillie, making her face heat fiercely, and twice as many for Ariadne. Roses, lilies, lavender, lilacs, carnations, and wild carrot flowers, amongst many others, popped from between evergreen and ferns and eucalyptus leaves. A different colored ribbon tied about the neck of each crystal vase held a card from whom the bouquet came.

"And whose fancy did you catch last night?" Ariadne asked, smelling the crimson rose closest to her.

A beat of silence as Emillie squirmed, looking at the cards and well wishes. "Lords Jaq and Moone, it would seem."

She chewed her lip. The flowers were lovely and the Caersans who had sent them were kind and respectful. There should be no reason for her to feel so hollow about receiving their affections.

"You do not seem to share their sentiments." Ariadne angled her head curiously, the color having returned to her cheeks since the distraction arrived. Anything to keep their minds away from what ended last night's festivities.

"It is not that," Emillie said slowly, rolling the corner of her linen napkin between her fingers. "I do not know..."

The weight of Ariadne's hand on hers startled her out of the dark pit she spiraled into. Emillie looked up to find her sister searching her, calculating. Heat burned her cheeks under the scrutiny, and she checked the room and corridor beyond to ensure they were alone before admitting, "I am not attracted to men."

Ariadne hummed as she took another bite of yogurt. She tapped the air with her spoon, swallowed, and said, "I figured that much."

"Wait." Emillie frowned. "What?"

A sly smile crept onto Ariadne's face. "Dearest sister, I have spent the last century listening to you sigh over portraits of goddesses and pinpoint precisely how a dress flatters a woman's body. You have recited just how much you adore the female form while sketching, and you gravitate to the most beautiful women in the room. Moreso, you have never turned into a puddle at a man's feet the way you do when Hyacinth Hooke enters a ball."

Emillie blinked once, twice. She gaped at her sister for a long moment, mind blank of any retorts. There were none. Everything Ariadne said was true. Even about Hyacinth, the most intelligent and beautiful woman she had ever met.

"Quite honestly," Ariadne continued, "I am a bit envious of you. Men are awful."

Emillie's composure broke. She threw her head back and roared with laughter. Never once in her entire life had she heard Ariadne say such things. Dancing around a difficult subject or making light of uncomfortable topics had been her specialty prior to a year ago. Since her return, she was far more blunt. Emillie loved it.

"Huh."

The monotonous tone caught Emillie's attention. "What is it?"

"There is no calling card on this." Ariadne frowned at the tiny vase hidden behind the rest, bearing a single flower. Six cream petals stretched out, each with a deep red streak up its center. "What even is it?"

Emillie lifted a brow. "One flower? It is a gladiolus tristis—the moonlight flower."

Her sister rolled her eyes. "It was probably Alek Nightingale. He would do something dramatic like this. 'A single flower to signify our life together' or something of the sort."

"What did he send you during your first Season?"

"Gods," Ariadne breathed and shook her head. "A bouquet too large to carry upstairs."

Remembering the event, Emillie snickered, much to Ariadne's bemusement. "Is there one from the General?"

Now her sister bit her lip, slim cheeks flushing with color so deep, it nearly neutralized the shadows beneath her eyes. She pulled forward the largest bouquet of a myriad of red flowers. "Indeed."

"Red is certainly his favorite color."

"He is passionate."

Emillie raised her brows. "It is a lot."

"I think he is kind," Ariadne said, pushing her nose into a carnation. "I think he truly likes me."

"Do you not think it odd," she said slowly, "how much he pines over you after Darien?"

It was the wrong thing to say. Ariadne stiffened. Her free hand gripped the napkin on her lap, and she turned back to her food without answering.

They finished their meal in relative silence after that, then stood together.

Before she could leave, her sister took her hand again. "We should visit Camilla soon to talk about your interests. Until you know how to approach it, know that Father will expect you to dance with both of those suitors."

Emillie's stomach dropped. "I know."

"I love you, Em." She squeezed her hand, then left, as quiet as a ghost.

She waited several beats after Ariadne's departure before following. Her mind reeled. Had she truly just exposed her deepest secrets just to be met with indifference? Not that she had expected her sister to be eager for more information, but she had been convinced she was able to hide the truth. If Ariadne had figured it out, had her father done the same?

Just outside the breakfast den, Emillie ran smack into a large body. She gasped, took a step back, and tilted her gaze up to find Madan watching her wide-eyed. Odd for him to be up there so early in the night.

"I'm terribly sorry, Miss Harlow," he said, straightening his jacket. "How are you feeling this evening?"

"Oh!" Emillie gaped at him. "Not entirely well, if I am honest."

"I'm sorry to hear that," Madan said and took a step back. "If there's anything I—or my cousin—can do to be of assistance, please let us know."

Emillie gave him a tight smile. "Thank you."

After a brief bow from the guard, she swept past him. Glancing back over her shoulder, she frowned. Madan stared at the collection of vases on the table, his mouth forming a thin, tight line. What did he see that she had not?

Azriel lounged on a frayed couch in the common room at the end of the servants' basement hall. He kicked his legs out before him, a bowl of porridge in hand and sword within arm's reach, to watch as Madan stomped past the bedroom doors. The vampire's face twisted at the sight of him, and every one of Azriel's senses went on high alert.

"Morning," Azriel grunted, shoveling another bite of plain gruel into his mouth; he didn't want to get into it with him again.

"What the fuck?"

Azriel lifted his spoon to point it at Madan. "You told me not to curse here."

"Not in front of *them*." Madan shook his head, running his fingers through his hair with a groan. The other guard turned to look around the room littered with mismatched chairs and old furniture as though to check they were alone. "You sent her a fucking *flower*?"

Azriel blinked once. Fuck. How'd he find out? He grunted by way of response and shoveled more porridge into his mouth.

"So it *was* you."

Another grunt. Another spoonful. He didn't have to answer that.

"What the actual fuck?" Madan stepped closer, fists tight at his side.

Azriel felt the proverbial hackles rising at his approach. Like a rabid animal locked in a cage. He could smell Ariadne on him. What was he doing wandering the manor at nightfall?

"You know what would happen to you if anyone found out?"

"And who would tell them it was me?" Azriel leveled a cold gaze at him in challenge.

Madan threw his hands up. "You're acting like a real asshole, you know that?"

"*You* brought me here."

"I didn't think it'd turn you into your father."

Azriel froze. It had been an unspoken agreement between the two of them not to mention his father. The man had been kind to them and treated Madan like his own child when he was around, but he hadn't been around often. Therefore, when his father lost his temper, it made an impression.

And the apple never fell far from the tree, did it?

In a flash, Azriel stood a breath away from Madan. Fear flashed in Madan's eyes at their size difference. Azriel had never lashed out at his only remaining family member, but bonded fae were unpredictable.

"I won't do it again." The words were low, and he could not keep the disturbing images from plaguing his mind. "But never speak of him again. Is that understood?"

"You'll need to talk about it at some point."

"He's dead." Azriel turned away and, scooping up the bowl and sword, made for the exit. "Let him rest."

"Az—"

"Don't, Madan."

"No." Madan grabbed his arm, stopping him from leaving. "Something else."

Azriel turned his head enough to see him over one shoulder and lifted a brow in question. What else could he say? What else could he do? He'd done enough, imprisoning Azriel here with her.

"I haven't seen Whelan in months."

That wasn't what he expected. He turned back toward him with a sigh. "I told you to visit him."

Whelan, Madan's fae partner, had been a valuable ally long before the two had finally admitted their feelings for one another. Being gay in a world of heteronormativity created problems Madan had avoided by pretending to fit into the mold expected of him.

He'd tried for so many years—decades, really—to be what he believed everyone wanted. When Whelan came along, every careful brick of his façade crumbled. Azriel had watched, heartbroken, as Madan had struggled to face what made him different. Different and so perfectly who he was always meant to be.

Strange, really, for a Caersan who'd been raised in such alternative ways. The village in which Madan had lived after his parents were gone had no issues with anyone expressing their sexuality however they wished. It was a natural part of life. Yet those distant ties to the Society and their strict rules kept the vampire from being comfortable with himself.

The night Madan had finally told Azriel, it'd been obvious that he'd anticipated reservations. Questions about why he believed himself to be gay.

But when the words finally came, Azriel frowned and said, "I know."

Azriel had wrapped his arms around the last shred of family he had left and held Madan as he cried. He didn't need to explain himself. He didn't even need to even say anything. Azriel had known and accepted him long before the conversation had ever occurred.

Then Azriel held him at arm's length and said, "Now go find Whelan and tell him."

Madan never even had to speak the name of the fae he loved—the fae who'd bonded to him and struggled the same way Azriel now struggled.

Madan's brows pinched together in concern. "Would you be alright without me for a couple weeks?"

"Of course." Azriel didn't meet his gaze. Alone with Ariadne for two weeks could spell disaster without Madan.

"Don't lie to me." He gripped Azriel's arm and gave it a squeeze. "I won't be here to keep your head on straight."

Azriel slanted his head and looked him over. He could manage a fortnight without his personal leash. When he finally spoke, he did so quietly. "You haven't had a day to yourself in far too long. Take your time—and send Kall my regards."

Tension eased from Madan's shoulders, and he loosed a sigh of relief. He knew that even seeing Kall, the fae who kept Whelan from losing his mind much like Madan did for Azriel, would be a reprieve. The vampire worked too hard.

"Have you not spoken with Kall?" Madan frowned.

Azriel shook his head. "Razer's too far."

"What's he doing?"

"Guarding the clutch with Mhorn."

By the way Madan's eyebrows show high, that hadn't been what he expected to hear. They hadn't discussed sending their friends to ward off the dhemons—Azriel had made that decision alone. "Are they safe?"

With a huff of wry amusement, Azriel shrugged. "I don't know. Maybe check in on them with Whelan?"

"Thank you for this."

"I'm going to check in with the grounds guards," Azriel said, hoisting the sword onto his back and fastening the latches. He shrugged his shoulders to adjust its weight, then added, "Go confirm your absence with the Princeps."

Madan nodded and followed him into the hall. Back past the doors, to the steps leading from the manor's lowest floor, he paused again. "Az—"

"Stop." Azriel didn't look at him, choosing instead to focus on a point at the top of the steps. "You're right. I've been an asshole and have already pushed the line with that fucking flower. It won't happen again."

"If I'm not here—"

"I'm fine, Mad." He rotated his shoulders, discomfort creeping in. "Please trust me."

"More than anyone."

"Good. Go see Whelan."

With that, Azriel launched himself up the steps three at a time and shoved through the door at the top. He slipped down the routes most often used by the servants, avoiding the main corridors. Each step further into the manor constricted his breath a little more. Amongst other scents, Ariadne's lingered in every nook and cranny.

Helping Madan pull Ariadne from the dhemon keep had cost them both more than they were willing to admit to themselves. Madan's imprisonment by the monsters. Azriel's torture. Their knowledge of the keep's location aided their rescue-gone-awry. A pity there hadn't been time to tell more soldiers where to bring help. Perhaps they would've rescued Ariadne sooner if they had.

Time had been of the essence. Stopping to tell anyone what to do or where to go could have led to dire consequences. They couldn't risk it.

So once they'd gotten Ariadne out, Madan had left Azriel to find his own way to Algorath, and he'd become Lord Harlow's most prized personal guard.

It should've been Azriel.

The Harlow Estate, relieved of its bloodstains, was a real beauty. Loren admired the construction from its foundations, laid by skilled masons, to its soaring ceilings propped by carpenters. A manor—gods, a castle—built for a king.

For that is what the Princeps was in the Society and the position Loren worked towards obtaining with every breath he took. As the General, he answered only to Markus Harlow. The rest of the Provincial Council held equal status, but despite his father holding one of those seats as a governor, Loren desired more. A side-step to a desk would never do. Only a step up into the seat with the most political power would suffice.

Therefore, Loren appraised the manor with the eye of its future master. With no sons to take it over, it would pass to one of his daughters' husbands, and Ariadne, the first-born, would likely be the one who inherited it.

So he played the game required of him to obtain the two things he desired most: the Golden Rose's hand in marriage and a solidified position to become the next Princeps. That included asking after Ariadne's well-being and making pleasantries with her father.

"Walk with me," Markus said as their conversation found its natural conclusion. "Captain Jensen should be arriving at any moment."

Loren inclined his head in agreement and stepped aside to let Markus lead the way from his study to the foyer. "I am disappointed the Captain was not on duty last night."

"He seemed to enjoy himself at the ball."

"Yes," Loren agreed, remembering his friend dancing to his heart's content and filling his gut with wine. "Yet had he been in charge, the ambush would have never made it to the manor."

Markus nodded, expression grave. "He would have done well."

"I will be doubling our security for future events." The reassurance eased the tension in the Princeps' shoulders, so Loren pressed on, "This Season shall not be thwarted by ruthless beasts."

Markus stopped as they reached the foyer where Captain Nikolai Jensen stood. He did not greet the officer right away but turned to Loren and held out his hand. "Your perseverance in the face of such crises is what gets me to sleep each morning. You are a Caersan of honor."

Chest swelling, Loren grasped the outstretched arm. "My Lord, I will do everything in my power to ensure the Society's safety."

"Very good."

They turned in unison to Nikolai, who watched with visible interest. His dark hair, shorn short, flopped just to his brow, and his brown eyes glinted with anticipation. At their sudden attention, he placed a hand over his heart and bowed. "Princeps. General."

"Thank you for joining me, Captain," Markus said and stepped forward to clasp arms with the Caersan. "Both of my daughters should be finished breaking their fasts."

"Captain." Loren squeezed his friend's forearm in greeting next before standing back and asking, "What brings you back to the Harlows so soon? Did the younger Miss Harlow catch your interest last night?"

Nikolai laughed and shook his head. "No, sir, that would be a breach of trust."

"Is that so?" Loren glanced at Markus.

The Princeps nodded in agreement. "Very good. Yes, Captain Jensen has been the Elit to both Ariadne and Emillie for the last year."

A strange, ugly feeling curled in Loren's gut. Elits, contracted Caersan men, provided blood to unwed women. Feedings were an intimate matter, closely watched for all young Caersan women until they married and took only from their husband's vein. For Nikolai to be the one who sustained Ariadne after she returned knotted Loren's stomach.

It should have been him.

But if that had been the case, he never would be allowed to court Ariadne, just as Nikolai could no longer entertain the idea of garnering Emillie's favor. An Elit signed away the rights to ever court the woman they fed so no attachment could be made or abused.

All the same, Loren did not like the idea of Ariadne's fangs in Nikolai's wrist. He particularly hated that it had been Nikolai's blood that nourished her body for the last year. Soon it would be his blood and his blood alone.

"The Harlow women are fortunate to have such an honorable Elit to see to their needs," Loren bit out after a moment to collect himself. He slid a smile into place before inclining his head. "I must be on my way."

"Thank you again," Markus said, mimicking the gesture, "for looking in on Ariadne's well-being. I hope to see you at the next ball."

Loren nodded. "I would not miss it."

"General." Nikolai bowed again before turning back to Markus and saying, "Lead the way, my Lord."

The two took to the stairs, and Loren watched them disappear at the second-floor landing in the direction of the drawing room. He shoved the burning bite of envy away before pivoting to the front door. His heart leapt, hand twitching to the sword at his hip.

The new Harlow guard stood in front of the doors, closing one behind him. The bastard's gaze flickered from the place Markus and Nikolai had vanished to Loren, where it settled with cold calculation. For a long moment, neither of them spoke.

"General Gard." A bow, fist over heart, though his eyes never left him.

Loren did not so much as nod. "Remind me your name."

"Azriel Tenebra, sir."

"Indeed." He surveyed the hulking mutt with distaste. It was no secret the guard had a muddled heritage. Not only did it say so in the employment paperwork from a century earlier when he began his training, his build harked back to fae lineage. Even his ears had a slight point to them. His father had been high fae and his mother a disgraced Caersan woman long abandoned by Society. The guard did not deserve the faint blue veins on his throat and therefore did not deserve to be treated as someone with Caersan parentage. "Strange for you to be coming in the front doors."

Tenebra inclined his head. "I'll take better care in the future."

"You watched my dance with Miss Harlow last night," Loren said, ignoring the implied apology. "Then you were with her outside when the dhemons attacked. You have a habit of lurking about. Why?"

Something flickered in the guard's eyes. "It's my job, sir, to look after the Harlow family."

"Your job." Loren nodded. "Do not forget that."

"I might ask the same of you, sir," Tenebra said, ignoring Loren's words just as easily. "You, too, seem to have a habit of lurking about the Harlows."

A fire lit in Loren's chest, and he drew himself up. Though the guard might be too tall to look at directly, he would do his damnedest to try. "You forget your place."

"My place is here, sir, ensuring the Harlows' safety."

"You will do well," Loren said, his jaw stiff and lips hardly moving, "to remember to whom you speak. I am the General of Valenul, and you are but a guard. As such, you fall under my command."

Tenebra cocked his head, something between a sneer and a smirk curling his lips. "I answer to the Princeps."

"You answer to *me*," Loren snarled, then caught himself. He sucked in a deep breath and forced his voice lower. "Consider this a warning. I mean to make my intentions clear to the elder Miss Harlow so you will see me often. Make yourself accustomed to that fact."

To that, the bastard had no reply. Tenebra stiffened, and a muscle flexed in his jaw before he nodded. After a tight-fisted bow and a mumbled "General," the guard disappeared down the corridor.

If that great oaf believed he could stop Loren from wedding Ariadne, he had another thing coming. No one—no vampire, fae, or mage—could stand in his way. Any who tried would be put down without mercy.

CHAPTER 4

Madan's absence brought about more troubles than Azriel would ever admit. After Markus granted Madan's request for leave, Azriel found himself in charge of the estate guards, their schedules, breaks, and positions around the grounds. Though a timetable remained posted in the guard house at the entry to the estate, it appeared the men's ability to read it properly depended solely on Azriel's verbal instructions. He'd never encountered such uselessness in his five centuries of life. No wonder Madan woke up as early as he did to get everyone into place—nightly meetings were required.

Luckily, the Rusan day guards did not require as much hand-holding. Although Azriel's half-blood heritage allowed him to go out in the day without it causing the lethal sun sickness, aegrisolis, he didn't want to be awake at all times. Madan had clearly assigned the more independent guards during the hours he couldn't check on them regularly.

Overall, Madan's organization made Azriel's life easier. It'd always been that way between them. Madan planned. Azriel executed. Without Madan's meticulous lists and charts, Azriel would've died several times over. The one time he'd been forced to plan anything due to Madan being incapacitated, he'd nearly killed them both and dragged Ariadne down with them.

Azriel's skin crawled at the memories. The burn of a whip, a desperate scramble for Madan's shackles, and Ariadne's inability to *run*. He hadn't calculated her trauma into the escape plan, and it cost them lethal seconds in which the dhemons almost took her again. Thanks to Madan's quick thinking, he'd adjusted and gotten her safely from the keep.

But Azriel hadn't been so lucky. When Ehrun had rounded the corner to see only he remained, the dhemon seethed. He'd charged forward and swung his massive sword, which Azriel dodged, then parried the next strike, but his strength was no match. Ehrun's fury had rained down on him again and again, and only one thing kept Azriel from collapsing under the blows: each moment he distracted the dhemon earned Madan and Ariadne more time to outmaneuver the rest of the beasts.

"You fool. You bonded with her, didn't you?" Ehrun had snarled at him when he finally hit the ground. The dhemon's foot came down on Azriel's femur, snapping the bone like a twig. His screams had almost drowned out the next words: "She would *never* love a half-breed bastard like you. I'm doing you a favor, really."

The words still echoed in Azriel's ears as he paused while leaving the guard house on the Harlow Estate and gripped his thigh. Aches radiated from it occasionally despite the mage healer's work. Phulan prevented the injury from twisting his leg, though recovery had been difficult.

Yet that memory and those aches were nothing in comparison to the agony of watching that monster cut down his father. His last-minute appearance gave Azriel enough time to escape, drenched in his father's blood.

Sucking in a deep breath, he shook the image from his mind and continued back toward the manor with quick but uneven steps. Too much to do tonight to sulk over the past. His lamentations would have to wait.

Azriel slowed his gait at the front door where four horses stood, leads held by stablehands awaiting the riders. His, the large black stallion, stood amongst them with his worn saddle and fraying reins. Jasper eyed him from beneath his ebony forelock and huffed with indignation. Azriel glowered back. It'd been days since he'd been to the pasture. Apparently, that was too long for a horse being pampered in the finest stables of Laeton.

The stablehand, Thom, bowed to Azriel and passed him the reins before stepping aside. He stroked the long, glossy neck. "Are you angry with me?"

Jasper bumped him with his nose as though to say, *You think?*

"You prissy little shit," he muttered, shaking his head, but made the mental note to visit to keep the beast content.

The front doors opened, and Markus swept out, flanked by his daughters. The Princeps wore a simple suit of brown trousers, a white shirt, a cream and russet houndstooth waistcoat, and a matching jacket. Emillie, hair twisted into a bun at the nape of her neck, wore a navy, long-sleeved dress, and brown lace-up boots. Half of Ariadne's raven hair fell about her shoulders while the rest remained braided back to keep it out of her face. The forest green dress, cut in the same fashion as her sister's, hung looser on her thin frame. Her face, however, held more color than it had a couple nights ago. As much as he hated to admit it, the Elit's duty was necessary.

And damn, she was radiant.

"Princeps." Azriel bowed, fist over heart, to the lord first before addressing the women. "Miss Harlow. Miss Harlow."

Markus inclined his head as the women bobbed their curtsies. He then held out his hand, a more personal greeting than previous nights. Azriel grasped his forearm as the Princeps said, "I have business at the Hub tonight. I will be back before dawn. Take care of them."

"Yes, sir." Azriel looked to the women with a trained, neutral expression. "They're safe with me."

"Very good." Markus turned and, approaching his horse, hoisted himself into the saddle with ease. "I am trusting you, Tenebra."

Trust. Not something Azriel had in himself when it came to Ariadne, yet there he was. As the bond clambered forth, demanding to be met, he stamped it back down with equal force. If Ehrun had been right about anything, it was that one assessment: she would never—could never—love him.

"Safe travels, my Lord."

Without a farewell to his daughters, Markus clicked his tongue and spurred his horse forward. He disappeared down the dark drive lined with tall, regal hedges and lit at intervals by lanterns. The flames, encased in glass, flickered as he passed but did not extinguish.

Azriel turned back to his charges for the evening. "We should get going."

"Eager to return?" Ariadne angled her head at him. "Do you have other plans?"

He almost laughed and strained to keep the amusement from his face. "No."

He just didn't need to spend any more time with her than was necessary.

Emillie lifted a brow, then fit her foot into the first stirrup. Thom, steadying her mare, held out an arm for her to grasp as she mounted. Beside her, Ariadne followed suit without assistance.

With them settled, Azriel stepped into the saddle, his leg sending a sharp pain through him for the first time in weeks. That's what he got for thinking about it too much. He swallowed back the grunt, turning it into a cough to cover the discomfort.

"What's our first stop, Ladies?"

Ariadne swept her analytical gaze to him. "Madame Ives's."

Heat prickled his skin. "Lead the way."

The Caersan women started down the drive, and he followed a few paces behind. He twisted in his saddle to look back at the manor, a massive stone building at the top of a hill to overlook the grounds. Its lawns and gardens, complete with a small lake and endless walking paths, were immaculate. The Rusan groundskeepers kept everything trim and tidy, working throughout the daylight hours to maintain its splendor.

It would be a shame to one day leave its finery. Azriel knew he couldn't stay beyond the Season. The rules of the Society and the suffocating presence of the Caersan aside, every moment spent in Ariadne's presence dug him a deeper grave. Watching her get swept away by the man of her dreams would be more difficult than putting a rope around his own neck.

Though, gods, did a rope like that burn.

Azriel's hand drifted to his throat to feel the smooth, almost imperceptible scar that ringed it. To imagine he wouldn't have been able to deflect that bolt aimed at Ariadne's heart if Madan hadn't cut him down soon enough.

They passed the guard house and gates and turned down the lane leading to the market of Laeton. The road, darker than the well-lit drive, opened overhead as it widened to let in the moonlight. Caersan vampires didn't require much illumination for their eyes to adjust and improve their vision. Azriel's, however, did not regulate the darkness as well, and so he strained to make out the shadows around them.

Constant vigilance, the first rule of guarding someone. Be prepared for the unpredictable. For Azriel, that meant determining whether each movement was a threat, a passerby, or merely a swaying tree branch. It made his head hurt. He depended on his keen sense of smell to make out potential threats.

"You are rather quiet," Ariadne observed, drawing his attention again. "For being family, you and Madan are quite different."

Emillie shot her a warning look. "Ari, you and I are like night and day."

Ariadne waved her off. "I am merely inviting him to speak. No need to be so sullen all the time, Mister Tenebra."

Azriel shifted in his seat and studied her for a moment. "Madame Ives is a Caersan of the Society, is she not?"

"She is."

"Yet she owns her own business?"

"Yes." She lifted her chin a bit at that, appearing more regal and confident than he'd yet seen her. "And she is a dear friend."

Azriel cocked a brow. "Do you employ all your friends?"

"Mister Tenebra," Emillie cut in as Ariadne gaped at him imperiously, "would you care to tell us about yourself? I fear we know very little about you, and it would put us both more at ease."

A beat of silence. Talking about himself never sat high on his priority list. "What would you like to know?"

"I have been made aware your father is not Caersan," Emillie said, once again shooting her sister a sharp look. "From where does he hail? Did you know him well?"

Loaded questions. "He's fae. I spent most of my life with him, and when Madan's parents died, he joined us."

"You told me you grew up in Asterbury," Ariadne said, eyeing him suspiciously. "The high fae live in the west."

Azriel frowned. "My mother was born in Eastwood Province. My father met her there and settled in Asterbury to remain close."

"And your mother's name?"

"Maribel Tenebra."

"You took your mother's surname?"

"Many fae don't have family names," he explained, cool dread curling through him. They were prying, and he didn't care for it. The complexities of his family history made him stand out from the other vampires too much. "If I might ask, ladies, why do you want to know this?"

Emillie pursed her lips in thought. "Our father does not tell us much."

Odd, though not uncommon, for Caersan men to keep the women in the dark. Their customs were old, outdated, and relied heavily on traditions that had once kept them safe. When the curse was placed on the vampires thousands of years ago, the women were stripped of the one thing that kept the playing field even: their magic. The men once again became stronger and capable of overpowering who they believed to be the weaker sex. As the Caersan men rose above the rest, the Caersan women had no choice but to adapt or be disowned.

There was a reason mages and fae often believed themselves greater than the vampires. Their societies were not nearly as strict.

"You now know everything there is to know about me," Azriel said, twisting the reins in his hands. "Half fae. Half Caersan. Full guard."

"Do you have any magic?" Ariadne's eyes flickered to the rounded points of his ears. "It is not often we see high fae magic."

Azriel shook his head. "I fear you're to be disappointed once more. My father possessed no such gifts."

"Pity." Emillie turned to look ahead again.

A pity, indeed. He'd always wished for magic. After his first visit to Algorath as a child, he lamented his sire's lack of it. That feeling never truly left him.

The homes squeezed closer together as they made their way deeper into Laeton. The estate gardens turned into small strips of land divided by picket fences, then soon, the buildings butted up against one another. As they crested the hill into the city, Lake Cypher sprawled in the distance, reflecting the moon on its surface. The houses turned into apartments stacked above businesses, and more and more vampires roamed the streets.

In the crowds nearest the market, human mages in their bright, colorful clothes made appearances. The high fae with their long, pointed ears cropped up often with the occasional avian amongst them. Still fewer were the lycans, the race of fae cursed to remain in their wolven forms except on full moons as punishment for various crimes. The massive wolves, typically paired with a high fae merchant in servitude to reduce their sentence, cut broad swaths through the vampires and startled horses out of their way.

"Perhaps you could convince one of them to show you magic," Azriel said with a smirk.

But Ariadne had gone quiet and still in her saddle. She chewed her lip, gripped her reins too hard, and watched the crowds with wide eyes.

Wordlessly, Emillie reached across the distance between them and squeezed her hand once. Ariadne shuddered as she exhaled, looking to her sister with gratitude.

"Are you alright, Miss Harlow?" Azriel knew he didn't need to ask. She wasn't alright. A bustling city with all the people and noise could cause someone with half the experiences as her to shut down.

Ariadne looked at him, ghosts and memories swirling behind her wide eyes. It was a punch to the gut. A reminder of his failures.

"I will be," she said in a light, airy voice.

"How can I assist you?"

For a moment, she just stared at him as though studying his words and adjusting her response. "Stay close."

Azriel blinked once, his mind going numb at the words. *Nothing*, he thought she'd say. *I am fine*, or *It will be okay*. Anything but vulnerability. Still, she didn't have to tell him twice. He nodded and gestured for them to continue on, nudging Jasper close enough to bump into both women's horses.

They pressed through the throng, the horses naturally weaving along the path of least resistance. Many moved out of their way, not wanting to be stepped on or have their goods bumped from their hands. Others took one look at the women, then Azriel, and hurried away. Times like these made him thankful for the way his face settled into a scowl without thought.

He hated it anytime Ariadne glanced at him.

"Ari!" Emillie turned down a less-crowded street lined with fine, high-end shops not financially accessible to most Rusan vampires. "It is over here."

With a shake of her head, Ariadne followed her sister, and Azriel brought up the rear, frowning at her lack of awareness. That was something that needed addressing. For someone so vigilant in her own home, she became oddly befuddled in public.

Could he blame her? She'd been taken from her own bedroom—the haven in which she should've felt safest.

Outside Madame Ives's, Azriel dismounted and dropped Jasper's reins. The stallion had yet to wander away in all their years together. He took hold of both Caersan's horses, however, in case they spooked in crowds, and held a hand out to Emillie first. She took it with a quiet murmur of gratitude. Then he turned to Ariadne, who stared at his hand for a long moment before swinging a leg over the saddle and accepting his brace for the dismount.

The moment their palms touched, Azriel was certain the world exploded. Everything slammed into focus, and the din of the market faded to a low hum. His very skin seemed to alight with flames, bringing his attention to every minute detail, from the way the hairs on his neck stood on end to his raging pulse.

All too soon, Ariadne slid her fingers from his. He sucked in a breath at the frown creasing her brows, and she thanked him.

Had she felt it, too? Impossible.

"Of course, Miss Harlow." He inclined his head. "Would you like me to accompany you inside, or do you prefer I remain here?"

She chewed her lip a moment before saying, "Come inside, please."

"As you wish."

Madame Revelie Ives, Ariadne's close friend and favorite designer in Laeton, kept her seamstress shop clean and welcoming. Dresses hung displayed from mannequins in front windows lit by carefully placed candles, and bolts of fabric hung from the gold-trimmed walls. Peace lilies and pothos brought life to the otherwise sterile environment.

Entering the shop behind Emillie, with Azriel on her heels after tying off the horses, she felt like an intruder. The looming guard at her back only made things worse. When she looked at him, Azriel seemed at a loss. He crossed, then uncrossed his arms before refolding them over his chest. His dark clothes—black leather trousers and boots and an airy black shirt—made him appear like a shadow come to life.

"What can I do for you, my dears?" Revelie floated from the back room, her brown skin, complete with the vivid blue Caersan veins running up her throat and jaw, perfectly complementing the bright fabric of her dress. Thick, coiled, ebony hair bounced around her angular face, and her round, dark eyes gleamed with delight. "I have missed you."

The Madame was one of the few Caersan women to run her own shop. She debuted amongst the Society two decades earlier and, after being named the Season's Golden Rose, decided she wanted nothing to do with the ridiculous customs and rules. Her father, killed in a dhemon raid in Notten Province to the north, left the family estate to Revelie and her mother. While the latter continued living her lavish lifestyle and found another husband, the former took her share of the inheritance and pursued what she loved most: fashion.

Ariadne could not be more grateful. Revelie's dresses were the finest in Valenul, and her vantage point in the Society provided unique discourse on current affairs.

"We missed you at the Vertium ball," Emillie said, running her fingers over a violet fabric with a pattern of indigo flowers. "I believe Ari requires something special for the Season."

"Oh?" Revelie turned to Ariadne, her glossy, red lips pursed with interest. "Have you caught the eye of a suitor already?"

Despite her distaste for being a part of the Season, the Madame enjoyed the gossip and drama. That she had yet to hear of the priestess's choice for the Season was unlikely.

"I am the Golden Rose, it would seem." Ariadne's cheeks warmed, and when she turned to hide the inevitable rise of color by looking at fabric, she found Azriel watching her with a peculiar expression. His lips parted a bit, and after a sharp inhale, he looked out the window.

Revelie's eyes glittered with mischief, her smirk revealing the tips of her fangs. "I had heard as much but did not want to take Miss Tare's word. She is far from a reliable source."

Indeed Miss Silva Tare, a known rumor mill and heavy drinker, could hardly be considered a trustworthy bearer of news. The Caersan's last three Seasons without finding a husband gave her plenty of time to spin tales. Despite her sly tongue, Ariadne was forever grateful Silva kept her speculations about her disappearance last winter to herself.

"This time, she was correct!" Emillie held out the violet cloth. "I love this pattern."

"I have something already in the works with that one," Revelie said, crooking a finger at her to follow. "Come see if you like it."

The two disappeared into the back room, the seamstress chalking up her absence from the ball to being too busy and tired from making dresses for the start of the Season. Beside the window, Azriel shifted, those sharp eyes piercing the swinging door they had gone behind.

"She is fine," Ariadne said, voice low. "There is no back door."

Azriel frowned. "Why not?"

"Revelie prefers her business to remain honest." Ariadne brushed her fingertips along a soft, dusty rose-colored fabric. "One door in and out means everyone can see precisely who she works with. No one can claim they saw a rake sneaking into the back alley."

"Concerned about her reputation?"

"No." Ariadne shook her head. "She is protecting the legacy she is building by following her dreams."

"Respectable."

"Admirable."

Something heavy slunk into her gut, a weight she knew well yet had difficulty placing its cause. She did indeed admire

Revelie's business and courage for stepping out of the Caersan Society's web. Listening to Camilla on Vertium gave her a similar feeling. Was it the need to break from conformity or the desire to merely wield the strength needed to live on her own terms? She did not know.

"That color would look lovely on you," Azriel said after a beat of quiet.

Ariadne turned back to him, dropping the cloth. "While I appreciate your candor, I am not certain that comment is appropriate."

"Apologies, Miss Harlow." He cast his gaze to the floor and shifted toward the door again, shoulders tight.

The weight in her stomach pressed down more. She swallowed hard. Those were the words of her father, not her. She did not believe Azriel to have been disrespectful. If anyone had walked in and heard, however...

Emillie burst through the swinging door wearing a half-sewn, half-pinned gown. The rich purples made her skin glow warm, and the delight in her eyes banished Ariadne's unease.

"What do you think?" Emillie turned in front of the full-length, gold-framed mirror.

"That color is lovely on you," Ariadne said and watched in the mirror as Azriel glanced their way, brows pinched. His mouth twitched.

"I would love this one," Emillie told Revelie, who clapped her hands together and nodded.

"And for you, my Golden Rose," the Madame said, "I have the perfect fabric."

She pulled a bolt from the corner where she kept the newest stack. The iridescent azure fabric flowed over her fingers like a tropical waterfall, its shine picking up the light from the sconces around the room.

"I am envisioning," Revelie said, holding the fabric up to Ariadne's face, "long sleeves and high waist with rose embroidery—in gold, of course."

Ariadne's heart stumbled over the Caersan's words. She could picture how the final product would look. Perfect. The fabric, the same color as her eyes, would stand out amongst the paler springtime gowns.

Yet even as she nodded in agreement and handed over the gold for the dresses to be made to their specifications, Ariadne could not help but think of that dusty rose fabric and the way Azriel looked at her from across the room.

CHAPTER 5

T he Dodd Estate overlooked the small city of Udlow on the western edge of the Central Province, an hour's ride from Laeton. Though the distance allowed frequent visits, it also meant taking several nights of correspondence to plan a midnight tea. Why Caersans had yet to employ mages to communicate more swiftly was lost on Emillie.

When she received a letter from Camilla confirming a date and time for her and Ariadne to call, they leapt at the opportunity. Though Revelie wished to join, her booming business did not allow it. The journey to Udlow had been a quiet ride along a wide, well-lit highway accompanied by Azriel. No one spoke much—a normal evening for Emillie, but strange for Ariadne to keep silent for so long.

In fact, the past few nights had been oddly quiet. It began after the trip into Laeton to be fitted for dresses. She had overheard her sister speaking with the guard in the front room, and while she knew something had occurred between the two of them, Emillie had no idea what. She did notice, however, the quiet acquiescence to Revelie's choice of fabric despite Ariadne's fingers repeatedly finding the pale rose-colored cloth and the way Azriel's eyes followed her every move.

His hawk-like gaze continued during the ride to Camilla's. Though he kept pace behind them and he studied each passerby with cold calculation, he always looked back to Ariadne. Each time Emillie caught him, his jaw tensed, and he refocused elsewhere.

To call it abnormal was an understatement.

Yet the strangest part of it all was Ariadne's blissful ignorance. Since her return from the beasts in the Keonis mountains, her sister remained on edge at all times—except under Azriel's watchful gaze. Perhaps the trust arose from the guard's familial ties to Madan. Perhaps Ariadne did not even realize what she was doing.

Emillie could not help the pang of jealousy at how quickly her sister relaxed in the presence of the new guard. Though she knew she should be glad of Ariadne's readjustment into Society over the last year, that she had never succeeded in what Azriel did without provocation did not sit well with her.

When they arrived at the Dodd Estate, the long drive curved up an easy slope lined by low-hanging, overlapping willows. At the top of the hill, the tunnel created by the branches formed a picturesque frame to the manor beyond. The broad, regal exterior of tan limestone stretched into the dark sky with elegant fixtures along the parapet wall. Firelight flickered in most windows, casting a golden glow along the enchanting night-blooming landscaping around its edge.

No matter how many times Emillie visited the Dodds, the home continued to take her breath away. Aside from her own residence, the manor was the largest and most grand in Central Providence.

At the foot of the stairs leading to the front doors, Azriel dismounted and, as usual, left his stallion to assist them both from the saddles. Emillie accepted his hand down without fuss, but Ariadne was already halfway to the ground by the time Azriel turned to her. He shot a hand out to steady her back, recoiling before they touched.

Emillie narrowed her eyes. Not many Caersan, particularly those within the Society, knew of or understood her sister's opposition to touch—particularly on her back. In fact, even Emillie received a verbal lashing for trying to comfort Ariadne by rubbing a hand across her shoulders.

She still did not know what had happened to cause the reactions, and she was far from the only victim of Ariadne's sharp tongue. Their father, Madan, and a number of handmaids fell to her onslaught. Not one of them had so much as glimpsed her bare skin, let alone been told the cause of her aversions.

They could only wonder, and such thoughts never landed anywhere pleasant.

To see Azriel pick up her sister's cues so quickly told Emillie just how much he paid attention. What had given it away? Dancing at the ball? The way Ariadne pulled back from hugs too soon?

"Misses Harlow," Azriel said with an incline of his head, "would you like for me to remain out front?"

"It is cold tonight," Ariadne said, eyeing him with an unreadable expression. "Give the horses to the stablehand and wait inside. I will have tea delivered to the parlor for you."

His eyebrows twitched together, but he nodded nonetheless. "As you wish, Miss Harlow."

With that, Emillie and Ariadne mounted the stairs and entered the manor as the butler swung the doors open. Warm light enveloped them in the foyer, forcing Emillie's eyes to adjust to the illumination. She blinked long and hard to clear the spots dancing before her vision, and when she opened them again, Camilla stood before them.

"You arrived earlier than I expected!" The Caersan flounced forward, her blonde curls bouncing around her shoulders as she flung her arms first around Emillie, then Ariadne, who pulled away fast. "The cooks are preparing a light midnight meal for us to take in the drawing room. Come!"

Camilla made to usher them away as the front doors opened again, this time so Azriel could slip through. The Caersan froze at the sight of him and turned, her lips curling into a smile.

"You must be the new guard," she cooed and held out an elegant hand.

Azriel's eyes flickered to Ariadne, then back to Camilla. He took her hand and bowed, brushing his lips along her fingers. "Azriel Tenebra, Miss."

"Welcome to the Dodd Estate." Camilla, comfortable with expressing her attraction to anyone, remained calm and collected. Not a flush of her cheeks or wave of her hand to create distance between them. "Shall you be joining us?"

Another glance to Ariadne, who said, "No. Perhaps some tea for him to warm up in the parlor, however?"

"Pity." Camilla gave him another once-over before turning to the butler. "Jasmine tea and cake in the parlor for Mister Tenebra, please, Norman."

Norman, a handsome Rusan vampire with a round face and full figure, bowed low before sweeping down the hall toward the kitchen.

As he disappeared, Camilla gestured to the yellow and gold room off the foyer with a crackling fire and plush, upholstered ivory chairs. "Make yourself comfortable, Mister Tenebra. Please do not hesitate to call on me for *anything* you might need."

"I'm certain Norman will take good care of me thanks to you, Miss Dodd." Azriel curled his lips in a warm smile that did not quite reach his eyes, bowed, and made his way into the parlor.

Camilla turned back to them, her eyes glittering with mischief as she guided them away. In an instant, Emillie's thoughts turned from the curiosity of Azriel's soothing presence to the purpose of their visit. Her stomach knotted.

They did not speak on their way up the stairs and down the hall to the large drawing room. The powder blue damask walls and cream accents matched much of what had been in fashion during the manor's construction centuries before and therefore appeared very similar to the Harlow manor. They sat on two ivory couches assembled near the fireplace. Emillie sat beside Ariadne, with Camilla seated opposite and a low table between them.

"How have the two of you fared since the Vertium ball?" Camilla adjusted the skirt of her dress, glancing at the open doors nearby.

Did she expect Azriel to come in and sweep her off her feet? Emillie would not put it past her friend for thinking so, or at the very least, hoping.

"It was difficult at first," Emillie admitted, then bit her lip and looked to Ariadne, who did not meet either of their eyes. "And yourself?"

"It was absolutely frightening," Camilla said, though she did not sound perturbed. "I have never seen a beast so fierce before. How are you coping, Ari?"

Ariadne blinked twice rapidly as though pulling herself from her thoughts and lifted her gaze back to them. "Perhaps everyone now understands the threat they pose to the Society. I am, oddly enough, doing better than I expected."

Emillie did not believe it for a second. The ghost which haunted their manor for the nights following the attack resembled her sister with very little of her casual demeanor attached. Even the uncertainty she had shown in Laeton's market crowds had been alarming.

Luckily, Camilla did not seem to accept the reassurance, either. She leaned forward to study Ariadne's face and said, "You are allowed to be upset—fearful, even."

A pained smile slunk into place as Ariadne shook her head. "It was distressing, but it is done. We are safe, which cannot be said for those who fell that night. Let us be thankful for that."

"Safe this time, yes," Emillie said and laid a light hand on Ariadne's knee, "but not free from those nightmares."

Something dark and angry flashed through her sister's eyes. "You know nothing of nightmares."

Emillie pulled back and turned to Camilla for help. The Caersan merely sighed and shrugged before saying, "You are right. We do not."

Ariadne rubbed her brow, closing her eyes briefly. "I am sorry."

"Do not be, doll." Camilla offered a sweet smile. "We understand."

At least as much as Ariadne allowed them to understand, which, admittedly, was not a lot.

Interrupting her thoughts, three servants swept in, each laden with a different tray. The first set was a silver tower filled with honey, spiced, and plum cakes. Beside it sat three teacups, each filled before them with steaming lavender tea. The last, another tower, was piled with small cuts of bread layered with different toppings such as butter and herbs, roasted tomatoes, tapenade, and cucumber with dill.

"Delightful!" Camilla clapped her hands. "Thank you, Sephone."

"As always, Miss Dodd." Sephone, a gorgeous brunette Rusan with dark amber eyes, bobbed a curtsy. Her dress, cut low to reveal her ample cleavage, hugged her curves in all the right places.

Emillie stared. The maid was beautiful, and the sudden curiosity to know what Sephone's lips felt like brought a flush to her cheeks. Sephone, noticing her attention, bit her lip to keep from smiling. The simple motion sent a ripple of butterflies through Emillie, who shifted in her seat and quickly looked away.

But not quickly enough. As Sephone retreated from the drawing room, her wide hips swaying a little more than when she entered, Emillie found Camilla grinning at her like a cat cornering a mouse.

"Dearest Emillie," she crooned, plucking up a slice of honey cake, "what is it you wished to speak about during your visit?"

All thoughts escaped her. For a long moment, her mind reeled in search of something—anything—to say.

Ariadne, teacup to her lips, paused with wide eyes.

"I was hoping," Emillie said, an aching hollowness replacing the butterflies, "you could tell me how you knew you were attracted to women?"

The feline smirk returned. "Well... Ariadne, how did you know you were attracted to men?"

Ariadne choked on her tea. "I have no idea. I just... am."

"Well," Camilla said with finality, "there you have it, doll."

Emillie looked between them helplessly. "That explained nothing."

Chewing her cake, Camilla held her arms wide as though to gesture to the world itself. She swallowed, dropped her hands, and said, "I am uncertain what you mean. Attraction is just that with no other explanation needed."

"Em," Ariadne said, taking her hand and giving it that familiar squeeze, "do you ever get that light feeling in your stomach when you are around someone? Like when you think there is an extra step at the top of the stairs?"

Sephone, then Hyacinth and Revelie, jumped into her mind. Her stomach twisted pleasantly. "Yes."

A small curve pulled Ariadne's lips as she glanced at Camilla. The look of mischief passed between them was one Emillie had not seen in quite some time. Not since the dhemons. The familiarity of it put Emillie at ease.

"And when you get that feeling," Ariadne continued, "is it when you think of a man or a woman?"

Heat rose to Emillie's cheeks. The Society, though not cruel to those who preferred Caersan of their own sex, did not support it. Often those who had such attractions were married off to someone of the opposite sex, then left to their own devices within that marriage. Some hid their affections behind closed doors. Others, like Camilla, were not shy about it. Could she ever be so brave?

"Women," she admitted after a long moment. "It is when I think of women."

"Well, then." Camilla picked up her teacup and raised it in a salute. "There is not much to discuss, is there?"

Emillie chewed her lip. "You are so carefree about it. I could never—"

"Wrong!" Camilla smacked her lips and set the tea down. "I appear carefree because I refuse to let those mulish bastards on the Council dictate my life. My father tried for years, and he can continue to try as much as he likes, but I shall not change."

"You are braver than I."

Camilla clicked her tongue. "Then go at your own pace, but do not let them tell you what you can and cannot do."

Them. The Council. The Caersan vampires who controlled everything about their lives, from how they dressed to how they portrayed themselves to how they submitted in defeat. And her father, the Princeps, led them all. Fantastic.

"What did your parents do when you told them?" Ariadne asked as though sensing Emillie's failing courage.

"Oh, Father was furious." Camilla sipped casually and popped a small bite of cucumber-laden bread in her mouth.

She chewed pensively. "Mother did not mind, though she admitted in private to being worried for me."

Ariadne glanced at Emillie before asking, "Did your father do anything to you?"

"Gods, no!" Camilla's eyes widened as she looked between them. "Do you believe yours would?"

Emillie had no idea. Her father had the temper of a mad bull when provoked, and anything that did not go as planned could be the cause. She had seen him lift a hand to a servant who accidentally spilled a drink on him, threaten another Caersan's life for speaking out against him, and use a crop too brutally on his horse. Though he had never said anything negative about Camilla, she knew he did not approve of her provocative lifestyle and only tolerated her due to their long-time friendship.

"He is not known for his subtlety," Ariadne admitted when words failed Emillie. She would know; she had been on the receiving end of his anger before.

Camilla huffed indignantly and shook her head. "Well, then, fuck him."

Emillie's sharp inhale made her friend smirk. "Camilla—"

"If he cannot stomach his daughter as she is," the Caersan said, "then perhaps he should not be a father."

Ariadne laughed, the sound at once startling and beautiful. "At least with you being gay, he does not have to worry about premarital pregnancy."

A grin curled Camilla's mouth again. "Good thing he never had a son, then."

Camilla's outgoing, fun-loving, and passionate personality helped reawaken the Caersan Ariadne had once been. The liveliness thrummed through her veins as she and Emillie mounted their horses and made their way back down the long, willow-lined drive with Azriel at their backs.

She had not missed the number of times he looked at her during his introduction to Camilla as though searching for permission. The unspoken desire to know if what he did would be considered correct by her confused her. Then again, he did not know the ins and outs of the Caersan Society, and with her being the elder Harlow sister, it made sense he would look to her for guidance. At least, that is what she told herself.

So Ariadne ignored how often she caught Azriel looking her way as they returned home. She stamped down the rush she felt from his unwavering attention, reminding herself of her intention to ingratiate herself with Loren. The Season had just begun, and if she could settle down with General Gard, she would be more than satisfied. To entertain wild fantasies about a guard...

"Did you enjoy your tea, Mister Tenebra?" Emillie asked, breaking the silence.

Azriel grunted in response, then seemed to remember his manners and said, "Yes, thank you."

Emillie glanced at Ariadne before continuing, "Ride closer. It is strange to have you so far away."

As he edged nearer, Ariadne gripped her reins tighter. Did he have to loom over them so much? With Madan, things were simple. He did not tower above them like a wraith.

"Do you enjoy riding, Mister Tenebra?" Emillie asked, filling the quiet night with words.

A beat of silence, then he shifted in his saddle and said, "I do. And yourself?"

"I do." Emillie looked at Ariadne again, browns raised. "Not as much as my sister. She is the one who insists we forgo the coach so often."

Azriel blinked in surprise and turned to look at Ariadne. His sudden scrutiny made the hair on the back of her neck stand on end. It was a familiar feeling she could not place, though the studiousness reminded her of Madan. Families resembled each other in more ways than one.

"Do you ride often, Miss Harlow?"

Ariadne lifted her chin a bit. "Quite. It is a favorite pastime of mine."

"Why is that?"

"Why the interrogation?"

"Two questions is hardly an interrogation."

"Be nice, Ari," Emillie hissed, her mouth twisting as she fought to keep the smile from her face.

"Horses do not ask questions," Ariadne said, making a face at Emillie. She looked up at the guard, and her breath caught at the intensity in his eyes. "Spending time with Astra helps me."

"Interesting." Azriel tilted his head, then looked away to scan the tops of the trees. "I find riding helps me as well."

Ariadne almost laughed. The bastard guard, raised by a high fae in a town as fine as Asterbury, could have hardly found himself in much trouble. Petty crimes like theft or pickpocketing, perhaps, but nothing greater than a tavern brawl. The likelihood of him running from anything was so slim, she could not help the small smile that swept across her face.

"Helped you get this job?"

He did not look at her. When he responded, his gravelly voice lowered. "Yes, Miss Harlow, it helped me get this job."

Something about the way the words crackled told Ariadne she had hit a nerve. Her stomach churned. She should not have said that. If Madan had done the impossible and retrieved her from the dhemon keep, there was no reason to believe Azriel did not have a similar skill set.

"Well," she said, hoping to lighten the mood again, "you are an excellent rider."

Now he looked her way, a brow arched. "As are you."

"It must be all the riding you both do," Emillie said, her eyes trained ahead. She was acting strangely.

"Indeed," Azriel agreed.

Ariadne clicked her tongue. "I do not believe it is the number of hours that creates a skilled rider."

Now it was Azriel's turn to huff back a laugh. "And what would you attribute it to?"

She mulled it over for a long minute. She swept a hand down her mare's silky gray neck. The muscles flexed and twitched under her touch. "Passion and a love for the horse."

"That's all?"

"Without those two things," Ariadne explained, "there is nothing to strive for. You believe mere practice would be sufficient?"

He raised both brows now. "Yes."

"Riding is like anything else in life," she said, her voice rising with untamed imperiousness. "One will not maintain consistency or enthusiasm without having a love for it. The most beautiful dancers? They adore what they study. Cooks with the most delicious meals? Food is their passion."

"So you believe the dancer or cook doesn't practice their crafts?"

"I never said that."

"You implied—"

"Someone could dance every day of their life," she said, her pulse racing at the back and forth, "and maintain mediocrity. It is the person who loves dancing every day who will become proficient."

"So you admit practice is necessary."

Ariadne huffed and pursed her lips at his refusal to back down. "Practice does you no good in riding if you are too tense or uptight. The horse will know and respond accordingly."

She looked to Emillie for help, and her sister shrugged. "Perhaps a race to determine the better rider? Passion versus practice."

Where a cool and calculating glint had been, a spark lit in Azriel's eyes. He had come to life over the course of their conversation. The mention of a competition piqued his interest even more.

The heat in Ariadne's veins spurred her on as well. With Camilla putting wind back in her sails and Azriel lighting the fire of rivalry, she, too, felt more alive than she had for a long time. In those moments, a weight lifted from her shoulders, and she breathed easy. The world felt right.

"Well then, Mister Tenebra," she said, adjusting her seat and gripping the reins, "I am ready when you are."

A genuine smile cracked across Azriel's sullen face. The sudden shift highlighted the best of his features, including a set of dimples she had not noticed before. Her heart skipped a beat.

"Perhaps your sister would do us the honor of counting down." Even his voice sounded different—lighter, smoother, and less pained.

Emillie grinned. "I will count back from five, then say go. Whoever reaches home first wins."

Adrenaline dumped into Ariadne's blood. The last time she felt the rush of it, she had been running barefoot through the

Keonis mountains on Madan's heels. Then, it had been from fear. Now, excitement danced through her gut.

"Five..."

They came to a halt side-by-side. Her heart felt ready to leap from her chest.

"Four..."

Azriel's leg bumped hers as he shifted in the saddle. She glanced up at him, and he winked at her.

"Three..."

Ariadne gaped, then swallowed hard and shook her head to clear it, and looked ahead again. Blood pounded in her ears.

"Two..."

She squeezed her knees, ready for Astra's sudden lurch forward when she gave the signal. The mare twitched beneath her, ready to spring at the slightest touch.

"Ah! I am glad I found you three!"

Sucking in a sharp gasp, Ariadne turned to find her father making his way up the highway. She deflated at the sight of him. There would be no race today.

Her father rode his stallion, a large bay by the name of Titan, closer. She had not realized they were so close to Laeton already.

"Is everything alright?" Her father looked between them all and inclined his head to Azriel. "Mister Tenebra?"

Gone was the mirth; Azriel's face had returned to its stony neutrality. The guard's mask. He placed a fist over his heart and bent at the waist. "My Lord. All is well. We paused to admire the sky in this rare break of the forest."

Indeed, the stars were beautiful. Ariadne tilted her head back to study the inky heavens where a dark shadow—a low-flying bird, perhaps—swept overhead and plastered a warm smile into place for her father. Her hands shook nonetheless from unused adrenaline now fading from her system. "You return home already?"

"The Council could not meet as we had hoped," he said. "Lord Caldwell's condition is worse than we were aware, and he cannot travel at this time."

"What is his condition?" Emillie asked as they all nudged their horses forward.

Their father sighed. "Lord Governor Caldwell is quite old, my dear. First generation."

Emillie hummed through pursed lips. "I thought he was an Original."

"His wife, Lady Caldwell," her father explained, "is an Original. She has fared better than he, it would seem."

An Original. Those who had been alive when the curse had been placed upon them. Once powerful mages of the northern plains, their ancestors had chosen to feud with nearby clans who took it upon themselves to strip them of magic. They had intended for the newly created vampires to kill one another from their insatiable bloodlust. What they had not expected was for the vampires to hunt down every mage of those clans and feed from them instead.

The Society pretended to be founded on chivalry and morals. In truth, it was a façade for the heinous murders they committed in retaliation. Ehrun had done well in reminding her of their true history.

"Is there nothing to be done?" Ariadne asked, shoving the intrusive thought of the dhemon away, and Azriel shot her a strange look.

"No." Her father shook his head. "I have sent correspondence to his estate asking for the name of his heir, but it appears to be in his Will and therefore sealed until his death. He is refusing to answer when conscious."

Ariadne frowned. "Did he have no children?"

He stiffened at the question, then angled his head. "None still alive."

His tone told Ariadne the conversation was over just in time for them to turn onto their estate drive. Too many questions oftentimes caused more trouble than good. Between the insights from Camilla, Azriel's peculiar behavior, and now her father's cryptic reply, Ariadne was glad to finally be home.

CHAPTER 6

Councilman Kolson held the second ball of the Season almost a fortnight after the first. Loren did not blame the Lord for pushing the date back. After the chaos which ensued on Vertium, Kolson first approached Loren to ensure his soldiers could provide all safety measures. Ever the humble servant, he provided a small company to maintain a perimeter around his lush estate.

When Loren arrived at the front gates of the sprawling manor, he paused to speak with the lieutenant in charge.

"General Gard." The Caersan swept into a bow, fist over heart. "All accommodations have been met. Soldiers are stationed at intervals with special consideration near the forest and back gate."

"You have done well, McTavish." Loren clapped the vampire on the shoulder. "Send a house guard with regular updates throughout the evening. I want to know everything which transpires out here. If so much as a party arrives late, I want to know why."

"Yes, Sir." Lieutenant McTavish inclined his head. "Will Captain Jensen be in attendance tonight?"

Loren nodded once in confirmation. "The Captain is available for non-urgent questions. Do not interrupt me except for updates and matters of the utmost importance."

McTavish nodded and gave a final bow as Loren nudged his horse forward. The Kolson Estate sprawled before him with its gently sloped lawns and small, neat gardens. At its heart, the manor curled around a large pond alight with floating candles. Caersan couples and families milled around the water's edge from the open doors of the ballroom. Loren followed the drive up and around to the main entrance, scanning for his soldiers in their crimson uniforms along the perimeter of the grounds.

No dhemons would infiltrate them this time.

At the front of the manor, he dismounted with a sweep of his red cloak and handed the stallion off to a waiting servant. The lords and ladies he passed on his way up the steps to the doors paused to bow or curtsy. His chest swelled. By the time he reached the bright ballroom with its dark wood floors and gold accents, his confidence soared.

"General!" Nikolai Jensen raised a short liquor glass in salute from an alcove away from the dance floor.

At the call, several heads swiveled in Loren's direction. More bowing, curtsies, and Caersan debutantes hurrying forth to have him sign their dance cards. He did so, though he scanned the room for only one face.

Ariadne was nowhere to be seen. Yet. The Golden Rose could not miss the event.

Loren thanked the women seeking his favor and continued on to where Nikolai stood with two other officers. Captain Pietro Niil, a tall, thin Caersan with short, sandy blond hair, greeted him alongside Colonel Trev Wintre, a stalky vampire sporting long, brown curls tied back at the nape of his neck.

"General, welcome!" Trev called at his approach.

Pietro poured a fourth glass of whiskey from a crystal decanter. Loren accepted the drink, and they tapped glasses.

"I did not expect to see you tonight," Loren said to Pietro. Nikolai, he knew, would be present for the dances, then the after-party planned for the single Caersans back in town. Trev, married the previous Season, attended for his new wife's enjoyment.

Sighing, Pietro rolled his eyes. "My father is adamant I find a suitable wife this Season."

Nikolai snorted. "As if any Caersan would be willing to settle with the likes of you."

"As if I want to settle," Pietro growled, "when I could partake in Rusan women as I wish."

With a smirk, Loren turned to the sandy-haired Captain. "I doubt Lord Niil will be pleased to hear you admit to bedding a ruddy Rusan."

"You do not have to stop," Trev pointed out with a wink. "So long as you return home and keep the missus happy, she need not know. Even if she did, what would she do to stop you?"

Nikolai tipped his glass at the Colonel. "Speaking from experience, Sir?"

"What Lizbet does not know," Trev said, "does not hurt her."

"Well, then!" Pietro grinned, swirled his drink, and took a sip. "Perhaps this experience will not be as terrible as I imagined it to be."

Loren rapped his knuckles on the small table. "Or perhaps you take the time to find a Caersan you actually enjoy."

"Not everyone has the power of being the General," Nikolai said. "Who do you have in mind?"

"As you said," Pietro cut in, "he is the General. He has the first pick."

Loren clicked his tongue and took a sip before saying, "I will not settle for anything but the best."

"The Golden Rose, then?" Trev asked and tilted his glass toward the far side of the room.

Following the Colonel's gaze, Loren turned. Ariadne had arrived. Her dark hair piled on top of her head with a series of braids and kept in place with a rose pin of gold. She wore a gown of rich blue, stitched with gold, that hugged her bosom and waist before flowing to the floor like a waterfall at midnight. Her lips, painted dark red, formed the perfect, sensual pout.

"Indeed," Loren said, voice huskier than he intended.

"Nikolai," Pietro said, the words drowned out by the sudden rush of blood muffling Loren's hearing, "you are the Harlows' Elit, correct?"

The Captain, with all his wisdom in Loren's presence, merely said, "It is a duty I take on with the utmost respect."

"Do tell us, though," Trev said a bit breathlessly, "what her lips feel like on your skin?"

Now Loren turned back, the heat in his blood shifting from lust to fury in a matter of seconds. "Do not answer that. As their Elit, you signed a contract to maintain confidentiality."

Both Pietro and Trev shrank back, glancing at one another. It was not often Loren's temper lashed out at them. They were, after all, his trusted officers. Their questions, however, went too far.

"Of course, General," Nikolai said, holding his ground and turning from Ariadne in disinterest. "I would not dream of tarnishing that trust."

"Apologies, General," Trev added after a beat. "That was disrespectful."

"To say the least." Loren glared at him. "My conversations with the Princeps have gone well thus far, and I do not need my subordinates to ruin my progress."

The officers nodded. At least they could all agree upon one thing. Caersan women were not to be slandered. They could taint a Rusan's name as much as they desired. Those women meant nothing to him.

"I imagine your family's standing with the Harlows is already high," Pietro said, edging around the awkward lull. "What with your brother's proposal a couple years ago."

Loren flexed and unflexed his fingers. He did not enjoy being reminded of Darien's hand in creating the opening to the Harlow family. His younger brother should never have been introduced first, and he knew well of Loren's intentions to seek the hand of a Harlow woman. Had he not met his untimely demise, Emillie would have sufficed, but it was Ariadne who always drew Loren's eye.

"Our union would complete the arrangement our families had previously agreed upon," Loren said, turning to scan the crowd again. Ariadne had disappeared. "I believe Darien would be pleased to know I intended on caring for his beloved."

A look passed between Pietro and Trev, their mouths curling with an unspoken joke. Loren could guess at what they wanted to say but were now too scared to voice. He did not blame them. The venomous glare he shot over his shoulder would be enough to silence the most outspoken Caersan.

"It seems," Trev said, raising his glass, "that congratulations shall be in order soon, then?"

That kicked up a smirk for Loren. "Let us not get ahead of ourselves. I do not wish to curse the fortune brought to me by the gods."

No matter if it meant Darien had to die for him to get what he wanted. He had lamented his brother's death long enough. Now it was his turn to finish what was started with Ariadne.

The music hit its crescendo, drawing Loren's attention to the dance floor where he found Ariadne being led through a minuet with Alek Nightingale. She smiled up at the councilman and laughed at something the Caersan said, sending a spark into Loren's veins. That man was the bane of his existence and the number one threat to claiming Ariadne's hand.

"If you will excuse me, gentlemen," Loren said, finishing his whiskey in a single swig and slamming the glass onto the table. "I must claim what is rightfully mine."

"Do not fear, General," Nikolai said. "Rumor has it the Lord Governor has fallen out of favor with the Harlows over recent years."

Loren shook his head. "Do not believe everything you hear, Captain."

With that, he wove his way through the crowd of Caersan vampires, keeping an eye on his target as he moved. Women dipped into curtsies as he passed, perhaps hoping to be asked to the next dance. He ignored them. He had eyes for only one, and she was in the arms of another man.

The final notes of music faded, and the dancers parted ways. Alek held onto Ariadne's hand a beat longer, whispering something in her ear that made color rise to her cheeks. The fire in his blood burned hotter. The governor was not known for his subtlety or respectable manners. Not only did power come with his position but protection from the rumors of bedding his servants and even harming them in the process.

Loren did not believe for a moment that Alek remained guiltless and therefore did not trust him to be so close to the one he would one night be putting the engagement necklace onto.

To his delight, however, Ariadne's gaze found him as soon as the Lord Governor stepped aside. That beautiful mouth curled into a smile, and her oceanic eyes sparkled. He could not recall her ever looking at his brother that way—a mixture of relief and joy.

"Miss Harlow," he murmured, taking her extended hand and kissing her knuckles.

"General Gard." She bobbed a curtsy.

"Will you honor me with the next dance?"

Her smile grew, flashing the sharp points of her fangs. Gods, he would give anything for those to dig into his neck. She was perfect in every way. He would have her—one way or another.

"I would love to," she said as the other dancers took their places for a waltz.

At that, Loren took her hand and led her to an opening so when the music began, he was ready to sweep her into his arms. She sucked in a sharp breath, the first steps taking her off guard. He caught her, though, and shifted her through the steps with ease.

"I am pleased," he said, "to have the opportunity to dance with you without sharing."

Group dances like the quadrille belonged in the past. He preferred the intimacy of the more elegant dances.

"As am I," she breathed, turning her body when his hand slipped to her back.

"Tell me..." He spun her out, then back to him. "What do you think of the ball?"

Ariadne turned her eyes up from watching their feet and blinked twice before answering. "It is lovely. The Kolsons have such a beautiful home."

The niceties were forced, he knew. Lady Dierdre Kolson did not care for Ariadne, and the feelings were mutual. Though they had been cordial prior to her sudden disappearance, the respect fell apart in its wake. With most of the Society not knowing what she had endured, the speculation made Ariadne the hot topic for many months.

"I believe yours was far superior." He pulled her closer on the next turn and inhaled the rich scent of lavender clinging to her hair.

"You are too kind."

They spun in unison with the other dancers, and beside the open garden doors, he spotted Azriel Tenebra. The bastard was everywhere. His sharp eyes followed them like a predator stalking its next meal.

Loren glared at him, his gut twisting with distrust. "Your watchdog is quite attentive."

"Watchdog?" Brows pinching, Ariadne twisted her head around to follow his line of sight. She bit her lip. "He is."

"One might say," he said, annoyed at her sudden shift of attention, "a little too attentive."

Ariadne snapped her gaze back to him with a light laugh. "My father is adamant about our safety."

"And where is the other guard?" Loren liked him better. He did not intrude and made himself far less visible, as a guard should. Tenebra did not know his place. Loren would teach it to him if he must.

"Madan is on a well-earned break visiting his family home in Asterbury."

Ariadne squeezed his forearm, bringing his attention back to her. Her aquamarine eyes glittered like gems. Yes, it was much better looking at her beauty than the half-fae filth across the room.

"When does he return?"

"Soon, I suspect."

"Good."

A light line formed between her brows but disappeared in a blink. If memory served, she had not seemed thrilled about Tenebra's appointment at first. What changed?

The dhemon attack. She had been with Tenebra when Loren spotted her amidst the panic. The guard, not keen on letting her out of his sight at first, acquiesced only after Madan's reassurance of her safety. Now Ariadne trusted him.

Loren would put an end to that.

Waltzing with Loren was like a dream. He guided Ariadne through each step with the same assurances she had felt with Darien. His sure footwork masked every one of her stumbles, making her appear more capable than she felt.

His questions about her guards, however, were off-putting. He did not like them; that much she knew. Azriel least of all. Perhaps he did not approve of Madan at first, either. She did not recall much of those early days after her return.

The music ended. Ariadne pulled back from Loren to lower into a departing curtsy, and for the second dance in a row, her partner held onto her hand and pulled her close. Alek had whispered into her ear that her beauty would inspire him for many days to come. Loren, however, let his lips brush her cheek before speaking.

"It pains me to see you dance with others," he murmured. "I hope to one night be the only one for whom you search."

Warmth curled low in her core. Her breath caught. The spark she once felt with Darien came to life, telling her to find Loren in a dark, unseen corner. They would kiss, and his hands—perhaps even his lips—would drift from her face to her throat to her breasts. Up her skirts to bare flesh and—

Icy cold doused the fantasy when Loren pulled away and she found Azriel watching them, having not moved an inch since the start of the dance. His peridot eyes shimmered, face unreadable. Even from a distance, she could see his throat bob as he cast his gaze elsewhere.

"Perhaps," she said, still watching Azriel. "One night."

Loren followed her path of sight and frowned, releasing her. "Do I need to speak with him?"

"No!" Ariadne grabbed his arm as he turned. The last thing she needed was for Loren to make a scene with their new guard. "Let me. Please."

"Miss Harlow—"

She stepped in front of him. "I will correct this."

A beat of silence from Loren, then, "I will be close by if you need me."

"Thank you, General."

Ariadne bobbed another curtsy, then wove her way through the ballroom. To her surprise, Azriel remained where he stood in the corner. He did not, however, meet her gaze as she journeyed closer. Several Caersan men paused to ask if she would care to dance, and she held out her card for their names before moving on.

The next song picked up, creating a path as guests moved to the dance floor. With every step, Ariadne failed to decide what to say once she reached him. On one hand, he had been an excellent guard thus far, always ready to perform his duties without complaint or hint of annoyance. Escorting her and Emillie to and from the market and Camilla's seemed a menial task, but he took it seriously and managed to make each trip relatively enjoyable.

On the other hand, perhaps he took it too far in places such as this. The likelihood of dhemons crashing through the doors for the second ball in a row was slim. Besides, he always seemed to be watching *her*. Where even was Emillie?

"Mister Tenebra." Ariadne stood right before him, yet Azriel did not look at her.

"Yes, Miss Harlow?" His typical rough voice sounded hoarser than usual.

"I must ask," she said, angling her head to catch his gaze, "why are you always watching me?"

Azriel swiveled his pale eyes to her, sending a strange jolt through her middle. The corner of his mouth twitched. "Correct me if I'm wrong, Miss Harlow, but I was hired to keep you safe. That would require my attention to be on you."

"I believe you were also assigned to my sister." Ariadne struggled to keep her voice low. This was not the place to have an argument with a household servant. Too many ears listened.

"Your sister is on the dance floor."

"I need you to relax when we are at balls."

He frowned. "Again, I was hired to keep you safe."

Ariadne let out an exasperated breath. "I am in no danger here."

Azriel opened his mouth to reply, then shut it twice. She could guess what he had wanted to say, and discomfort curled through her. She thought she had been in no danger at her own home, also. Twice now, she had been wrong.

In her mind's eye, she could see the dhemon pushing in from her veranda door. She felt the spike of panic and recalled the mad rush to reach the corridor behind her. He had barreled after her, scooping her into his arms and hauling her back, screaming. Her fingers had slipped from the handle, and she got one word out before his hand clamped down over her mouth: *Darien*.

"I don't trust even the Caersan of the Society," he finally bit out, shocking her back to the present. "I consider everyone a threat."

Preposterous. Amidst the Society, she was safest. Even Alek Nightingale posed no danger to her despite the dark rumors. She was most in danger when alone.

"General Gard?"

Something flashed in his eyes, and he glanced over her head to where the general no doubt stood, overseeing the discussion. She prayed to any god who would listen that he could not hear them over the din of the room.

"Especially General Gard."

Ariadne almost shushed him. She whipped up a hand to halt whatever he planned to say next and closed her eyes against the audacity of his words. "General Gard is the protector of all Valenul. He has looked after me personally for years—this last year in particular—and is your superior."

"He doesn't care for the Rusan who—"

"Enough," Ariadne hissed, glancing at a passing group of young debutantes who eyed Azriel with interest. She bared her fangs at them, something she had not done since Darien, and felt a rush of pride at the fear which flickered in their eyes. Turning back to Azriel, she shook her head. "General Gard deserves no less than the praise of subordinates like you."

Nostrils flaring, Azriel's mouth turned into a thin line. "I will not argue with my charge about how to do my job. Return to the dance. I won't bother you again."

She opened her mouth to tell him off, her blood heating, but he turned and stalked away before she could speak. Not for the first time, his massive form in his all-black clothing reminded her of a wraith. Only, this time, it was not one she feared but one she found frustrating.

Collecting herself, Ariadne turned back to the ballroom. Loren watched from where he had stationed himself in an alcove with his fellow officers. He lifted a brow—a silent question—and she raised her hand, shaking her head. She was fine.

In fact, between the feelings Loren had reawoken within her and the surge of power from her conversation with Azriel, she almost felt like her old self. All she needed now was the boost of confidence from Camilla or Revelie, and maybe, just maybe, she could approach the remainder of the ball with the same tenacity she had during her first Season.

Ariadne slipped into the crowd to search for her sister and friends. She took a turn around the ballroom, greeting other Caersan women and thanking Lady Kolson for the lovely ball. When she finally found them, they were on their way to the dance floor. Camilla laughed at something Captain Nikolai Jensen said while Emillie gave Captain Pietro Niil a tight-lipped smile. Even Revelie, so often insistent on remaining on the sidelines, held the arm of Alek Nightingale.

"Miss Harlow," said a voice from behind her. She jumped and turned to find Lord Bast Moone, his dark skin shimmering with a light layer of perspiration from dancing. Black hair braided back from his face in intricate designs and ended at his shoulders. His warm, black eyes searched her face. "Will you join me for a dance?"

Ariadne glanced at the others taking their places for the next song, then nodded. "It would be my honor, Lord Moone."

CHAPTER 7

T he ball ended just before dawn with no sign of dhemons or disorder. Ariadne returned home with her sister, father, and guard with enough time to draw the curtains before the sun rose. She had finished out the early morning hours at the Kolson Estate dancing until her feet were numb, laughing with her friends, and enjoying herself more than she could remember doing in a long time. Even Camilla noted her change of demeanor.

But it did not last. The joviality required her constant presence in the moment. If her mind wandered for even a second, the darkness crept in. And it did so every time she looked up above the throng of guests, expecting to spot those cool green eyes and finding nothing.

Azriel kept his word. She did not see him again until they departed, and even then, he kept his distance.

Guilt settled heavily in her gut that morning when she lay down to sleep. The heavy curtains of her bedroom ensured no sunlight could reach her four-poster bed. They did not, however, ward off the discomfort she felt for scolding Azriel.

He had been doing his job. Despite the General's distrust, Azriel had been doing precisely what her father ordered: keep them safe.

When she woke the next evening, Ariadne did not feel any better about what she had said. She dressed without her hand-maid, Penelope, as usual since her return, and braided her hair over one shoulder. The style, though casual, maintained the simplicity and elegance she embraced. Her makeup, light and simple, highlighted her eyes and lips while adding some color to her pale cheeks.

Ariadne relied on Penelope to help with ensuring her face was presentable since she did not like looking at herself in the mirror. Try as she might to appear as she once had, she knew it to be impossible. It was better to pretend she still looked as she had before the kidnapping than the shell she had become.

After thanking her maid, Ariadne made her way down the stairs to the second-floor breakfast den. She passed by the balcony looking down over the ballroom, and she paused to glance over the rail. The pine floor gleamed in the moonlight, no sign of the blood which poured over it a fortnight prior. All evidence of the pain had been washed away just as she was expected to ignore the torment of her past.

She touched the tip of the scar peeking out from her dress. The brand, hidden below the green fabric, haunted her. It was the one reminder of what had happened that she could see each day. The design did not belong to the dhemons but everyone who praised the god of the Underworld, Keon. Even the vampires used the symbol, making it prevalent in her night-to-night life.

And each time she saw it, Ehrun's face, twisted with sadistic glee, looked back. She could still feel the burning, the met-al digging into her wrists to hold her in place, and the salt smeared into the open wound to ensure the brand scarred over. Her screams still etched into her mind, mixed with his wicked laughter. *He's our god, not yours.*

"I am due to meet with the Lord Governors tonight." Her father's voice, drifting from the drawing room, collided with the memory of Ehrun's.

"A pity," replied another voice Ariadne recognized immediately as the General's. "I had hoped to promenade in Laeton Park with the elder Miss Harlow."

Ariadne's heart skipped a beat. Loren wanted to spend time with her beyond a ball. A walk in public meant his interest was not only genuine but serious. It would display to the rest of the Society, for gossip spread like wildfire, what his intentions were.

Her father hummed in thought. "I can assign a guard to chaperone in my stead."

"What of Emillie?"

"Mister Antaire arrived home early yesterday morning. He will attend to her."

A pause as both Caersan men considered the option. Ariadne knew Loren would prefer Madan chaperoning their walk, but to say so could come across as an affront to the one vampire who outranked him in the Society. Her heart hammered at the thought of having the Caersan she hoped to marry in close range with the guard who did not trust the General.

Emotions competed within her. Hardly two weeks into the Season and already Loren's intentions turned serious. It thrilled her to have caught the General's attention, the only Caersan she hoped she would. His connection to Darien, however, complicated her feelings. While their similarities made it easier to see his positive attributes, they also made her heart throb with grief.

Darien had died trying to protect her after tracking them through the mountains to the dhemon's keep. He had not lasted long. Though the dhemon who stole her from her home roared with contempt at the sight of him, it was not he who landed the killing blow on her fiancé.

Ehrun had.

No one else came to her rescue for almost a week. Even when Madan arrived, they almost did not make it out alive. Whatever distraction he orchestrated had been a miracle.

Lost in her thoughts, Ariadne headed to the library. If there was one place in the entire manor that could get her out of her own mind, it was the room filled with books. She devoured the tales which lined the shelves with a particular fondness for fantastical romances from the city of Algorath.

Yet the hope for a moment alone did not come to fruition. Ariadne pushed into the room, zeroing in on a bookcase holding her favorite authors. Not two steps across the threshold, however, she froze and turned. A strange lightness took over the knots in her stomach, and for a long moment, all she could do was stare, lips parted in surprise.

Azriel sat at the far end of the library, dressed in his typical black ensemble with his hair knotted at the top of his head. Beside him, leaning against the couch he occupied, was the long sword he strapped to his back. The book in his hand, larger than most yet thin, appeared out of place.

Of all the rooms she expected to find the disgruntled guard, it was not here.

"Miss Harlow." He shot to his feet, tucking a finger between the pages to keep his place. "My apologies. Excuse me."

She shook her head to jostle the thoughts awake in her brain before holding up a hand. "No, please."

Azriel stooped to pick up his sword. "I will give you your space."

"Please." She motioned for him to return to the couch. "Sit. Read."

"But this morning, you said–"

"I know what I said." She swallowed hard and chewed her lip. "I am sorry for that. I was...crass. You were only doing your job."

He surveyed her for a long moment, eyes wide and wary. A glance at the book, then the sword in his other hand. Several long, quiet seconds passed before he eased back onto the cushions, watching her like a caged animal.

It was not the first time he let his neutral mask slip into what appeared to be fear and, like the last time it occurred, Ariadne was uncertain what to do with it. So she stepped closer with what she assumed was a pleasant expression.

In response, Azriel sank farther back on the couch.

How in the world was someone as intimidating as that guard so frightened of her? She did not hold the same power over him as her father, and the vetting process for personal guards was so thorough due to the nature of their assignments, he was to be trusted with her in all instances. That included private settings such as the library.

To avoid making him more uncomfortable, Ariadne switched directions and pulled an old classic from the shelf. The tale of a young mage imprisoned by a shapeshifter to save her family from his wrath and unwittingly falling in love—a personal favorite of hers.

She plopped into a chair near Azriel and looked at him over the edge of her book. "What are you reading?"

Azriel held up the book in his hand to reveal the cover. A collection of illustrated fae tales. It did not surprise her, what with his high fae heritage.

"Why did you choose that?" She flipped through the title pages of her book to find the beginning.

"My mother used to read them to me."

Ariadne looked up fast. That was not what she had expected. He did not speak much about his mother. Too often, the focus was on his father, the high fae who never married the Caersan vampire he had sullied.

"What happened to her?" The question left her without much thought. She snapped her mouth shut, covering it with a hand, and added, "I apologize. You do not have to answer."

"It's not a problem." Azriel ran a finger over the embossed lettering on the front of the book. "She was murdered by a man I trusted."

Ariadne's heart sank. Her mother had also been killed, though now she knew who had done it. Ehrun had haunted her family much longer than she realized. Until, of course, the dhemon recounted the tale of how he snapped her mother's neck in front of her and her father.

She had not realized they were the same dhemon until that moment.

Empathy rolled through her. "I am very sorry to hear that."

Azriel's gaze flickered up to search her face, his brows pinching with sorrow. "It's why I became a personal guard."

"What?" She gaped at him.

"I want to protect others from the same fate." He pulled his finger free of the pages, letting the book close. Turning his attention to the bookshelf beside him, he stood and slid the fae tales into the empty space with care. "The Caersan who killed her was an officer in the army."

Ariadne's heart crashed against her ribs. Everything made sense. His incessant watchfulness and cool, solid temperament. Why he had yelled so frantically when the dhemons attacked. The frustration when she told him to leave her alone. All of it was because of what happened to his mother—what happened to *him*—by someone they should have been able to trust.

"Did..." She bit her lip again. "Did you see it happen?"

He turned back to her but kept his gaze downcast. "I begged him to stop hurting her." His mouth twisted, and he exhaled hard through his nose, those eyes snapping back to her face. They shimmered as they had the morning before. Tears. "I was too young to *make* him stop."

"Azriel..." She sucked in a breath, the impropriety of her addressing him by his first name halting her train of thought.

His jaw tightened, and he closed his eyes for a long moment. "I should go, Miss Harlow."

Stooping again, he picked up the sword and swung it onto his back, fastening the straps with sure fingers. Ariadne watched, uncertain what to say next. When neither of them spoke, Azriel stepped around her chair, heading to the doors.

Without thinking, she grabbed his wrist. "Wait."

He froze, gaze trained ahead.

"You are a fantastic guard," she said, the words cracking. "I am honored to have you looking after me for as long as you are willing."

A pained smile curled the corners of his mouth, and he turned to her, taking her hand in his and kissing her fingers. When he spoke, his voice was soft and lovely. "Until the very end, Miss Harlow."

The library doors snapped open as he released her hand. Ariadne whipped around in her chair to find her father and Loren standing in the doorway. Azriel took a big step away from her and bowed deep, fist over heart.

"Strange," Loren said coolly. "The library is hardly a place where she needs a guard."

Her father shot him a questioning look. "I am glad to find you both here."

"How may I be of service, my Lord?" Azriel asked, the usual rumble back in his tone. The switch from soft and smooth to rough and gravelly was so sudden, it took a beat for it to register to Ariadne's ears as the same voice. It itched at the back of her mind, as it had the night they met.

"You will chaperone tonight, Mister Tenebra." Her father then looked at her. "General Gard is requesting your company for a turn at Laeton Park."

Ariadne got to her feet, dropping the book on the chair behind her so she could sweep into a curtsy beside Azriel. "I would be honored."

"I have business to attend to in town," her father explained. "I will escort the three of you as far as the Council Chamber."

With another quick bow, Azriel said, "I will have the horses readied immediately."

Then he was gone. Ariadne watched his retreat, a hollowness forming in her chest. Even as Loren smiled at her and bowed, taking her hand in his to press his lips to the same place Azriel had just done the same, she could not feel the same sweep of anticipation she once had.

"Madan, *please.*" Azriel stood at the stable, one hand gripping Jasper's reins and the other shaking at his side. His heart ached, and nothing he did filled the emptiness expanding in his chest.

"You know as well as I," Madan said without looking at him, "we can't change our assignments. The Princeps ordered me to go with Emillie."

He swallowed hard, throat burning. "I've done everything you've asked. Please do this for me."

"I'm sorry, my brother." Madan finally turned and laid a heavy hand on Azriel's shoulder. He squeezed once. "You have to do this."

He did. He knew he did, but it still hurt. In order to continue his life, he must harden himself against the bond. There would be no way to stop the inevitable nuptials between Ariadne and Loren. The best way to do so was to put himself into a position to face it as often as possible.

"It won't be much longer," Madan said after a beat. "Brutis said he's only getting worse. If you can delay the engagement—"

"No." Azriel grit his teeth and pulled Jasper toward the open stable doors. "I won't take the position. They'll never accept me anyway. She's better off with the General."

"Az—"

"Stop it," he snapped and shook his head. For the first time since his arrival at the Harlow Estate, he struggled to hold back the side of himself he hated most. It reared its ugly head like an inferno too wild to contain within his own skin, and fear flickered in Madan's eyes. Azriel sucked in a deep breath, counted to ten, then said in a forced, even tone, "This is for the best. I know it is; I just have to get the rest of me to understand it also."

Madan glanced over his shoulder. "Well, get the rest of you in line quickly."

Azriel grunted, shoving the horrible sensation down into a dark corner of his subconscious to lock away. When he felt composed and trusted himself enough not to explode, he turned to watch the Harlows descend the front steps alongside the General in his billowing crimson cloak.

Stable hands rushed forward with the horses in tow, and for a long moment, Azriel merely stared. Stared and wondered if he really could go through with it.

"Let's go," Madan said, quieter this time. "You can do this."

"You have far more faith in me than I ever will."

Yet he mounted Jasper and closed the distance between him and the front of the manor. Madan kept pace astride his paint, Rune. They said nothing when they took up their position behind the group of Caersan. Only one looked back at them, and Azriel couldn't bring himself to return the smile she offered.

The first to split off from the small company of vampires was Emillie, escorted by Madan. The younger Harlow sister reached across the distance between her and Ariadne. They clasped hands a moment, each giving a silent squeeze before she left. Madan nodded once to him, the only encouragement he had to offer, before following his charge for the night.

Riding into Laeton with the Princeps and General was more difficult to endure than Azriel imagined. Neither of them spoke to Ariadne, nor did they invite her into their conversation. She rode in silence, like him.

"Will there be voting on provincial laws tonight?" Loren asked without looking at the Head Councilman.

Markus clicked his tongue. "Always curious about what is happening in the Chambers."

Straightening a bit, Loren's chest seemed to inflate with self-importance. "It will be my duty to uphold any new laws. It's imperative I am prepared. The latest proposal from Lord Governor Nightingale intrigued me."

"I will not condone the enslavement of any peoples–imprisoned or otherwise." Markus gave Loren a sharp look. "The proposal did not make it to the floor."

Loren raised a brow. "As I suspected."

"If you must know," the Princeps continued, "we are gathering to discuss the absence of Lord Governor Caldwell."

Azriel watched both Caersan from the corner of his eye. How much did they know about the Eastwood Governor's condition? He twisted his hands over the reins, the leather creaking with the tightened grip.

"He is not expected to make a recovery, then?"

"No." Markus sighed. "And he has yet to name his successor. We are putting together a contingency plan for if he were to fail to do so in his Will."

"May I ask who you plan to place as the steward?"

Now Ariadne turned to look at them, curiosity blooming in her eyes. She shifted her gaze from father to suitor, collecting and storing the information she overheard. No wonder word traveled so fast within the Society. Men forget who's around when speaking, landing their secretive details in the laps of those with little power beyond communication.

"That is the topic for the evening," Markus confirmed. "We will discuss the merits for any names brought forth."

A ringing picked up in Azriel's ears at this. He knew whose name would be in that Will. At the rate Lord Caldwell faded, it would be some time before anyone else read it, however. What he needed was to know who the Council planned to put into power.

Too many Caersan men had the potential. Even Loren could take up the mantle if he so chose, forgoing his position as the General to vie for the position of Princeps later on.

The very thought made Azriel sick.

Before long, Lord Harlow parted ways from their group. He bid Ariadne goodbye and gave Azriel a meaningful look. His priority was to keep the daughter of the Princeps from being perceived as anything less than her pure status expected.

They rode on, weaving through the streets of the capital until they reached Laeton Park. Rusan groundskeepers rushed forward upon their arrival to look after the horses while they enjoyed the rolling lawns, well-kept walking paths through gardens, and the southern beach of Lake Cypher. Loren handed the two vampires a gold coin each, to which they bowed deeply and thanked him.

Azriel scowled. That was not generosity. It was a way to flaunt his wealth.

He followed the General and Ariadne at a distance respectable enough to keep them in sight while also providing privacy. The last thing he needed was for Loren to become volatile. By the way the Caersan had been staring Azriel down at the ball the night before, he knew it would be the next step. One toe out of line, and he'd face the General's wrath.

Azriel did not fear the prospect. He knew Ariadne carried scars from the dhemons. So did he. Of all the monsters who crawled through the Keonis Mountains, Ehrun haunted his nightmares most often. The dhemon's blazing red eyes and twisted smirk would loom from every shadowy corner for the rest of Azriel's life.

Compared to that, Lord Gard was nothing.

Ariadne's laugh jolted him from the dark recesses of his past. He refocused on the two walking ahead of him, their elbows bumping together every few steps. What had the General said that could be so funny?

Pain lanced through him. What he wouldn't give to be the one she looked up at with that smile. The monstrosities he would commit for one night–just one night–where he could show her that he could be anything and everything for her. He'd tear the world apart to prove his worth.

He grit his teeth. That was the problem. His solutions always included destruction of some kind. For so many years, he'd been taught that peace required leaving ashes in his wake.

But Ariadne didn't need any more atrocities in her life. She deserved someone who could bring together the broken pieces of her spirit and hold them in place. Azriel would never be able to do so, not just due to his status as half-fae but because of every terrible part of his history.

Ehrun's words still rang true. "She will *never* love a half-breed bastard like you. I'm doing you a favor, really."

He should have let the dhemon kill him. From the moment he realized the soul bond had snapped into place, connecting

Azriel to Ariadne, he knew it would be impossible to act upon it. It was what made him put the rope around his neck. His very being would never be satisfied so long as he was kept from her, and there was no way to ever solidify the bond.

Not even that name in Lord Caldwell's Will.

So as much as Azriel hated it, he was thankful for Loren Gard. The General obviously cared for Ariadne more than most of the greedy Caersan men who tried to dig their claws into her influential dowry. He looked at her with reverence and—much to Azriel's disgust—desire. She meant something to him.

Though it would never compare to what she meant to Azriel.

Ariadne was the very breath in his lungs and his reason to open his eyes every night despite awakening into an agonizing existence without her. He would do it, though, for as long as she needed him to. Until the very end.

What that end was, Azriel did not know. The end of his employment with the Harlows? The end of her needing him around? The end of his life, the only peace he would ever find without her?

Another laugh from Ariadne, and he swallowed hard, watching her with pinched brows. His throat burned, but he refused to let anyone see how difficult it was for him to be there.

Then she turned to look back at him. Something changed in her face at that moment. The smile faded, and her lips parted as her eyes scanned him from head to foot. Her face softened, and she blinked a couple times as though to clear her vision. She rolled her lower lip between her teeth, biting down. A flush of red washed across her cheeks, and when Loren spoke, she didn't look at him at first.

"Miss Harlow?" The General paused his walking and turned to her, concern on his face.

She whipped back around to him and smiled sweetly. Loren cocked his head to the side and slid a hand onto her lower back to guide her forward. In a single, graceful motion, she twisted out from under his touch.

Loren looked back at Azriel, his pale eyes darkening with loathing. In return, Azriel raised his brows and said, a little louder than necessary, "May I remind the General to keep his hands to himself?"

Passerby paused and stared for a moment before whispering behind hands or fans.

The General glared at him, baring his fangs, and for a moment, Azriel was almost content.

CHAPTER 8

A zriel sat at the edge of his bed when the door snapped closed, signaling Madan's return from the Dodd Estate. He didn't turn to look. Didn't move at all, in fact. Didn't see or even hear anything beyond the screaming silence echoing in his mind.

Again and again he saw her broad smile, heard her beautiful laugh, and felt his heart—his soul—shred a little more.

"Azriel..." The voice sounded so, so far away.

It wasn't until the knife was pried from his fingers that Azriel's mind even acknowledged Madan's presence. His sleeves, rolled up to his elbows, exposed the perfect escape he had been too cowardly to take while alone

He'd tried once. Gods, he'd almost succeeded. Madan had found Azriel hanging from a rafter after he'd so brazenly kicked the chair out from under himself. If it hadn't been for the sound, he doubted he'd have been found in time.

That had been a mere two months after saving Ariadne from the dhemons.

This time, Madan slipping the knife from Azriel's hand was simple. Firm hands gripped his wrist and pried his fingers open. The weight of the weapon dropped from his palm, and he watched numbly as the blade clattered across the room.

"What happened?" Madan sat on the bed across from him.

The room slid back into focus around him. It was small and sparsely furnished, like most servants' quarters. Their beds, no more than five feet apart, had a set of drawers against the wall between them. Beside the door sat a small table with two mismatched chairs. Nothing decorated the walls, though Azriel had seen other rooms with small portraits of old family members or loved ones hung on the plaster.

Madan tried again, "How did it go?"

This time, Azriel slowly slid his eyes to him. "I think she loves him."

Madan frowned, concern twisting his expression at whatever he saw on Azriel's face. "Excuse me?"

Though the Season had just begun, Loren's frequent visits to the Harlow Estate only meant one thing. How many more nights had Loren visited before Azriel's arrival? The two had a history. Opportunities to get to know one another and build a relationship.

"The way she looks at him," Azriel said, his voice distant and hollow. "She comes alive when he's around. He makes her laugh, he—" The words cracked. "He is everything she needs."

With a sigh, Madan leaned forward so his elbows rested on his knees. "You knew this would happen when you took the job."

"I know, but..." Azriel groaned and pressed his closed fists against his eyes as though the pressure on his face could relieve that in his heart.

"Nothing is for certain yet."

"Markus approves of the match."

"There's still time." Madan knew better than to close the distance between them. "If Garth dies soon, you could—"

"Enough!" Azriel shot to his feet, unable to contain the terrible, crashing waves of emotions. He stalked to the door, stopped, and turned back. "She will *never* love me. I am *nothing* next to the *General.*"

Madan stilled. "Don't, Azriel. You are more than he could ever be."

"You didn't see them together!" He braced himself on the back of the nearest, spindly chair. The wood creaked beneath his weight.

"You're right, I didn't, but—"

His body reacted before his mind could catch up. One moment he leaned on the chair, and the next it splintered into pieces as he threw it against the far wall. A wail escaped him as every fiber of his being lit like an inferno. The unclaimed bond consumed him, ravaging his heart and mind. He pounded a fist against his chest. The steady beat mimicked the slow shatter of his heart.

"Stop!" Madan grappled for his hand.

Azriel cried out again, weaker this time, and sank to the floor. He tilted his head back against the wall with a low, feeble moan. Tears streamed down his face, creating cool, damp paths from eye to jaw to neck.

They sat there together for what felt like an eternity, Azriel's gasps for air the only sound. Beside him, Madan settled in to wait it out.

Why Madan continued to put up with his outbursts, Azriel didn't know. The vampire had always teased him: ridiculous size, ridiculous emotions. Though he'd always done well to keep them from boiling over in front of others, Madan had seen them all. Seen them and loved him regardless. Azriel owed him everything.

When the tears slowed, Azriel choked past his tight throat, "I can't keep doing this."

Madan said nothing. What could he say? Don't leave? Don't worry, things will get better? No. Though Madan had never given up on him, he couldn't solve Azriel's problems. He had to do it on his own, for better or worse.

"But I can't leave her," Azriel croaked after another moment of contemplation. A fresh wave of tears ran down his face. He could never live with himself if he didn't ensure her safety with Loren first.

"I need to ask you something," Madan said slowly, "and I need you to hear my words before you get upset."

Azriel rolled his head to the side to look at him, suspicion creeping in. "What is it?"

"Is this all because of the bond?" He held up a hand, keeping Azriel from snapping a response. "Is this the bond... or do you truly *love* her?"

Silence. It wasn't a bad question, even if it lit a new fire within him. The bond made fae males possessive and unruly. They acted uncharacteristically and often became volatile when separated from their mates. However, there were also cases of fae bonds beginning and ending with that—no love attached.

"And," Madan added with caution, "if you *do* love her... why? What has she done to earn your love?"

"Bonds are often tied with—"

"That isn't what I asked," Madan cut in. "Don't speak to me about how bonds work. Whelan bonded to me. I know what it's like from a fae's perspective, even if I don't feel the same soul connection."

Azriel snapped his mouth shut and turned his gaze back to the ceiling. What had she done to earn his devotion? When did it start? Because if it were just the bond, his heart wouldn't feel ready to wither away. He'd only feel the rage of the bond instead. At least that was what he'd always been told.

"I love her." He spoke the words in a whisper. "The bond connected me to her, sure, but I can't think straight when she's around. She's the only one I see whenever she's in the room. I can't stop thinking about her, what makes her happy or sad or angry. She's the breath in my lungs, my reason for getting up each night, the only light in my dark world."

Madan sighed. His only response.

"She is kind," Azriel continued, his voice tight and rough. "She's intelligent and funny, and I want to make her laugh. I want to speak with her about anything and nothing and..."

"Azriel—"

"And I hate her," Azriel cut him off. "I hate her so much for doing this to me. She ruined *everything*, and I would do absolutely anything to stop feeling this way, but I can't. I can't, Madan, and it hurts so, so much."

"I know." Madan put a hand over his. "I wish I could take it away for you."

Azriel shook his head, closing his eyes. "I just want her to be happy... and she would never be happy with me."

"Everything could change."

"No," he whispered, "it can't. Because as much as I love her, I couldn't ask that of her."

Madan squeezed his hand. The gesture had passed between Ariadne and Emillie a multitude of times. This time, Azriel squeezed back. Perhaps it could mean something to them, too, for there were no words he could use to express the pain of his broken heart.

Emillie knocked on Ariadne's door after returning from the Dodd Estate. A quick acknowledgment of her request to enter and Emillie slipped into the room, closing the door behind her with a snap. She needed to hear how the walk with Loren had gone and to discuss everything she and Camilla went over.

Inside the suite, Emillie found Ariadne pulling her own curtains closed against the impending sunlight at the balcony doors on the far side of the sitting room. Over the last year, those doors had never been so much as unlocked. Her sister's last suite in a wing across the manor still bore the marks of the struggle which took place inside it. No one went in there anymore.

Ariadne's new sitting room, lit by several candelabras and a fireplace, included two small couches and several plush chairs. A low table sat in the midst of all the cushioned seats, and two tall bookshelves took up the wall opposite her bedroom door.

It was similar enough to the other suites of the manor to be familiar without it being a replica of the rooms Ariadne now hated.

Her sister turned, her dark braid reflecting the candlelight like spun obsidian. Those eyes, so much like her own, glittered as Ariadne smiled. She closed the distance between them and held out her hands, which Emillie took. The gesture, more common in public, set off warning bells in her mind.

"How is Camilla?" Ariadne asked, pulling her to the couch and sitting.

Emillie settled in and slumped back against the cushions. With anyone else, she would never slouch, but this was different. The last year changed more than just her sister's manner-isms.

"I do not know how she does it all," Emillie said in a rush.

Ariadne raised a brow, mimicking the relaxed position on the couch, and turned her head to look at her. "What do you mean?"

"She exudes confidence," she said, staring at the ceiling. "I do not think I will ever be like her."

A soft chuckle from her sister, then, "What did she do to make you think this?"

Waving her hands before her, Emillie struggled to put words together. "Everything!"

"You are being oddly specific," Ariadne teased. "You had tea. What could have possibly happened?"

"It was *not* just tea!" Emillie sat up and stared at her wildly, mind reeling at the events of the evening. "She invited Dier-dre and Belina. Revelie could not attend."

When she had arrived at the Dodd Estate, Emillie expected her friends and no one else. What she discovered, however, was that Dierdre Kolson and Belina Fletcher had overheard Camilla's invitation to Emillie, Ariadne, and Revelie at the ball and immediately invited themselves. As prominent wives of Central Province's Councilmen, it would have been imperti-nent for Camilla to deny them.

"You've got to be joking." Ariadne's voice was flat, and Emil-lie could not contain her smirk at the slip into Rusan colloqui-al language.

"I wish I was." Emillie rolled her eyes and fell back against the couch again. "They would not stop asking about you. I did not know what to do, so Camilla warded off all their questions."

Ariadne shook her head. "Thank the gods for Camilla."

Neither Dierdre nor Belina had been particularly kind to Ariadne over the last year. They had been less than civil prior to her sister's sudden disappearance and, as wives of Councilmen, they knew more than most of the Society. What they did not know was *why* Ariadne vanished or why every soldier in Eastwood Province was sent to find her.

"What did Camilla say?" Ariadne's voice was quieter then as the understanding took hold.

Emillie blindly found her sister's hand and gave it a squeeze. "She told them, in her most diplomatic way, that neither of us had the authority to divulge any information on the matter."

Ariadne snorted airily. "I doubt that dissuaded them."

"Hardly." Emillie sighed, her heart kicking up its speed. "They asked if the rumors about you and Darien were true."

Her sister went painfully still but said nothing. She did not need to. The rumors surrounding her and Darien were just that: false information passed around to make trouble. Some said Darien had deceived her into running away with him and, when she refused, he stole her before being brutally murdered by soldiers. Others claimed it had been Ariadne who lured him into the mountains, where she killed him in an old, forgotten mage ritual like the one which brought about the vampirism curse. Still more swore they eloped and ran away together before being discovered by her father.

No matter how much Emillie tried to shield Ariadne from the whispers, she knew her sister heard them all. None, of course, were true, and Emillie knew that even if she only knew part of the story herself.

"Camilla told them to stop believing all the gossip," Emillie said after a moment. "When they pressed the matter and made some rather backhanded comments about you being the Golden Rose, Camilla told them to either shut their mouths or leave."

At that, Ariadne gaped at the ceiling. "She did not."

"Oh, she did." She chuckled at the memory. Both Dierdre's and Belina's faces had gone ghostly white with disbelief. "They were so taken aback that they actually stopped."

A small smile curled the corners of Ariadne's mouth. She closed her eyes for a long moment and said, "I would have loved seeing the looks on their faces."

"It was perfect," Emillie admitted. "But that is what I mean: I would never have the same confidence as Camilla to put an end to their nagging so quickly."

Turning her head, Ariadne frowned at her. "You are far more courageous than you believe."

"Hah!" Emillie shook her head, unable to scrape up a single incident in which she felt remotely brave. "Not like that."

"Perhaps not," Ariadne agreed. "But I have seen you face off with Father many times and walk away victorious, and he is one of the most frightening Caersan I know."

That had not occurred to Emillie. While in many circumstances, she stood up to their father in order to protect Ariadne from his onslaught of constant questions, never once had she believed herself to be brave because of it. It had only been natural to keep her from suffering through the same round of interrogations over and over.

"Tell me, then," Emillie said slowly, "why I cannot seem to talk to him about..."

"About liking women?" Ariadne sat forward again and looked at her. "Because when you told him off before, it was for me. Not you."

Not promising, then. "I do not think I can."

"For this," her sister said, squeezing her hand again, "I cannot tell him for you, but I can be with you when you do it."

Emillie swallowed the sudden lump in her throat and blinked back the burning tears in her eyes. "Thank you."

A silence descended upon them for a long moment. Emillie did not know when she would tell her father the truth about her preference for women, but she knew it needed to be soon. If she was to continue through the Season, he needed to understand that she would never make a decision about a suitor. He would have a fight ahead of him if he wanted her to marry a Caersan man.

"How was the visit with the General?" Emillie asked, grappling for anything to keep herself out of her head. At least by deflecting, they could speak of something more pleasant.

Ariadne loosed a long sigh, her cheeks coloring. "He is everything I desire in a husband."

That was not what she had been expecting to hear. "How so?"

"He makes me laugh and reminds me of..."

"Of Darien?"

"Yes," she breathed. "It is strange, though, how much he seems to dislike Mister Tenebra."

Emillie raised a brow at that. Why her sister bothered to worry about their guard, she had no idea. "What happened?"

"Well..." Ariadne glanced at her. "I had been in the library with him when Father and General Gard came in."

Her jaw fell open, and she turned her entire body to face her sister. If anyone had heard about that, the scandal it would cause would be one for the ages. "You were in the library alone with him?"

But Ariadne laughed. "He is our *personal guard*, Em. Are we not often alone with Madan as well?"

She had a point. Nonetheless, Emillie could not help the rush of curiosity and excitement from their strange rendezvous. "True. But why *were* you in the library with him?"

Ariadne gave her an exasperated look. "I had not planned it. I went to read, and Mister Tenebra was already in the room."

Emillie hummed, detecting no lies. "Alright. Why do you believe the General dislikes him?"

"The look of disgust when he entered the library." Ariadne chewed her lip. "And he was not pleased at all to see him at the ball last night."

"That does not sound like he dislikes him specifically," Emillie pointed out, "but is merely protective."

"He called Mister Tenebra a watchdog."

Emillie frowned. "Well, then."

"Mister Tenebra has done nothing wrong that I can tell." Ariadne continued to worry her lip, pulling her hand free from Emillie and twisting her fingers together in her lap. "Have you noticed anything that would make him out to be less than trustworthy?"

She took a moment to consider it. Over the last fortnight, Azriel had been the only guard to look after them. Though quite different from Madan and far more sullen, Emillie could not pinpoint a moment in which she ever felt uncomfortable. He was respectful and caring and took notice of little things, which put them at ease, even if they did not recognize it at the time.

"Never," Emillie admitted. "He has always been perfectly gentile. Although..."

Ariadne frowned. "What is it?"

"He *does* look at you a lot."

"What?" Ariadne's cheeks reddened, her hands stilling.

Emillie scrunched her nose. "Have you not noticed?"

The blush deepened. Her sister was hiding something. "Not entirely..."

"Well," she mused, "maybe the General has taken notice of Mister Tenebra's...careful observations and believes it to be something more."

Her sister continued to chew her lip but said nothing.

"Ari," she continued slowly, "*is* there something more?"

In true Ariadne fashion, her sister scoffed loudly and shook her head despite the brightness of her face. She looked away as a sparkle picked up in her eyes. "The very question is preposterous. There is nothing, and there will never be anything between me and Mister Tenebra."

"Even I can admit that he is handsome," Emillie said with the hopes of drawing out more from her sister.

Ariadne glanced at her, visibly fighting back a smile. "He is."

"It is a shame he is not a part of the Society," she said a bit wistfully.

"His mother was."

"And you know this how?" Emillie laughed and shook her head in disbelief. "Well, maybe his father was a secret fae king or something."

Her sister smiled broadly. She knew that one would get her to smile. Ariadne adored her fae tales and all their fantastical elements—something Emillie never truly understood.

"And what if he was?" Ariadne said, sitting back again. "Even then, he would not be considered good enough for a Caersan woman."

"But!" Emillie held up a finger. "He would be a prince in disguise. That has to count for something, right?"

They both laughed. Emillie could not remember the last time they had found so much entertainment in something so simple. Yet despite the jokes, she could see her sister's thoughts swirling. As much as Ariadne claimed to want to marry Loren Gard, a piece of her came to life around Azriel Tenebra.

CHAPTER 9

A zriel avoided Ariadne over the next week. With Madan back from his visit with Whelan and Kall, it became easier to fade into the background. He took over the schedules posted in the guard house, which got him away from the manor more often, and the one journey into Laeton was made more simple with Madan entertaining both Ariadne and Emillie. Visits from potential suitors required their presence to oversee interactions, and that was all.

The main event of the week, a dance at Councilman Fletcher's estate, allowed him a chance to breathe. Madan took to circling the ballroom, and Azriel kept outdoors, battling against the urge to burn the entire manor to the ground.

"We're going to town tonight," Madan informed him while they broke their fast together in the common room the following evening.

Azriel grunted by way of response and picked up his bowl of porridge to tip the dregs into his mouth. Another night, another menial task to drag himself through. Going to town, at least, didn't require much thought on his part.

"We leave in thirty minutes."

He nodded and pushed back from the table to clean the bowl in the washtub. What else could he say?

"Azriel." Madan's voice was sharper than usual. "This has to stop."

Looking over his shoulder, he frowned. "What?"

"This." Madan gestured to Azriel as a whole, and when the half-fae merely looked down at himself, puzzled by what was implied, he pressed, "You."

With a grunt, he turned back to the bowl, rinsing the suds from it in clean water before propping it on a rack. "I'm no different than I was before."

Madan sighed and joined him at the washtubs, dunking his own bowl into the soapy water. "They're starting to notice."

"Who?"

"The Harlows."

"How do you know?" Azriel dried his hands on a towel and stalked back to the table, where he swung his sword onto his back. The familiar weight comforted him.

"I've been asked about your well-being." Dishes clinked behind him as Madan stacked his bowl beside Azriel's. "By Ariadne."

The sword almost dropped to the floor as his fingers fumbled over the fastenings. His stomach knotted, and the porridge threatened to find its way back out of his body. Readjusting the straps back to their normal place, he shoved the leather through the appropriate loops.

Taking his scrabbling as an indication that he was listening, Madan continued, "You can't just stop talking to them out of nowhere."

"I didn't talk to them much anyway," he muttered and yanked the tie from his hair. A black curtain fell in front of his eyes just long enough for him to run his shaking fingers through it and shove it out of his face again. It took several tries to retie the knot.

Madan appeared before him. "Make more of an effort."

"I'm making as great of an effort as I can." Azriel refused to look him in the eye. It would give his feelings away—as if Madan didn't already know. Their telepathic connections to Brutis and Razer had exposed them to one another. He knew how Madan's mind worked just as Madan understood his own thought processes.

"Don't lie to me." Madan walked to the door and paused. "We need to ready our horses. Let's go."

Azriel watched him leave and, after taking several deep breaths, followed. By the time he reached the stables and had Jasper's tack in place, his mind was at once more clear and cloudy.

Why had Ariadne asked about him? She made it abundantly clear she didn't want him around too often, and yet their conversation in the library had been very different. The mixed signals were getting confusing.

He mounted Jasper, silently wishing it were Razer to take him away through the clouds, and followed Madan to the front of the manor, where they met with the Harlows. Markus, it appeared, would be joining them as well. Azriel had half a mind to ask Madan if he could be excused for the evening since they were well taken care of by the two of them.

Then Ariadne turned toward him and smiled. "Good evening, Mister Tenebra."

Fuck.

Azriel inclined his head. "Miss Harlow."

She opened her mouth as though to speak again, but Markus nudged his stallion forward to stand between them. He nodded to Azriel and said, "You are up to speed on tonight's events?"

"Yes, my Lord." Azriel bent at the waist, fist over heart. They would be going into Laeton for shopping, then partaking in the midnight meal in town. Madan shared the information on their way to the stables. They were to join in case a suitor asked to speak with either Harlow sister and required a chaperone.

"Very good." Markus then set off and to his daughters said, "Come, girls, or we will be late for our reservation."

They made good time on the trek into Laeton with minimal conversation. Even Madan didn't find a moment to ask any questions. Markus, the ever-busy Princeps, didn't seem to want to inquire about his daughters' potential suitors.

Until, of course, General Loren Gard made an appearance outside the capital's Court House.

"Princeps!" Loren hailed as he descended the steps to the street.

Markus dismounted, and they clasped forearms. "Good evening, General."

In unison, Azriel and Madan dropped to their feet, and each held out a hand to the Harlow women. Emillie balanced her weight on Azriel's while Ariadne hardly touched Madan on her way down. Once standing, they curtsied low to the General in greeting.

"Miss Harlow." Loren kissed Emillie's hand first, then took Ariadne's and let his lips linger a breath longer before saying, "You look very well, Miss Harlow."

"You are too kind, General." Ariadne's cheeks flushed.

Azriel bit back a scowl at the discomfort in her eyes as she pulled her hand from Loren's.

Madan dug an elbow into his side and hissed under his breath, "Hold it together."

He grunted in response and averted his gaze.

"What brings you to the Court House tonight?" Markus looked up the steps behind the General, a light frown forming.

"Drunk and disorderly conduct during training," Loren explained. He adjusted his weight so he turned his back to the women, cutting them off from the conversation.

Madan shot Azriel another warning look as though taming a rabid dog.

Markus, however, appeared unphased by the adjustment and nodded. "A pity to see such behavior within the ranks."

"I do not see such recklessness amongst the Caersan ranks," Loren said and lifted his gaze to Azriel. The corner of his mouth twitched, and he continued, "Poor breeding makes for a half-rate soldier."

Heat sparked in Azriel's veins at the jab. He grit his teeth and glared back at the General. Holding his tongue, though difficult, was pertinent in moments like this. The need to prove him wrong outweighed the desire to shut him up. Besides, he'd heard worse before.

"I hardly think it has anything to do with lineage." Ariadne's voice was the last thing Azriel expected to hear at that moment. By the look on her father's and Emillie's faces, he was not alone.

Loren, however, smirked. "Miss Harlow, what would you know of this matter?"

She drew herself up, cheeks rosy. When she spoke next, she did so with a strong voice and looked Loren in the eye. "The pressures of the military are likely to cause a breakdown of morale. Perhaps instead of insulting your men's parentage, consider addressing their trauma."

Azriel watched in disbelief. Was she defending him? Madan's eyes widened. Emillie paled. Even Markus looked at his daughter as though she'd grown a second head. No one spoke for a long moment.

Then Loren laughed. He *laughed* at her and stepped closer. "Oh, Miss Harlow, you are amusing."

The corners of Ariadne's mouth tightened, the anxiety melting away in a flash to reveal a woman Azriel had yet to see. Her words left her low and hard, "Excuse me?"

"What would a Caersan woman know about the pressures of the military?" Loren shook his head, still grinning. "Your most exciting days in the Society are trivial at best."

Madan seemed to understand what was happening before Azriel registered what he was doing. The other guard's body blocked his path with one hand pressed against his chest. The edges of his vision turned dark, and his head throbbed.

"Gods damn you, Azriel," Madan hissed. "This is not what I meant."

"Remind me, General," Azriel growled over Madan's head, "when the last battle you fought was?"

Loren pivoted to glare at him. "That is none of your concern."

"If you've forgotten," Azriel's voice grew louder with each word, "she has seen and endured more than most of your pampered Caersan officers."

"Tenebra, stand down," Markus snapped, eyes flaring.

But Ariadne gaped at him in astonishment. He didn't know what she saw in his face, but whatever it was didn't appear to frighten her. She said nothing, though, and looked to Loren. Only then did her expression give in to fear, and damn if it didn't add to the fire in his blood. She feared him.

"You gained your title as General from your *fortunate* breeding alone." Azriel pressed forward, Madan's open hand curling into a fist against his chest in warning. He ignored it. "You wouldn't last one minute with what Ariadne went through."

"You do not have the right to speak of her with such informality." Loren stepped closer, face white with rage. "Cease immediately, or there will be consequences."

Vampires paused on their way in and out of the Court House, drawn in by the sudden argument between the General and his subordinate. They whispered and watched with piqued interest. He didn't care. He couldn't care about any of them. Not so long as that man attempted to demean Ariadne Harlow in front of him.

"And you have no right to speak to her as though she is nothing but dirt beneath your boot." Azriel pushed past Madan to stand a breath from Loren. The extreme height difference forced the General to tilt his head back to look him in the eye.

"Tenebra!" Markus snapped from behind Loren. "Final warning!"

"Get out of my face, or you will be the next thing under my boot," Loren snarled, hand drifting to the sword at his hip.

Azriel angled his head and bared his fangs. "You are a pompous asshole who uses a worthless title to elicit fear. Ariadne Harlow deserves better than the likes of you."

Madan pushed between them and shoved at Azriel's chest. Azriel took two steps back, still pulling his lips back in a snarl. His hands shook at his sides, and he blinked hard to clear the pounding in his head. It did nothing.

"Return to the manor immediately," Markus ordered him from behind Loren. "I will deal with you when we return."

Holding up a hand, Loren shook his head. "No."

"He is my responsibility," the Princeps said.

"And all personal guards fall under my jurisdiction." Loren motioned at the soldiers standing outside the Court House. They hurried over. "Arrest him."

Ariadne watched in horror as the soldiers unbuckled Azriel's sword and yanked his arms behind his back. Thick-chained shackles clanked as they locked around his wrists. He did not resist, choosing instead to glare at Loren the entire time. Only when the soldiers gripped his arms to lead him away did his line of sight shift.

Something big swelled in her chest as his eyes collided with hers. The peridot shimmered, and the hardness fell from his face. He opened his mouth once, then closed it without a sound. What Loren was doing was wrong. Disagreements should not equate to an arrest.

"Father, he cannot do this," she said, reaching for him.

Her father pulled away. "Tenebra stepped out of line with a superior officer. He must face the consequences."

"But he was only—"

"For the sake of the gods," he snarled, "hold your damned tongue and learn your place."

Ariadne gaped at him, speechless. He spoke as though he blamed her words for Azriel's response. What Loren had said had been out of line—for his soldiers and the implications he made about their guard.

Perhaps she *was* to blame for what Azriel said. He had been defending her, just as she had tried to refocus Loren's words. They had been cruel and out of character for the man she saw as her future husband.

"General, please," she said quietly, slipping closer to Loren. He looked down at her, brows furrowing, and she laid a hand on his arm. "I spoke out of turn. This is my fault."

Loren scanned her face for a long moment, then spoke to the soldiers. "I will determine his punishment at a later date. Take him away."

"No—please!" She turned to her guard, flanked by and dwarfing two soldiers. Were she not mortified by the events unfolding around her, the sight would have been comical.

Azriel searched her face for a long moment before he stumbled forward, the soldiers marching him toward the back of the Court House. To the prison, unseen from the street.

"Ari..." Emillie's soft voice behind her did little to settle the sudden urge to vomit. Her sister's hand slipped into hers and squeezed. "Ari, it is done. You have to stop."

The words, faint behind the ringing in her head, did little to calm her down. As Caersans who stopped to watch the drama continued on their way, her father turned to Loren, lips thin and nostrils flared.

"You made a fool of my personal guards," he said in a low hiss. "A fool of me."

Loren pivoted back to him, cool and calculated—a wholly atypical expression to what Ariadne was accustomed to. When he spoke, his tone was even and the words loud enough for onlookers to hear. "My apologies, Princeps. Your guard was out of hand. I will remind him of his place and return him to your services once he has been dealt with."

"What punishment do you believe he is due?"

"You and I can determine that later." Loren straightened the cuffs of his sleeves as though everything was business as usual. It only made the hollowness in Ariadne's stomach grow. "I do not feel it appropriate to leave you with an insubordinate guard. He will be corrected."

"Publicly or privately?"

Loren's mouth curled up at the corners. "As I said, my Lord, you and I can determine that later, though I believe the fine people of Laeton will wish to witness what happens to a personal guard who steps out of line."

A beat passed as Ariadne looked on in horror, then her father nodded. "Very good."

He could not be serious. A public punishment for speaking out of turn? Even for how much Loren hated Azriel, it was extreme. The Caersans who lingered to overhear the words passed between her father and the General seemed pleased, however, and hurried off with excited whispers.

Ariadne squeezed Emillie's hand without looking at her sister. It would be too much, as the memories of her own *punishments* threatened to drag her below the surface of her thoughts.

"Just remember," Ehrun had said to her, filling the fresh cut he made on her back with salt, "that this is what happens to vampires who forget their place."

She could barely hear the words above her screams, but he had made sure to lean in close to her ear. His breath smelled of rotting meat, and when she did not look at him, he grabbed her face to force her head to turn. Crimson eyes burned down at her, filled with a hate she did not understand.

"Do not despair," he had continued, brushing her tears away with surprisingly gentle fingers, "I will send you home soon to share your lessons with the rest of them."

What most of those lessons were or why they were inflicted upon her, Ariadne could not recall. After Madan rescued her, she never looked back. When she tried to claw through the memories of what happened, she could piece none of it together. Some hours had disappeared completely, while others were muddled and confusing. She had no timeline, no sense of what happened to her first or last—just pain.

Pain and flashes of suppressed memories that surfaced at the worst times.

Such as in front of a Court House, surrounded by strangers.

"Miss Harlow." Madan stepped closer to her and held an arm out to gesture to Astra. "May I help you onto your horse?"

Ariadne blinked at him until the words registered. She looked around to find her father swinging back up into his seat, Emillie already sitting on her mare, Lily, and Loren mounting Azriel's empty saddle. They were leaving, then. Just like that, they moved on from whatever had just happened.

Exactly as the dhemons had moved on after Ehrun crushed Darien's skull in front of her. Her fiance had been led away in chains, much like Azriel. The next time she saw him, his fangs were removed, and when he tried to fight back, Ehrun put a permanent end to the first vampire she ever loved.

Watching Azriel being led away muddled her thoughts.

She searched Madan's marbled eyes for a moment, desperate to claw her way back to the present. How he had kept himself professional through it all, Ariadne could not fathom. From the moment they met, he had never faltered under the pressures of his job.

"Thank you." It was all she could muster as she turned to Astra and accepted Madan's extended arm to swing into the saddle.

"Since you are down one guard," Loren said, turning the stallion to face Markus, "may I join you for the evening? I will be happy to return this stallion to your manor when you have finished your business in town."

Her father nodded, if a bit stiffly. "Much appreciated, General."

Their group stopped first at Madame Ives's, where she and Emillie picked up new dresses for the next ball. Revelie, sensing the tension, did not pry. She spoke quietly with Emillie as she handed over the short-sleeved yellow dress embroidered with green leaves and cut with a classic empress waist. To Ariadne, she merely gave a tight smile, then handed over the dusty rose dress.

"I will see you soon," Revelie promised before moving on to her next customer.

Ariadne looked at the color, folded so perfectly in its box, and tried to ignore the pang she felt in her gut.

That color would look lovely on you.

What would happen to Azriel the next time she saw him?

Their parcels were secured to Madan's and Azriel's horses, and they turned toward the businesses along the edge of Lake Cypher. In the distance, Ariadne could make out Laeton Park stretching along the lake's banks. How different the night had been when she strode with Loren along the fantastical walking paths. He had been so light and humorous, at ease and approachable.

Now he felt rough and distant. The shift from callous to business-as-normal unnerved her. Had he always been that way? Perhaps she had merely never noticed before.

Or was it her fault? Her father had been right; she should not have spoken. It was not her place to comment, and in doing so, she had gotten Azriel into dire trouble.

But why—*why*—did he say anything at all? She would have let it go. The encounter was hardly the first time she had been laughed at or spoken to in that manner. Such was life for a Caersan woman in the Society.

Nonetheless, it had been dealt with whether she liked the outcome or not.

The bistro added Loren to their reservation without fuss. After all, who would deny the Princeps and General their midnight meal? With the whispers that followed them all the way to their table overlooking the lake, Ariadne could only guess how many of them witnessed or already caught wind of what happened outside the Court House. She dared not listen to what the onlookers said for fear of hearing the worst.

Once seeing them to their table, Madan bowed. "My Lord, would you prefer I remain nearby or at the front doors?"

"Remain at the doors," her father instructed without looking at him.

The guard's mouth twitched, and he inclined his head again. "Very well. Enjoy your meal."

A tightness took hold of Ariadne's chest as he walked away. Not only was she uncomfortable having Madan—or, she supposed at this point, Azriel—so far away when in public, but she knew he worried for his cousin. Unlike Azriel, Madan struggled to hide his emotions from his face, and the pinched brows said more than he could.

"Was a conclusion reached for Lord Governor Caldwell's successor?" Loren asked.

Her father eyed the sampler of white wine as it poured into his glass. He swirled it, sniffed, and sipped. With a quick nod to the server, she filled his glass before moving on to the rest of the table. Once satisfied, he turned to Loren and said, "We still await the final ruling due to the undisclosed documents in his Will, but I believe we have come to a conclusion for a steward."

Ariadne sipped her wine, one hand twisting the skirts of her dress in her lap. Positioned with her back to the rest of the room, she could not find it within herself to relax her shoulders. She stared, unseeing, at the paper before her describing the courses set for the midnight meal.

"Lord Veron Knoll would become the Lord Governor Steward if no other successor is named." Her father eyed Loren for a long moment. "Do you plan to take your father's place one day?"

Loren's mouth curled into a smile. "One cannot play soldier his entire life, no?"

Chuckling, her father nodded. "Indeed, General."

"I believe taking the same route as you," Loren said, "would be the wisest course of action if I am to one day have a family."

His sapphire eyes slid to Ariadne. At once, she felt butterflies in her gut and an unexplainable desire to hide.

There was no doubt in her mind that, of all the suitors thus far interested in her, Loren made the most sense. In fact, she desired no other Caersan man but the General. His increased attention on her over the past several weeks was all she had wanted since the beginning of the Season.

So why did she suddenly recoil? She should be able to overlook his treatment of an unruly subordinate.

Then Ehrun's voice crept in from the back of her mind alongside flashes of the dungeon below the dhemon keep. "No one will want to marry a sullied Caersan. Isn't that right?"

Her stomach roiled at the memory of phantom hands sliding down her body and the very thought of creating a family with *anyone* tied directly to that moment. Hands shaking, she gripped her skirt again and looked anywhere but at the two Caersan men beside her, who took no notice of her sudden rocking.

"Ari?" Emillie whispered, reaching across the distance to untangle her hand from the fabric. She squeezed once, long and hard.

Ten...

Ariadne sucked in a breath, squeezing back.

Nine...

Exhale. You are home. You are safe. You are loved. A mantra she often forgot until she felt her sister's hand in hers.

Eight...

Inhale. How could she possibly marry someone who did not even look at her except as a puzzle piece of his future?

Seven...

Not even her father noticed her discomfort. Oblivious, useless Caersan men.

Six...

Ariadne looked to Emillie. Her sister held firm, her eyes studying her without expectation. Just calm, cool understanding. What would she do without Emillie? She could not leave her—ever.

Five...

The first course set down before them—a creamy soup of some sort. It smelled delicious, yet still, her stomach churned.

Four...

She pulled in another long breath and closed her eyes, steeling herself for the moment she had to reopen them and become a functioning member of the Society once again.

Three...

The air left her in a rush, eyes snapping open.

Two...

Pulling in a final breath, she looked up at her father and the General. Loren did not so much as glance in her direction, and a realization hit her like a horse's hoof to the chest.

One...

Ariadne picked up her spoon with her free hand and slid it into the bowl as she grappled with the thought that now plagued her: Azriel would have cared.

Ordering Azriel Tenebra's arrest was the highlight of Loren's week, without a doubt. He could think of nothing sweeter than the incarceration of the Harlow family's bastard watchdog. From the way he interjected himself at the worst of times to how he watched Ariadne with too close an eye, the gods damned guard was nothing but a nuisance.

And if that was not good enough, Loren would be in charge of doling out the punishment. What an absolute dream.

The evening following the arrest, he met Markus outside the Laeton prison. While dropping the Harlows off at their estate, he had arranged the meeting in order to discuss the appropriate manner of discipline.

"Good evening, Princeps," Loren said with a bow, then extended his arm.

Markus took it with a nod. "General. Shall we see if time in the brig has done its job?"

Mouth curling, Loren nodded. He would not let Azriel get away with his actions so easily but played along nonetheless. Markus did not need to know his plans just yet. Not while he still hoped to regain his guard so soon.

"Does this mean you wish for him to return to your estate?" Loren stepped to the front door of the prison, and the soldier standing guard bowed before opening it for them. "Or would you prefer I find you a suitable replacement?"

"Ah, that will not be necessary."

"May I ask why?" Loren schooled his face into neutrality though the disappointment dripped from his words.

Markus sighed as they made their way through the reception room to the first set of locked doors. Another soldier stepped forward, a key ring in hand. With a few clangs from the tumblers, the door swung open.

"You must understand," the Princeps said once out of earshot of the soldiers, "the precarious position it would put me in to exchange guards so readily."

Loren raised a brow. "I am certain I do not know what you mean."

Pausing outside an empty cell meant to contain low-level criminals for a day, Markus crossed his arms. "You know and understand to some extent what my daughter's condition entails."

Condition. As though Ariadne were incurably ill. While there was a chance some professionals would state her to be such, Loren did not believe it. She had been a mess upon her return from the mountains, but the strides she had made over the last year were admirable. She partook in dinners again, and the balls were livelier with her presence.

But it was not Ariadne's mental fortitude which Markus addressed. Loren knew precisely what he meant. The pains she had suffered at the hands of the beastly dhemons were unmentionable.

"Of course, my Lord," Loren inclined his head. "But what does that have to do with this simple guard?"

"You are well aware of the lengths I have gone to conceal the details of her disappearance last winter." Markus shook his head as though the entire ordeal had been an annoyance at best. "Do you know why I find it necessary to do so?"

Loren gestured for him to continue.

"The war against the dhemons has been plaguing my family for centuries." Now a deep frown formed on the Princep's brow, and he did not look at Loren directly. "I have worked hard to minimize the impact of my personal history on legislature and militaristic strategies."

"I beg your pardon?" Loren cocked his head. "Your personal history?"

Markus raised a hand to silence him. "What I am about to tell you has been stripped from the history books detailing the lineages of the Society. There is only one Caersan man still alive with ties to my past, and he is well on his way into the next world. Do you swear, as your own father swore, to never speak of this information again?"

Now he had Loren's attention. There were few secrets left in the Society, what with the loud-mouth lords and ladies who made it their business to spread gossip and rumors. To be privy to a final scrap of hidden knowledge would be one of Loren's greatest achievements.

"My Lord Princeps, I swear by my life blood to hold your secrets as my own from now until my dying night." Loren placed a fist on his heart and bowed deeply.

"Very good." Markus nodded, seemingly satisfied with the vow. "As you know, I married my wife, Jezebel, a little over a century ago. What many will not acknowledge is that I was married once prior."

This was not what Loren had expected to hear. He blinked hard and refocused without interrupting.

"My first wife, Mariana Caldwell, was murdered by the dhemon you know as the Crowe." Markus clenched and unclenched his fists at his sides. The memory clearly still haunted him, as it should.

The Crowe, a dastardly monster who many considered to be the king of the dhemons, held jurisdiction over the Keonis Mountains until last year. Then, the Crowe disappeared, and Ehrun, his dhemon army's general, took his place.

When Loren took up the mantle as General, the Crowe was gaining ground in the war against the vampires. More and more villages fell to the raiding parties and hundreds of Rusans died in each attack. Keeping up with his incessant movements was taxing at best, impossible at worst.

Until it all came to a sudden halt half a year before Ariadne's abduction.

"He targeted my family due to my position as the General at the time." Markus shook his head with a scowl. "I vowed the same fate would not reach my new wife—my new family. Then Jezebel was killed and Ariadne, tiny as she was, escaped by the tip of her fangs."

Loren frowned as Markus went silent. "Pardon me, my Lord, but how does this connect to Tenebra remaining in your service?"

"In order for my personal guards to maintain the appropriate level of security," Markus explained, "I believe it to be necessary for them to understand the full history of my family. Not only does Tenebra know about Mariana and Jezebel, he has been briefed on the details of Ariadne's disappearance."

So the bastard knew all of this before Loren. The thought soured, and Loren could hardly contain his disgust.

Markus continued before Loren could speak, "He has sworn an oath to remain quiet. If he is released, he may choose to forgo the oath to undermine me."

"To break an oath such as that holds greater consequences than what he has already done. Why would you entrust him with such information?"

"Because I trust him explicitly."

Loren scoffed. "What could a half-breed bastard have done to gain such loyalty from the Princeps?"

With a cock of his eyebrow, Markus studied him for a long moment. "He assisted Madan Antaire with Ariadne's rescue."

"That is absurd." Loren could not stop himself. "By the gods, how was he involved?"

"As Mister Antaire explained, Tenebra provided a safe haven after he escaped with Ariadne," Markus said simply. "Madan specifically requested Tenebra to join him this Season due to their mutual connection to that event."

Loren could not believe what he was hearing as secret after secret poured out before him. From Markus's first marriage, to his family being hunted by dhemons, to Azriel fucking Tenebra's involvement in Ariadne's rescue—it was all too much.

And he knew that one outburst would do little to cast the bastard from the Harlows' employment.

Fuck.

Then he would have to make the half-breed suffer in whatever way he could.

"Well," Loren said with a shake of his head, "now that I understand why Tenebra will continue as your personal guard, shall we continue on to determine the discipline appropriate for his behavior last night?"

"Lead the way, General."

They continued on in silence through the next set of doors, this time unguarded. The room they entered, however, had soldiers stationed at each set. It was a wide room with high, barred windows where the prisoners were allowed to move farther than their cells provided. Loren did not approve of it, and therefore, very few vampires roamed through.

Soldiers unlocked the next set of doors, and they entered a long corridor lined with the small, dark cells. Most prisoners within the dark confines awaited trial or their final sentence; others merely waited for the final payment to be made by their families to free them from the prison once and for all.

Azriel sat on the floor of his cell halfway down the corridor. He looked up, appearing relatively at ease in the prison. Probably not his first time behind bars.

"Mister Tenebra," Markus said. "How do you fare?"

The bastard stood and bent at the waist. "To be quite honest, my Lord, I am in prison and therefore not faring well."

To Loren's surprise, Markus chuckled. "Do you understand why you are in that cell?"

Those cold eyes slid to Loren. "Indeed. My sincerest apologies, General. I'm ashamed of the way I lost my head last night."

He would lose far more than that if Loren had any say in the matter. As it were, the very public offense would not be seen as a crime punishable by death in the eyes of the Society. To give the bastard such a sentence would reflect poorly on Loren.

"I am not here for apologies," Loren said coolly. "We are here to inform you of your punishment."

The corner of Azriel's mouth quirked up. Loren would punch him right in that smirk if he could.

"Your impudence," Markus said, "and attempt to smear General Gard's name in public was witnessed by far too many Caersans to let go so lightly. You are to be made an example of—publicly. As it was the General you insulted, it will be the General who decides your final sentence."

Now it was Loren's turn to smirk as Azriel's face returned to neutral. A muscle ticked in the guard's jaw as he turned his attention to him. Loren reveled in it for a moment before speaking.

"Fifty lashes three nights from now." He turned to Markus. "I believe a few extra nights in a cell will do him some good."

The Princeps considered it for a moment, then nodded. "Very good. Fifty lashes in three nights. The flogging post outside will be sufficient."

When they both looked at Azriel again, he inclined his head. "I will see you in three nights, then."

CHAPTER 10

Returning to the Court House for Azriel's discipline sat low on Ariadne's list of priorities. Her father refused to tell her what punishment they decided on. That he was forced to remain in the prison for three more nights told her what came next would not be pleasant.

"Mister Tenebra's outburst," her father explained when she asked to stay home for the third time, "was due to your lack of control."

So being forced to witness whatever came next was as much a punishment for her as it was for him. At least it felt that way. She should have guessed, really, based on the way her father avoided speaking to her over the last few days. Whenever he did deem her worthy of his attention, it was to discuss the next ball and suitors with whom to dance—with the General at the top of the list.

The first time Ariadne attended a prisoner's sentence in public, she was thirty years old. She watched the prisoner—a young Rusan man—branded on his face as a thief and could not stomach it. She learned later he had stolen coins to feed his young wife and child. That man she did not know. Now the one she would witness being harmed was someone with whom she had become familiar.

By the time they reached the courtyard outside the prison, a crowd of Caersans and Rusans alike had gathered. News spread like wildfire in Laeton, and everyone available would arrive to watch.

So much for being civilized.

Ariadne stood beside Emillie and their father toward the front of the throng. Madan took up his place behind them, the ever-dutiful guard placing himself between the crowd and his charges. Yet no matter how much he tried to be at ease, Ariadne sensed his tension.

A hush fell over the onlookers as Loren stepped out of the prison and mounted the steps to the raised platform before them. Stocks, a pillory, hang-man's noose, and a flogging pole loomed behind him. Everyone waited with bated breath to hear what would happen to the guard who spoke down to their General.

"As many of you know," Loren said, his voice imperious, "a personal guard under my command defied his superiors."

Caersans and Rusans alike murmured around them, curious about the vague statement. Their voices rose as Azriel stepped out, shackles around his wrists and ankles clanking. He stood tall despite the hisses of disapproval, staring out above the heads of the crowd and avoiding eye contact with anyone.

"Azriel Tenebra," Loren explained, "will continue his role as personal guard to the Harlow family after today's lesson in humility, but his libelous claims against me, your humble General, will not be forgotten."

Several nearby Caersans leaned in to ask her father why he would continue to employ such an insolent guard. To her surprise, her father did not entertain any of the questions and merely gestured for them to watch and listen.

"Moreso, however," the General continued, "his indirect threat to my life by attempting to intimidate me will be addressed in tonight's punishment."

Ariadne frowned. Behind her, Madan went very still. Even her father narrowed his eyes. This must not be something he had discussed with Loren. Azriel never threatened Loren—why would he claim such a thing?

"My intent is to impress upon Mister Tenebra," Loren said, "and every guard and soldier under my command the importance of maintaining order and following the instructions of authoritative officers."

"Father," Ariadne whispered, unable to look away from what unfolded on the stage, "he did no such thing. You know this."

Her father shook his head once. "It is not my place to decide how the General perceived Mister Tenebra's insubordination. We discussed the appropriate level of discipline."

Despite his confident words, her father did not appear convinced Loren would adhere to their plan. He watched the General with a tense jaw and sharp eyes. Something was not right.

"To make my statement," Loren said, sweeping his gaze across the crowd for emphasis, "Mister Tenebra will receive two hundred lashes."

The world dropped out from under Ariadne as a unified cry rose up from the crowd around her. Both the Caersan and Rusan vampires were hungry to watch the blood spill, no matter if the crime had been inflated. None of them cared. None of them knew what really happened.

"Father," she choked out, though she did not dare grab his arm in public again. The world spun. "Do not let him do this."

Emillie turned to them. "Two hundred lashes...that could kill him."

When their father did not respond, his face stark white and lips thin, Ariadne turned to Madan. The guard she had come to love like a brother stared up at the stage, eyes wide and mouth slightly agape. He knew as well as she that Azriel did not deserve such severe punishment. Neither of them could act.

"Please stop him," Ariadne said, turning back to her father.

"There is nothing left to be done." Her father shook his head. "If I interfere now, it will undermine the General's control over his subordinates."

"What if he dies?" Ariadne watched as Azriel was led to the flogging post. Though full-blooded Caersan vampires healed faster than most fae or mages, his half-Caersan lineage would almost certainly reduce the speed at which Azriel healed. Only fae with magic healed as fast as them. He had none. He was no better off than a Rusan vampire facing that level of flogging.

"He won't," Madan assured her quietly, still not looking at her. "Trust me."

The wrist shackles were removed along with Azriel's shirt. Ariadne's heart thundered as the crowd sucked in a collective breath. His muscular chest was covered in scars ranging from long, razor-thin stripes to broad, short reminders of daggers or knives.

On his left pectoral, however, was the one scar that made her throat tighten: a crescent pointing to the sky with three lines, each shorter than the last, descending from it. The mark of Keon—the same brand she bore in almost the exact same place.

He had been burned by dhemons, too.

Azriel's face twisted at the sounds of shock, unable to conceal his shame and discomfort at being scrutinized by them all. When he turned to have his wrists locked into the chains dangling from the flogging pole, the onlookers inhaled again, and his muscles rippled as they stiffened. If his chest had been bad, it paled in comparison to his back. Lumps of scar tissue criss-crossed along his skin, and it was obvious that this was far from his first time getting flogged.

By the gods, what had he done to deserve such fates?

In that moment, Ariadne knew Emillie was correct: two hundred lashes could very well kill him. His body did not heal like a Caersan's, and whatever fae blood he possessed did nothing to aid him.

"Please stop this," she begged her father. "Please. This is my fault—I am sorry! Please make him stop."

Her father turned his golden eyes to her, jaw tight. "No."

So it *was* her punishment. To watch Azriel suffer for his defense of her at the hands of the man she thought she could trust. With each slow, agonizing second, that trust dripped away.

On the platform, Loren shrugged off his jacket and unfurled a whip. The long, thin end hit the wood underfoot with a dull smack. He took one last look at the crowd, then lifted the handle and let it fly.

A whistle, then a crack as it connected with Azriel's back. His hands twisted in the shackles to grip the chain overhead, muscles flexing all down his arms and shoulders. Yet he made no sound as the second and third strikes landed.

A low murmuring rose over the crowd. Surprise, perhaps, at his lack of visceral reaction to pain? Ariadne did not know.

What she did know was the lightheadedness that overcame her as the skin split on Azriel's back. Blood poured as the tenth lash ripped across the old scars, pooling at the guard's feet. As suspected, he did not heal like a Caersan would. Sweat dappled Loren's forehead, but the General reeled back and struck again.

A phantom pain radiated from Ariadne's back where cut after cut dug into her flesh. Its permanence, thanks to the salt, itched beneath the dark blue dress she wore.

Her breathing turned ragged as she watched, counting each lashing.

Fifteen... sixteen...

Despite actively avoiding prisoner punishments after that first experience, Azriel's flogging was not the first she witnessed. The memory clawed its way back into the forefront of her mind as Azriel's knees began to quake.

Twenty... twenty-one...

The last person she had seen whipped had been a dhemon at the keep. What he had done to deserve such a punishment, Ariadne did not know, nor did she ask. It had not been possible for her to wonder or speak as she was dragged down the dungeon corridor to her small, dark cell. The dhemon, chained up to the wall, stood firm against the beating, and all she could remember thinking was *good*.

Now, she wanted it to end. Needed it to end.

She could not breathe. Her head swam, losing count of the wet slaps of the whip on mutilated skin. Worse, each strike was delivered by a man for whom she had ached mere nights ago. Now, his smirk twisted his face from beautiful to nightmarish. His cruel enjoyment of Azriel's pain, reminiscent of Ehrun's sick pleasure, seared into her mind.

Mere nights ago, that face had smiled down at her, making her light with elation. Those hands held hers with such care.

Now, they tortured the one man who ever stood up for her.

"Ariadne," Emillie breathed, catching her as she swayed on the spot.

Shaking her head, Ariadne took a step back, running smack into Madan's chest. She heaved in a rattling breath. "I cannot..."

Ariadne turned and pushed through the crowd, aiming for their carriage on the far side of the Court House. If she could reach it, she would be able to catch her breath. She just needed to sit—to get away from the bodies pressing in on her and the sound—that terrible sound. It echoed in her mind.

"We will go," Emillie offered, taking her arm to steady her.

"No," Madan cut in and pulled Emillie away. "Stay with your father. I will watch after your sister."

Ariadne tripped, and Madan's strong hands steadied her by the arms. Not the back—never the back. He never touched her there, just like Azriel never had, either. Now she understood why: he, too, held a history of pain in his skin.

"The carriage," she croaked, pushing through the crowd. Some onlookers chuckled under their breath while others cried. Their expressions, hazy in her desperation to get out of the throng, ranged from wicked delight to horror.

To her relief, Madan said nothing. No soothing words or expectations. His silent company as she stumbled past the outskirts of the crowd was more than enough to show his solemn support. Even as they reached the main street outside the Court House and he opened the door to the carriage, he did not so much as speak her name. Instead, he extended a silent arm for her to balance herself against while clambering into the darkness beyond.

The journey home felt like an eternity for Emillie. She sat across from a blank-faced Ariadne, who stared out the carriage window without saying a word. Their father, after ensuring both his daughters were safely within the carriage, stayed behind as Madan escorted them home.

"What are you doing?" Emillie asked him before he could close the door on her.

Her father shook his head once. "I must speak with General Gard and arrange for Mister Tenebra's return to the manor."

Emillie held a hand out to block the door as he tried, once again, to close it on her. "Will he be returning tonight?"

"Yes." The door snapped shut behind him, leaving Emillie to sit back and process everything she had witnessed.

Ariadne left her side as the fiftieth lash struck Azriel's back. It was clear at that point that Loren, sweat dripping down his face, enjoyed every second. His Caersan muscles did not fatigue as a Rusan vampire's or even a mage's did. Each strike was done with strength and purpose.

Somehow, though, Azriel's knees never gave out. When they reached the hundredth lash, his entire body trembled. He adjusted his feet and slipped on the blood-soaked wood. The chains kept him upright as he corrected his stance, hands still gripping the chains above his head.

Emillie did not blame Ariadne for leaving. Her stomach had roiled with each hit.

In the end, Azriel's back was stripped almost entirely of its flesh. Soldiers stepped forward with caution, not wanting to fall into the puddle of blood that, by then, had leaked onto the dirt beneath the platform. They released his wrists, and for a moment, Emillie believed Azriel would fall. His legs, accepting the weight back onto them, shook violently, and his arms hung limp at his sides. He did not look at the crowd before being led down the steps and disappearing into the prison.

On her way back to the carriage, Emillie had nearly lost the battle of wills against her stomach. It churned again and again, and she fought the tremors of shock at seeing Azriel in such a state.

"Is it over?" Ariadne had asked when she sat back against the carriage cushions.

Emillie confirmed, and that was the last she heard from her sister.

Back at the estate, Ariadne hurried out of the carriage and into the manor. Emillie stood at the foot of the front steps and watched her go. She could do nothing to help her sister with this. Only time and patience would see her through.

"Miss Harlow." Madan's voice shook her back to the present.

She turned to the guard, his grim face attempting a small smile. "Yes?"

"I must ask you to return indoors." He gestured to the manor. "I am needed to...help."

To help Azriel.

Emillie looked beyond him as the carriage pulled away. A prison wagon made its way up the drive but took a turn down a side path reserved for servants and deliveries. Her father rode his stallion at the back of the procession.

"Mister Antaire," she said and squeezed his hand like she would her sister's, "I am sorry."

He huffed and shook his head. "He knew full well what he was doing when he got himself into this mess, but he's been through worse. He'll be on his feet in no time."

Emillie frowned, not quite understanding what he meant by any of it. "I hope so."

The guard bowed and mounted his horse again, taking off in the direction of the wagon. Once gone, Emillie started up the steps into the manor, where she found the staff quieter than usual. None of them looked at her as they mumbled their greetings and passed. Odd, though not uncommon when one of them got into trouble.

Maintaining her distance from the servants, Emillie stopped Penelope as she passed. "Is my sister in her room?"

The Rusan woman curtsied. "Yes, Miss Harlow. I saw her go in."

She nodded. If Ariadne did not wish to speak, there would be no changing her mind. Eventually, she would come out, and Emillie would be ready to help her overcome this as she had overcome everything else.

Before the maid could slip away, she asked, "Do we still have Algorathian salve?"

"Yes, my Lady." The maid smiled. "It's in the clinic. Would you like me to fetch it for you?"

"No," Emillie said with a shake of her head. "I can get it myself. Thank you."

With another quick bob, Penelope disappeared, leaving Emillie alone in the foyer again. She hurried toward the servant halls where the small clinic room lay. As Caersan vampires rarely became ill and healed quickly, the clinic's main purpose was to assist the Rusan servants with any ailments they had. It remained stocked with bandages, medicines, and ointments of all kinds. Some were locally sourced, while others, such as what Emillie sought, were imported from the fae or mages.

Emillie opened the medicine cabinet and pushed jars aside until she found the Algorathian salve. The glass jar, filled with a thick, clear, gel-like substance, was too large and heavy to hold in one hand, even for a vampire. She tucked it against her body, distributing its weight across her forearm instead.

Back out of the clinic and further down the servant's hall, she ignored the strange looks from the household staff as she passed. Odd though it may be for her to be in spaces most often occupied by Rusans, Emillie was on a mission and refused to let their uncertainty dissuade her.

At the end of the hall, she opened the door leading to the basement and started down the steep and narrow staircase. Some steps whined underfoot, and she hesitated on each one, her heart skipping a beat. Still, she continued on to the bottom, where she stared down the long hall of doors.

Everything about the place kept for the Rusan servants made Emillie uncomfortable. With little she could do to improve their accommodations, she merely chewed her lip before continuing forward. It was not her first time down there, and she did not anticipate it being her last.

At the end of the hall, Emillie paused in the doorway of the common room. Two Rusans, a man and woman, leapt from the couch to greet her as customary. She waved them off.

"Where can I find Madan?" Emillie asked, glancing over her shoulder again.

The woman stepped forward and pointed back down the hall. "The fifth door on the left, Miss."

Emillie inclined her head. "Thank you."

She backtracked the way she came and, stopping outside the fifth door on the left, she knocked.

For a moment, no one responded. Emillie worried her lip again. Perhaps he had yet to return to his room. It had not been long since she saw the prison wagon, after all. Could he have gotten Azriel to his bed already?

The door cracked open just wide enough for someone to look through, then Madan slipped into the hallway.

"Miss Harlow," he said, scrubbing his hands on a cloth. Deep crimson peeled away from his fingers, and a metallic scent wafted from the room as the door closed behind him. "What can I do for you?"

Emillie pried her eyes from the cloth covered in Azriel's blood, hesitated, then held out the jar. "This is an Algorathian salve. It will help."

Madan frowned and stared at the jar presented to him. "I've been ordered not to heal him with magic."

Absurd. Barbaric. She stayed her tongue, though she allowed her features to convey her thoughts on the matter. She pushed the jar into his hands. "A good thing it is not magic, then."

"An Algorathian salve is—"

"Merely a mixture of ingredients that anyone, mage or otherwise, could concoct." Emillie moved his hand to accept the weight of the jar. "It was founded in Algorath and most of it is produced in the desert region, thus its name. But mage, fae, or vampire could make it."

He chuckled and took it. "You know a lot about it."

"As you know, I prefer to indulge in facts over fiction," she said with a shrug. "Medicinals are one of my favorite subjects."

"Well, then," Madan said, patting the lid of the jar, "thank you."

Emillie sucked in a breath and looked at the door behind the guard. "How is he?"

A ridiculous question, given it had been a mere hour since the final blow struck. Caersan vampires could heal from such malicious beatings within a day or two. Rusans, if they were lucky to survive, would likely take over a week. With Azriel's strange heritage—a fae father with no magic—she could not even begin to guess how long he would take to heal. Assuming, of course, his Caersan blood saved him.

"Not well," Madan admitted after a moment. "He's sleeping right now."

Good. Rest was good. The likelihood of seeing Azriel on his feet anytime soon was slim, then. The thought perturbed her.

"I think there is another jar in the clinic," Emillie said, nodding to the one in his hand. "In case you run out. It really should help."

"Yes." Madan smiled down at her and rested his hand on the doorknob. "I will try it."

Heart kicking up its pace, Emillie motioned for him to wait. He did, watching her curiously as she gathered her thoughts. There were some things only Madan knew that she doubted he had told anyone before. She needed to know now.

"What was Ariadne like?" She chewed her lip, then added, "When you found her, I mean."

Madan went very still, his dark brows lowering over his eyes. He searched her face for a long time before saying simply, "Your sister and what she went through made Azriel's punishment tonight look like midnight tea."

Stomach twisting violently, Emillie swallowed hard to keep nausea at bay. She had suspected it to be bad, but the comparison underscored the reality of what Ariadne endured. So long as time was given to heal between sessions and the blood of another provided, a Caersan vampire could survive torture indefinitely—whether they wanted to or not.

"Thank you for your honesty," she whispered after composing herself. "Please... tell Mister Tenebra I am sorry."

"I shall," Madan said and, as she turned, he continued, "but, Miss Harlow...none of this was your fault. Or your sister's. He made his choice, and now he is dealing with the consequences."

Emillie grimaced back at him. "Speaking up for what is right is not a choice. It is a responsibility not all of us are ready to take on."

CHAPTER 11

L oren entered the Harlow Estate the next night with sure steps. He handed his cloak to the butler at the door before being led into the parlor to await the Princeps. Arriving unannounced, frowned upon by anyone of lower status than he, meant traversing the unfamiliar waters of waiting. Markus needed time to prepare himself for whatever conversation he believed Loren intended on having.

After their brief conversation following the lashing, he expected all of it. Markus had expressed his deep displeasure at what occurred, and perhaps Loren had stepped out of line with two hundred strikes.

But perhaps the half-bred bastard should have died like he had intended.

Disappointment was uncomfortable, to say the least.

Turning back to face the foyer from his position near the low-flame hearth, Loren found the butler speaking to a Caersan that, for a moment, he did not recognize. Madan's features shifted into focus when he pivoted, dark brows low. His lips barely moved as he explained something, one hand brushing his back over his shoulder. Then his eyes snapped up to sear into Loren with such scathing heat, he could not help but smirk.

Azriel's healing incompetence, underscored by his absence, alighted hope in Loren's chest. If he did not kill the bastard, at least he wounded him enough to keep him off his feet for a bit. Perhaps now he would put distance between himself and Ariadne.

Madan's top lip peeled back, flashing his fangs.

"Good evening, General Gard," Markus called, appearing and then crossing the foyer in a few languid strides. As he passed his servants, Madan disappeared out the door, and the butler swept down the hall. "I was not expecting you."

Loren extended his arm, which Markus took with a firmer-than-usual grip. "My apologies for the intrusion, my Lord Princeps. I came to inquire after the elder Miss Harlow's welfare. Her sudden departure last night concerned me."

"Ah." Markus nodded, then gestured out of the parlor. "Let us speak in my study."

Down the hall to the regal office, Markus barked an order for food to be delivered at a passing maid, then closed the door behind them with a snap. The long study, with its two side walls bearing floor-to-ceiling dark wood shelves, invited conversation around a low table between a pair of blue velvet couches. Before the bay of windows at the far side sat a large, dark desk covered in stacks of paper, and a high-backed leather chair.

"Sit." Markus turned to the credenza near the door and poured two glasses of amber liquor as Loren settled onto one of the couches. "I must apologize for the mess. Lord Governor Caldwell's illness has grown worse, and I am up to my fangs with paperwork."

Taking one of the glasses, Loren tipped it to the Princeps before sipping. The whiskey burned deliciously on its way down. "Not a problem, my Lord. You are a busy man. Is there no hope for a recovery?"

"At this point," Markus sighed, "there is naught to be done. Garth Caldwell is old, and this has been long overdue."

"A pity." Loren felt none of it.

"Truly a shame." Markus sounded more exhausted over the situation than saddened. "What brings you to my home this evening, General Gard?"

Loren settled for a regretful expression. "I must apologize, my Lord, for my sudden change of plans last night."

Markus had not said much to him before departing from the prison, but his fury was palpable. The last thing Loren needed was the Princeps to bear him any ill-will if his plans to wed his daughter were to come to fruition.

With a sigh, Markus took his seat across from him and rested his free arm over the back of the couch. "I am disappointed you felt the need to punish Tenebra so severely. Speaking out of turn has never demanded such a heavy hand in the past. I believed my explanation of why I needed him well would have been enough to dissuade you from such harsh consequences. I was wrong."

"My personal feelings about him influenced my decision more than I anticipated." Loren swirled his drink, studying the Princeps's reaction.

Not even a flinch revealed the High Councilman's thoughts. "Your personal feelings?"

"Indeed." Loren sat forward, leaning an elbow on his knee. "While his cousin has done a fine job over the last year, I have found Tenebra to keep a strangely close eye on your elder daughter. Perhaps I am looking too far into it due to my own desire to protect her after all she endured."

Markus lifted a brow and nodded once. "I understand your concern, General, though despite his outburst in town the other night, I believe his intentions were to protect her as well.

I would think you would find it comforting to know someone to be keeping her safe when you are not around."

"After my brother died," Loren said with as much sorrow as he could muster, "I have felt a deep desire to remain close to Miss Harlow."

"Very good." The corner of Markus's mouth twitched up. "I am pleased to hear this from you. While your brother's death is regrettable, I have always found you to be a Caersan of worth. Your actions to care for my family, Ariadne in particular, have proven this time and again."

Loren's pulse quickened. He smiled back at the Princeps and sat a little straighter. "It has been my intention for quite some time to ask for her hand, my Lord. Would you find this acceptable?"

A knock at the doors drew their attention, and after Markus's invitation to enter, the young maid from earlier entered with a tray of breads, fruit, and cake. She curtsied, then set it down and asked, "Is there anything else I can get for you, my Lord?"

"Not at this time, Penelope, thank you."

Penelope smiled at Loren, her pale cheeks flushing, before retreating to the doors. Before she disappeared, he raised a hand and said, "Actually, Penelope, I have a request."

"Yes, General?" She turned back to them.

"With the Princeps' permission," he said, looking to Markus, "I would like to speak with the elder Miss Harlow."

Markus gave him a curt nod, then turned to the maid. "Please ready Ariadne for a visitor. Have her wait in the parlor."

With another quick curtsy, Penelope said, "Yes, my Lord. Right away."

Then she was gone. Markus turned to the food set before them, took up a small slice of bread smeared with salted butter, and popped it into his mouth. He sipped his drink to wash down the remains. "I believe a match between you and Ariadne is serendipitous."

Loren leaned into the back cushion, the corners of his mouth ticking up and his chest swelling. "I am honored, Princeps."

"In fact, I had originally hoped for this match," Markus said without looking at him. "Though your brother was a fine Caersan, I had intended on more for Ariadne. I mean no disrespect to Darien, of course."

With a low chuckle, Loren snatched up a slice of the lemon cake and pointed it at the Princeps. "No disrespect at all. It had been my intention to ask for Miss Harlow's hand a long time ago. My brother made himself known first."

"Disappointing, really." Markus's eyes glittered in the candlelight. "So much pain could have been avoided had he stepped aside for his elder brother. I am confident this last year's debacle would not have occurred had she been engaged to you."

Finally, someone understood Loren's annoyance at the situation. He had loved his brother dearly and mourned his death as any sibling would have. Unfortunately, Darien had not been equipped to handle such a task when he went after Ariadne's abductor. Had Loren been the one she had called for that night instead, the dhemon would not have made it to the treeline.

"And I am confident," Loren said after swallowing a bite of the cake, savoring its tartness in such a glorious moment, "nothing of the like will ever occur again with Miss Harlow under my direct protection and that of the army."

"Very good." Markus held out his glass, and Loren tapped his against it. "To a bright future."

Ariadne, having abandoned her post in the parlor, backed away from the study door, a hand over her mouth. She had not overheard much of the conversation, but it was enough.

Her father had never approved of her engagement to Darien. Loren, his own brother, believed him to be unfit to provide for her. Loren's visit held a separate intention than what she had thought: to ask for her father's blessing to marry her. If the wishes for a bright future were any indication, the General had received it.

Stomach twisting, Ariadne hurried back to the parlor, where she steadied herself on the back of a chair. Her eyes burned, and her throat swelled. After everything Loren had done the night before and the pure epicaricacy he received from Azriel's suffering, she was certain the last thing she wished was to marry a man of such countenance.

That her father would not consult her beforehand only proved both their lack of compassion.

Yet the utter helplessness she felt outweighed it all. It hollowed out her gut and squeezed her chest. Speaking against her father's wishes would not go well. Insulting Loren by denying a proposal would destroy any future prospects with suitors.

Then she would never be free of her father's relentless control. His incessant desire to dictate every aspect of her and Emillie's lives kept them both afraid. Her sister feared speaking the truth about whose company she wished to keep, and Ariadne feared telling him *no*.

All her life, she had agreed to his every whim. The only time she felt free to choose had been when he accepted Darien's request for his blessing. For the first time in her life, she had chosen something substantial for herself, and he had said *yes*.

Now she knew it had been done reluctantly.

This engagement? Ariadne knew well she had no choice. She could attempt to put it off for as long as possible, and yet, she would not prevent it from happening. One night, she would have no option but to accept.

Unable to maintain her composure, Ariadne turned and headed for the stairs. She needed to lose herself in her books—to pretend the world around her did not exist and instead, she was a character on the page, moving through the motions of a life beyond her own with better prospects than she.

"Miss Harlow."

Not three steps up, she froze at the sound of Loren's voice. She swallowed hard and forced the rising bile back down her throat. Taking a deep breath, she cursed herself for not taking the time to count back from ten in the parlor. Instead, she plastered what she hoped appeared to be a sweet smile on her face and turned to look down at him.

"General Gard," she said and descended to accept his outstretched hand. The feeling of his fingers curling around hers—the same which had gripped the whip the night before—made her skin crawl. His lips brushing her knuckles felt like barbs. How quickly she had gone from craving his attention to recoiling from it. "I was uncertain if you were still visiting."

His lips curled into the smile that made her melt a mere week ago. The glint in his pale eyes, which she once thought to be a look of affection, only appeared as deviousness and triumph. "I am glad I caught you, then."

"As am I." Her voice, quieter than she wished, squeaked.

The discomfort, however, seemed only to appeal to him more. His smile grew. "I came tonight to inquire about your health."

Lies. Ariadne frowned. "My health, General?"

"You left so suddenly last night," Loren explained, still holding onto her hand, his face growing serious. "I was concerned you were unwell."

She peeled her fingers from his and clasped her hands together, swallowing hard. Vampires did not get ill. His concern was unfounded. "I found the display to be... unsettling."

Loren's brows knitted together with worry despite it not reaching his eyes. In fact, she did not miss the uptick of his lips. "I am very sorry to hear that. Perhaps we should caution against bringing Caersan women such as yourself in the future."

Heat bubbled forth and flushed across her cheeks. "I do not believe that to be necessary."

"May I ask what you would suggest?"

So now he wanted to hear her suggestions? Now he was willing to listen to her words? Or, perhaps, it was merely another dig at her incompetence as a woman. Ariadne shifted her shaking hands behind her back, praying to the gods he could not spot her unease.

"I would suggest," she said with as much confidence as she could muster, "allowing each woman to determine her limits, just as you would a man."

He angled his head. "Would that be fair to the Caersan women who do not yet know their own limits? I seek to understand, Miss Harlow, how one will know whether or not they are capable of handling such displays."

Ariadne gave him a tight smile. "Allowing Caersan women, as you do men, to determine when it is best to bow out without criticism would be an excellent first step."

"Ah." Loren held up a hand and smiled. "I apologize if I offended you. That was not my intention at all."

"Thank you, General." Ariande bobbed a quick curtsy. "If you will excuse me, I was just—"

"I had hoped," he cut in, grabbing her wrist as she turned to take hold of the banister, "you would accompany me into town—chaperoned, of course—where I could purchase you a gown for the next ball."

A scream started in Ariadne's head at his firm grasp on her. She swallowed the growing lump in her throat and gripped the rail to hold herself steady. "I am sorry, General, but I must decline. As you know, I purchased a gown already."

Loren held firm for another agonizingly long moment. When he released her, she whipped her hands behind her back again and smiled up at him. Blood pounded in her ears. Each breath felt like fire in her lungs.

"I must admit I am disappointed," he said, inclining his head. "I merely hoped to spend more time with you."

"Perhaps another night." Ariadne curtsied again. She needed to get away from him. "I look forward to dancing with you, General. Another waltz, perhaps."

A true smile flashed across his face. It almost worked to warm her up to him again. "I would like that very much, Miss Harlow. I hope you have a restful evening."

Foregoing the traditional farewell by ignoring his hand, outstretched again to kiss hers, Ariande turned and picked up her skirts to ascend the stairs. Each step was a calculated motion. Too fast, and she would appear eager to get away—despite that being her intention. Too slow, and he could interpret it as an unwillingness to leave his presence.

Fortunately, she made it to the next floor and, when she looked back, found Loren still watching her with an expression she knew well: possessive and determined. Her stomach roiled, but she smiled back and raised a hand in farewell before continuing down the hall.

Once out of sight, Ariadne clutched her chest and picked up the pace until she made it safely to the library, her closest haven. She shut the door behind her and gasped for breath.

How had she never noticed how cold and empty his eyes were? How had she been so blind as to believe he looked at her with any kindness? It never had been. It had always been that same look. As though she already belonged to him.

Gods, it made her want to run from him.

She could not live out her long life with a man who found pleasure in hurting others, and there was no denying he had enjoyed every moment of what he did to Azriel. The twisted look on his face reminded her of that from her nightmares.

Ariadne crossed the room and, before plucking up a familiar title, caught sight of one sitting just out of place. She pulled the large, heavy book from the shelf and stared down at the gold-stamped lettering on the cover. *Tales of the Fae and Other Short Stories*.

The book Azriel had been reading.

Sinking onto the nearest lounge, she let the book fall open. It settled on a page with a bright illustration of a terrified woman in a beautiful garden. Though Ariadne could not see who the woman feared, a depiction of a shadow along the wall behind her silhouetted a massive beast with a bear-like snout and long claws poised to strike.

How appropriate. She, too, felt trapped like the woman on the page, only she did not face a beast this time. No, she had done her fair share of withstanding monsters when she had been dragged from a dark cell each night by Ehrun. Now Ariadne faced something far more sinister: marrying a man no better than the dhemon who reveled in her pain.

CHAPTER 12

A riadne refused to leave the estate for almost a fortnight following Azriel's public lashing. With no balls to force her out of hermitry due to Councilmen traveling back to their respective provinces, even her father could not push her. They would return, however, and there would be no more hiding when the time came.

Until then, she kept to her rooms, where Emillie sat with her in near-total silence for hours as Ariadne read and her sister sketched. The library became a frequent stop for her during the rounds through the manor, and only twice she went out to ride Astra around the fields.

No less than five messages arrived from Loren, asking Ariadne to accompany him into town or to walk Laeton Park. She declined each, claiming to not feel well or to be busy. Each time, her father scowled at her. What did he want her to say? He did not care for her feelings on the matter, only that she did as he told her.

So when she descended the stairs for the next ball wearing the dusty-pink gown she had collected from Revelie on that fateful night, Ariadne came face to face with her father. He stood alone in the foyer, arms crossed and lips thin.

Pausing at the foot of the stairs, she watched him warily. "Good evening, Father."

"Daughter." A muscle in his jaw twitched. "You look lovely tonight."

"Thank you." She gestured to the door. "Shall we?"

"No." He continued to glare down at her, then took a step closer. "I assume you are aware of General Gard's intentions—that he wishes to ask your hand in marriage."

Ariadne swallowed hard. It took all her self-control not to step away from him. She twisted her fingers into the skirts of her gown. "Yes, Father."

"These last few invitations by the General have been declined by you."

Not a question, yet still she said, "Yes, Father."

He sighed and tucked his arms behind his back, pacing away from her. "I will have you know that General Gard has spoken to me of this, and he is displeased."

Uncertain of what else to do, Ariadne nodded. "I am sorry—"

"No." He turned on his heel to face her again, face white with carefully tempered rage. "No. Sorry is not good enough, Ariadne."

"Yes, Father." Her voice, smaller now, cracked. He did not often direct anger like this at her. The last time she could recall such fury was when she had lied about visiting Camilla and, instead, met Darien in town unchaperoned. It had been the one and only time he had struck her.

"Fortunately for you," he continued, nostrils flaring, "the General's interest has not waned."

She said nothing as he marched back toward her. Shrinking away, she watched him with wide, burning eyes. Her heart thundered in her chest. Surely he would not strike her before a ball? Even with her quick healing, she would arrive with a bruise.

The front door opened, and Madan appeared. His eyes narrowed, taking in her father's flexing hands, then the way she leaned back from him. "The carriage is ready, my Lord."

"We will be out in a moment," her father snapped.

Madan hesitated. "Will you be needing anything else at present?"

He turned to face the guard. "No. Go. Now."

"My apologies." Madan inclined his head, lines forming between his brows as he watched Ariadne. "I will be just outside."

The door closed behind him, and for a fleeting moment, Ariadne pictured her father turning back to her quick as a viper to bring his hand across her face. She recoiled as he turned, preparing for the blow.

Instead, he let out a shuddering breath and did not look at her again. When he spoke next, his voice was quiet and filled with an unspoken promise, "You will *not* jeopardize this engagement." His fingers flexed in and out of fists. "When he asks for your hand, you *will* accept."

Ariadne tilted her head back and blinked back the tears threatening to spill and ruin her makeup. "Yes, Father."

"Very good."

With that, he yanked open the front door where Madan, indeed, stood just outside and hurried down the steps toward the carriage driver. Ariadne watched him go, then looked to Madan. He did not speak. His face said enough.

"I am fine," she whispered more to herself than to him, blinking fast and tilting her head back again. One hand she laid over her mouth and the other over her chest as she turned away.

For a long moment, she stood there as wave after wave of tumultuous emotions crashed through her. How she had managed to hold it together in the face of her father's wrath,

Ariadne did not know. She had broken in the face of lesser assaults.

By the time Emillie stood at her side, Ariadne felt composed enough to face the night beyond the foyer. She followed her sister out, and Madan, who had remained at the top of the steps for the duration of her silent countdown, closed the front door behind them.

Markus stood at the carriage and nodded once to them before climbing inside. Ariadne swallowed hard, descended one step, and froze.

Azriel appeared from around the back of the carriage, each movement slow and purposeful. He looked up to his cousin and asked if they were ready to go, his gravelly voice a balm for her nerves. He wore his usual black clothes and boots. His hair remained in the top knot. The only difference she could tell was the position of his sword. Usually strapped across his back, it now hung from his waist. It looked odd there.

She shifted her gaze to the ground before he could catch her staring. Beside her, Emillie picked up her dark blue, velvety skirts and stepped into the carriage. She settled in across from their father, leaving enough space beside her for Ariadne.

Thank the gods. The last thing she needed was to sit beside her father right now.

Sucking in a deep breath, she gathered a fistful of her gown in one hand, then approached the carriage. She lifted her free hand for the handle to hoist herself up, and instead, a firm, steady hand gripped hers.

Ariadne paused, one foot on the carriage step, to turn wide eyes to Azriel. He searched her gaze for a breath, and in that moment, the world fell away.

He survived.

Against the odds and everything Loren had done to keep him off his feet, Azriel survived. After ten days of wondering, unable to fully immerse herself in the books she so desperately clung to, she could see with her own eyes that he was, indeed, alive and well. Or as well as he could be after such abuse.

Then he was gone, and the void left behind threatened to swallow her whole.

She watched him go, holding the hand he had used to support her against his chest. The skin where they had touched tingled, and when she sat beside her sister, Ariadne laid the hand in her lap, palm up to stare at it.

No one spoke on the ride to the Jensen Estate. Though Emillie had not witnessed the verbal lashing Ariadne received from their father, she had had enough sense to not ask about it when Ariadne appeared to be on the brink of an emotional collapse back in the foyer. Moreso, she knew to say nothing in front of their father.

Ariadne ran her fingertips along her palm as they trundled down the road to the ball at the Councilman's home, and watched the darkness shift by outside the window. Trees and sky were all she could see, with the occasional glimpse of a dark horse. The stallion moved from behind the carriage to beside it frequently, dousing his rider in the golden light of the lamp dangling from outside the coach.

Azriel's eyes stayed fixed straight ahead, narrowing every so often when they moved through a particularly dense crop of trees. Though he had never said anything of the sort, she got the impression he could not see well in the dark.

What would it have been like had Azriel Tenebra been brought up as one of the Caersan men in the Society? His mother had been a lady within the aristocracy, yet his status as a bastard kept him from claiming his rightful place within it. Archaic laws were all that maintained such boundaries.

How different her life might have been if Azriel had been in the ballroom, asking her to dance before Darien had the chance. Rather than follow the younger Gard brother around like a vapid puppy, perhaps she would have found herself swept away by the tall, handsome half-fae. It would have been him, not Darien, who danced with her the night she had been stolen away, and with him there, perhaps she never would have made it to the dhemon keep.

Ariadne snapped her fingers closed. Such thoughts were not helpful. She needed to put Azriel from her mind and do her best to find something—anything—to look forward to with General Loren Gard.

The carriage rumbled to a halt at the entrance to the Jensen Manor. Emillie waited for the door to open and looked on as Ariadne accepted Madan's assistance to exit. Shifting over, she took Azriel's outstretched hand to step down from the interior. Behind her, their father clambered out on his own. Though lines had begun to form on his face, he remained young and strong in the eyes of Caersan vampires. He had no intention of appearing weak before anyone.

Emillie picked up her skirt and hurried to catch up with Ariadne as her sister marched away. Too many eyes followed their entrance, so she kept silent until they entered the front doors and followed the crowds to the cream ballroom with its golden motifs. Before either of them could be bombarded by suitors asking to dance, she grabbed Ariadne's hand, squeezed it once, then pulled her to an empty alcove.

"What is going on?" Emillie asked, searching her sister's face. Loose strands of dark curls framed her pale face like wisps of shadows. They stood out in stark contrast to the refined makeup Ariadne wore with the pink gown.

Ariadne smiled a bit wistfully, and when she spoke, her voice was lighter than usual—a clear sign of her hiding something. "Father was just telling me that the General plans to propose."

A hollow feeling took hold in Emillie's gut. She shook her head. "The Season has just begun."

"And I am the Golden Rose," Ariadne said, the last words cracking despite the serene expression. "Perhaps he acts quickly to ensure others will not impede on his plans."

"You are allowed to decline." Emillie squeezed her fingers again.

"No." The word left Ariadne on a quick breath, her eyes snapping to the entrance of the ballroom where their father paused to speak with a lord. "No."

Something was not right. Emillie chewed her lip and looked from their father to her sister several times. "Ask him to wait just a bit longer, maybe?"

Ariadne closed her eyes for a long moment. When they flew open, they refocused with hard determination. A light line formed between her brows. "By the gods, Em, why would I ever want to do that?"

That was not the voice of her sister. She knew that voice—it had been carefully curated to hide discomfort and lies. Emillie shook her head. "To give yourself options!"

"Marrying the General..." Ariadne swallowed hard and sucked in a deep breath with a shake of her head. "Marrying the General is everything I have ever wanted. I have said it before, remember?"

"Yes, but—"

"Please." Ariadne squeezed her hand in response, harder than usual. She stared at Emillie with wide, pleading eyes. "Please, Emillie..."

"Ari, what did Father say to you?" Her knees shook, and she looked over her shoulder at their father again. His hawklike eyes found them and narrowed almost imperceptibly. "What happened?"

For a long moment, Ariadne did not reply. Her gaze remained focused over Emillie's shoulder as though having a silent conversation with their father before returning to her. She smiled again and shook her head with a light, false laugh. "Nothing!"

"Do not lie to me."

Ariadne loosened her grip, patted the back of Emillie's hand, then let it go. "Why would I ever lie to you, Em? You are my sister."

"Ari—"

"Do not speak of this again." Her sister's voice turned dark and stony with warning. She cleared her throat, returning the next words to the airiness they had had a moment before. "I am honored the General wishes to marry me. I *will* be saying yes, and that is the end of it."

Emillie opened her mouth to speak, but Ariadne turned and disappeared into the throng of party guests. The sudden departure spoke volumes more than her sister's words. She avoided an uncomfortable conversation and took to the one thing she hated most to escape it: walking through a crowded room alone.

Whether her sister admitted it or not, something was wrong, and it had to do with their father. Moreso, Ariadne's interest in marrying Loren, though evident several weeks ago, had waned after the public lashing. Her avoiding the General's requests only highlighted her discomfort at the very notion of being alone with him—chaperoned or not.

So why did she claim to want the proposal so badly?

Emillie looked to her father again. He followed Ariadne's path through the ballroom while maintaining the conversation he engaged in. If he had frightened her sister enough to make her agree to marry a man she no longer found interest in, then what was he truly capable of? She had seen him lose his temper in the past, even witnessed him slap Ariadne with all his strength, but Emillie never imagined him to threaten his own family.

Snatching a wine glass from a passing servant's tray, Emillie downed the entire thing in one fell swoop before setting it on the nearest table and pushing into the crowd. If she could not get Ariadne to listen, maybe Revelie or Camilla could talk some sense into her.

Everything hurt. Azriel stood as still as possible in the corner of the ballroom, ignoring the disgusted whispers not hidden from him. Word of his lashing spread fast to those who hadn't been present, and more officers than usual lingered uncomfortably close, no doubt told to keep an eye on him. Being at the manor of Captain Nikolai Jensen's parents only worsened matters.

Why Markus didn't just fire him, Azriel had no idea. It would've made both their lives easier. Instead, it appeared the Princeps enjoyed torturing him mentally just as much as the General reveled in his pain.

If it weren't for Madan's diligent care, Emillie's aid of Algorathian salve, and the generosity of Rusan servants sharing their blood, he would've succumbed to his wounds. Night after night of bandage removal had put him in such agony, he'd half-wished they'd let him die. That no one in the household above heard or said anything about his screams had been a miracle unto itself.

Returning to work, however, put Azriel in a new waking terror. At least when he'd been forced to remain on his too-small bed he'd been distracted by the pain of his injuries. Back on his feet, he could no longer ignore the pain in his heart.

Stuck under the vicious, leering gazes of the Caersan vampires, Azriel did his best to shrink into the corner of the ballroom. Too much movement pulled at the scabs on his back. Too little, and his muscles grew stiff. Damned if he did, damned if he didn't. So was his life.

As if his physical agony were not enough, Azriel couldn't bring himself to stop watching Ariadne. The General had made himself clear before: stay away or die.

"Do not forget your place," Loren hissed as he'd unfurled the whip all those nights ago. "You are a bastard."

The first crack across his back had hurt, certainly, but it hadn't broken the skin. It'd been easy to bear. The second sent a shock through his body. The third, laced with Loren's next words, burned red hot.

"I see the way you look at her." *Crack.* Four. Five. Six. "She would never lower herself to give you a second thought."

It was true, of course. She'd never so much as given him a reason to believe otherwise. He couldn't help it. The bond still dragged out the best—and worst—of him.

"You are nothing." Fifteen. Sixteen. "And your pathetic pining will only cause more trouble."

Azriel closed his eyes and angled his face away from the dance floor where Ariadne twirled with Nikolai. She wore that dusty rose fabric he'd found so beautiful, and as he'd imagined, it made her ethereal. His heart ached as much as his back.

"If you recall nothing else of this lesson," Loren had hissed in his ear as his wrists were unshackled and his knees threatened to buckle under him, "remember this: I will not stop next time. If I see you so much as breathe in her direction, I will kill you and everyone you love."

Oh, Azriel remembered the threat. Even if the latter half of the lashings faded in and out of memory, he wouldn't forget the way the General squeezed his face between his fingers and sneered, almost nose to nose. The crowd, a distant roar behind him, did not see when their military's leader spit in his face. All they saw was the bastard guard receiving the punishment he deserved for his insubordination.

Opening his eyes again, Azriel grit his teeth as he studied Ariadne's movements. Each step appeared stiff and more un-coordinated than usual. She clung to the Captain's arms to steady herself, eyes fixed on their feet.

Then her gaze snapped up to him, her brows pinching together as her mouth turned down. His stomach flopped over, and he swallowed hard. Something was wrong. He could see it in her eyes—a silent, desperate plea. For what? He didn't care. If she needed him, then he'd be there.

The song ended, and Azriel lurched forward, fire ricochet-ing down his back. She curtsied to Nikolai before turning to face him again.

Fuck Loren's threat. He was her guard, and gods be damned, he would help her with whatever she needed. At least...that's what he told himself. Her *guard*.

Azriel pushed through the edges of the crowd, and Ariadne, gaze fixed on him, started across the ballroom to meet him. His heart hammered against his ribs hard and fast. Every movement, every bump to his body, made him ready to shat-ter into a million pieces. That wouldn't stop him. Nothing could stop him from getting to her when she needed him.

A soft song started, neither one for a dance nor an inter-mittent tune, as new dancers took their places. It called the attention of the Caersans, and everyone slowed to a halt to turn and look.

Still, Azriel moved forward. Ariadne's face paled, and she, like the others, pivoted back toward the empty dance floor. Only then did he slow to watch in mute horror as Loren stepped forward and held his hand out to Ariadne.

The next few seconds slid by slower than he'd ever experienced before. Ariadne looked over her shoulder at him, lips parted in what he imagined as a small, silent scream. The corner of her eyes shimmered, and slowly—oh, so slowly—she turned back to Loren and laid her hand in his.

A single, ear-splitting note rang through Azriel's head. By the on-lookers' lack of reaction, he knew it wasn't something they could hear. Only he suffered through the mind-numbing sound as Loren pulled Ariadne closer.

"Miss Harlow," the General said, and it sounded so, so far away. The words, distorted as though echoing through water, interlaced with the note slamming through his brain. "The Golden Rose of Valenul. These past weeks have been the most magnificent of my life."

This wasn't happening. Not now. The Season had just begun. There was still time. Still time. Still—

"I have been fortunate enough to have spent many wonderful nights alongside your family this past year," Loren went on, attention unwavering. "Over this time, I have found your grace and kindness to be unyielding. I admit, it was a shock to have been so drawn to you after losing my brother, but I have prayed to the gods many mornings asking for answers."

Fuck.

Azriel took a sudden step back. Someone cursed at him, but he heard nothing aside from that ringing and Loren's speech and his heart shattering.

"It is with the greatest respect that I, General Loren Gard, ask you, Miss Ariadne Harlow, to accept my hand in marriage."

He was going to vomit. This wasn't happening—it couldn't be. She wouldn't say yes, would she? Not after what Loren did—not after all he said to her. How he'd belittled her.

"Will you do me the honor?" Loren held her hand fast in his, scanning her face.

Something slid down Ariadne's cheek. It glinted in the brightly lit ballroom and shone like diamonds. Her shoulders shuddered. She exhaled a breath as everyone else in the room held theirs. Not a single person spoke. No one moved.

Except Azriel. He had to get away.

"Yes." Ariadne's answer left her on a breath.

The world fell out from beneath Azriel's feet. He grit his teeth to keep from screaming and balled his fists to lock up his body and stop the shaking. His back roared in protest, and as applause rang out, he shoved backward out of the crowd, unable to turn away.

Loren pulled out a long, thin box and opened it to reveal a crimson lace choker sewn with diamonds. An engagement necklace. He stepped around Ariadne and laid it across her throat, the sign of his claim to her.

The song shifted into something lively and romantic, and within a measure, Loren had Ariadne in his arms. Others joined in, shouting their congratulations to the newly engaged, and soon, the dance floor was alive again.

Azriel's stomach churned. He lurched out the doors to the garden steps and nearly landed on his face in his desperation to escape. Stumbling into the darkness, he found a bush to disappear behind where he could empty the meager contents of his stomach on the dirt.

Again and again, he retched until nothing but bile appeared. Even then, his muscles contracted as though even his soul attempted to claw its way out of him through his esophagus. It burned like wildfire.

"Azriel..."

He shrank back as Madan appeared around the bush. Something hot ran down his back. The scabs must have broken open from all his heaving. The physical pain remained secondary to everything else.

"Go away," he choked, wiping his mouth with a kerchief from his pocket. He blew his nose into the fabric, then tossed it under the bush as he fell onto his ass and stared at the lawns.

"I'm so sorry," Madan said, crouching down beside him. "Azriel, I just...I never expected—"

"Leave me alone."

"What can I do?" Madan studied him, dark brows pulled tight and silver rimming his eyes.

Azriel lifted his gaze to him and shook his head. "You should've let me hang."

"You know I could never do that."

"Well, congratulations," Azriel said, baring his teeth. "This is a fate far worse than death."

Madan gaped at him. "Please don't say that."

"I knew it would happen eventually." Azriel pressed his fists into his eyes and buckled forward to suck in a ragged breath. The air rushed into his lungs like fire. "But I thought I'd be gone before it did."

"I'm so sorry." Madan laid a heavy hand on his shoulder, and Azriel, too exhausted to pull away, let it rest there as he let out a low moan.

Tears pushed past the barriers he'd hidden behind, and he dropped his hands as he sobbed, shaking his head. Nothing could be done. He knew this night would come. He knew he had no right to be upset, and yet the gods damned bond had other plans.

"I can't go back in there," Azriel said after several long minutes of crying. "I don't trust myself. I can't."

"Alright," Madan said in a quiet, soothing tone. "Alright. I'll come get you when it's time to leave. Stay out here."

Azriel nodded once. It's all he could manage. The rest of him felt numb. Broken. Would he ever find himself again? No telling. An unfulfilled bond drove most fae toward uncontrollable violence and twisted, unreasonable thoughts. Now he felt shoved down that path.

As Caersans made their way into the garden again, speaking animatedly about the impending wedding, Azriel wiped his face dry before shoving to his feet. They already believed him to be a criminal. He didn't need the next round of gossip to include how someone found him curled up beside a pile of vomit.

He kicked dirt over the sick he left behind and meandered back toward the manor. Going inside was not on his agenda—not unless he planned on getting ambushed by soldiers as he caved in Loren's face. Standing outside, though? He could handle that.

Maybe.

Or maybe he would burn the entire manor to the ground just to hear the screams.

Song after song played, echoing through the garden doors, and he watched the moon slide across the dark sky. Every so often, a chorus of congratulations raked across his ears, turning his blood cold. A group of young Caersan suitors, excited to have the attention removed from them for the time being, wandered outside.

Azriel envied them. All of them. They never had to feel what he felt.

"Mister Tenebra."

Fuck. He was going to vomit again at the sound of Ariadne's voice. Yet he turned in time to see her brushing off her skirts and making her way to where he stood in the shadows.

"Miss Harlow." Damn him, his voice cracked. He looked away and swallowed hard before saying, "Congratulations."

Ariadne did not respond right away, and he turned back to her, heart threatening to crack his ribs. She didn't look at him as she said, "How are you?"

"Well enough."

"I must apologize," she said, flicking those perfect eyes back up at him, "for not stopping them when they—"

"Don't." The word left him in a harsher tone than he intended, and she flinched. He grit his teeth, then continued, "Get back to the ball. Celebrate. The General—apologies, your *fiancé*—would have my head if he saw me speaking to you."

Ariadne froze and gaped at him for a long moment. She glanced over her shoulder at the party, eyes shimmering, then nodded to him. "Alright..."

Azriel's head swam. All he wanted was to pull her to him and tell her the truth. Tell her how much he loved her, then get on his knees and beg—*beg*—her not to go back to the General. To choose him, the bastard guard instead.

But that wouldn't be fair to her, so instead he said, "Good evening, Miss Harlow."

She turned to go and paused again. "Thank you for what you did."

Bracing himself, he asked, "What do you mean?"

Ariadne looked back at him and smiled a small, sweet smile that threatened to crack his composure. "No man has ever stood up for me the way you did with the General."

He had no words. The ringing started up in his head again, and his body lurched forward involuntarily.

Her smile turned sad. "For what it is worth, I am sorry you were punished because of me."

Then she was gone. Azriel watched her go, the pieces of his soul crushed into a fine powder. She blamed herself for the lashing, and he hadn't been able to find his voice to tell her he'd do it all again, given the chance. He'd do anything for her.

Even if it meant letting her go.

CHAPTER 13

O ver the two weeks following her engagement, Ariadne could not stop replaying those moments at the ball in her head. Again and again, she felt the flood of hope as Azriel pushed through the guests, aventurine eyes wide and concerned. He knew. Somehow, he knew she needed him in that moment—him and the freedom he would certainly sweep her away to.

Then the dread set in as, over and over, she heard the chords of the song, making her turn to find Loren standing before her, hand outstretched. He looked regal in his usual red and leveled that expectant expression at her. She knew what it meant. No escape. No freedom. No Azriel.

She played it through, searching for a way she could have gotten out. There had been none. Over Loren's shoulder, at the edge of the dance floor, stood her father, arms crossed and mouth a hard line. Though he said no words, she heard his voice daring her to refuse. Daring her to walk away. She knew the consequences if she tried, and she would end up with that necklace nonetheless.

The tears as she had turned away from Azriel and took Loren's hand were not of joy, though she forced her mouth into a smile. A hollowness had opened in her gut, swallowing her whole from the inside. She had heard nothing he said. All she had known was that would forever be the moment she lost any semblance of freedom she once had. Her life was forfeit.

So when she had finally pried herself away from the throng of congratulatory guests and made it outside, Ariadne went straight for the man she hoped would make it all go away. But he had abandoned her—scolded her for speaking to him.

It had been a kick to the gut. A kick she deserved after all he endured for her at Loren's hands.

Yet spending a fortnight reliving those moments in the rare quiet had been nothing compared to the tasks set before her now. The night of her engagement to Loren ended with her father informing her of the wedding date just over a month away. Every decision was up to her, from the decorations to the location to the invitation list—as if she had a true say in who would be present. If anyone in the Society was left off the guest list, the scandal it would cause...

Night after night and even into the late hours of the morning, Ariadne poured over the papers scattered across the table of the drawing room. Piles of ribbons and paint chips and fabric squares needed sorting. Invitation designs required precise decision-making. Not only did she make every choice on her own for the wedding, but for the announcement ball as well.

Occasionally, Ariadne hid from the mind-numbing work. She locked her suite doors and claimed to suffer from terrible migraines. Other times, she took Astra out for rides around the grounds without telling anyone. These worked, though not to the extent she hoped. Too often, her father unlocked the door and dragged her from the solitude, or she fled back inside by Madan's sudden appearances to keep watch over her.

It was not until Camilla's arrival at the Harlow Estate that Ariadne received the mental break she craved. For the first time in nights, her father did not demand she spend time inking personal replies to those in the Society who accepted the engagement ball's invitation.

"You need to get out of this place, doll," Camilla announced upon her entrance to the drawing room at almost midnight. Behind her, Emillie wrung her fingers and looked over her shoulder toward the stairs leading to their father's study. She had tried to drag Ariadne away many times only to be berated by the Princeps.

Relief rolled over Ariadne, teasing out the tense muscles in her shoulders. She shook out her writing hand and stood. "Please."

"Where are we going?" Emillie asked, following as Ariadne hurried up to the next floor to her suite. "Shall I change?"

Camilla huffed behind her. "Just into town, darling. We will eat and shop to our heart's content. Perhaps we can pry Revelie away from her fabrics."

Ariadne shot her a tense look. She had already sent notice to Revelie to not only be a guest but to create a crimson dress to match Loren's militaristic aesthetic for the announcement.

"Worry not!" Camilla winked. "No talk of the wedding allowed."

Turning to her sister, Ariadne smiled. "Did you do all this?"

Emillie's cheeks flushed red. "You were miserable, Ari."

"To be honest," Ariadne said with a sigh, "it was."

It. It was—not that *she* was miserable. If anyone heard her speaking ill of the upcoming nuptials, there would be no end to the berating she would receive from her father. Pronouncing herself as miserable would be considered a slight to her new fiancé.

So, true to Camilla's word, she did not hear any questions from either Caersan about the planning as she dressed for town and headed to the front of the manor where their carriage stood at the ready. A horse stood saddled beside the coach. Ariadne's heart skipped, then sank.

Only Madan would be joining them today.

Oh, how things had changed since she wished Azriel to be gone, leaving them to their lives with only Madan chaperoning their ventures into town. She loved the guard like her brother, and he joked and protected her and Emillie with just as much familial caring. Those feelings never left, but her heart had made room for the newcomer. She told herself he watched over them with just as much platonic love, but she did not want to truly believe it.

With the way he looked at her...Loren had every right to be jealous.

Azriel looked at her with eyes that did not see a sister, like Madan. And Ariadne could not deny how her breath caught at seeing him.

Over the last fortnight, Ariadne's traitorous heart launched into action each time she glimpsed him in passing. Even during the daylight hours when she should have been thinking of her future husband as her hands explored her body, it was Azriel she imagined running his lips across her skin.

Some nights he would stop and open his mouth to speak, but he never said a word. In fact, she had not heard his voice since he had told her off at the Jensen ball.

They all clambered into the carriage and, as though reading her mind, Camilla asked, "Where is Mister Tenebra? Should he not be joining us in town?"

Emillie shrugged. "I have not seen him much."

"We also have not left much," Ariadne pointed out, gazing out the window as they pulled away.

"Too right you are, doll." Camilla clicked her tongue. "It has been too long."

"I must admit," Emillie said, "it is strange he has disappeared so suddenly after the excitement at the Jensen's."

Strange indeed. Ariadne watched her sister curiously for a long moment. It was strange the guard had found any interest in her in the first place and far more curious that the interest floundered so suddenly.

Unless, of course, her abrupt engagement made the difference. Had he only watched her with such intensity because of her availability? Now that she was bound to Loren, was it possible he saw her as something soiled or unappealing?

Ariadne brushed her fingers over the crimson lace necklace around her throat. It made sense the half-vampire would not find her desirable now she was no longer eligible. She had not thought of him as such a rake in the past, but now she could see it. Maybe Loren had been right. He watched too closely for someone of his status. She deserved something more.

Perhaps the General would be that for her after all—if only she could stop hearing the sounds of the whip.

Emillie watched Ariadne with a light frown as they made their way into Laeton. Her sister fidgeted with the engagement choker and looked out the window despite the constant reassurance that she was, indeed, fine. The last two weeks had been difficult for her. It had been difficult for Emillie, too, to watch her sister succumb to the pressures of the Caersan Society. Her introversion, not unlike what she had displayed upon her return from the Keonis Mountains, erupted.

Even Camilla and Revelie could sense it, and she had not seen much of either of them over the last couple of weeks.

Letters were all that passed between the three of them. So when Camilla entered the manor earlier that evening to Emillie pacing the foyer, the Caersan had swept her into her arms and held tight.

"She will be okay, doll," Camilla had told Emillie as they broke apart and started up the stairs to hunt down Ariadne in the drawing room. "We will help her through this, as we have done before."

Now as they trundled along, Camilla leaned forward and placed a gentle hand on Ariadne's knee. "How are you doing, really?"

Her sister turned her blue eyes up to their friend and smiled. "Fine. Tired."

"What have you been doing to make you so tired?"

Emillie shot Camilla a warning look. They had agreed not to talk about the wedding, and she had told her friend everything she knew. There should be no reason to pry into it further.

"A lot of planning," her sister said, dragging her attention back inside the carriage.

"On your own?"

Ariadne glanced at Emillie. "Yes."

Their father had not permitted Emillie to help, insisting the entire process was traditionally done by the bride alone. For her to interfere could poorly influence the outcome of the engagement ball, wedding, and subsequent marriage. Still, Emillie's face burned. She should have snuck in more often to lend her support.

"Absurd." Camilla shook her head. "Well, the bistro I have planned for tonight will be exactly what we all need to relax a bit."

Emillie frowned. "I thought we were going shopping."

Something devious sparkled in Camilla's eyes, and she shrugged. "It will be more enjoyable once we relax a bit, do you not think?"

"I look forward to it," Ariadne cut in and smiled at both of them. It did not reach her troubled gaze. "Thank you. Both of you. This is much needed."

As the carriage rumbled to a halt, Camilla clapped her hands and opened the door before the coachman could do so. She leapt from her seat as Madan dismounted, his brows low over his marbled eyes. He turned in place, then looked up at the sign hanging above the establishment. The Drifter's Inn and Bistro.

"Excuse me," Madan called up to the driver. "I believe we are in the wrong place."

"Nonsense!" Camilla waved him off, then gestured for Emillie and Ariadne to follow her. They did so, looking around at the brightly lit street. It was off their usual route, yet still well-kempt, and the vampires who wandered by were well-dressed. "This is precisely where I wished to go."

Madan turned to her and Ariadne and shook his head. "I must insist we leave. This is no place for either of you."

"This is precisely why I pay Gerard to not accompany me into town," Camilla muttered, referring to the personal guard with whom she could be rarely found. Though Lord Dodd tried to keep his daughter on a leash, she had found ways of cutting those ties.

Yet Ariadne did not seem to hear him either as she followed Camilla through the front doors of the bistro. Chatter and music flooded out as the door opened, then dampened as it closed behind her sister and friend.

Emillie paused and looked around. "I see nothing wrong with it."

"Miss Harlow." Madan grimaced. "Please."

A strange, uncomfortable feeling curled in Emillie's gut. She did not often do things to upset others, and it was rare for Madan to instruct them against any plans they had. He had seen them through many outings which were less-than-pleasant. A market night that ended with brawling in the streets, an over-indulgent evening at a fine restaurant at the edge of Lake Cypher, and numerous events which left him shielding Ariadne from the crowds so she would not get overwhelmed.

Despite all of that, this was the first time Emillie could recall Madan looking panicked.

"They are inside." Emillie gestured to the door. "Let us go in, have a bite, and then we will leave. It will be fine."

Madan's jaw flexed. "If you insist, Miss Harlow."

"I do."

With that, Emillie turned and pushed through the front doors of the Drifter's Bistro. Two steps into the establishment, she froze. Rusan vampires of every status, from servant to guild leader, turned to look at her. The wood floor creaked underfoot, and the tables scattered across the space wobbled at the center of mismatched chairs. A loud band played in one corner and a long, tall bar surrounded the back wall, stacked with liquor bottles.

Ariadne and Camilla stood at the bar like roses in a field of dying weeds, leaning in and accepting an unidentifiable liquid in small, questionably clean glasses. Emillie gaped and rushed forward, pulling her skirts out of the way of her feet. Clouds of tobacco smoke stung her nostrils, and leering gazes followed. She stumbled over several loose boards before coming to a halt beside her sister.

"Ariadne," she hissed under her breath. "Maybe Madan was right."

"Nonsense!" Camilla pushed a glass of liquor at her. "I come here all the time."

That did not make Emillie feel better. She loved her friend more than she could ever express, but she knew what Camilla did when left to her own devices. She likely found the bistro thanks to a Rusan vampire she met by chance, if not by a servant of her own household.

Ariadne, on the other hand, ignored Emillie completely. She picked up the next glass of liquor and tossed it down her throat with ease. No grimace of displeasure or gasp for breath.

This was the Ariadne she remembered. This was what her sister had been like—almost as troublesome to their father as Camilla was to her own parents.

"Your sister has no self-control," he had ranted to her one night after Ariadne had returned home from the Dodd Estate stumbling drunk. "She will never find a proper suitor when the time comes."

That had been almost five years ago, before Ariadne's first debut. Before they were pinned under the expectations of the Season. Before Darien and the dhemons and everything which changed her sister forever.

"Ariadne," she hissed again and looked over her shoulder at a mortified Madan who watched on. "We can find another place and have a glass of wine—"

"I do not want wine." Ariadne tapped the bar, and the tender poured another glass. She threw it back as easily as the others. "I want to forget."

Emillie gaped at her. "Forget *what*?"

But Ariadne did not respond. On her sister's far side, Camilla leaned toward a young, handsome Rusan man who appeared more interested in her ample cleavage than her face. Except, maybe, her mouth.

This could not be happening. Emillie turned to Madan, who stepped forward and leaned in so both Ariadne and Camilla could hear him over the boisterous music. "Misses, it is time to go."

"No," Ariadne said, turning to glare up at the guard. "If you do not like being here, then leave."

Emillie sucked in a sharp breath.

Ariadne whipped around to her. "Do you wish to leave as well?"

Truthfully, no. Emillie had not seen her sister so at ease in a long time, particularly in a crowded and unfamiliar place. She would not ruin that. Not tonight.

"No." She chewed her lip and looked apologetically at Madan.

The guard crossed his arms. "Fine. But as soon as this gets out of hand—"

"Relax, doll!" Camilla crooned up at him, placing a hand on his chest and adjusting the collar of his shirt. "I swear by the gods we are safe here."

Before he could reply, Ariadne ordered a tall, foggy glass of ale and shoved it into his hand. "Please, Madan. I need this."

"Fuck," he swore loud as the music died down. Heads turned in their direction. He shook his head and stepped aside, setting the glass down without drinking.

Camilla wandered onto the dance floor, where a Rusan man swept her into his arms, and she laughed as they spun to the next jaunty tune. Emillie watched for a long minute before Ariadne pushed a small glass into her hand, tapped it with her own, and downed the liquor before raising her eyebrows expectantly. She sighed and shot it back, the fiery tang burning her throat as she swallowed. It pooled in her gut like lava.

"How are you drinking this?" She wiped her mouth on the back of her hand.

Ariadne laughed. Gods be damned, she *laughed* and ordered another for each of them. With the quick healing of a Caersan, they did not need to worry too much about alcohol's effects. That did not mean they could not get drunk. It just took twice as much as a typical Rusan. The greedy bartender lingered nearby, racking up their tab with each glass.

After three more, Emillie's head felt lighter. She turned back to the dancers, and before she knew what was happening, Camilla grabbed her hands and dragged her forward.

"This is Kyra," her friend said, introducing her to a beautiful, round-faced Rusan woman with long, fiery red hair and dark, enchanting eyes. "Kyra, this is my very dear friend, Emillie."

Kyra's smile lit up her features and revealed dimples in both cheeks, sending a jolt of lightning straight through Emillie's core. "Miss."

Camilla clicked her tongue. "No formalities here."

With a wink, Kyra held out her hand and, after a moment of hesitation, Emillie accepted. The Rusan pulled her against her soft body. Emillie's breath caught, and Kyra led her through the first steps of a commoner's dance she did not know. It was at once terrifying and thrilling.

It took only a few steps before Emillie's shoulders eased away from her ears, and she knew without a doubt that this—dancing with a beautiful woman—was what she was meant to do. Not once in her long life had a man's touch ever elicited such a heated response in her blood. Kyra had only held her for a few heartbeats, and Emillie never wanted to leave again.

When Nels, a young Rusan kid, appeared at the servants' entrance to the Harlow manor shaking and white-faced, Azriel knew without needing to be told that trouble had found Madan and his three charges. He'd asked to be left home—the women couldn't have possibly needed two guards for a turn about Laeton—and now regretted his decision.

"Madan needs you," Nels squeaked and pointed in the direction of Lake Cypher. "He sent me on his horse to—"

"Fuck." No one touched Rune if Madan could help it. That he'd sent a pre-transitioned vampire on his stallion to collect him told Azriel all he needed to know. He launched forward, and the kid shrank out of his way, eyes wide with awe. "Where are they?"

"The Drifter's Bistro." Nels followed, hot on his heels.

"What's happened to them?"

Nels froze at the barn doors to gape, wide-eyed as Azriel buckled his sword on his shoulder. "He told me to get you, sir. Nothing else."

"Where's this place?" He'd heard of the infamously raucous bistro before but had yet to investigate himself.

Thom the stablehand, in all his wisdom, already tightened the straps for Jasper's saddle. The black stallion huffed and shifted his weight in anticipation of a fast ride. Azriel swung up into the seat and pulled the reins around to face the exit.

"West Shore." Nels hauled himself into Rune's saddle, almost falling off the far side.

Azriel squeezed his legs, and Jasper launched forward. Rune did his best to keep up. Nels' poor handling, however, held the stallion back.

Azriel wasn't certain at what point he lost the kid, but it was somewhere near the heart of Laeton. If he'd thought at any point the women would stray from their plans, he'd have joined them. As it were, he'd worked too hard to keep his distance from Ariadne to ruin the microscopic progress he'd made in taming the bond.

Shoppers hurried out of his way and cursed him as he passed without slowing. Caersan, Rusan, mage, and fae parted like a river around a boulder. Without more information from Madan, he had no idea what to expect when he arrived at the Bistro. He couldn't risk taking his time.

Reining in Jasper, the stallion pranced to a stop mere feet from the familiar grey carriage outside the bistro. Azriel handed the reins off to the driver and stalked to the front door. It wasn't until he laid his hand on the knob that he finally saw Nels, clinging to Rune, appear around the far corner. At least he'd made it back in one piece.

Inside, Azriel reeled to a halt. Music slammed into his ears, tobacco smoke choked his throat, and his eyes struggled to adjust to the sudden dim light. Those sitting closest to the door turned to size him up, then quickly averted their eyes, much like the way Nels had stared in awe before focusing on the floor.

At least Azriel liked to believe it was awe and not horror or disgust.

He wove through the tables, scanning the room. A pair of provocatively dressed women eyed him with interest while a handful of Rusan men scattered about glared in silent challenge. Had Madan been met with such ire? He doubted it. Everyone loved him.

Then he saw the first of the trio closest to the bar. In one hand, she balanced a tall glass of amber liquid, and in the other, she poised a dart. The hem of her gown, hiked up high enough to reveal her thigh, was tucked into a leather belt she had likely gotten from the Rusan man with loose trousers she stood beside. Ariadne's dark hair, braided into a knot at the nape of her neck, gleamed in the light of the chandelier overhead. At his entrance, she swung her oceanic gaze in his direction, and her rosy lips parted. Then the man said something, she grinned, and she threw the dart. It stuck in the outer ring of the board.

At the bar, Madan stood, his head on a swivel. Relief washed over his face at Azriel's approach.

"Gods," Azriel growled, "what the fuck is happening here?"

Madan shook his head. "They're *drunk*, and I've never had such a difficult time getting them together—the *elder* Miss

Harlow in particular. The barkeep has been watering down their drinks for the last hour."

Azriel glanced at her again, collecting her darts from the board with the help of the Rusan. His blood roiled. "Where are the others?"

The other guard nodded in two directions, and Azriel pivoted on his heel to follow each. Emillie stood against a wall on the far side of the dance floor with a beautiful, round-figured Rusan redhead. Emillie's hands, buried in the Rusan's hair, kept them entangled as their mouths wandered from lips to jaw to neck. The redhead's hands, however, wandered. One kneaded Emillie's breast while the other had pulled the Caersan's dress high enough to leave nothing to the imagination—particularly when Emillie tilted her head back with a low moan.

Not much farther back in the room, Camilla could only be half-seen. While she had been wise enough to keep to the shadows, it was not enough to hide her secrets. The way she straddled the vampire in the corner with her skirts hiked up and hips rocking, little guesswork was required.

If anyone worked out who they were...

"What the *fuck*, Madan?"

"They look to Ariadne," Madan said, glaring at the perpetrator at the dartboard, "and she's been completely unmanageable. I was hoping that *you* could help with that."

"I'm not your fixer."

"And I'm not a fucking babysitter!"

"How have you made it this far if you can't control three Caersan women?"

Looking ready to slam Azriel's face into the bar counter, Madan stood to his full height and bared his fangs. "They're grown-ass women. This is *not* my job. I'm here to keep them safe."

"You call this safe?"

Madan snarled. "Are you here to help me or berate my incompetence?"

A smirk cracked across Azriel's face, and he crossed his arms. "So you admit it."

"What?"

"You're incompetent without me."

"Shut your fucking mouth," Madan said, but a grin curled the corner of his lips. "Just help me."

Azriel chuckled and nodded. "Focus on Camilla and paying their tab. I'll get the sisters."

With a nod, they parted. Madan hurried to the shadowy corner as Azriel crossed the dance floor to the two women. It didn't take long for the Rusan vampire to notice his approach and retract her tongue into her own mouth, hands dropping to her sides. Emillie, however, continued her prowl across the Rusan's throat, fangs dragging across skin.

"Miss Harlow."

Emillie froze. Turned. Paled.

"It's time to go."

She looked across the room at Ariadne, still playing darts, and chewed her lip.

Stepping into her line of sight, he crossed his arms over his chest. He dropped his voice in a low rumble. "Now."

"Em?" The Rusan looked at her, worried. "Is everything alright?"

Emillie took her hand and squeezed—a motion Azriel thought to be special between her and Ariadne. "Yes. I must leave...for now."

"From this place?" Azriel gestured around himself. "You must leave forever. Want to see each other again? Go to Laeton Park. With a chaperone."

"But I—"

"Meet me outside, Miss Harlow." Azriel gave her a meaningful look. "Don't make me carry you out."

For the first time since their introduction, Emillie glared at him. Maybe Madan was on to something when he said they were being difficult. Nonetheless, she turned and spoke quiet goodbyes to the Rusan. Azriel stepped away to give them a moment of privacy, then turned to Ariadne.

The Rusan man playing darts with her stood at her back, chest almost pressed against her. She shifted, putting space between them, and took a drink before throwing. The tip stuck just center of the outer ring. Before she could throw the second dart, the Rusan shifted to help her line up her hand and gripped her wrist to do so. Ariadne's reaction, though slowed, was as he'd always seen. She shrank away and turned to face the man with wide eyes.

Azriel was by her side in a heartbeat.

"It's time to go," he said in her ear and pried the last two darts from her fingers.

Ariadne's unfocused eyes glimmered up at him, and a small smirk curled her lips. She ran her fingers across his chest. He froze, the touch sending jolts of lightning through his blood. Something inside him hummed with satisfaction. Something else screamed the reminder: she was *engaged* to another vampire.

"You are quite handsome," she said, walking her fingers up to one shoulder before sliding her palm down his bicep.

Fuck. For a moment, Azriel stared at the ceiling and prayed to all the gods that his cock stayed put. She was engaged and not to him. She was the Princeps' daughter. The Golden Rose of Valenul. Untouchable. The one who would never, *never* love him back.

The Rusan man beside them puffed out his chest, then cut across his thoughts. "We're playin' a game, boy. Walk away."

Azriel ignored him. He set the darts on the nearest table and pointed to the door over Ariadne's shoulder. "Come now."

"I said," the Rusan man growled, "we're playin' a game. Now leave."

When Azriel shifted to face him and drew up to his full height. Placing himself between the Rusan and Ariadne, he cocked his head to the side and set his jaw. "You put your hands on the Princeps' daughter. You'll be lucky if I don't turn you inside out."

His face paled, but he didn't back down. "She asked me to show her how to play."

"And now she's done."

Beside him, Ariadne scoffed. "You don't tell me what to do."

It took all of Azriel's self-control not to yell in frustration. No wonder Madan had called on him first. If the other guard had put his hands on Ariadne—even to get her out of a filthy tavern masquerading as a bistro—he knew what Azriel's wrath would look like. With enough drinks in her to loosen her tongue, Ariadne's self-assurance flew skyward.

"Tonight, I do."

"No." Ariadne made to step around him, the glass still in her hand swinging precariously. "Tonight, I do what I want."

"There's a good girl." The Rusan man held out a hand.

As Ariadne went to reach for the stranger, Azriel slapped the man's arm away, slid between them, and slammed his fist into the Rusan's face. The man stumbled back, blood dripping from his nostrils, and growled. Without a word, he charged forward and swung.

Azriel blocked the punch with ease. He caught the arm, slid to one side, and pinned the arm down tight. In one fluid movement, he grabbed the Rusan, shifted his body, and lifted the man onto his back before dumping him on the floor. The Rusan landed like a stone, the air rushing out of his lungs. Before he could stand again, Azriel kicked his head.

He straightened again and looked around the room. Those nearby stared, wide-eyed, as the band continued playing.

Azriel swept a hand across the top of his head, peeling flyaway hairs from his forehead and smoothing them back into place.

"Let's go," he grumbled to Ariadne.

"You are going to do that to a stranger and then expect me to go with someone like you?" She watched him, incredulous.

Sighing, Azriel shook his head. "No. I don't."

"Then leave me be."

"Not an option."

"Then what—"

Before she could finish her question, Azriel grit his teeth and stooped, slinging her over one shoulder. Ariadne inhaled sharply, then after a moment, she shrieked in outrage and pounded her fists on his back.

"Put me down!"

He didn't deign to respond. Not only was it childish behavior on her part, but he didn't want to think of the last time he'd done something like this. So instead, he focused on the door ahead, ignoring the turning heads and Rusan men standing, contemplating what to do next.

Yet no one followed as Azriel stepped into the bright moonlight and walked toward the carriage where Madan, Camilla, and Emillie stood waiting, then far enough beyond for him to speak with her in private. He knew Madan's tendencies and didn't want him dropping any eaves.

Satisfied by the distance, Azriel set Ariadne back on her feet, where she swayed dangerously.

"Enough," he said.

Ariadne, however, hadn't had enough. She pulled back her hand and let it fly. The sound of her palm across his cheek cracked through the night. His head jerked to the side, and when he faced her again, it was with deadpan annoyance.

Face twisting with fury, Ariadne growled in frustration and slapped her hands against his chest. "How *dare* you!"

"Are you trying to hurt me?"

"Yes!" She kicked his shin and winced in pain.

"You'll never hurt someone like me by hitting like that." Azriel held out his hands to block her onslaught until she slowed. He took her hand, loose enough for her to pull away if she chose, and rolled her fingers into fists. Tapping the first couple of knuckles, he continued, "Hit with this part of your hand or you'll break it."

Holding her fists aloft, Ariadne stared at him for a long moment, rage still simmering in her eyes. Azriel's shoulders slumped. Teaching a Caersan woman to defend herself was useless. Not when she had someone like the General to look forward to marrying.

Then her fist collided with his temple. He stumbled to the side, the sheer strength of the impact taking him by surprise. Behind him, Madan barked a laugh. He grumbled over his shoulder, then looked back at the Caersan before him.

"Well done."

A light frown formed between her brows. "Your face is bleeding."

Azriel ran his fingers over his cheek and, indeed, they came away crimson. "It'll heal."

She sobered a bit, her fingers loosening and hands falling to her side. "How long?"

He went still. "What do you mean?"

"How long does it take you to heal?" She wasn't looking at his face. Her gaze lingered on the slope of his shoulder—his back. The rage dispersed as fast as it'd sprung to the surface, and concern lay in its place.

His heart cracked. "It'll be gone by morning, Miss Harlow."

But a Caersan's face would heal within the hour. The flesh stitched together quickly and without scarring; it was as though the damage had never been there. Again and again, he cursed the magickless fae who'd sired him. Even a drop of healing magic could make up for his missing vampire blood.

"Will it scar?"

"Maybe."

"I am sorry."

"Don't." Azriel shook his head and stepped back. "Don't apologize. Ever."

He'd wear the scar like a badge of honor. There would come a night, sooner rather than later, when she'd marry the General. After, she'd leave him behind, and in her absence, he could look in the mirror to remember.

Remember that he deserved every second of his torment.

CHAPTER 14

The doors of the Harlow manor opened before Loren reached the top of the entry steps. Warm, golden light swept across the stones and, upon his entrance, the butler took the crimson cloak from his shoulders while a maid held out a crystal glass of whiskey. Home. This was what home looked and felt like, and one day, the massive building and its surrounding grounds would be his. The Harlow Estate would shift to become the Gard Estate when he took his place as the leader of all Valenul vampires.

What came next from the butler, however, was not picturesque.

"Good evening, my Lord General," the Rusan man said with a bow. "I regret to inform you that the elder Miss Harlow is not well and has requested your patience as she readies for the evening."

Loren's heart skipped a beat, and he gripped the glass in his hand a bit harder than necessary. For a Caersan vampire to feel ill, they would need to be on the brink of death. It was only the lack of panic in the household which told him she could not be so poorly. That only left one possibility, however, that could cause her to hide away. If anyone had laid a hand on her, he would have their head. As for the guards meant to be watching over her—he would skin them both alive for their incompetence.

"What do you mean she is unwell?" Loren turned his attention up the stairs where Markus appeared at the landing above. He bowed quickly and stepped closer. "My Lord, how is she?"

Markus sighed, motioning for Loren to ascend the steps. At the top, the Princeps said, "She is not answering at the present, and Emillie refuses to speak of what happened."

"Where did they go?"

"Into town," Markus said. "I was with the Council and unable to attend."

Just as he suspected. Those damned personal guards were useless. "Who attended them?"

"Both guards." Markus led him down a wide corridor, then up another flight of stairs. This was the furthest Loren had ever been in the manor. When Ariadne had returned, she stayed in a room on the second floor before demanding she move suites. The more he saw of the house, the more impatient he became to own it.

"And two grown men could not keep track of two women?" Loren rolled his eyes. "Will another lesson need to be taught to them both?"

"No." Markus did not so much as glance in his direction. "From what I saw of Emillie and Camilla—"

"Miss Dodd is present?"

"Indeed." The Princeps shook his head. "They are also unwell from too much drink."

Perhaps he should have guessed. If there was one thing vampires, Caersan or lesser, succumbed to, it was alcohol. Not even he was safe from its vicious grasp.

Nonetheless, if Tenebra and Antaire had been doing their job properly, the women would not be in their predicament.

Markus halted before a set of doors and rapped his knuckles against the wood. "Daughter."

A pause, and then, "Father."

Interesting. Drunk Ariadne was gutsier than he was used to. The sharpness of her tone spoke volumes, and by the way Markus tensed, he knew the Princeps heard it too.

"Your fiancé is here with me." Markus crossed his arms and glared at the door.

Another long pause. In the suite beyond, he heard a thump, crash, muttered curse, and then a stumble before the doorknob twisted. The door cracked open a fraction, and Ariadne's face appeared there, her eyes glassy and cheeks flushed.

"Good evening, General," she said with a curl of those pretty lips. "I must ask for another few moments to prepare myself."

"Enough of this." Markus laid a heavy hand on the door and pushed.

Eyes wide, Ariadne stepped back so he could step in. She wore a purple dress that elegantly hugged her lithe curves, and her dark hair, hanging in waves around her shoulders, gleamed in the candlelight. Loren looked forward to the mornings he could finally tear the gowns from her body to ravish every rise and hollow.

Gods, if Markus had not been in the room with them, he might have done more than the bow he swept before her.

"Please, Father—General—" Ariadne said, speech slurred, "just a few more moments."

Loren wanted to throttle the men who let her get to this point. Beautiful though she was, her behavior was appalling. The wife of the General could never be seen in such a state.

"By the gods, Miss Harlow," Loren said, steadying her as she swayed, "where did you go tonight? Did Tenebra let this happen?"

"I want to know the same," Markus chimed in. He widened his stance and crossed his arms, ever the ex-General.

Ariadne's head snapped up to look at them. "*I* went to the Drifter's Bistro, and *I* chose my drinks. Neither Mister Antaire nor Mister Tenebra had anything to do with it."

"But they were with you?" Markus pressed.

"I am the Golden Rose," she slurred, "and those guards do not tell me what I can or cannot do."

Loren raised a brow and turned to the Princeps. "That establishment has been a thorn in my side for ages. I should have shut it down decades ago."

Ariadne's eyes widened, and she lurched forward. She clutched the back of the nearby couch and looked between him and her father. "Wait. Shut it down?"

"Very good," Markus said, blatantly ignoring his daughter. He turned to go as though that was the last of what he wished to hear. "It is a scourge on Laeton if it cannot keep its patrons from over-indulging."

"No, wait!" Ariadne caught Loren's hand as he made to follow the Princeps. He paused at the sudden sound of panic in her tone. This was an intriguing shift from her stubbornness a moment before. "Do not ruin a business because I made a bad choice."

He angled his head. "Excuse me?"

"Please," she said, voice smaller now.

The way she sounded when she begged sent a warm flush through his veins. The things he would like to do to demonstrate how much he enjoyed it. He would need to find reasons, once they were married, to get her to do it more often. A small smile curled the corners of his lips at the possibilities.

Before he could speak, Markus barked from the door, "What is it, Daughter?"

Her eyes flickered to her father, then back up at Loren. When next she spoke, it was so quiet, he was certain the

Princeps could not hear her words. "Please, General. Let them be. I will not go back again."

"Speak up!" Markus turned now, frowning.

"Do it for me," Ariadne simpered, gripping his wrist a little tighter.

Fuck, he was going to lose his mind if she kept that up. He kept his voice even and loud enough for Markus to hear, "As you wish, Miss Harlow. I will not shut down the bistro so long as you do not return."

"I promise," she said a little too quickly and, releasing her hold on him, took a step back. Her face paled, and she swallowed hard.

"Ariadne, are you alright?" Markus took a step closer.

She shook her head. Loren moved forward, confused by her sudden withdrawal. He had thought, for a moment, she had been feeling the same tension he had.

Then she puked on the floor.

After vomiting onto Loren's boots, Ariadne could not bring herself to look him in the eye. She apologized repeatedly, mortified and stunned at the lack of self-control. First, she told Azriel how handsome she thought he was, then her loose lips betrayed her again by allowing the sick to escape. She had held it back from the moment they pushed through the doorway and had hoped they would leave long before she succumbed to the vile sensation.

Dinner, however, became an entirely new villain to overcome. Though emptying her stomach of its contents and drinking ginger tea alleviated the nausea, she had not been prepared for the very sudden mental clarity.

What the *fuck* had she done to keep Loren from ruining the Drifter's Inn and Bistro? She did not speak like that to anyone. Not even when Darien would taunt her and all she wanted was to feel his lips on hers.

She certainly did not wish for Loren to do so, though it was inevitable with their engagement ball and wedding on the horizon. Once they were officially announced, small displays of affection would be allowed and expected. If she refused to accept his advances, particularly in public, it would cause an uproar of gossip.

That was a problem for another time.

Making it through dinner with Loren and a handful of his officers, including Nikolai Jensen, was the problem of the evening. The Captain had been called on immediately after her gruesome display in her suite sitting room to provide her and Emillie with fresh, untainted blood. Alongside Markus, Loren had remained to oversee her feeding.

When Ariadne sank her teeth into Nikolai's wrist, something primal had sparked in the General's eyes. Her father chatted casually with Nikolai, as he always did, and prodded her fiancé with questions, which he answered without removing his gaze from her. His nostrils flared, and he shifted in his seat on the couch across from where she drank.

She knew what he was thinking. She knew he imagined his own wrist in place of Nikolai's. She knew he struggled to contain the lust in front of the other Caersan men.

Feeding, after all, could be an erotic connection between married vampires.

Ariadne also knew she should have those same feelings for Loren. One night, she would be drinking his blood for survival, and he would partake in hers. It was said to connect Caersan partners much in the same way as fae bonded. She should, then, look forward to sharing those moments with her future husband.

But she did not. It was not Loren she thought of as the Captain's blood gushed across her tongue before being diverted up her hollow fangs to mingle in her veins. It was not Darien, either, though once it had been.

It was Azriel.

The dream that somehow, someway, he would save her from the looming nuptials eclipsed the shame of the very thought.

Impossible, of course. A bastard-bred, half-fae guard had no place in the Caersan Society. The only other option would be to run away with him, and that was as fantastical as getting out of marriage with the General.

So as she pushed the food around on her plate, ignored as usual by the Caersan men who sat around her, Ariadne felt more distant and alone than ever before. She stared out the bay of windows beyond Loren, unable to muster a smile anytime he looked her way.

"It was very kind of the Captain to come tonight," Emillie whispered to her as the men laughed boisterously around them. "I am feeling much better. Are you?"

Ariadne did not respond. Her very soul ached, and absolutely nothing she did made it end. Every time she looked across the table, she remembered precisely what her life thus far had amounted to: becoming the prized broodmare won by the highest bidder.

"Ari?" Emillie took her hand and squeezed once.

A single, silent squeeze was all she could muster in response. What could she say? She was not thankful for Nikolai nor for the engagement forced upon her by a father who did not care for her happiness. Her safety was only his priority, so she could one day become the wife he had trained her to be. Quiet. Subordinate. Accepting.

That Ariadne had not adhered to those virtues her first Season was his ultimate shame. He allowed her to accept Darien's proposal to save his own reputation. Nothing more, nothing less.

"How is Lord Governor Caldwell faring?" Nikolai asked as the laughter died down. "Last I heard, he had entered his final sleep."

"Ah," Colonel Trev Wintre said with a grimace and pulled out a small slip of paper. "I received word this evening of his passing two nights ago."

Everyone fell quiet. Even Ariadne's pulse slowed as the understanding set in. The Lord Governor of the Eastwood Province was the last Caersan vampire of the first generation. An elder who had lived through the very making of the Society after the curse and the second most powerful voice on the Council after her father.

"Let us raise our glasses," her father announced suddenly, standing with his wine in hand, "to the Lord Governor, Garth Caldwell. May his soul rest with the gods."

The Caersan officers stood, saluted their cups, and said in unison, "Rest well, Lord Governor Caldwell."

She and Emillie raised their glasses of water as well. They said nothing, as was customary of women. To do so would be impudent.

As the men returned to their seats, Nikolai asked, "Has his Will been read yet?"

"I should be receiving it soon." Her father tucked back into his meal, the thoughts of a dead Councilman doing nothing to upset his appetite. "Though it could take several weeks for the Legal Guild to sift through the records and parcel out the inheritance."

"How is Lady Caldwell?" Trev sipped his wine.

"I am uncertain," her father confessed. "She has yet to reach out."

"Mourning can be a tricky thing," Loren said. "Let us speak of something more positive."

Nikolai turned to Ariadne. "Yes. How are the plans for the engagement ball coming along?"

She choked on her water. "Fine."

"We are looking forward to celebrating the two of you," he said and winked at the General.

Ariadne forced a small smile and avoided her fiance's gaze. "It will be stunning."

"Will there be a theme?" Trev asked.

"No." She pushed her potatoes to the far side of her plate.

That ended the questions directed at her. Ariadne felt no disappointment as they turned back to discussing matters they deemed inappropriate for Caersan women. She and Emillie fell silent again.

Before long, the dinner plates were removed, and dessert set before them. Chocolate mousse with a cream whip on top. Ariadne's favorite.

Yet three bites in, she looked to her father. "I am quite tired. I believe I will retire for the day."

He pierced her with his sharp gaze, then nodded once.

Loren stood as she did. "May I escort you?"

Ariadne gaped at him for a long moment before saying, "Thank you, General, but I am fine. Please stay and enjoy the food and company."

He swept around the table and bowed, taking her hand in his to kiss it gently. "Good day to you, then, Miss Harlow."

With a quick curtsy, she left the dining room and half-ran to the stairs in the foyer. Her heart thundered—a mix of exertion and panic. Up one floor, and she paused. A new book. She needed a new book to distract her. Even something as droll as history would be better than nothing.

Ariadne turned down the hall to the library and hurried through the closed doors. She shut them behind her and closed her eyes.

Leaning back against the wood, her head made a dull *thunk* as she inhaled deeply to calm her racing heart. Counting back from ten, she followed the steady rhythm of the numbers to slow her pulse. The last thing she had wanted was to think about the wedding. About a future with Loren.

At one, Ariadne opened her eyes again. Through the dim candlelight of the library, she found Azriel standing rooted to the spot before a chair, book in hand. The cut on his cheek, still red and blossoming with a bruise, stood out in stark contrast to the rest of his features.

Her heart leapt and started off on its wild race again. Cheeks flushing with warmth, she bit her lip and mumbled, "Sorry," before turning back to the door.

"Stop." His deep voice was soft, and she looked over her shoulder at him. "Stay. I'll go."

"You were here first." But she did not turn the knob. She only watched him and wanted nothing more than to throw herself into his arms and cry.

But that was not how she left him last. No, after he had dragged her from the darts game and she punched him in the face, she refused to speak with him again. Gods be damned if she did not keep up that façade. She would not let him see her break.

"I'm done anyway." Azriel set the book on a table and stepped closer. "Excuse me."

Ariadne turned back to him and set her jaw. "Why are you acting like this?"

Azriel frowned, searching her face for a long moment. "What are you talking about?"

"Gods!" She stepped forward. The anger rushed back as she recalled the last two weeks. "First, you stand up for me and nearly get yourself killed. Then you pushed me away. You pushed me away when I *needed* you."

Tears swarmed her vision. She blinked them back, the heat in her chest boiling over. No, she could not let him see her upset. Her throat burned as she held back the teeming emotions.

"Miss Harlow," he said and swallowed hard, "this is inappropriate. I must leave."

Ariadne moved closer again. "No. *No.* You *abandoned* me these last two weeks. Just disappeared!"

"Please." His voice cracked. "I have to leave. If the General finds you alone with me, he will have my head."

"Leave him out of this," she hissed. She could not bear hearing him speak Loren's title. "That is not what this is about."

"But it is," he breathed. "It is."

"You were supposed to be my friend, Azriel," she said, unable to keep the pain from her words. "My *friend* and you left me."

Azriel froze, eyes wide, at the sound of his name. He shook his head, and a muscle ticked in his jaw. "We were never and can never be friends."

"But why not?" Her lips quivered, and his gaze dipped to her mouth, brows pulling up in concern.

Gods, they were so close now. She wanted him to hold her. Needed him to wrap his arms around her and shield her from the world. To reassure her that everything would be alright. To kiss her. It was all she could think about now that she was alone with him.

When next he spoke, it was a whisper on a breath as he searched her face. He pushed a curl back from her face with steady fingers, tucking it behind her ear. His thumb lingered against her cheek as he shook his head. "It would be wrong, Ariadne."

She wanted to scream. The way he said her name made her skin alight. It was like a skeptic begging the gods for forgiveness—filled with worship and infinite devotion. She could survive on the luxurious bass of his voice saying her name alone.

"Maybe," she whispered, so close to him now that if she were to inhale deep, they would touch. "Maybe I do not care anymore."

The library door opened in a rush. Azriel lurched back, creating space between them in an instant. It gaped wide, like an ocean separating continents that tried so hard to meet. Ariadne whipped around to face the intruder, already missing the feel of his hand on her face.

Emillie stood in the doorway, eyes wide as she looked between them.

All it took was one call from her to their father, and that would be the end of everything. For them to have been found alone and so, so close would have dire consequences. Ariadne would be punished most severely by her father for such a thing.

But Azriel? He would be killed.

Pure panic coursed through Ariadne's veins as she awaited her sister's decision. Each heartbeat became an agonizing eternity.

Then Emillie turned her wide gaze to Ariadne and whispered, "They are coming."

Someone screamed. Maybe it happened in Azriel's head alone, but the scream echoed so loud that every other sound in the world disappeared. Nothing else existed aside from her. Ariadne was all that mattered in that moment—gods, she was all that mattered in any moment.

And to have been so close...

How he'd managed to control the bond's urge to pull her to him and claim her mouth with his, he had no idea. Yet he had long enough for that damned door to open, ruining everything.

Azriel didn't look at Emillie as she closed the door behind her, those words clanging around his brain. *They are coming.* They didn't make sense even as they struck terror into him. Who was coming? Why should he care?

Emillie shut the door and looked at him with eyes so much like Ariadne's. "You need to leave. *Now.*"

Everything slammed into focus. He shouldn't be here. Not with Ariadne—not alone with her like this. Least of all when Loren lurked about. If they caught him with Ariadne, it'd be his life on the line and her reputation.

Icy panic leached into his gut, twisting it from the inside like a vice. His breath hitched, and he looked from sister to sister. The younger chewed her lip. The elder pointed to the veranda at the far end of the library.

Azriel opened his mouth to speak—what? He didn't know. To tell her he was sorry for abandoning her? That he loved her? To ask her to run away with him? He could do none of those things. Not in this lifetime.

Voices echoed down the hall. A loud laugh he recognized as the Colonel's drew closer. Why they were heading to the library, Azriel could not fathom. Aside from the Princeps, none of the Caersan men from dinner this morning were studious.

"Why are they coming here?" Ariadne hissed to her sister and motioned again for Azriel to get to the veranda.

"Something about genealogical history?" Emillie picked up the book Azriel had abandoned and plopped onto the couch. She glanced at the title and frowned at him. More fae tales.

"Go!" Ariadne said, desperation dripping from the word. "Please."

Finding his legs, Azriel launched into action. He crossed the room and snatched his sword from its place against the couch. Unlocking the veranda door with steady fingers, he paused. With a quick glance over his shoulder, he found Ariadne ripping a book from the shelf and sitting beside Emillie, her eyes still latched on him.

Azriel's heart stumbled. He shouldn't be leaving her. Not again. But the plea in her gaze pushed him through the door so he could close it behind him. He flattened his back against the outer wall of the manor to stay hidden, heaving in a deep breath of cool spring morning air.

And not a moment too soon. The library doors opened with a chorus of voices.

"A Steward Governor would be fine for a time," Markus was saying as he entered the room, "but a direct descendant of the Caldwells should take the seat."

"Miss Harlow." Loren's tone was one of surprise and, to Azriel's disgust, pleasure. "I thought you had retired for the day."

A beat of silence. Azriel could see her stand and curtsy in his mind's eye. Her cheeks would still be flushed from their encounter as she said, "General. I desired a book before turning in."

"A pleasant surprise." Nikolai's voice was closer, almost to the veranda doors.

Azriel gripped the rail beside him with one hand and, in a single, swift leap, launched himself down from the second floor. He landed, knees bent and heart racing, in the grass at the same moment the doors opened where he'd stood a breath before. Voices spilled into the early morning air behind him, and it took all his concentration to not look up at them right away. Instead, he picked up a casual gait toward the servant's entrance near the kitchen.

"I admit I am pleased to have another chance to speak with you," Loren said behind him. "Are you feeling better?"

"Yes, thank you." Ariadne's tone was tight.

Azriel looked over his shoulder then, unable to stop himself from ensuring she was, in fact, safe. On the veranda, Loren stood behind Ariadne. She gripped the rail Azriel had just leapt over, and the General, body almost close enough to touch hers, laid his hand beside hers so their fingers brushed together.

Azriel's throat tightened. That should be him. Every instinct in his body demanded it be him standing beside her, their bodies a mere whisper apart. Not Loren.

Ariadne shifted away from the General and snapped her gaze to Azriel. Her mouth formed a tight line. His footsteps faltered until she shook her head almost imperceptibly. *Do not turn back*, she seemed to say.

Azriel dipped his chin, then turned away again. Gods, he was in trouble.

CHAPTER 15

E millie dressed the next evening in a simple green gown meant for home wear. As she braided her hair and slipped on soft-soled shoes, her mind remained restless. It leapt from the bistro to the dinner to the library in a steady rotation.

Already she missed Kyra. The Rusan woman, so open and proud of her affinity for other women, had felt...right. Her hand between her legs had felt even better. She envied her and, most of all, wished she had had more time to get to know her.

Meeting with Kyra again would be almost impossible. After Ariadne had gotten sick all over the General's boots, their father decreed they were no longer permitted to Laeton without his accompaniment. Azriel and Madan's presence would not suffice since they had ignored their efforts to steer them home. Even if she could get word to Kyra to meet her somewhere, her father would not allow them to be seen together in public.

The horror of her father insisting Camilla return home before dinner had eclipsed Emillie's regret about not asking Kyra for a way to get in touch again. Her friend had taken the suggestion well, claimed she needed to get home before dawn, and left with Madan as her escort.

That had then left her alone with a quiet, withdrawn Ariadne throughout dinner, surrounded by military officers who did not care to engage her in conversation. It was obvious from the start of the meal that her sister had not been fully present. The journey into town had been meant to loosen her up—and it had for a while—but the moment the General arrived, the Season's Golden Rose wilted.

To walk into the library and find her with their personal guard had therefore been a surprise greater than anything Emillie had ever experienced. The two were standing more intimately than she had seen many Caersan vampires with their wedded spouses. Azriel's head had angled so that if he had bent just a bit, their mouths would have met. Ariadne, in turn, had curved her back to meet his body with so little space dividing them, Emillie doubted she would have been able to slide her hand between their forms.

And that was the one thing she could attempt to solve tonight. Kyra would have to wait, and Camilla knew she would be welcomed back once their father realized his mistake—as he always did.

Emillie knocked on Ariadne's door, and it opened much sooner than she was accustomed. On the far side of the threshold, her sister gave her a tight smile and stepped aside as a silent invitation to enter. Ariadne still wore her sleeping gown and a long robe, which she pulled closer to herself.

Settled onto one of the sitting room couches, Emillie tracked her sister as she slipped a couple of books onto her shelves. The only one she left out was the same book from the previous morning. It had been many years since she saw Ariadne reading simple children's stories. Even her fantastical-loving sister, who typically read of love and worlds in which objects such as carriages operated without manual assistance, rarely stooped to the tales of their childhood.

"How are you?" Ariadne asked as she slid onto the chaise across from Emillie, tucked her feet up and under her robe, and pulled her long, dark hair over one shoulder to twist and curl around her finger.

She studied her sister for a long moment, noting the subtle nods to her discomfort. "Better tonight. Yourself?"

Ariadne suddenly became very interested in the ends of her hair. "Much better, thank you. Last night was an interesting experience."

It certainly had been on many accounts. Kyra flashed through Emillie's mind again, and she pushed the image of the redhead aside to focus on what she had come to discuss. "What happened between you and—"

"Nothing." Ariadne pulled her lower lip between her teeth, exposing the tips of her fangs as she bit down softly. "Mister Tenebra and I had a disagreement that had carried over from earlier."

"When you hit him?"

Her sister's cheeks flushed. "Yes."

"I recall a conversation we had weeks ago," Emillie said cautiously. "About him. Do you remember what you said?"

Ariadne stilled, her hands dropping from her hair to twist in her skirts instead. "Indeed."

"Please, Ari." Emillie glanced at the door, worried it might open at any moment. Someone could be listening in the corridor beyond. "That was no argument I saw last night. If anyone else had walked in on you..."

With a shake of her head, Ariadne smoothed her robe out over her legs again. Anything to avoid eye contact, it would seem. "I was telling Mister Tenebra how unprofessional he had been by making Madan escort us into town last night. If he had been there from the beginning—"

"I am not stupid, Ariadne." Emillie sat forward as her sister's eyes snapped up to scan her face.

"I never said you were."

"Then stop treating me like I am!" she said, dropping her voice into a harried whisper. "I am your sister, and I tell you *everything*."

Mouth agape, Ariadne merely stared for a long moment before she said, "As do I."

"Lies!" After everything they had gone through, she could not understand why her sister would want to hide her true feelings. "Again and again, you have lied to me. Please, Ariadne, I know you are not fine. I can see you struggling every single day. Let me help you."

"I am not lying."

"Swear it," Emillie said, swallowing back the heat building in her throat. "Swear on our mother's ashes that you are not lying to me."

Ariadne scoffed. "This is an affront. How could you think so lowly of me?"

"Swear it!"

"I was overwhelmed last night," Ariadne said, and Emillie did not miss how she skirted around the demand. "After everything at the bistro, then the General... I needed a moment to myself. Mister Tenebra was there, and he got the brunt of my frustration."

Still no acknowledgment of her request. No swearing. It stung to see how desperately her sister wished to avoid speaking the truth.

"Are you happy?" Emillie asked after a long moment of grappling with her frustration.

"I told you," Ariadne sighed, "I am overwhelmed."

Emillie shook her head. "No. Are you happy with your engagement?"

Another pause in which Ariadne did not look up. Her fingers twisted around the hem of her robe again, and when she finally spoke, it was quieter than usual. She looked up at the ceiling, and her eyes shimmered. "Of course I am happy. Anyone in the Society would be thrilled to be engaged to the General."

"Ari..."

Her sister smiled tightly and stood. "I need to get ready for the night. If you will excuse me."

Emillie followed suit and made her way to the door. "Join me for tea later?"

"Of course." Still, Ariadne did not look at her.

Closing the suite door behind her, Emillie took a deep breath to temper herself. She knew her sister well enough to know that every word out of her mouth had been more lies. The only problem was that Emillie had no way to help her escape the inevitable, and with the engagement ball looming on the horizon, those lies were about to become her reality.

Over the next week, Ariadne found herself lingering in uncommon places. Confined to the manor, except for the rare instances when her father was willing to take her to town, she had little to keep her occupied. Reading, painting, and practicing the steps to ballroom dances were how she maintained her sanity. With the engagement ball quickly approaching, she needed every possible activity to distract her.

The top spots to loiter around the manor included those where she would be most likely to see Azriel. The first night, she lingered near the small lake near the driveway he walked down each night to check in with the estate guards. At first, she was not certain he noticed her on his way out.

Upon his return to the main house, however, was another matter.

"Good evening, Miss Harlow." He looked around, a light frown forming between his brows when he found her unaccompanied. The cut she had given him had healed. A small, shiny scar remained amidst the yellowed bruise. "Are you alone?"

Her heart picked up its pace. "Yes."

In response, he started down the hill to where she sat on a bench and extended a hand to her. "Your home though it may be, I must ask you to return to the manor with me."

"I quite like it out here," she said, taking his hand. Rather than standing, she tugged him closer. "Sit."

Azriel inhaled sharply. "Miss Harlow, it would be—"

"Inappropriate." Ariadne sighed and loosened her grip on his palm. His fingers, though, held fast. Her breath hitched.

"Please, Miss Harlow."

"I wish to stay outdoors, Mister Tenebra." She twisted her hand from his, missing the warmth of his touch as soon as it disappeared. "Stay if it pleases you."

He stood for a long moment in silence, then said, "As you wish."

So she sat that night, languishing in the moonlight with Azriel standing nearby. They spoke infrequently, his presence enough of a salve to her anxious tendencies.

The next night, she kept to the parlor. When she saw him again, her stomach fluttered. She put her book on her lap, and he paused halfway through the foyer and leaned a shoulder against the opening.

"Good evening, Miss Harlow."

The way he said her name had changed over time. At their first meeting, he had been stiff and cold. His face gave nothing away, and his answers to any questions were short and filled with gravel.

Now his tone was softer, sweeter, and more of a purr. Though he distanced himself in the presence of others, he let a smile slip through his expressionless mask when they were alone.

"Mister Tenebra."

"Not out by the lake tonight?" His lips curled, and damn if they were not the most sensuous thing she had ever seen. His dimples deepened to show his genuine feelings.

Ariadne pulled her lower lip into her mouth, and his eyes tracked the movement. Warmth curled through her. "Not tonight."

"Pity." He straightened away from the wall. "I was looking forward to some fresh air."

"I could do with a walk through the lower gardens." She set the book aside and stood. "Stretch my legs a bit."

His pale eyes flickered to her long limbs and back. "Alright, then."

Ariadne strode forward, focusing on a point before her so she would not be tempted to look at him. Her blood thrummed through her veins, and she could not believe only she could hear its thunderous roar. She paused beside him, and her fingers brushed his hand. In response, he laced a couple with hers. She exhaled hard, then continued out the front door with her guard at her back.

Night after night, she found a way to spend time with Azriel Tenebra, the guard who listened to her. He showed her how to hold a dagger after a long argument about whether or not it was *appropriate* and what to do with it if she were ever in a situation she was not comfortable with. The time they spent together felt easy, and she looked forward to the distraction.

But the night before her engagement ball she understood what he had silently been doing: teaching her strategies for when he would no longer be around. As the realization set in, Ariadne felt her world drop out from under her. Loren's claim on her would be solidified at the following night's ball, with the wedding looming on the horizon.

Azriel would no longer be a part of her life, and he knew it. Each night since she had accused him of abandoning her, he had made up for his absence.

Heart cracking into what felt like a thousand pieces, Ariadne mounted Astra on her own and took off across the estate lawns. Eventually, someone would notice her disappearance. She had no doubt in her mind it would be Azriel. Still, she rode with the hope that each stride of her mare would alleviate the heaviness on her chest.

It did not.

In fact, the longer she remained outside on her own, the more prominent her self-imposed ostracism became. Emillie had hardly spoken to her over the week after seeing through her lies. Foolish of Ariadne to think she could keep anything from her sister. Now she had pushed away the one constant of her life. The one person she had been able to count on being there for her.

In less than a month, Ariadne would be taken from her home by a man she did not love and imprisoned by her new title. It was not unlike what happened to her a year ago. Only this time, rather than a stranger dragging her from her bedroom, it was a known villain with whom she would be stuck for the rest of her life.

Tears rolled down her cheeks as Astra galloped across the dark field. Whether it was from the ache in her chest or the wind in her face, Ariadne did not know. Nor did she care.

The rhythm of a second set of hooves grew louder, and she reined in her mare so she could turn to the newcomer. Azriel slowed to a halt beside her.

"Good evening, Miss Harlow."

She wiped the tears from her face, and his eyes narrowed. "Good evening, Azriel."

He stilled in the saddle and scanned her face as though searching for some sort of injury to her head. "Miss Harlow, please—"

"No." Ariadne shook her head. "I will call you whatever name I decide."

He weighed her words. "As you wish, Miss—"

"As should you." She locked her gaze with his as he frowned. He opened his mouth to argue, but she cut him off for the third time, "I do not consider it inappropriate. Please. I know what you have been doing. Give me this before I must leave."

Azriel moved his stallion close enough to brush knees with her without taking his eyes from her face. She tightened her grip on the reins and swallowed hard. He had already done so much for her—the least she could do was remove the barrier of rank between them.

"Well, then," he said, voice a quiet rumble, "Ariadne."

Her name on his lips stroked through her like a warm caress. She closed her eyes to relish the sound. With a hum of satisfaction, she looked at him again and smiled. "Thank you."

"You being out here has reminded me of something," he said, nudging his stallion forward so his thigh rubbed the length of her own.

Ariadne's mind went blank for a moment as the pleasant sensation of his touch warred with dark memories. She took two deep breaths before asking, "And what is that?"

"We never determined who would win in a race."

Their argument over what made a good rider slid back into her mind. She had worked so hard to hide how much she liked him at that point—even from herself. Ridiculous, really, considering where she was now.

"You are correct," she said, then pointed to the manor. "First back to the front doors?"

"Alright." Azriel grinned. "From here?"

"Yes."

"There are fences between us and the end goal." His eyes sparkled mischievously in the moonlight.

"Again, Azriel," Ariadne said with a wink, "you are correct."

His grin broadened, and he gathered his reins in a fist. "On three, then... Ariadne."

A flutter kicked through her stomach, and she nodded. "One."

"Two."

"Three!"

They launched forward in unison, their horses stretching their legs into a gallop. Within the first few beats, Azriel pulled ahead. The stallion, with his longer limbs, ate up the distance between them and the first fence surrounding the field.

Ariadne laughed again as Astra hurdled over the first barrier, the rush through her gut sending those butterflies into the ether. Halfway through the second field, she caught up with the half-fae and his steed.

The stallion flagged. Larger though he was, it meant he had more weight to carry—plus the huge guard on his back. In comparison, Astra's lithe build and Ariadne's slender body made for better aerodynamics.

By the time they launched over the second fence, she and Astra were in the lead by a head. She looked back at Azriel, who let out a breathy chuckle. No doubt she looked ridiculous with the loose strands of hair flying in front of her face.

"Come now, Azriel!" She laughed. "You can do better than that!"

The final fence had Astra a full body length ahead, so when they shot around the corner to the front drive, winning the race, Ariadne threw her hands up in victory. She turned in her saddle to watch Azriel slow behind her, face alight with more excitement than she had ever seen. His peridot eyes gleamed with life, and he trotted up beside her.

"I told you," she said, "I would win."

"But was it due to your love for riding?" He smirked. "Or your skill?"

Ariadne scoffed and went to slap his arm playfully.

"Well done," he said and stopped her hand before it could land its blow, kissing her knuckles without taking his gaze from hers. "You win."

Warmth flushed across her cheeks. She liked the feeling of his lips on her skin, and the very thought sent heat rushing to her core.

Something in her periphery moved, and Ariadne froze. She pulled her hand back and turned to find Loren standing at the front doors, his face drawn with fury.

In an instant, her smile disappeared. All sense of victorious elation vanished, replaced by dread. She did not dare look at Azriel as Loren strode forward, striking down the guard with his glare.

"Miss Harlow," Loren said and held out a hand. With the other, he gripped her reins to hold Astra in place.

Ariadne swallowed hard, accepted his hand, and dismounted so she could curtsy. "General Gard."

"I will take it from here, Mister Tenebra." Loren's voice, cold and accusatory, cut like daggers.

Finally, she looked from her fiancé to her guard. The former's quiet anger rippled through the night. The latter's quick switch from open and excitable to cool subordination made her stomach knot.

"Yes, sir." Azriel nodded once to them, then nudged his stallion into a trot, leaving her alone with the General.

Loren's hands shook at the effort of holding back his rage. The moment the pair had rounded the corner to the front drive, he could not ignore the way they looked at each other. Ariadne's face, flushed and bright, was beautiful as she laughed—happier than he had ever seen her before. Behind her, Azriel watched her move with longing.

Where Loren had his suspicions before, the sudden sobriety from their ignorant bliss underscored what he knew. It was not just Azriel who searched for Ariadne. She, too, found enjoyment with him.

And if that did not infuriate him beyond measure...

As Azriel rode away, Loren turned back to Ariadne and brought her fingers to his lips. "Miss Harlow, even flushed from victory, you are stunning."

"You are too kind, General," she said quietly, far more meek than she had been a moment before when she had teased the bastard guard.

A stablehand ran around the corner, likely sent by Azriel to collect Ariadne's mare, and he tossed the reins into the Rusan's hands. The servant bowed, then walked away in silence. At least some of the men around here had the common decency to do their job properly. When he took over the estate, centuries down the road, he would rid the place of anyone who believed themselves equal to the Caersan.

When they were once again alone, Loren turned to his fiancée. "You have been spending time with Tenebra?"

Ariadne chewed her lip. "Yes, General."

"Why?"

Her eyes widened, and she looked toward the front door as though expecting—perhaps *hoping*—someone would join them. "I do not ask him. It is his job. When I am out on the grounds, he has been appointed to look after me."

"Correct." Loren ground his teeth. "He is there to look after you—not *play* with you."

After all, Ariadne was his. His fiancée. His future wife. His *plaything*. He would not have another man, particularly not a low-born bastard, thinking he could touch what was rightfully Loren's. The half-breed had grown bold over the weeks, and it seemed time to teach the fucker another lesson since the last one did not take.

Ariadne, however, gaped at him. "He was not... We were not playing! It was a race. We tried... I asked him... I wanted—"

"Do you like him?"

Now she stared in utter shock, her face paling. Good. Let her know she has been caught. It was better she learned her place now.

But the hesitation boiled Loren's blood. She was looking for excuses and lies and pretty words to hide what she truly felt. If she did not love him, fine. He would still marry her and take what he wanted. He would not, however, stand by as she fawned over a lesser vampire.

"Az—Mister Tenebra is an excellent guard," she choked out, and he lifted a lip in a snarl at her slip-up. "He kept me safe at the Vertium ball. Do you remember?"

"I remember well." Loren grit his teeth and grabbed her wrist, yanking her toward the front door with him.

Ariadne yelped and tugged back. He tightened his grip. She would learn who was in charge, and it certainly would never be a Caersan woman. They were meant to serve their husbands, bring heirs into the world, and hold their tongues.

"You will not spend any more time with that guard," he snarled and started up the front steps. Still, she twisted her arm. To his pleasant surprise, she did not say anything. "Do you understand me?"

Again, she did not speak. Instead, she stared at his hand around her wrist and whimpered. Each attempt to free herself became more and more feeble. Tears streaked her cheeks, and she turned wide eyes up to him in a silent plea.

"Do you understand?" Loren snarled. He twisted her arm hard and drew her in closer so their faces were inches apart. She tried pulling her arm down to free it.

"Yes!" she gasped and cried out in pain. Again and again, she nodded. "Yes, I understand."

"Say it back to me."

"I will not spend any more time with him." She whimpered again and curled her shoulders in on herself.

"Look me in the eye," he ground out, reveling in the pitiful sight of a Caersan woman at his mercy, "and tell me you love me."

Ariadne lifted her silver-rimmed gaze and searched his face. When she spoke, her small voice shook, "I love you, Loren."

Fuck. He liked that a lot. He still had a month before he could show her just how much he enjoyed reminding her of where she stood. What a fabulous morning it would be. Until then, he needed to get his cock under control. The urge to throw her up against the wall almost won out.

Instead, he released her wrist. She gasped and swayed, bracing herself against his chest to keep from falling. Gods, if only he could get away with fucking her right there.

Ariadne straightened, looking up at him with wary, watery eyes. Her tears shone on her cheeks like diamonds. Beautiful. He brushed them aside with his thumb, and though she flinched, she did not pull away.

A heavy hand went a long way, it would seem.

"Good girl," he said, softer now, while dragging his thumb down her face to run across those perfect lips. They parted a bit. He would part them again in a couple weeks, and it would not be with his finger.

His cock throbbed at the thought. He would need to take a moment to himself before he could meet with the Princeps. Perhaps there was a maid with similarly dark hair he could fuck from behind.

"Now," he said, brushing a strand of her hair back behind her ear. Again she winced but stood still. A smirk cracked across his lips. "I came to discuss business with your father. You distracted me."

For a long moment, Ariadne did not reply. She breathed heavily through her nose, then finally, she whispered, "I am sorry, General."

Loren clicked his tongue, warmth sweeping through him again. "Oh, darling, I forgive you. You did not mean to."

She pulled her lip into her mouth. He almost groaned and instead set his hand on the doorknob to steady himself.

"I hope your meeting goes well," she said and gave him a small smile.

"I will see you tomorrow," Loren said and took up her hand again to kiss her fingers, "to celebrate our engagement before all of the Society."

With that, he pushed through the front door and went in search of a maid.

CHAPTER 16

A zriel paced the kitchen, the race and its abrupt end thanks to Loren fucking Gard replaying in his mind again and again. The cook offered him tea after noting his agitation, and he declined with a silent shake of his head. Tea wouldn't help this. Tea couldn't soothe the wildfire in his soul.

When at last he found it within himself to reenter the rest of the manor, he almost turned back. Madan stopped at the end of the hall, crossing his arms and glaring at him from the far end.

"I know," Azriel growled and pressed forward before Madan could even open his mouth. "I know."

"Do you?" Madan said, throwing his hands in the air. "What the *fuck* did you do?"

Azriel shook his head to avoid eye contact. "He hates me. You know that."

"I've been assigned to Ariadne exclusively."

A chasm opened in Azriel's gut. He stared at a distant spot, unable to think or breathe clearly. "What?"

"The Princeps has ordered me to look after her," Madan explained. "You aren't allowed near her anymore. I'm to stand guard outside her room, even."

"Ridiculous," Azriel scoffed. "Do they think I'd sneak into her room and whisk her away into the night?"

As if he were as devious as the dhemon who'd done just that. His stomach twisted at the thought.

"You're to watch Emillie. It's your last chance or Loren will—"

"I did nothing wrong." Azriel swallowed hard. "Nothing."

"He'll kill you, Az." Madan shoved his face into Azriel's line of sight. "Do you hear me? *Kill.*"

"I'd like to see him try." Darkness crept in from the sides of Azriel's vision. A rhythmic pounding took its place in his head.

"He's the General of Valenul," Madan hissed. "So even if we got the upper hand, you could never—*never*—come back."

Shaking his head, Azriel grit his teeth. We. At least Madan had not completely abandoned him. So many took one look at him and saw a dangerous criminal after that lashing. Madan remained the peaceful, pragmatic guard, beloved by all. They didn't know it was he who'd ensure no one ever found Loren's body when they were finished with it.

But killing Loren remained a hopeful dream. Azriel lowered his gaze and rubbed his eyes hard. When his fists dropped, the darkness eased and that horrible sensation in his mind faded.

"Is everything alright?" Madan asked, voice softer as he laid a hand on Azriel's shoulder.

"Fine." Azriel sighed. "You're right."

"At last." Madan chuckled. "You're finally seeing the truth."

Azriel scoffed. "Shut the fuck up."

"For far too long, you've ignored my wisdom."

"Well, then," Azriel said with a shake of his head, "you'll be pleased to know I've put in for a transfer."

Madan frowned, his face paling. "What?"

"You won't need me here much longer anyway." Azriel pulled away and leaned his back against the wall. His throat tightened, strangling the words. The bond writhed at the very thought of leaving her behind. Even his heart ached at the promise of being separated from Madan again. "She'll be married off, and you can handle Emillie on her own."

"You won't need a transfer," Madan said and pulled a folded letter from his pocket. "Caldwell's Will is being delivered to the Council the night after tomorrow."

Azriel whipped his gaze up to Madan, his eyes wide. He opened and closed his mouth several times, sorting through his numb thoughts, before shaking his head and returning his stare to his shoes. It'd still be too late. "I don't want it."

"You did before."

"If I accept," Azriel whispered, "I'll never be free of her. She'll haunt me forever."

Madan stepped closer. "You don't have a choice."

"I'll abdicate." He couldn't bear to take the position. Not now, not ever.

"To who?"

"You." Azriel lifted his eyes to him again. "You're a better leader than I could ever be."

Madan frowned. "You know you're wrong."

"Look what happened to my father." Azriel checked each end of the hallway for any sign of eavesdroppers. "I'm not made for it."

"No." Madan took Azriel's face in his hands and leaned their foreheads together. They both closed their eyes for a long moment. "That will never happen to you."

His voice cracked, "How do you know?"

"Because I'll be there," Madan said quietly. "I'll be by your side every step of the way."

After his mother's death, Azriel had watched his father spiral into a hatred he couldn't control. The link Azriel provided by carrying her blood is all that kept him from succumbing to the bond's nightmarish hold. Perhaps by some miracle Madan could be that anchor for him. A link to the world so he wouldn't become a shadow of himself.

"You can do this," Madan whispered and pulled away, one hand on Azriel's face. The familial warmth radiated through him. "I believe in you."

When Azriel opened his eyes, his vision blurred. "At least one of us does."

Loren did not linger long after dismissing Madan from the office. His business complete, he bid his goodbyes and started down the corridor toward the foyer. Halfway to the exit, he heard a pair of familiar voices. Of the two, the deeper, more rough tone made his temper simmer.

Killing the bastard guard would be easier than walking this fine line to protect what belonged to him.

He shifted closer to the servant hall to better listen to what Madan told his cousin. If he was expected to trust the vampire with his future wife, he needed to know what kind of man he was. That included how he went about following instructions.

"Caldwell's Will is being delivered to the Council the night after tomorrow," said Madan.

Why would a guard know the comings and goings of such official documents? He had no bearing on what those papers said.

"I don't want it." Azriel sounded somber.

Loren's blood ran cold. The Caldwell heir could not possibly be that bastard-born fae piece of shit. The second-most powerful Council position in Valenul could not be replaced by half-breed filth. It would be a disgrace to the very title.

"You did before," Madan said, quieter now.

The reply from Azriel, whispered, could not be heard from Loren's vantage point around the corner. His mind whirled. He had never heard of a blood heir to the Caldwell line—they died centuries ago. What could he do, then, to prevent this heinous ascension?

"You don't have a choice."

"I'll abdicate."

"To who?"

"You."

Loren had heard enough. He pushed away from the wall and returned to the front door. Outside, he called for the stablehand to return his stallion. He mounted the horse and yanked the reins to face the long drive. None of what he had just discovered would happen as far as he was concerned.

Those low-standing men would never be accepted as part of the Society. Whether they spoke the truth or not, he now had much to consider.

The strangest part of it all, he realized as he started toward the road, was their sudden appearance in all their lives. How had he not considered the oddity of it sooner? Both men, according to the paperwork he had read weeks ago on them, moved from simple grounds guards to personal guards at the Caldwell Estate almost a year and a half ago—not six months before Ariadne's kidnapping—and frequently requested to be stationed in Laeton.

Then Azriel joined his cousin at the Harlow Estate a mere fortnight after the first notice of Lord Governor Caldwell's illness.

Why did either of them continue in their positions as personal guards? If they knew they were to be named the heirs of the Caldwell Estate, they would have done better to join their distant family and take up the mantle of Steward as the lord passed in peace.

Unless, of course, they were hiding something.

At the old highway, Loren spurred his stallion toward town. Only one way to find out what they were hiding, and that required taking a deeper look into their lineage. Azriel Tenebra might be a bastard, but he needed to know how he connected to the Caldwell family.

CHAPTER 17

Ariadne could no longer wear the gown Revelie had made for the engagement ball. The short, capped sleeves would have been perfect for the late spring celebration, and everything she had put together during the weeks of planning matched it perfectly. Rich emerald garlands amongst sapphire and burgundy flowers paired well with the deep crimson fabric.

Long sleeves, however, covered the yellowing bruise on her wrist. She did not know if it was from not having fed since the night at the Bistro or the sheer strength of the General, which caused her arm to turn purple within minutes. What she did know was her strong vampire bones were all that kept her arm intact. Without them, Loren would have snapped it in half.

Nonetheless, Ariadne instead chose an older, less fanciful, powder blue dress to wear with sleeves long enough to hide the bruise. Sympathy did not pair well with celebration.

Though celebrating remained far from her thoughts as she settled into the chair before her vanity. Maids swept around her, pulling strands of hair into curls, swiping rouge across her cheeks, and lining her eyes with black. The first time she had gone through the preparations for the traditional ball, they had bathed her and dressed her. They had done neither since her return from the mountains. Dressing for the event was no different.

As they worked, Emillie entered in her pale green dress. The maids pinned her hair back and powdered her cheeks as well.

"You chose a different gown." Emillie's mouth tightened. "Why?"

Ariadne did not look her in the eye. "It is cooler tonight than I expected."

"You fretted over that dress," she said with a narrowed gaze. She did not miss much. "But you look beautiful no matter what."

"Thank you."

A silence stretched between them for a long minute. The brush combed through her gentle curls, and as one maid began braiding small strands, another fixed Emillie's. She focused on the strokes of the brush and sweep of powder across her cheeks to make the blue veins on her throat and jaw stand out.

"I overheard," Emillie said to break the lingering quiet, "the Lord Governor Caldwell's funeral pyre went well."

"I am certain the ceremony was beautiful."

Her sister hummed in agreement. "Have you heard who will be taking up the title as his heir?"

Ariadne parted her lips to allow for a rich red stain to be spread across. "I have not. Though, as far as I know, he only had one child."

"Mariana." Emillie sat back in her chair. "She died, did she not?"

"Murdered," Ariadne breathed. Her chest tightened at the thought. It was a brutal tale meant to frighten the recent generation of young Caersan out of the woods. "By dhemons."

In the mirror, she caught the maids glancing at one another before declaring themselves satisfied with their work. Emillie said nothing else on the matter. She did, however, reach out and take Ariadne's hand. The squeeze she gave was longer and stronger than most in the past. Ariadne squeezed back—a half-hearted, gentle press of her fingers.

Then Emillie left as swiftly as the maids.

Ten...

Ariadne sucked in a steadying breath to clear her mind of any memories tainted by dhemons. If Mariana had not died in those woods outside the Caldwell Estate, would she have suffered the same fate as Ariadne? No one could say, and to dwell on it meant losing herself to the dark halls of that dungeon once again.

Nine...

On and on the counting went, her breaths timed with the inhale and exhale. By the time she reached three, Ariadne stood and made her way out of her suite. Not a soul stood outside her door. Maybe Emillie warned any others away, knowing well she needed time alone.

Or maybe Madan, now assigned to her personally, stood just around the corner.

She crept down the halls, past a window overlooking the front drive flooded with Caersans of the Society arriving for the celebration. More, certainly, than the ball held in honor of her and Darien. In a matter of moments, the manor would be crawling with more vampires than she had ever seen in one place.

Until, of course, the wedding.

Down the first flight of steps she went and turned down the hall, away from the ballroom teeming with noise and toward the quiet sitting room. There, Loren would meet her before descending the final staircase, where both their fathers would introduce them as officially betrothed. Praise for the General capturing the eye of the Golden Rose would pour out while others looked for the next catch of the Season.

Ariadne made it halfway to the sitting room when, down a side hall, she saw *him*. Her heart lurched into her throat before kicking up the speed to hammer against her ribs like a drum. Exiting the small room meant for servants, a knapsack in hand, Azriel froze.

After a beat, a strained smile curled his lips, and he started toward her. "Miss Harlow."

No more first names, then.

She should not be with him. Her father had forbidden it after meeting with Loren the morning before. Still, she wanted to go to him more than the sitting room.

Ariadne bit her lip and nodded to the bag in his hand. "Going somewhere?"

He looked at it as though he had only then realized he had it in his hand. His throat bobbed. "Transfer."

Her blood ran cold. She had to have misheard him. She could not get through these last weeks of wedding preparations without him. Even if they could not interact, seeing him would be better than nothing.

"Congratulations," he said when she did not speak and took a few steps closer. His jaw, more tense than usual, flexed. "You must be ecstatic."

The air burned in her lungs. This could not be happening. None of it. Every evening was a waking nightmare. From the engagement to Loren's volatile jealousy of the guard to the one man trusted more than most leaving forever.

"Thank you." It was all she could choke out in response. Eyes prickling, she inclined her head, then turned back to the sitting room.

"Ariadne, wait."

Her name... oh, her name on his lips...

Then his fingers closed around her bruised wrist. Hissing in pain, Ariadne yanked her arm back. Unlike when Loren held her, however, Azriel let go. She curled the injured arm against her chest, cradling it away.

Brows furrowed, Azriel's nostrils flared. When he spoke, his tone was flat and low. "What's wrong with your arm?"

"Nothing." She dropped her hand to her side. "Good evening, Mister Tenebra."

Ariadne hurried away. She should not have stopped to speak with him. It only served to pain her more than the night already did. Entering the sitting room, pulse thundering in her ears, she did not notice his pursuit until he spoke next.

"Don't lie to me." His long legs overtook her, and he placed his huge body between her and the rest of the room. "What happened to you? You were fine when I saw you last."

"I *am* fine."

Azriel gaped at her, eyes wide. "I'm meant to protect you. I can't do that when you refuse to speak to me."

"You are transferring anyway," she choked and clutched at her throat as though the pressure could ease its tightness. "It was a reaction, not pain."

"I haven't transferred yet." He moved closer. "Please let me help you."

Ariadne shook her head. "You need to go. You are not supposed to be here."

"Not until—"

"If he catches you in here, he will have you killed." She pointed to the door. "Go."

In one fluid motion, he grabbed her hand and pulled her sleeve up. The yellowed bruise, clearly outlining fingers, stood out in the firelight. Azriel stared. He stared and stared, and Ariadne did not so much as see him blink or breathe. If he had moved at all, she would have been surprised.

"This." The word left him on a low, gravelly breath. "Who did this?"

In all her life, Ariadne had never seen a vampire so still. The green of his pale eyes seemed to shift in the firelight, flickering a muddied color from his rage. Yet his hold on her hand throughout it all remained loose and passive. The self-control as he teetered on the brink of blind fury should have frightened her. His ability to still see her—to still know her limits—through the rapid thoughts was enough to prove she could trust him, even in that moment.

When she did not reply to his question, he released her and took a step back, still staring at the bruise. She tugged her sleeve into place, but his gaze remained locked.

He growled, coming to the correct conclusion via her silence. "The General."

"It was an accident," she said in a rush, and finally, those fiery, molten eyes shifted to her face. They looked so strange in his quiet seething. Still, the lurch of her heart was not fear.

Azriel shook his head. "I'll kill him. I'll kill him for laying a hand on you."

That. That shifted her perspective as it was far from what she expected the guard to say.

She closed the distance between them. "No! Azriel, it was an accident."

"He *hurt* you." His voice broke, and his chin quivered. "I took an oath to keep you safe, and that bastard hurt you."

"He did not know—"

"How?" He swore under his breath. "How could he not possibly know?"

"I did not say anything."

"So?" Azriel searched her face, incredulous. He lifted a hand and stroked a curl back from her cheek, sending a shiver down her spine from the gentle touch. "You shouldn't have to say anything—he *knew* what he was doing. I would *never* hurt you like that."

His lips parted again as though to continue speaking, but whatever words he had caught in his throat. He shook his head and whispered, "You can't marry him."

A lump rose in her throat, and she released a shuddering breath. The weight of the Society's standards pressed hard on her shoulders. She stared back at the man she wished could take her away from it all and said, "I have no choice."

Azriel cupped her face with his large, warm hands, and for a long moment, the world fell away. His eyes drifted from hers to her mouth and back. "You always have a choice."

Ariadne did not know which one of them gave in first. All she knew was his lips on hers. His hands in her hair. His body pressing against her. His touch, all-consuming and raw with passion, curled hot in her core. She moved in closer as his tongue swept across her own, and she moaned soft and low.

He pulled away to run his lips along her jaw and whispered, "Choose me."

Ariadne's fingers curling into his shirt were all that kept Azriel and his bond tethered to the present moment. His blood roared, torn between two warring emotions: rage and passion. The soft sound she made as he drew a fang over her throat made every muscle in his body clench. He inhaled deep her delicious scent and knew he needed to pull back, to rein in the bond demanding more, more, more before he lost himself to it all.

Easier thought than done. She released his shirt and wrapped her arms around his neck, pressing every perfect curve of her body against him. He pulled her to him and kissed her hard, moaning against her mouth.

Heat exploded through his veins. Never in his entire life had he felt so satiated—so complete. Only Ariadne could complete the final piece that had been missing. Since the moment he laid eyes on her, the hole had gaped wide in his soul, threatening to swallow him up.

"I love you," he murmured.

She nodded, wordless, and slammed her mouth back to his. Her tongue slipped along his, each pulse of their rhythm raising his heartbeat a little more. Intoxicating.

Then somewhere beyond the endless sea of his bliss, a shout echoed. Words he couldn't make out, nor did he care about, rang through the room. It wasn't him, and it wasn't Ariadne—so none of it mattered.

Until, of course, someone ripped her from his arms.

Darkness, then crimson flooded his vision. Azriel blinked hard to clear the color, a telltale sign of his slipping grip on reality. He took a deep breath and refocused on the room, fangs bared.

Loren dragged Ariadne away, his grip like a vice on the same wrist he'd already bruised. Her sharp inhale, unnoticed by the General, sent Azriel's bond into a frenzy. In the doorway, her father watched in stunned silence as the events unfolded before him.

Azriel lurched forward as Loren released her, then threw a punch hard and fast at his face. The blow knocked him back a step, but Ariadne's scream for the General to stop kept him focused.

"I knew it," Loren snarled, advancing on him. "I knew I should have *never* trusted a filthy bastard like you."

To the Caersan's confusion, Azriel laughed. "Trusted me? Perhaps the Princeps should've never trusted *you*."

Markus frowned. "Excuse me?"

"Tell me," Azriel continued, leveling his gaze at Loren, "do you get off hurting women? Did you enjoy bringing her pain?"

The Princeps stilled and turned his attention from guard to General. "What does he speak of?"

For a long moment, Loren glared at Azriel. For once, the silver-tongued General couldn't concoct a quick enough lie to ensnare his audience. His complexion, however, paled a shade.

"Curious that your daughter chose to change her gown at the last minute after weeks of planning," Azriel said, crossing his arms over his chest and studying Markus over Loren's head. "Check her arms."

Without a word, the Princeps closed the distance between him and his elder daughter. Ariadne glanced at Azriel, brows pulled together with concern. When her father held out his hand, she placed hers on his. He held firm and tugged the sleeve up, revealing the yellowed bruise.

"I cannot believe the lies," Loren spat, rounding on them. "I would *never* harm my own fiancée. This beast, on the other hand, is always lurking about and clearly attempting to disgrace your daughter."

Azriel tempered his rising impatience and shouldered past the General. To his relief, Ariadne didn't cower away from him. To cringe back would be telling.

"May I?" he asked of both the Princeps and his daughter. When they both nodded, he loosely laid his hand over the bruise. The entire thing disappeared beneath his touch, then he removed it slowly. "The injury doesn't match my print."

Ariadne watched him with wide eyes as he stepped back. Though he had nothing to do with the harm caused to her wrist, he was far from innocent. The pain she held ran deep, and being caught in such a compromising way would only add to the hurt he'd caused. If either Caersan wished it, he could be killed for such transgressions.

"General." Markus nodded to Ariadne's naked wrist still in his hand. "You, too, have been accused. Care to prove yourself?"

Loren hesitated. He looked from Markus to Azriel and back. "That proves nothing."

"Then pray tell," Markus said calmly, "why you will not prove your innocence in harming my daughter?"

"If it was me," Loren said, stepping closer to Ariadne, "then it was an accident made in an attempt to assist her."

"Lies," Azriel snarled and jerked forward. Ariadne caught his gaze and gave a subtle shake of her head. He froze, fist curled at his side.

The General smirked up at him. "The true problem is yet unsolved."

"General," Ariadne breathed and pulled out of her father's grip. She straightened her sleeve. "I am sorry. Please—"

To Azriel's increasing irritation, Loren ignored her. "You defiled my fiancée. There are consequences for such bold behavior."

"No." Ariadne grabbed the General's arm. "Please stop!"

"Silence, Daughter," Markus snapped. "You have done enough tonight."

If Azriel could have killed both Caersan men, he would. Ariadne, though, would never forgive him. That understanding was the only thing staying his hand.

"A duel," Markus declared. "For her honor."

Loren scoffed. "A lowly guard? He should be hanged."

"And domestic violence was outlawed decades ago." Markus raised a brow. "Prove your innocence by fighting for her hand. The gods will make their judgment."

Again, Ariadne shook her head and whispered, "Do not do this."

"When?" Azriel trained his focus away from her, unable to withstand her pleas if he didn't concentrate. The bond, stoked by their moment of passion, pushed for him to abide by her commands.

A wicked smirk twisted Loren's face. "Immediately."

Not so long ago, it seemed the world had fallen out from beneath her in the most glorious way. Ariadne, wrapped in an embrace with a man her heart had chosen, did not think beyond her own desires. The rules and traditions of the Society were as troublesome as a fly—mere noise and no real bother.

What a fool she had been.

Now the world fell out from beneath her in the most horrific way. The duel, posed and accepted, determined her future with no thought as to what she would want. Given the chance, she would cloister herself away and tell every man who wished to speak with her to go away. She would grow old as a lonely spinster with no one but her sister for company.

That was not the reality Ariadne lived in, however. No, instead, she played the damsel to be saved, the maiden to be wed, and the Caersan woman silenced because of her gender. She hated each role. The first left her with scars better left hidden beneath her clothes. The second shackled her to the highest bidder like a broodmare. The last kept her muzzled so no one would listen to a word she said.

Even if she told her father the truth about the bruise, the General of their army held more sway. His daughter though she may be, Markus Harlow had never listened to her plights. The only reason he asked her about what happened in the mountains was to gather intelligence for Loren to use against the dhemons.

A Caersan woman's power came from her husband's position and the rumors she could spin to get what she wanted. It was all any of them had.

So Ariadne watched, heart racing, as the men filed out of the room. Her father lingered on the threshold, overseeing both Loren's and Azriel's departure, before following them out. That he did not lock her into the sitting room as they handled the duel was a miracle.

Ariadne followed them all at a distance. She clasped her hands together and wrung her fingers again and again. Her skin felt cool despite the dapple of perspiration on her forehead and neck. Blood pounding in her ears, she could not hear the hush that fell over the waiting guests when the four of them appeared at the top of the stairs leading into the ballroom.

Azriel was going to die. An excellent guard though he may be, the General's years of combat training and experience would overwhelm him. Despite the terms yet to be decided, she knew Loren would not stop until the half-vampire lay in pieces. Even if, somehow, Azriel managed to scrape by in the duel, he was not a Caersan nor a part of the Society and risked being hanged for what they had done.

No matter the outcome, she would end up with Loren, and Azriel would be dead. Once again, he would pay for her mistakes. Only this time...with his life.

"A most egregious development has occurred," Markus said to the quiet guests. "To settle a dispute, General Gard has challenged Azriel Tenebra to a duel."

"Speak plainly," Loren snapped. "The lowly bastard was discovered forcing himself upon Miss Harlow."

A collective inhale of breath from the Caersan, then eyes swiveled in her direction. Ariadne's heart flopped over, and at once, her face heated while her body shook from a sudden drenching of cold. In a dozen words, Loren had ruined her reputation, securing her to him. Markus glared openly at him, knowing well the consequences of what the General had said.

But Loren paid no mind. He barked a few quick orders to the soldiers present in the room, and they moved forward, clearing a space where the dance floor should be. No music played as they moved, and murmurs of excitement and surprise took its place from the Caersan.

Ariadne swayed and turned her gaze in a desperate search for someone—anyone—who might wake her from the nightmare unfolding around her. At the back of the room, standing in his usual place, Madan looked on with shock. His eyes flickered to her, and he shook his head slowly. There was nothing he could do.

A hand slid into hers. Ariadne jumped and almost ripped her hand away, but Emillie held fast. She squeezed hard and asked, "Are you alright?"

Words failed her. No. She most certainly was *not* alright, but not for the reason anyone was thinking as their judging gazes swept over her. Because of Loren, she appeared as a harlot who invited the advances of a guard. No matter that he claimed it was forced, the Society always blamed the women first.

Worst of all, he painted Azriel as an immoral criminal—again.

The dance floor cleared for the duel, and Azriel and Loren made their way to its center. The General held a hand out to his nearest soldier. A sword, produced with that song-like sound of steel being released from its sheath, passed to him. He had not brought his own, expecting the night to proceed as normal.

Across the floor, Azriel pulled his own sword from his back. The weapon was less flashy but just as sharp. Its edges gleamed in the firelight cast by the chandeliers overhead.

General and guard circled each other. A gleam sparkled in Loren's wintry blue eyes, his mouth curling at the corners into a wicked smirk. He shifted his shoulders in circles, warming up his muscles for what would inevitably be a short fight in high favor.

Across the dance floor, Azriel's expression descended into cold calm. It was how he looked the first night they had met. Calculating. Focused. He did not move like Loren did and instead kept his sword's tip pointed to the floor between them. His pale eyes almost darkened with the hate radiating from him.

Then the General struck.

CHAPTER 18

E millie did not understand what was happening. When she had entered Ariadne's rooms earlier that evening, it became painfully obvious how her sister felt about the engagement. Her reserved, ghost-like countenance said more than the reassuring words. It had been like stepping a year into the past when she had struggled to coax Ariadne from her new suite.

The moment Azriel appeared at the top of the stairs beside her father and Loren, Emillie knew something was wrong, as did the rest of the onlookers. Beside her, Camilla's sharp intake of breath drew her attention from the silent descent of the men with Ariadne trailing behind.

"Look at her lips," Revelie whispered from her other side, clutching Emillie's arm. "And Mister Tenebra."

Then she saw it. The ruined lip stain and the corresponding smear across Azriel's mouth told the truth. Loren lied, of course, as he had the first time he had tried to kill the guard with lashes. Now, he had the entire Society on his side.

Camilla covered her mouth. "Do you think he really—"

"No." Emillie shook her head. "No, I think this was a long time coming."

At least she prayed to every god listening that was the case. If it had been anything different, Emillie did not believe Ariadne would have come out with the men.

"I will be back," Emillie whispered, before moving to her sister's side.

Emillie slid her hand into Ariadne's, holding firm when her sister jumped and nearly pulled away. "Are you alright?"

The non-response spoke volumes. No, Ariadne was not okay. Not as the two men circled one another, swords in hand. The General moved like a predator stalking his next meal. In a way, he was. The Caersan had been targeting the half-fae for months. But the guard stared back, face drawn and nostrils flaring, as though he was ready to finish what he started.

Brave, considering the General's training and experience.

Loren lunged. Azriel blocked with ease and struck back. Metal clashed again and again, ringing through the ballroom to the response of gasps and hisses.

"What happened?" Emillie tried to engage her sister again, this time working hard to keep her mouth from moving too much. She did not want others to try guessing what she said.

Ariadne did not look at her. Eyes still glued to the duel, she said on a breath, "I made my choice."

Her choice? She chose the *half-fae guard* over the *Caersan General*? It was not so long ago that she had been fawning over the most powerful military figure of Valenul. Her eyes never left the Caersan.

Until Azriel spoke up for her and was lashed for it. Something broke in Ariadne then. Whatever glamour the General had held over her diminished, and she had never looked at him with the same passion again. Even if she never admitted the change of heart.

Until now.

The guard parried another attack, then slid into a quick riposte which nicked the General's shoulder. Azriel spilled the first blood, much to the astonishment of the crowd.

Loren lifted his lip in a snarl, twisted aside, and doubled down on his next attack. The strength of the swing forced Azriel back a step, though the guard did not look surprised by the move. Both swords swung hard, colliding with a rasp.

Footing regained, Azriel pushed back. Loren stumbled, and the Caersan onlookers gasped. For a beat, it appeared Azriel could land the fatal blow. He rushed forward, and the General righted himself quick enough to lunge in.

Azriel leapt back, body bowing around the point of the sword. A rivulet of blood ran the length of Loren's blade. When the guard stepped back, a dark ring of blood spread across his black shirt from the shallow stab.

Beside her, Ariadne tensed. Emillie turned her attention to her sister and squeezed her hand. She did not squeeze back, wide eyes trained straight ahead.

Emillie did not know what she would do when Azriel lost. If Ariadne chose the guard, for better or worse, she knew what would happen. A no-name, half-vampire guard against the General of Valenul? How did her sister believe such a match would be possible? Even if, by some miracle, he won, their father would never allow such an engagement to last.

A cry of alarm rose from the guests, and Emillie's heart stumbled. She whipped back around. Azriel stood weaponless. Loren had successfully disarmed the guard, sword tossed out of reach.

A small, sad sound escaped Ariadne as she lurched forward. Emillie held her fast. She could not be seen going down there for Azriel—it would ruin her more than Loren's damning announcement.

The General, though, did not hesitate. He swung hard, aiming for the guard's neck. A killing blow if she had ever seen one.

Azriel bent his knees, dropping his weight heavily onto his thighs. He drove forward, cupped the back of Loren's legs, and ripped the General's feet out from under him. The Caersan crashed to the floor, his back slamming against the marble, and the sword jostled from his hand, too.

Before Azriel could right himself, Loren wrapped his now-free arms around the half-fae's neck. The guard jerked his head up and leapt over Loren's legs to shove his shoulder into the General's throat. For a beat, it appeared nothing happened. Then Loren wiggled his arm free, releasing his hold on Azriel, and slammed his fist into the side of the guard's head.

Loren pulled the fist back to swing again, and Azriel grabbed his wrist to pin it to his chest. Knee digging into the General's gut, Azriel raised himself high and, using his free hand, rained punches down.

Emillie covered her mouth as blood sprayed from Loren's nose. This was an unexpected turn of events. Most Caersan men would have given up once they had lost their sword. But Azriel was not a Caersan, and Loren did not seem ready to end the fight.

The General twisted out from under Azriel's knee and kicked hard, landing a blow to the guard's chest. Azriel grunted, grabbed Loren's leg, and shoved it to the side. The Caersan rolled onto his knees with the force of the toss. He made to get back up, but Azriel moved faster than Emillie had ever seen anyone move before.

In a flash, Azriel slipped one arm across Loren's chest and the other under the General's arm. He clasped his hands together and hauled back—hard. Loren fell, back against Azriel's chest, and the half-fae wrapped his legs around the General's body. Azriel hooked one knee over his own ankle and squeezed hard.

Loren refused to give up. Though he could not move his body, he twisted his shoulders enough to elbow Azriel's head. The guard, unphased, adjusted his hold. In a single, swift movement, the crook of Azriel's elbow tucked under Loren's chin. With the hand of the arm wrapped around the General's throat, he grasped his own bicep and pressed his free hand to the back of Loren's head.

Together, they rolled to the floor. Loren squirmed, fingers grappling for a hold on Azriel's arm—to no avail. Before long, Loren's face turned red, and his eyes rolled back. His whole body fell limp in the guard's arms.

Azriel released the General and shoved the Caersan man's unconscious body away. He stood, stalked to where his sword dropped, and retrieved his weapon.

Another collective intake of breath echoed through the near-silent ballroom as Azriel stalked back to Loren. He stood over the defeated General and slowly pointed the tip of his sword at the man's throat. Everyone waited on bated breath to witness the demise of the military's leader.

But it never came.

Chest heaving from exertion, Azriel kept the tip poised so when Loren's eyes fluttered open, there was no mistaking the victory. The half-fae guard did not smile. He did not gloat. Instead, he turned to the Princeps expectantly.

"Azriel Tenebra." Her father's voice sounded louder than usual in the eerily-silent ballroom. "You have won."

Whispers picked up around Azriel from the crowd. His heart thundered from the receding adrenaline. There'd been no doubt in his mind that he'd win against Loren. The General gained his position through minimal experience and, most of all, family name. He'd learned to protect himself and defeat stronger opponents from a young age.

"What a shame," a Caersan woman whispered to her friend, eyeing him from her place at the edge of the crowd.

The other shook her head. "So sad for Miss Harlow."

Azriel forced himself to remain focused on Markus. If he showed his discomfort for even a moment, they'd take it as an admission of guilt. Despite the fact that Loren always twisted events to suit his own agenda, they'd all side with their General.

All Azriel had wanted was to collect items to tide him over as he awaited a new guard assignment. He had planned to speak with the Princeps for permission to leave after the ball. The Caldwell Will would be released the next evening, and Azriel wanted to put as much distance between Laeton and himself as possible to avoid accepting the inevitable.

This changed everything. Now he couldn't leave. He'd as good as signed that Will himself.

"How could the Princeps do this?" a Caersan man hissed next.

His companion sneered. "To accept a victory from the filth who forced himself on Miss Harlow?"

"Disgraceful."

Azriel's blood boiled. Never in a thousand years would he ever do such a thing. Not only was he driven by the bond to protect Ariadne at all costs, but he'd put a blade through a man for less.

Then there were the unwed women. They didn't speak much. Instead, they worked their way closer, whispering comments behind their hands that made one another giggle.

"Do you think they will marry?" a Caersan woman fanned herself and leaned toward her husband.

Now Azriel looked up. He let the sword fall from Loren's throat so the General could rise again. As much as he'd dreamed of marrying Ariadne, he'd never considered the possibility of it being real.

The man scoffed. "A bastard guard? Never."

"He may not have a choice," she pointed out. "No one else would touch such a—"

"Hush." Her husband cut her off with a warning look. "She is still the daughter of the Princeps."

Azriel slipped his sword into the sheath on his back. He studied the faces around him, including Loren's, white with anger and twisted into a snarl. Markus, to his credit, appeared unperplexed at the outcome. Ariadne, not far behind her father, didn't take her wide eyes off him, just as he'd struggled to do throughout the duel. Emillie gripped her sister's hand and gaped openly at him and Loren.

The General stood, swaying a bit from the rush. "Coward should have killed me."

Azriel turned, his vision darkening. If he lost control, Loren wouldn't be the only casualty. No soldier would allow him to attack their General again now the duel was finished.

Azriel glared at the General. "I'd rather be a coward than a man who abuses women."

Sound erupted from the crowd at the accusation. Gasps and calls for proof rang out. Soldiers' hands moved to their swords—the words as good as a threat to them.

Azriel, however, turned to Markus as though the Princeps could explain. As the onlookers took note of this, they, too, turned in that direction. Either their High Councilman would admit that Loren, the General of Valenul, was abusive or decline to comment. The former would be damning. The latter left enough to speculation that Azriel's accusation would hold weight. Either way, Loren wouldn't walk away without a mark on his reputation.

Markus said nothing.

More whispers arose, then someone called out incredulously, "You would let your daughter wed a servant?"

A laugh spread across the crowd as though such a thing was the most ridiculous thing any of the pompous Caersans had ever heard. Azriel stilled.

Madan's clear voice carried over the din. "He's not a servant."

"He is a half-blood bastard guard," Loren snarled, wiping the blood from his nose. "And you have no voice here."

Azriel whipped around, his breath catching. No. No, this couldn't be happening. Not now, in front of everyone. Madan leveled his glare at Loren and reached into his coat pocket. A moment later, he held out a thick letter, folded within its ivory envelope to Markus. "This is the late Lord Governor Caldwell's Will. Azriel Tenebra is the heir to the Caldwell Estate."

Silence descended over the ballroom. No onlookers seemed to move or even breathe as Madan stepped forward so the Princeps could take it. He did so and yanked the pages from the envelope.

Azriel gaped at Madan, the blood draining from his face. Every opportunity to disappear and leave the estate to Madan vanished. But that wasn't Madan's fault when he was foolish enough to act on the bond, leaving Ariadne ruined in the eyes of the Society.

"Impossible," Loren said. "No half-breed has ever held a title such as a Lord Governor."

"Correct." Markus's mouth tightened into a thin line. He looked over the papers at Azriel, a frown forming between his brows. "But there has always been a direct heir before now."

Several Caersan men shifted uncomfortably, glancing from their wives to the Princeps. Those who remembered Markus's first family. Who knew the name of the Caldwell who *would* have been heir and bore the responsibility of keeping it all a secret from the next generation so the Princeps could move on with his new family.

No one spoke the names of his lost children.

After a long moment, Markus read aloud, "It is with great pride that I, Garth Amon Caldwell, Lord Governor of the Eastern Province, Last of the First Generation, and Guardian of the Keonis Tree, pass my titles, estate, and seat on the High Council to my eldest kin, Lord Azriel Tenebra. His status should henceforth be recognized as Caersan and a full-blooded member of the Society, given the blessing of the Princeps."

Azriel took a slow, deep breath and raised his chin. Markus Harlow now held the power to either accept his position or cast the Will aside. If the Princeps chose to ignore Caldwell's final decree, his life and Ariadne's reputation would be forfeit.

"His father was not even a vampire." Loren addressed the crowd, gesturing to Azriel. "He does not belong amongst us. And you would give a half-breed bastard a seat at the High Council?"

Standing tall under such scrutiny became more and more difficult. Azriel's shoulders turned in.

Madan sighed and spoke quiet enough for no others to hear him, "My Lord Princeps, it's your decision alone. You've seen the truth of the man who your daughter would wed otherwise. Her heart doesn't want him. She made her choice, and you've experienced firsthand what happens when a marriage is forced... and when it's a union of love."

Nostrils flaring at the mention of his past—no doubt wondering how a guard knew his best-kept secrets—Markus pierced Madan with his amber gaze. For an instant, Madan shrank back under the unyielding stare.

Azriel swallowed hard, uncertain how he could lend his support in that moment.

"You speak of things you do not understand." Markus's lips hardly moved.

Madan took another step closer. "I understand more than you could possibly know."

Recognition flashed in the Princeps' eyes. His gaze narrowed, studied Azriel a moment, then flicked away as he turned to look at Ariadne. He whispered, "Love?"

The Caersan woman withered under his scrutiny. She looked from her father to Madan, then landed on Azriel. The single nod was all it took.

His heart skipped a beat. She had chosen him in front of everyone.

Markus pivoted back to the murmuring crowd. "This evening has been filled with surprises. We shall postpone the engagement celebration in lieu of continuing the Season as normal. Join me in welcoming our newest Lord Governor of the Eastern Province: Lord Azriel Caldwell."

Applause erupted from the Caersans. Whether it was an expected practice in moments such as these or due to his display in his fight against Loren, Azriel wasn't certain. What he *was* certain of was how drastically his life was about to change.

CHAPTER 19

T he drawing room—the bane of Ariadne's existence for the last fortnight—became a haven from the dancing, music, and gossip in the ballroom on the lower floor. Following her father's acceptance of Azriel's position as the next Lord Governor of the Eastern Province, what had been intended to be an engagement celebration turned into a rumor mill. Her father implored the guests to enjoy the party despite the change of plans. After all, no sense in letting the food and labor procured for the evening go to waste.

Servants moved across the ballroom to clean up the blood from the duel. The shallow, crimson puddles glistened in the brilliant light of the chandeliers, looking horribly like that first night of the Season. Just as easily as the opening ball, the carnage disappeared. Only gleaming pine wood remained.

As the music picked up and some Caersan swept onto the cleaned dance floor, her father folded the Will and tucked it neatly into the envelope from whence it came. He looked from the General to the newest Lord Governor in contemplation. Ariadne never considered herself an expert on her father. The one thing she knew, however, was how to avoid his wrath.

When his critical amber eyes landed on her, she sucked in a breath and cast her gaze to a spot on the floor somewhere in the distance so she could still see what happened around her. "Father, I—"

"You and I will speak soon." The flat, matter-of-fact tone made her skin crawl. Then he addressed the men before him, "Meet me in my office—all three of you. Madan, I trust you will keep the two of them from destroying my home."

"My Lord." Madan bowed and motioned for Loren and Azriel to follow him out.

Ariadne could not help looking up at the General as he passed, his nose no longer dripping but still purple from breaking. She opened her mouth to speak, but Loren avoided her searching gaze. He motioned for several officers to follow him before disappearing into the gawking crowd on his way to the study.

Azriel, however, paused to look her over closely. A bruise spread out from his temple where Loren had hit him, and he kept one hand pressed to the shallow stab wound in his gut. She swallowed hard and, again, opened her mouth to speak.

"Don't." He shook his head, then bowed, kissed her fingers, and whispered, "I'm sorry for keeping secrets."

Then he, too, disappeared. The guests parted for him as much as they had Loren. Some stared in awe, while others sneered and huffed before turning to a companion and whispering. Whatever they said did not phase the guard-turned-lord, and Azriel moved through with grace.

As soon as her father went to collect the members of the High Council, Caersan women stepped forward. Ariadne gaped at them as one question after another pelted in her direction.

"What happened?"

"Did you know he was the heir?"

"But what about the General?"

"Did he force you?"

"What did you *do*?"

No one asked if she was okay.

Not for the first time, Emillie yanked her away from the gaggle. Camilla pushed to the front, cursing them all and demanding they leave. Behind her, Revelie spread her arms wide to keep the women from moving closer.

"Come," Emillie whispered to her and motioned for Camilla and Revelie to follow.

Together, the four of them left the ballroom behind and cloistered inside the drawing room, where a maid brought a tray of herbal tea. Ariadne accepted the cup handed to her and held it in her palm so the heat of the porcelain warmed her skin. Without a sound, she lowered herself into the seat closest to the fire and stared into the flames.

Her friends murmured amongst themselves at first. She did not mind. Too much had happened over the last hour to entertain their questions just yet.

In fact, Ariadne was not certain she would be able to answer any of the questions herself. No, she had not had any inclination that Azriel was the heir of the Caldwell Estate—when he had told her he was leaving, she assumed he meant transferring to another personal guard position. Never in her wildest dreams did she believe he would ever be accepted into the Society.

If he even had. Accepted was a strong term even if his title and position had been finalized. Most members of the Council would likely react to his appointment just as Loren had: with disdain. That meant the entire Gard family—the one she had hoped to marry into for so long—would never truly accept him. The Lord and Lady would likely look down on her now as well.

Yet somehow, someway... Ariadne did not care. Perhaps that was the realization which shocked her most. Despite watching her fiancé lose a duel to the man she loved—yes, she understood it was love the moment her father asked—she was at peace with it all. The violence, the anger, and most of all, the outcome.

She had not known Azriel was so skilled. Each movement he had made throughout the duel appeared relaxed and calculated. Aside from the jab to his middle, it seemed as though he knew what Loren would do next. Mind-reading was a strong term. Studious seemed more apt.

How, then, did Azriel find the time to study the General's sequences? His tells? Ridiculous though it was, he looked as practiced in it as one would if they had fought before. Impossible.

Perhaps, when Azriel joined the lower military ranks as a personal guard, he had been taught to fight in a similar manner. It made more sense than him facing off against Loren in the past.

What seemed to take the General off-guard the most had been the moment Azriel took him to the floor. While Ariadne knew the soldiers in their military trained hand-to-hand combat from watching her father give orders at the Hub as a child, she could not recall them learning such techniques. Had Loren been expecting it, he never would have lost the grip on his sword. The movements, however, were still familiar to her.

A shiver worked its way down Ariadne's spine despite the heat from the fire and tea. She sipped it, relishing the cascade of brisk lemon and soothing honey. The steam worked its way across her face as she took a shaky breath.

Try as she might to ignore the similarities in Azriel's combat style and that of the dhemons she had witnessed fighting in the past, she could not shake it. Again and again, she saw the massive, horned men circling one another, weaponless and glistening with sweat. Ehrun, the dhemon whom she had come to know and hate, slammed the other—her kidnapper—to the ground in a similar manner to what she had seen tonight.

That Azriel knew the same moves told her precisely why he walked away victorious: he had faced off with those monsters many times and learned how to move like them to protect himself. It made sense.

"Did you know he was connected to the Caldwells?" Revelie whispered to Emillie and Camilla, drawing Ariadne's attention.

Emillie shook her head and glanced toward her. "Not at all. Neither of us."

"Will your father push for a marriage after the General's accusations?" Camilla sipped her tea, eyes bright.

Emillie chewed her lip. "I do not see why not. He made him the next Lord Governor, after all."

"No one will want me after this." Ariadne looked back at the fire, her chest constricting at the very thought. Why did she care? She had wanted to fade into the background like Revelie, free to live her own life. But if the Society now considered her ruined, would Azriel even want her?

"Ariadne—"

"I had the best match of the Season," she said and silently cursed the way her voice broke over her tight throat. Her father would still be furious. "I ruined it."

The three Caersan women moved closer and sat beside and before her around the fire. Emillie tucked in close, her warmth decreasing the quakes of her body.

"What did he mean about the General finding pleasure in hurting women?" Revelie asked quietly, leaning forward to look Ariadne in the eye. "Did he hurt you?"

Emillie tensed. "I cannot imagine—"

"Yes." Ariadne eased the sleeve of her gown up and held it out. "He is not a kind-hearted man."

Camilla scoffed, taking Ariadne's fingers and pulling her closer to inspect the fading bruise. "And you were going to marry him without saying anything?"

Blinking back tears, Ariadne nodded. "Yes."

"Why?" Emillie's wide eyes searched her for any hint of understanding. "I knew something was wrong."

"Because that is the poison of the Society," Revelie said. She sighed and gently pulled the sleeve back into place. "It tries to keep Caersan women in a position of weakness. It is not this way with Rusan vampires. Their women are hard-working and treated with respect."

Camilla, Emillie, and Ariadne stared at her for a long moment. Though they had discussed existentialism in the past, the reality of their status in the aristocracy felt suffocating. The only sounds were the distant music in the ballroom and the snaps of the fire. Ariadne always knew the Rusan had a different way of living. Their customs were not as strict in many ways. Women could do as they liked without permission from the men of their families, and they could marry who they loved. To say Rusan women were respected, however, implied Caersan women were not.

"There are many things that need to change," Camilla agreed after a beat of quiet. "Perhaps this will move things along."

"This?" Emillie asked with a frown.

"Mister Tenebra's—" Camilla cut herself off with a short, abrupt laugh. "Pardon me. *Lord Governor Caldwell's* appointment despite his—to be frank—criminal record."

"He is not a criminal," Ariadne whispered, cheeks heating. "Unless you consider standing up for me a crime."

Camilla placed a hand over her heart. "Apologies, doll. I meant no offense. His imprisonment is all I referred to."

Beside her, Revelie smiled grimly. "We need men like him in power to make any true changes in the Society."

"With you by his side," Emillie added with a squeeze of Ariadne's hand, "big changes could happen."

"By his side?"

"As his wife." Now her sister frowned and glanced at their friends across from them. "Will you not marry him?"

Ariadne scoffed. "The better question is if *he* will want to marry *me* after all of this."

She looked down into the tea in her hand. The translucent brown liquid reflected the candles overhead, turning and flickering on the surface. She focused on the gentle, shallow slosh as she shifted the cup from one hand to the other in a desperate attempt to distract her mind from the looming rejection.

A loud, boisterous laugh drew her attention back up. Camilla shook her head. "Are you blind?"

With a confirming nod, Revelie added, "I did not have the best of views from where I stood, but from what I saw, he could not stop looking at you."

"They are right," Emillie said quietly. "Every chance he got, he looked at you."

Ariadne did not remember this. Her mind was so abuzz with concern for what he had gone through. The blood on his stomach and dripping from his fist. It all made her head rush and unable to focus.

"Still," Ariadne said, trying to ignore the way her heart picked up its pace at the thought of him focused on her, "any other prospect of marriage would be ruined after this."

Emillie shrugged. "That *is* what you wanted for some time."

True. But that was before Azriel. She had never even considered the possibility of her heart yearning for another man after Darien and this? This was something else. Something more.

She delighted in and leapt at the opportunity to see her late fiancé, no matter the circumstances. It could have been a ball or a walk through the park or dinner with the family. All of it sent her heart racing and mind whirling. Now she understood it was all superficial. Naught but surface-level lust and puppy love.

With Azriel, everything felt deeper. It was a quiet, almost ancient sensation that drew her attention. His subtle glances and light touches sent her spiraling in a way Darien never could. Azriel's scent drifted through her dreams each day. His sharp, peridot eyes tracked her each night. He was a hunter, and she was his prey, too eager to be found. Every fiber of her being begged for his attention.

"But you love him," Revelie said quietly. "Do you not?"

Turning her gaze up to the Caersan, Ariadne chewed her lip. She should feel safe admitting it to her friends and sister. Still, admitting it to herself was difficult. So, as when her father had asked in front of hundreds, she nodded once.

"Well, then." Camilla sipped her tea and set the cup down a bit harder than necessary. "Since the *Lord Governor* is now considered Caersan... does that mean your other extremely handsome and gentlemanly guard is as well? Because I am quite interested."

Emillie and Revelie laughed. Ariadne choked on her tea, then joined in with the merriment. She shook her head at her friend, who winked back and poured another cup of tea.

The door opened behind Ariadne. Music, talking, and laughter spilled in from the corridor. She turned to see several Caersans paused nearby to peek in at the private gathering before Markus, standing in the threshold, leveled an icy stare at his elder daughter.

"I would like to speak with Ariadne alone." He took a step into the room and clasped his hands behind his back.

The three Caersan women stood, curtsied to the Princeps, then hurried around him to exit the drawing room. Last out, Emillie paused and threw her sister a small smile of encouragement before closing the door behind her. As she did so, Camilla's sharp warning for others to quit eavesdropping swept by.

Ariadne placed her teacup on its saucer. Her hands shook, and she did not need her father noticing her nerves. He would take advantage of her weakened mental state if he did, just as he had the night of Loren's proposal.

"Be at ease, Daughter." He took up the space left behind by Revelie and pierced her with his hawk-like gaze.

"Father, I..." Her voice broke. "I am sorry."

At first, he said nothing. He did nothing but stare. What observations he made by doing so, Ariadne could not tell. She would have been surprised if he blinked at all.

"I must know the truth of it," he said finally and nodded to her arm. "Who did that?"

Ariadne swallowed hard. "Please, Father, I did not wish to cause trouble."

He held up a hand to stop her from continuing. "You have caused more than trouble tonight. Now answer my question."

She winced and chewed her lip. What were the chances he would believe her? What were the chances he even cared?

"Was it the General?" His voice turned soft, lulling her into what she hoped was not false security.

Her hands shook, and she curled her fingers into her skirt to hide it. "Yes."

Her father sat back with an exasperated sigh, the cause of which she did not know. Loren had likely continued to lie, even in front of the other Councilmen, and he had been inclined to believe the General over Azriel. No matter the source of his contemplation, he surveyed her before saying,

"Young vampires of every walk—Caersan, Rusan, and those in-between—are often not in control of themselves."

"Please, Father," she whispered, "do not make excuses for him."

"No excuses." He leaned forward, elbows to knees and took her hand in his. She had half a mind of pulling away. Such an affectionate gesture was not common between them. "I know from experience."

By the gods, what did he mean by that? Ariadne did not want to know. He had held the title of General long before Loren and for good reason. It made for an officer willing to do what was best for Valenul, though perhaps not the best for everyone else.

"The General hurt me," she said, stronger now. She met his gaze and held it with as much force as she could muster.

"So could Lord Caldwell."

Strange, to hear Azriel's new name from her father. It felt foreign and as though he spoke of someone other than the black-clad guard who put the General of Valenul to sleep in front of everyone.

"I trust him," she said and knew it to be true in her heart. He would never harm her the way Loren had.

With a sniff, her father shook his head. "And I trusted the General."

He released her hand and sat back again. For the first time since entering the drawing room, he looked away. The fire reflected in his eyes, making the golden hue dance like the flames.

"For what it is worth," she said, "I *am* sorry. None of this was intended."

"I have spoken with Caldwell." Still, he did not look back at her. He spoke to the hearth. "He is ready to take his place on the Council, gods help him."

Ariadne's heart stumbled. She had guessed, of course, that he would do so to avoid certain death. Between their kiss and his victory over Loren, the safest place for him was amongst the other Lord Governors.

"Happy news," she said breathlessly.

His gaze finally flickered back to her. "And he will set this right by taking you as his wife."

She gaped at him for a long moment, stomach alighting with butterflies. Her breathing hitched. This had to be a dream. "You will allow it?"

Ice flooded her veins as his eyes narrowed. She knew that look. Sitting back a bit, she took in his minute movements. The flutter of the muscle in his jaw. A clench of his fist. This was the temper he had spoken of—the one he claimed only plagued the youth.

"Neither you nor I have much of a choice at this point, Ariadne."

He stood and swept past her. She held her breath as he moved, waiting for the hammer to fall. He had worked hard for the match between her and Loren. All for her to burn it to the ground by kissing Azriel.

She turned to see him open the door, letting in the sounds of joviality from below. He did not look back as he said, "For your sake—and your sister's... do not mess this one up."

Every plan Loren constructed for his life crashed around him the moment he had found his future wife in the arms of another man. Had that man been a Caersan of worth, he may not have cared, considering he would have won the duel against most men. Even if it had been Nikolai Jensen, who swore a blood oath to keep his distance from her, Loren would not have been angry.

But Azriel *fucking* Tenebra? That pitiful excuse of a guard who spent his nights leering at her did not deserve to live after what he had done. If it were not for the Will of a deceased Lord who had been cognitively declining for decades, Loren would have seen the filthy bastard strung up by his testicles.

As it were, the Princeps accepted the dirty fae's ill-earned victory *and* the words of a dead man.

Perhaps Markus Harlow was not one to be trusted.

Loren exited the Harlow Manor the moment the Council convened in the study. He pushed past the dumbfounded lords and motioned for Nikolai to join him. The Captain, loyal as always, loitered in the foyer, awaiting the next command.

"What happened?" Nikolai followed him out the front doors as Loren called for their horses to be brought forth.

"*My* wedding is canceled." Loren tugged on his leather riding gloves and adjusted his cloak. "Ariadne's is not."

Nikolai frowned, blanching at the informal use of her first name. "How is that possible?"

The General chuckled darkly as the stable hand hurried over. He snatched the reins unceremoniously and swung up onto his stallion's back. Beside him, the Captain did the same.

"She is now betrothed to Lord Governor Caldwell." He spat the name like something foul on his tongue, then yanked the reins to start down the drive. "There is a bastard half-fae now sitting on the High Council."

"Ludicrous!" Nikolai shook his head. "Have they all gone mad?"

"They may very well be." Loren ground his teeth, beating back the inferno building in his chest. The embarrassment of losing his fiancée and a duel to that disgrace was too much to think about for long. "He has poisoned their minds, just as he did to that bitch."

Nikolai barked a laugh. "Fae magic, perhaps?"

"Tenebra does not have the capacity to see beyond his own cock let alone harness any significant magic." They turned onto the Old Highway and started toward Laeton proper. "That duel should have ended the moment I disarmed him."

"Right you are."

"Perhaps they are well-matched," Loren mused with a scoff. "She hardly has two thoughts to string together. Quite the empty-headed pair. It is no wonder he was able to seduce her so easily."

Another boisterous laugh. Nikolai shook his head to clear the mirth away. "You will get your revenge—of that, I have no doubt."

Loren let his own smirk drop. "Indeed."

"I know that tone." Nikolai raised a questioning brow and turned in his saddle to look at him fully. "You have a plan?"

"Knowledge, Captain." Loren could not keep the sneer off his face. "I have been building my knowledge on this matter."

"Is that so?"

"I overheard those low-life guards speaking about the Caldwell Will just last night," Loren explained, "and how they knew they would be claimed as heirs."

A frown creased Nikolai's brow. "Suspicious."

"To say the least."

"What have you discovered?"

"Supposedly," Loren said with a roll of his eyes, "the bastard's mother is a distant Caldwell relative. Maribel Tenebra. I cannot find any records of her aside from the forms he filled out for guard duties."

"Maribel Tenebra?" Nikolai looked contemplative. "The name is unfamiliar."

Loren had thought the same thing as he stood in the Princeps' office with the pages of the Will spread across his desk for inspection. The Councilmen, as perplexed as he, muttered their dissent. Many preferred the Lord Governor Steward and asked whether or not they could, instead, place him at the helm of the Eastern Province. To his credit, even Azriel had appeared in agreement.

Which did not bode well when Markus had said, "A Caldwell has ruled that region for millennia. We are to change it now?"

That had shifted many perspectives. A half-breed though he was, Azriel Tenebra was still a Caldwell and the eldest male heir to the title, with Madan second in line.

"Given a proper wife," Markus had continued, "he will produce a Caersan vampire heir to continue the lineage."

All eyes had shifted to Loren at that. Heat rose to his face. There had been no mistaking what the Princeps implied by that choice of words. He had been defeated in the duel for Ariadne's honor and no longer held the right to her hand.

"I have already voiced my decision before the Society," Markus had said as no one spoke. The attention shifted away from the General. "But I will heed the Council's vote."

So Loren had watched on in horror as nearly every member of the Council voted in favor of instating a bastard-born guard with zero training to the position of Lord Governor—one of the highest seats of power in Valenul. The only men who declined were his own father and those present from his home, Notten Province.

Loren had spoken to no one as he left, not even his father, who remained to congratulate the newest Lord Governor despite his vote against him. Traitor.

Dragging his thoughts from the recent memory, Loren returned his attention to Nikolai. "Evidently, Maribel Tenebra is a distant cousin of Garth. There are no other men still alive in the Caldwell line."

It did not surprise him, really. The Caldwell family had been hit hard from the beginning of the vampire era in Valenul. As the first to settle on the northern side of the Keonis Mountain range, they were targeted by dhemons who lived nearby. If nothing else, that reason alone upheld Azriel's claim to the seat. For a family as hardy as the Caldwells to be wiped out would be considered a crime.

"What will you do?" Nikolai asked after a beat. "I have never known you to let something like this stand."

The humiliation, of course. Though unsaid, Loren knew precisely what Nikolai meant. Not once had he allowed anyone to best him without exacting his revenge. It was how he climbed to the position of General so quickly.

"I will find a way to discredit him," he mused aloud. "What I need is to track down more information about his fae father. No fae of worth settles amongst vampires, only criminals."

"We do not carry records of fae lineage."

"But I have his name," Loren said, a dark hope brimming. "Azazel."

Nikolai's eyes sparkled with the same vicious glee he felt. "No surname. Fascinating. Do you have contacts with the high fae?"

"I have worked with their general before against the dhemon blight." The path cleared in Loren's mind just as they exited the trees and were drenched in moonlight upon entering Laeton. "We shall work together again to rid me of this plague as well."

CHAPTER 20

The plan had been to leave. Run away before the release of the Will. Azriel had wanted to put as much distance between himself and Ariadne as he could—to leave her to a happy, calm life with the General. It's what she deserved after everything she'd gone through.

The last thing he wanted was to be a Lord Governor. For so long, he'd learned to hate the Caersans and their insufferable Society. He raged against them, what they'd done to his mother, and how they'd ostracized him and Madan. Together, they planned to destroy it all. Then wisdom came with age, and before either of them knew it, they stood in the foyer of the Caldwell's Laeton manor bearing the name they'd run from for so long.

The staff of the house, lined up along the far wall, looked at them with a mixture of uncertainty, reverence, and hope. Garth Caldwell wasn't known for being the kindest Caersan. In fact, his rough upbringing and the terrible things he'd endured turned the late Lord Governor into a wretched excuse of a man.

Did the servants see his face, albeit a bit younger, when they looked at them? Azriel didn't bear as much resemblance to the Caldwells as Madan did. Only the green of his eyes and quirk of his mouth alongside the blue veins along his jaw shared a hint of Caersan lineage. At least... that's what he was always told.

The house, not nearly as grand as the Harlow's, was two floors tall with soaring ceilings and massive chandeliers in every room. Whereas Azriel had grown accustomed to the pale colors used to brighten the rooms of the Harlow Estate, the dark wood and jewel-toned walls were at once comforting in their warmth and claustrophobic.

"Welcome home, my lords," said a Rusan man with vibrant red hair who stepped forward to bow low. "My name is Petre, and I am head of your staff."

Azriel stared for a long moment. He'd never get used to people bowing to him. It felt foreign and wrong.

"Thank you, Petre." He glanced at Madan, seeking approval and receiving none. The other new Caldwell appeared just as at a loss. "I'm grateful for your help. I..."

His words faded, and he looked around again. The parlor opened to his right with a low fire and well-maintained furniture. Overhead hung a crystal chandelier that flickered with candlelight. He'd never imagined himself standing on this side of it all. Ownership of a fine manor was never on his list of things to accomplish.

Sighing, Azriel scrubbed his face with his hands. The room tensed, the servants inhaling collectively. He lowered his hands to find Petre rooted to the spot, his freckled face blanching at his signs of distress.

"Petre," Azriel said, hoping his voice sounded as calm and controlled as he intended. "To be completely honest with you..."

A mousy-looking woman shifted, clearly uncomfortable. She noticed his attention and looked quickly at the floor, the light brown bun on her head wobbling precariously.

"All of you," he said a little louder, then pointed to the parlor, "come and sit."

Everyone hesitated. No one seemed to breathe for a long moment before another Rusan woman with brown skin and her twists pulled into a low bun said, "My Lord, that is not customary."

Looking to Madan, who shrugged, Azriel said, "And I'm not Garth. If you won't sit, then I will."

At that, Azriel stepped around Petre and sat in the middle of the foyer. If they wouldn't accept his offer to sit on the furniture, he'd make them watch as he refused to use it as well.

"I need your help." He looked over his shoulder at Petre.

The Rusan seemed lost. He knew he shouldn't be standing above the master of the house in such a manner but was also too accustomed to following traditions. Eventually, Petre stepped closer and slowly, cautiously, sat on the floor beside Azriel.

"How can we help you, my Lord?"

Madan sat on Azriel's other side and stretched his long legs out in front of himself. He said nothing. Instead, he watched the other servants expectantly. One by one, they moved forward and sat as well.

"To be frank, Petre," Azriel said and leaned back on his elbows. It'd been too long since he'd sat in such a position. "I have absolutely no fucking clue what I'm doing."

Beside him, Madan burst out in laughter. The others stilled again and watched. Then a few of them cracked smiles. Slowly, oh so slowly, the temperature of the room warmed.

"My Lord?" Petre looked from Madan to Azriel in confusion.

"I'm not a Lord Governor." Azriel shook his head and elbowed Madan to shut him up. It only served to prolong the mirth. "I was a guard. Before that, I was nothing. I grew up a half-breed, bastard-born, amount-to-nothing failure. Getting all of this—" he gestured to the house in general "—was never my intention."

The servants looked at each other in confusion. The Rusan woman who spoke before sat forward a bit and said, "Then how did you become the Lord Governor?"

Now it was Azriel's turn to still. He didn't speak of his past for a reason. He certainly didn't admit that everything the Caersan Council knew of him was, ultimately, wrong. If they knew the truth, not one of them would deny his place amongst the Society. Especially not Madan's. Bastard though Azriel had always been, there'd be no denying his heritage.

So rather than expose every secret, he edged around the truth. "My father hid Madan and me from the Caersans. You may have heard that the two of us are cousins?"

A collective nod.

"Madan is my little brother." Azriel watched with grim amusement as they gaped back at him. "We agreed to tell the Caersans we're cousins to protect him were anything to happen to me."

"What did you expect to happen?" The Rusan woman's dark eyes flared with interest.

Azriel chuckled darkly. "I'm sure you all heard about my imprisonment a while back?"

Again, they looked at each other nervously. Some mumbled their apologies for what happened to him, while others merely nodded.

"I'm not exactly known to follow the rules." He gestured to himself, sitting on the floor with them. "And the last thing I need is for my brother to bear the brunt of my mistakes."

Madan smiled at him grimly. "This is not something we tell you all lightly. In exchange for our transparency, we expect this to be kept a secret until we're ready."

"Of course, my Lords," Petre said a bit breathlessly. "Of course."

"If there's one thing I can promise you all," Azriel said, voice darkening, "it's a swift end to anyone who breaks my trust. I'm a man of the sword first—words and forgiveness don't come easily."

Every servant looked at one another. Many swallowed hard while others gave a friend or family member a sharp look of warning. Those were the gossips, no doubt, and prone to spilling secrets. He'd keep an eye on them.

"Now," Azriel said, looking at each of them with purpose. "Like I said, I need your help figuring all of this out."

They all sat a little straighter. The uneasiness dissipated from the group, their shoulders dropping away from their ears.

"I need to learn a lot in very little time," Azriel said and sighed. "How to dress, eat, speak...all of it. Can you teach me?"

A small smile curled Petre's mouth, and he looked to the rest of his staff. They nodded to him and began standing. Azriel followed suit with the butler, Madan doing the same behind him.

"We have our work cut out for us," the Rusan woman whispered to her friend, who giggled behind her hand.

"You'll find I'm a quick study," Azriel told them with a wink. "Where do we start?"

The staff moved in unison. Some picked at his hair, others at his clothes. A man whipped out a measuring tape and nearly throttled him for a neck measurement while an elder Rusan clicked her tongue at the scars on his hands and arms. Yet another servant began rattling off rules of etiquette and Caersan grammar.

Azriel immediately regretted it all. Who was he kidding? He wasn't cut out for any of this. It was like a game of make-believe that, once started, he could never escape. An incessant list of responsibilities and appearances he didn't know how to maintain long-term. Sooner or later, everyone would discover the truth: he was a fraud.

But for Ariadne, he'd do anything. Even if it meant pretending to be someone he could never truly be.

So it was Ariadne he thought of as they pruned him into a more palatable vampire for the Caersans to consume. Whether they considered him a Caersan or not, he could put on the mask required of him, and it would all be for her. Because it's his fault she couldn't continue on with the life she was meant to live with Loren.

By the time he stepped into the Council Chambers a fortnight later, he was a different man. He'd signed away his surname and become a Caldwell and let the staff smooth out his rough edges. By the time he looked in a mirror in the long hall leading to the Chamber, Azriel couldn't recognize himself.

The clothes in the manor from the previous Lord Caldwell had been too small for him, so they'd all gone to Madan. Instead, tailors crafted a new wardrobe to his measurements. He wore a white shirt and deep green and black brocade vest, dark brown trousers, and fine, new black leather boots that reached his knees. The black jacket, fashioned with double buttons, stopped at his waist in the front while hanging almost to his knees in the back.

He adjusted the cravat at his neck and winced at his appearance. The staff had called in a local mage to tend to the small scars in visible places. His face was now smoother, including the newest addition given to him by Ariadne the night of her drunken escapade. Though he asked to keep the length of his hair, they'd insisted on a trim. It now hung to his collarbones, half of it tied up in a smaller top knot than he was used to.

Still, the soap they'd used in it made the dark curtain of hair shine more than he'd ever seen it before.

He certainly looked the part, much to his chagrin. Whether or not he could play the part had yet to be determined.

Continuing down the hall, Caersan men he recognized from the balls stepped out of his way with a bow. Some watched him with reverence, while others demonstrated their respect with resentment. The former outnumbered the latter. Whether it was because of his new position or that they'd watched him win against their esteemed General, he wasn't certain. Nor did he care.

The Chamber lay beyond a pair of massive doors carved with the history of the vampires. From the Great War between the two largest rival mage clans of the plains to the curse of night and blood put on their people. Azriel studied it for a long moment, tracing a finger over the young Caersan vampires who settled in Valenul to escape the long summers. They thought they'd escaped the carnage wrought by the Rusans who'd destroyed their plains enemy. What they hadn't realized is that they'd merely traded one for another—the dhemons.

His finger twisted over the spiral of a dhemon's horn, then he pressed his palm to the wood and pushed open the door.

Inside, the massive Chamber was made up of a series of desks for all the Councilmen. To the left, two massive desks faced off against two more on the right with a wide aisle between them. A single, wing-backed chair sat behind each. These were for the four Lord Governors of Valenul. Further back were long tables with five chairs each for the Lower Council. Straight down the room, facing the door, sprawled a massive hearth with a large, crackling fire. Overhead hung a chandelier which provided the light otherwise inaccessible by the fireplace.

Markus Harlow sat in his chair and studied Azriel's entrance with an unreadable expression. Behind him, several more Councilmen entered and found their seats. Only one stood and stepped forward, arm outstretched in greeting.

After spending the last two weeks practicing the formal embrace, Azriel stood tall and grasped the Caersan's forearm. Too firm and it'd be perceived as a threat. Too light and he'd be viewed as incompetent. Too close to the wrist? Frightened. Too close to the elbow? Overly familiar. To his relief, he hit the mark with the lord—a perfect, neutral grasp.

The man had long black hair and eyes the shade of coal. His sharp, handsome face twisted into a smirk as he said, "Welcome, Lord Governor Caldwell. I am Alek Nightingale, Lord Governor of the Waer Province."

He'd heard of Nightingale. His name was almost as shadowed by rumors of terrible deeds as Azriel's was of poor breeding. "Thank you, Lord Nightingale. I am honored to be here."

Chairs scraped back from their places at the tables, and before long, a slew of Councilmen stood before him. One after another, Azriel met them all. Even those who glared upon his entry and cursed him under their breaths at the Harlow manor moved forward to exchange greetings.

Then everyone stood back to let through the Princeps. The Caersan around him stilled, watching carefully at what was to come next.

"My Lord Princeps." It took all Azriel's self-control not to bend at the waist while addressing the man who'd employed him for months. Respect amongst the Councilmen didn't come in physical submission but through words and actions.

Markus's fiery gaze, however, sent a wash of cold through Azriel's gut. The Princeps studied him for a long moment. When he finally stretched out his hand, he said, "Lord Caldwell. Welcome."

The tension eased from the room and Azriel's shoulders as he took the offered gesture. "Thank you, my Lord."

As one, the Councilmen returned to their seats. Azriel watched as they moved, paying close attention to where the Lower Councilmen sat. He followed the five from his province and took his place at the large table to the right of the door nearest the hearth. Markus lowered into his chair, facing him.

At a small desk in the corner across the room sat a Caersan man Azriel did not recognize with a pile of papers. He shuffled through them a moment, dipped his pen into an inkwell, and said, "I am ready, my Lord Princeps."

"So begins the first Council meeting with Lord Governor Azriel Caldwell." Markus eyed him before turning to the others in the High Council. "It has been brought to the Council by the Lords of Notten Province that the dhemon raids have not only continued but have increased over the last two months."

Azriel watched the other Lord Governors out of the corner of his eye. Alek Nightingale beside him scrawled notes on a paper and, upon spotting his curiosity, gave an almost indiscernible nod toward his own stack of blank papers. He pulled one close and jotted down *dhemon raids - Notten - two months.*

Lord Governor Damen Gard, silver hair gleaming, stood and leaned heavily on his hands. He took the moment to glare openly at Azriel before addressing the room. "The villages farthest north have suffered the most in all aspects. Our people receive the least trade, withstand the harshest climate, and are now watching their neighbors burn."

A murmur of agreement rose and fell. Azriel studied the expressions of Notten's Lower Council. None appeared surprised or alarmed. This was a normal occurrence, and none of them expected much from this conversation.

"The soldiers we receive are still green," Damen continued. "They fall under the blades of the dhemons again and again. We require more experience to stave off the attacks."

"You forget," Alek said without looking up from his notes for a long moment, "we are all struggling in this war."

War. It was the first time Azriel had heard the struggle against the horned fae called such. Raids and small battles were commonplace with the dhemons—but to consider it a *war* made the assumption there was something more for the vampires to gain.

They'd already taken land and valuable resources from the dhemons. What more was there? Anything else, and they'd move swiftly into genocide.

As the newest member of the Council, however, it wasn't his place to say such things. Given time and experience, his voice would gain the weight needed to introduce the wild concept of *diplomacy* with the Caersans. The dhemons had their land ripped away from them, and the vampires lamented when there was retaliation.

Leashing his tongue, however, was not among his strengths.

"None so much as those holding the front lines," Damen said, glaring at Alek. "Your steep mountain passes provide the protection needed from continuous assault, whereas the ice fields allow free passage."

Heart thundering, Azriel leaned forward. "Forgive me, but the eastern mountain passes provide clear access to Eastwood and Notten alike. From what I have studied, a similar situation is occurring on those major trade routes and highways."

All eyes swung to him. He was going to puke. This was the part of leading he hated—it's what Madan excelled at. If there were ever a reason for his brother to take his place...this was it.

"Perhaps if we were to provide a heavier presence in the east," he continued with as much power to his voice as he could muster, "we could provide relief to Notten as well by impeding the free passage from east to north."

Despite the urge to look away, Azriel held Damen's hard, icy gaze. The Lord Governor's jaw twitched, and he flattened his lips into a thin line. When, finally, he moved, it was to turn toward Azriel and give him a stiff nod.

"Perhaps." Damen then tilted his head a bit. "What are the statistics of your province?"

Azriel made a show of flipping through the notes provided by the province's Steward, Lord Knoll, the only missing member of his Lower Council. "It would appear no one has taken the time to collect the information."

"And what information would you need?" Markus leaned back in his chair. It was a test to see how much Azriel knew about this position and to see if he was even capable of handling such tasks. The Princeps knew well enough the information required to make such judgments.

Little did any of them know, this was something Azriel understood. Working with pompous lords and military officers wasn't what he enjoyed. Planning in advance was Madan's strength. Gathering information and acting upon it, though? He could do so in his sleep.

So Azriel stood, his imposing height forcing everyone to crane their necks to see him. "I need data. I need to know the time of day or night these attacks are occurring, their frequency, and where it happens most often. Give me information on who is being targeted or if it is random."

"And how do you propose this information be gathered by dead men?" Damen glared at him, nostrils flaring.

"I will position small companies of soldiers along the main highways to begin narrowing down the information." Azriel lifted a quizzical brow at him. He'd assumed this would be considered standard. "Each will operate with a messenger who will be dispatched to relay as much information as possible back to their base of operations."

Damen scoffed. "Do you truly believe those beasts will let a messenger get away?"

Without missing a beat, Azriel spat back, "Do you truly have so little faith in your son's men?"

Every Caersan in the room froze. Even the note keeper looked up with wide eyes. Perhaps they weren't the wisest choice of words for his first night on the job. He refused to back down despite the rising color in Lord Gard's face.

"I, for one," Azriel continued, "have witnessed firsthand the valiant skills of our army. I believe them to be far more efficient than you give them credit for."

A small smirk curled Alek's mouth, and he sat back with an appraising look. "Here, here, my Lord."

Damen shot Alek a sharp, warning look before returning it to Azriel. "You have now derailed my motion to ask for assistance in my province in favor of your own."

"I am happy to step aside in favor of your ego." Azriel raised his hands before him. "With the dhemons coming down through Eastwood to get to Notten, I assumed you would want my assistance. Bold of me to presume the provinces work together, I suppose."

A trickle of laughter sent a shock of red into the Lord Governor's cheeks. Schooling his expression, Azriel took a seat and leaned back. He glanced at Alek, who waited for Damen's response, then turned to Markus. The Princeps had been surprisingly quiet through all of this.

"A vote." Markus looked around the room. "Those in favor of sending additional troops to control the raids in Notten?"

A smattering of hands raised. Azriel's heart pounded. Had he been too harsh with his words? The Gards had done nothing to win his favor, but speaking so openly during his first meeting may have turned too many Councilmen against him.

Markus made a note on his paper. "Those in favor of sending additional troops to monitor in Eastwood?"

Hands raised, including Alek Nightingale's, to show their support. Azriel didn't dare look back at the lords of his own province. If they didn't vote for him, it'd speak volumes.

"Additional troops will be sent to Eastwood to monitor and make reports of dhemon movements through the mountain passes." Markus scrawled another note on his paper without looking at any of them. "We will reconvene to discuss the status of Notten in one month. Any other business to attend to?"

For the rest of the meeting, Azriel remained quiet. He'd asked enough of them and gained more support than he'd anticipated. Damen Gard refused to look at him, and when they adjourned for the night, he stood, collected his things, and departed without a word to anyone. Azriel capped his inkwell, took up the pages he wrote on, and started for the door in his wake.

"Lord Caldwell!"

He froze, then pivoted to face Alek Nightingale. The Caersan's black eyes glittered, and Azriel started back.

"Lord Nightingale." Azriel held out his hand, which Alek accepted heartily. "I must thank you for your support."

"Please," he said as others funneled out of the Chamber, "call me Alek."

Azriel nodded once. "Of course."

"You must join me for a drink," Alek said with a smirk. "I am fascinated to learn more about you."

"I am free this morning."

The smirk grew into a broad grin. "Fantastic."

Chapter 21

M usic drifted from the powder-pink Teaglow Estate ballroom on waves of laughter. The young Lord and Lady of the house swept from place to place, welcoming guests and thanking them for joining their first-ever ball. Ariadne watched from afar as Lady Teaglow, last Season's Golden Rose, laid a hand over her swollen belly and turned her sparkling blue gaze up to her husband with his wide grin and thick beard.

She had done well at hiding from the spotlight since the engagement celebration. As soon as Ariadne walked into the room, the attention would turn from the newlyweds and their sweet blessing to the drama-filled, current Golden Rose of Valenul.

What really happened that night? Did Azriel force himself on her? Was she compromised? If not, why would she ever choose a simple half-vampire guard over the General? Did she know he was the heir to the Caldwell Estate?

Absolutely none of the questions or attention enticed her.

So she lingered on the outskirts as her father peeled away to speak with the other Lords and studied the partygoers.

Several passing officers shot daggers in her direction. Most Caersan women lingering in the corridors whispered amongst themselves and only looked her way as she drifted by. The one person she had hoped to see did not make an appearance.

For two weeks, she had heard from Azriel only twice, and both times were in a short letter apologizing for his absence. The thought was sweet. He remembered the insecurities she had expressed that night in the library and made strides to reassure her that he had not abandoned her. Not again. Never again.

Fingers slid into her palm.

"You are pacing." Emillie gave her a firm squeeze.

Ariadne bit her lip and scanned the foyer and hall leading to the ballroom. "He is not here."

"He may be waiting for you."

"Perhaps." She turned to where the music and joviality sprung. Showing her face in such a crowd after the last ball made her palms sweaty. "What if he did not come? What if he decided against the betrothal?"

Emillie laughed. "The man who has written to reassure you of his intentions?"

Heat flushed Ariadne's cheeks as her sister tugged her toward the ballroom. "Emillie, I do not think—"

Guests nearest the door fell quiet as they entered. Like a wave, the boisterous conversations fell into an excited whisper. Caersan women leaned closer to chitter to one another while the men drew others' attention with a sharp prod of their elbow. Eyes shifted to her, and like a wedge driven into the crowd, bodies parted to create a path forward. At the end stood Lord Governor Azriel Caldwell.

Ariadne faltered. Emillie gave her hand one last squeeze, then released her. Alone, she continued on with her blood pounding in her ears, drowning out the whispers.

Azriel, otherworldly handsome as always, looked vastly different than the last she had seen him, covered in blood and bruises. His raven hair, no longer all in a knot, hung mostly loose around his shoulders, with only the top half pulled back. Those pale, peridot eyes locked on her face and sent shocks through her body.

The strangest part of seeing him standing at the edge of the dance floor was the exchange of his guard's clothes for those typical for a Caersan man. High, polished black boots and finely tailored black trousers remained while the white shirt appeared out of place. The dark damask vest shone with the thin, silver threads woven through like iridescent spiderwebs flickering in the light. His tailed jacket, the latest in fashion amongst the Caersan, only accentuated the width of his shoulders and, thus, his bastard lineage.

He met her curtsy with a bow and swept her hand in his to kiss her fingers, eyes lingering on her face. "Apologies for the delay."

"Not at all," she said, voice quiet. "You look…"

"Ridiculous," he finished and flashed her a grin, then pulled from his pocket a long, thin black box. "You, however, are missing something."

Heat rose to Ariadne's cheeks as Azriel opened the box to reveal an obsidian velvet choker. Embedded at its center rested a large dark ruby. Thin, silver chains hung from it, interlocked and twisted into intricate lacework. When he pulled it from the box, the chains sparkled with dozens of tiny diamonds. Women gasped at the sight of it, echoing Ariadne's own sharp inhale.

"I fear," Azriel said in a low voice, the tension in his shoulders displaying his discomfort, "I have no beautiful words to say before everyone, except—"

"My Lord, you need not—"

"Except that I love you."

Ariadne's heart stuttered. She snapped her gaze up at the new Lord Governor, lungs burning as she struggled for breath. Those words, spoken loud enough for those nearest to hear, were all she wanted—needed—from him. Though not his first time uttering them, to have his feelings reiterated after a fortnight of wondering soothed the aching part of her.

He slid the empty box back into his pocket. "May I?"

"Please," she breathed and shifted her dark curls out of the way.

Azriel stepped around her, draping the silver chain lace across her collarbones, and clasped the necklace in place. The third and—she prayed—final piece of engagement jewelry she would ever don. She shifted under the new weight of it and of the eyes swinging back to her.

It was Azriel's touch that guided her attention, though. His fingers brushed down the slope of her neck, sending a wave of goosebumps across her arms before landing heavily on her shoulder. She turned her face up to him, heart full, and took in the sharp angles of his face. The scars she had grown used to were either faded or gone entirely. A shadow of a beard graced his jaw—a newer style taken by the younger Caersan men.

But Azriel did not return the look. He stared straight ahead, eyes blazing and mouth taut.

Ariadne followed his line of sight and froze. Across the dance floor, Loren glared back at them. His fingers curled hard around the glass in his hand, knuckles white. Despite his defeat at the ex-guard's hands, he did not flinch away. Whether it be his position as General or his own foolhardiness, Ariadne did not know.

What she saw in his icy gaze, however, sent chills down her spine. He was not yet ready to forgive.

And it appeared Azriel had no intention of letting him forget, for he slipped his hand down her arm, slow and purposeful, to grasp her hand without looking away and said, "Dance with me."

She bit her lip. The very thought of not only stumbling through a dance, and Azriel stumbling as well, made her heart sink from its lofty heights. Two weeks as Lord Governor. When did he have time to learn the steps?

"We do not have to," she whispered as the first note of the music struck and he started to the floor.

Azriel did not respond. Instead, he squeezed her fingers once and pulled her in close, free hand on her back as he lifted their clasped pair into the air. The perfect starting position.

Within a beat, they began. Azriel guided her through the steps of the waltz with uncanny ease. She watched their feet—his sure and rhythmic, hers delayed and hesitant. Like every other ball, Ariadne thanked her only saving grace—the length of the dresses Caersan women wore.

"How?" She dragged her gaze from the floor to him.

Azriel's eyes glittered with mirth, and his mouth twisted with a hidden grin. "You forget I have overseen quite a few of these dances by now."

"And you learned just from watching?"

"No." He chuckled, shaking his head before spinning her out, then back in. As their hands connected again, he continued, "My mother taught me as a young boy."

Strange to know nothing of this man's family when she was set to be bound to him for life. With Loren, she knew his parents and brother—intimately. Knew his past and future hopes. Azriel was a stranger from a strange part of Valenul with strange connections to the Society. He held a well of secrets for her to dip into and satiate her thirst for discovery.

Because somehow, despite her usual reservations about anything new or unknown, it sent a thrill through her. This man she had grown to love surprised her at every turn. It only made her love him more.

All around them, more dancers took to the floor. Their evaluation of Azriel's skills complete, many deemed it appropriate to join. Caersans courting the young, available women sought out their first partners and swept them in broad circles.

They turned and turned again, and for the first time that Season, Ariadne fell into a comfortable rhythm. Her shoulders fell away from her ears, and her feet found the steps they once knew—if poorly. To be held in the arms of a fiancé she had chosen made all the difference.

And as the music crescendoed, the room fell away. The other dancers and party guests ceased to exist. Only the arm holding her close and the solid, muscular body brushing against her mattered.

When she turned her face up to him, the air caught in her lungs. His eyes blazed into her, and she knew by the intensity of his gaze that he had not looked away since they began their dance. Heat pumped through her veins, licking through her chest and straight to her core. It settled heavily there, and she stumbled, her thighs pressing together.

If she thought his look had been intense before, it could not compare to the dark shift in them at that moment. His nostrils flared, and she suddenly wished she had taken the time to read more factual books about fae. She knew enough to remember their keen sense of smell.

Keen enough to smell her arousal, it would seem.

"Ariadne..." Azriel said, his low voice hoarse as he dropped all pretense and formalities. He closed his eyes for a long moment, blindly spinning her out, then back as the final note struck home. They snapped back open, and he dipped her low, then righted her before releasing his hold and stepping back to bow.

She almost forgot to curtsy. "Yes, my Lord?"

Inhaling deeply, he raised his brows at her and held out his arm. "Nothing at all."

Warmth flushed her cheeks as she accepted his arm and fell into place beside him. He moved with slow purpose, conscious of her smaller gait and how the skirt hindered each step. The guests parted for them both like a river splitting around a boulder.

"Lord Caldwell!" A paunchy Councilman with dark red hair extended a hand.

Azriel accepted without releasing her arm, stepping into the formal embrace while ensuring she did not get forgotten. "Lord Theobald, a pleasure to see you again. I must extend my sincerest appreciation for your support last night."

"The pleasure is all mine," Theobald said with a grin that flashed longer fangs than Ariadne had ever seen. "Eastwood Province must band together as a united front. My house will always support the Caldwells."

Azriel inclined his head. "You honor me."

"Pish posh." Theobald waved a dismissive hand. "When will you return east?"

With a quick glance at Ariadne, Azriel took a half-step back. "May I introduce you to my fiancée, Miss Ariadne Harlow. Miss Harlow, Lord Oren Theobald is a Councilman from Eton."

Ariadne curtsied. "A pleasure, Lord Theobald."

"The Golden Rose. A pleasure indeed." Theobald extended a hand, and she laid her free palm in his so he might kiss her fingers. "So it is you who shall be keeping our Lord Governor from his seat, I take it?"

Again, she flushed, but Theobald laughed merrily and winked at Azriel as though to say it was all a joke.

"Correct," Azriel said and grinned back. "I intend to remain in Laeton for the duration of our betrothal. We shall return to Monsumbra together."

Theobald nodded once. "Very well, my Lord Governor."

"I shall be sending my cousin, Madan Caldwell, to tend to business just after the wedding." Azriel cast his sights around the room and tipped his head in the direction of the vampire. Like Azriel, Madan's finery looked odd on her ex-guard. Nonetheless, he laughed with another lord, drink in hand, and seemed completely at ease amongst the Caersan as though he had always meant to be with them.

"And he has been made aware of our business?" The Councilman's mouth tightened.

"My Lord," Azriel said lightly, "Madan is very much aware and equipped to handle everything per my instructions. I trust him explicitly."

Another, more terse, nod. "Very well. I shall not keep you from your lovely fiancée any longer. Do enjoy yourself, Lord Governor."

"And you as well." Another incline of their heads, and just like that, Azriel's attention returned wholly to her. He guided her away and blew out a breath. "How'd I do?"

Ariadne gaped at him. Never in all her life had any male vampire of the Society sought her approval even for anything as simple as a conversation amongst Caersans. To ask a woman for reassurance made most believe they appeared weak or incapable.

"You are a natural," she said after realizing the honesty of his question. "As though you were always destined to be a Caersan."

"Can I tell you a secret?"

Another blink of surprise. "Yes, of course."

"The servants at my manor taught me." He chuckled under his breath and shook his head. "I haven't stopped studying speech patterns and customs long enough to get a good day's sleep."

"Truly?"

He nodded. "It's part of why I haven't visited. I'm sorry."

"You need not change anything for me." The words surprised even herself. Ariadne bit her lip, uncertain if they were the right thing to say in the face of his hard work.

He loosed another breath, and tension eased from his shoulders. "Thank you."

Pausing, Azriel snatched two glasses of red wine from a passing servant's tray. He handed one off to her before starting forward again. She sipped the drink as they walked, the first notes of the louder, more prominent dance music beginning.

Ariadne turned to look back at the dance floor and pulled Azriel to a stop. "Look."

Madan guided Emillie through the start of the song, his less-practiced movements more prominent in contrast to her sister's fluidity. He smiled down at her and said something to make her laugh before she swept to another partner in the quadrille. Her lavender dress billowed out in unison with her brown curls as she returned to his arms.

"They look good together." Azriel tilted his head in observation.

"A pity," Ariadne said and sipped her wine. "That they cannot be together, I mean."

Azriel raised a brow. "Can they not?"

She cast him an exasperated look. "Do not play coy. You saw her at the Bistro."

His laugh boomed louder than she had ever heard him before. The sparkle in his eyes danced as much as their siblings moving about the floor. "Well, Madan's partner wouldn't be very pleased, anyhow."

It took a long moment for the pieces to click together. Azriel's careful use of the term *partner* kept Madan's private life from scrutiny by any eavesdroppers. Despite her time knowing the vampire who had dragged her from that damned keep, she did not, in fact, know anything about him.

The understanding, once settled in her mind, sent a jolt of joy through her. She clutched Azriel's arm and turned a big smile up to him. "Then they can be the best of friends instead. Who is his partner?"

Azriel subtly moved them away from the Caersans now turning interested gazes their way before speaking. "His name is Whelan."

She frowned at the name. Foreign—certainly not Caersan or classical vampiric. "Where is he from?"

They continued moving. Lingering too long in one place could be dangerous for his cousin. "Southeast."

"A mage?"

"Fae."

"Like you?" She smiled up at him.

Azriel hesitated, face paling. For an instant, he looked to the door as though considering a quick exit. Then he closed his eyes, took a deep breath, and nodded. "Yes. Like me."

"I am sorry." She pulled him to a halt and touched his chest with her fingertips, wineglass teetering precariously. "I know it is not something of which you wish to speak."

"One night, we will," he said with a grim smile. He took the wine-holding hand from his chest and kissed her fingertips before letting her go. "For now, I wish to...play the part as much as possible."

"Understood." Ariadne sipped her wine again as she slid her hand down his arm and across his palm to entwine their fingers—a motion she had not made since Darien. Only here, beside Azriel, did she feel comfortable and safe enough to express her feelings so openly in public.

As they continued their turn about the large ballroom, pausing here and there to accept congratulations and speak with the Councilmen still analyzing Azriel, she could not help realizing how very new and strange all of it was. On top of knowing very little about her fiancé's past, their previous conversations had been so brief and superficial, she could not even pinpoint his favorite color or preference between white or red wine. Aside from their tense, almost competitive interactions, she had no reason to have chosen him over the General of Valenul.

Except, perhaps, his keen observations of her—almost as though he saw into her very soul. He sensed her shifts in emotions, knew when and where to touch her, and protected her with more care than anyone. Even Darien. As much as she trusted Madan, Azriel kept her safe and saw her as more than a woman.

It was clear, long before she realized her feelings for him, that Loren had been right. Azriel loved her and would do anything for her—even leave so she may marry the General. Until he knew she would not be safe with him.

"Thank you," she said suddenly after setting her empty glass on a table in passing.

Azriel's brows furrowed. "For what?"

"Keeping me safe."

His face relaxed again, and he turned to face her, taking both hands in his to press his lips to them. "Since the first moment I saw you, it's all I've desired. But it's you, Ariadne, who's kept me safe."

"From what could I possibly keep you safe?" She took in, not for the first or even fifth time that night, his broad shoulders and muscular arms. His massive frame held enough strength to defeat any adversary—even dhemons.

"Myself."

Ariadne's heart sank. She recalled the pain in his eyes the night of her engagement ball when he told her he had to leave. He could not live through watching her marry another man.

"Well," she said with a small smile, "we need not worry about it anymore, no?"

He swallowed hard. "I need not worry about anything so long as you're by my side."

"Until the very end."

The corners of his mouth curled at the same words he once said to her. He kissed her fingers again, then released her hands. "Until the very end, Miss Harlow."

"Well, well, well," said a crooning voice behind them.

Ariadne turned as Camilla slid between them. Her pale hair fell in waves of curls from a braided crown to hang around her bare shoulders. The light green dress, cut to her usual scandalous specifications, revealed more skin than a handful of Caersan women in the room combined. She appeared to have stepped straight from a painting of the fae.

"Good evening, Camilla," Ariadne said and hugged her friend with a grin.

"I have never seen either of you quite so happy." Camilla curtsied to Azriel, who bowed in response, before turning back to Ariadne.

"I have never *felt* quite so happy." Ariadne's cheeks heated.

"That necklace looks good on you." Camilla winked at Azriel. "Much better than red lace."

Azriel's gaze snapped over their heads as Camilla made a disgusted face. Ariadne turned to follow his line of sight to find Loren watching them again. The General set his jaw into a hard line at her sudden attention, then turned back to Nikolai beside him.

Were it not for Azriel standing behind her, Ariadne would have wilted under the General's angry scrutiny. She rubbed her wrist absently, the memory of his grip an echo on her skin.

"Agreed," she said quietly after a moment. "Much better than red lace."

Every second of the ball sent Azriel's nerves over the edge. While Ariadne may be more accustomed to the eyes following her—for better or worse—he hated it. Blending into the shadows and drifting unseen, inconsequential, put him at ease. To have his movements analyzed and discussed churned his stomach. At least the last time he'd been the center of attention, the speculation and gossip faded before he'd been well enough to return to his guard duties.

For Ariadne, though, he'd endure anything. Nights of scrutiny, duels for her honor, and incessant rumors were nothing in comparison to the very thought of spending a lifetime without her.

More speculative eyes turned their way as Camilla joined them. Beautiful though she was, she paled in comparison to Ariadne, even in her form-fitting gown.

Again and again, he felt out of place. As his fiancée—he'd never get used to using that word for her—chatted with her friend, he stood back and ignored the leering gazes. Too many sneered at him like an imposter. A wolf amongst sheep.

He didn't blame them. He felt as out of place as they believed him to be.

"Lord Governor."

Azriel gave a start, dragging himself out of his thoughts to turn to Markus Harlow. Camilla fell silent, and Ariadne turned to her father with an anxious expression. He stepped forward, extended his hand, and loosed a breath of relief when the Princeps accepted.

"My Lord Princeps." Azriel ignored Camilla's grin at his change of tone to one of more seriousness. Caersan vampires closest to them grew quiet to inspect their interaction. What better gossip than tension between the man who won the hand of the Golden Rose and her father?

"I admit I am impressed," Markus said, "by your performance before the Council last night."

Ariadne's eyebrows rose, and she shifted closer to Azriel. Her proximity soothed the tension in his muscles.

"You honor me," Azriel said with an incline of his head.

"It is not often we have untrained newcomers." Markus surveyed him in a way that said they *never* had untrained newcomers. Everyone on the Council had been born and raised to take their position. "Your quick decision-making in the face of so little information is not something of which many would be capable. You gained more support than I anticipated."

Azriel nodded once, something like pride swelling. "Thank you, my Lord."

It wasn't his first time synthesizing data to create an actionable plan, though he knew it wasn't his strongest attribute. Azriel's strengths came from observing his brother. There was a reason Madan succeeded in rescuing Ariadne when he fell short. There was a reason Azriel struggled to lead, whereas it came to Madan naturally. That's why his brother led the guards at the Harlow Estate. His mind worked wonders.

Azriel prayed to continue channeling Madan's skills at future meetings.

"I look forward to working with you more," Markus said, loud enough to be heard by surrounding Caersans over the dance music. "You and I have much to discuss. We shall meet soon, you and I, to further your knowledge to best serve your province."

"Your guidance is much appreciated."

In an instant, the mood of the Society vampires around them shifted. Suspicion and haughty superiority simmered into interest. Their cold shoulders turned open and welcoming.

Markus made this approach on purpose. No doubt he'd noticed the tension everywhere Azriel went with his daughter and wished to quell the storm with his public support. Whether his praise was truthful or calculated didn't matter. In a few dozen words, the Princeps turned the ballroom from a hostile cage to an open field.

Which only invited hunters to shoot.

The Princeps stepped aside, and a flood of Caersans swept forward. As a young child, Azriel attended a single engagement celebration and witnessed the swarm of well-wishers upon the newly betrothed couple. What happened the moment Markus stepped away was no different.

"Lord Governor Caldwell," said an older lord with silver streaks in his brown hair, extending his arm to him. Azriel accepted, and the vampire continued, "I am Lord Jon Tiln of Asterbury. This is my wife, Lady Valencia Tiln."

A lord of Eastwood Province—of the very town from which he hailed. He tucked the information away for later use. "A pleasure to meet you, Lord Tiln—Lady Tiln. May I introduce my fiancée, Miss Ariadne Harlow."

Beside him, Ariadne curtsied. "My Lord. My Lady."

"The pleasure is all ours." Lord Tiln bowed to them both. "May we officially congratulate you both on your engagement. A surprise turn of events, to be certain."

Azriel inclined his head. "Thank you. I admit my own surprise to find my name on that Will."

"A fortunate change!"

"I thank the gods every night." Azriel looked down at Ariadne at that. Her cheeks flushed with color, and his chest swelled with pride. "I look forward to visiting you in Aster-bury, Lord Tiln."

The Lord bowed low. "To host you and your exquisite future wife would be an honor."

With that, Lord and Lady Tiln stepped aside, and the next Caersan family came forward. They exchanged the same formalities again and again, each as enthusiastic as the last. For the first time in a fortnight—gods, for the first time in his adult life—Azriel felt accepted. Even if these vampires turned around and hissed terrible things about him the moment they departed, he'd never been so welcomed.

Until, of course, Lord Governor Damen Gard stepped forward with his wife, Giselle. All the ease in his body fled. Making an enemy of Damen spelled disaster in the Council Chamber. Attempting to befriend him meant suffering Loren's presence more often. An undesirable outcome no matter his route.

Ariadne went rigid beside him. A small, uncertain smile crossed her lips, and she slipped a little closer.

"Lord Governor Gard." Azriel extended his arm, heart hammering in his chest.

What felt like an eternity passed before Damen accepted the gesture, squeezing harder than Azriel, and responded with a calculated attack. "Caldwell."

No *Lord* or *Governor*. No rank, title, or term of status. In a single word, he made his thoughts on Azriel's new position known to all.

"Damen," Giselle hissed, her red hair shimmering as she cast her husband an exasperated look. Her brown eyes blazed at him with warning. "We talked about this."

"Lord Governor," Damen amended. "We extend our congratulations on your engagement."

Giselle leaned closer to Ariadne and spoke in a low voice. "Please know we respect your decision, though we are saddened you will not be joining our family."

"You have been like a mother to me for so long." Ariadne took Giselle's hand in her own. "Thank you for all you have done."

"And shall continue to do." The elder Caersan shot her husband another stern look.

Azriel opened his mouth to thank her for her generosity but snapped it closed as Loren slid between his parents. His red cheeks and slight sway suggested a heavy consumption of the Teaglows' wine. Giselle sucked in a sharp breath, and Damen paled at his son's belligerence.

Loren's sapphire eyes shot to Ariadne's throat, scanning the necklace which had replaced his own. "I should have known you were damaged when even the dhemons let you go."

The closest Caersans' collective inhale at the insult drowned out the music for a beat. Whispers whisked through the crowd, the rumors around Ariadne's disappearance put to rest. Giselle grabbed her son's arm, but he yanked it away without thought. Even Damen's eyes widened in alarm.

As Ariadne shrank back from the attack, Azriel stepped forward, blinking back the shadows creeping in on the edges of his vision. "You no longer speak to her."

"No." Loren raised his unfocused gaze to him and smirked. "Apparently, I speak with the Bastard Lord who stole her from me."

"Loren!" Damen snapped. "Enough!"

But Loren ignored him and took another step forward. "Tell me, Tenebra, are you proud to sully the name of the Caldwells?"

"You are trying to bait me, General." Azriel's patience thinned. He wanted to put an end to the incessant prejudice, but the middle of a ball was not the place for it. Not again. "I will not bite."

Loren's smirk turned into a sneer. "You think you are better than me?"

"I think you are drunk," Azriel said, moving again to ensure Ariadne remained behind him. "Do not embarrass yourself."

"You are an embarrassment to all of Society." Loren shoved at Azriel's chest. "Do you truly believe anyone here takes you seriously?"

"They are free to make decisions as they see fit."

Loren shoved again. "And now you have stolen a name, a title, and *my* fiancée by poisoning her mind against me."

Azriel drew himself up and stepped forward now. "You did that bit yourself. I was prepared to leave her with you until you almost *broke her arm.*"

More excited murmurs rose up around them, and Giselle grabbed her husband's wrist in alarm. "Loren!"

"Enough!" Markus's voice boomed louder than Azriel had ever heard it before. The Princeps shoved to the front of the gathered Caersans. "*Enough.*"

Azriel stepped back to stand beside Ariadne. She took hold of his fingers with a shaking hand, and he focused straight ahead. If he saw any semblance of fear in her face, he'd snap.

"You have overstepped, General." Markus placed himself between them, face pale with rage. "I am more proud of my daughter's *choice* of fiancé than I could ever be if I had allowed her to marry a *boy* who treats his woman like an object."

Whipping his gaze to Markus, Azriel struggled to hide the shock from his face. Those were not the words he expected to hear from the Princeps—ever. He'd resigned himself to the fact that he'd be the unwanted son-in-law, tolerated only for the sake of his wife. If Markus meant what he said, it changed everything. If he'd said it as a mere jab to the General, it no longer mattered. The Society had heard it loud and clear: the Princeps preferred Azriel.

Azriel's chest swelled with pride, and he leveled a victorious glare at Loren.

Loren gaped at him for a long moment. "My Lord Princeps, as your General, I must insist—"

"No." Markus shook his head. "Take leave, *Mister* Gard. Your position in the army will be reevaluated by the Council at a later date."

"My Lord—"

"Your behavior tonight has been appalling," Markus continued, "and not fit for your position. I recall you serving punishment to inebriated soldiers not too long ago, and the General is never truly off duty. Do not make this worse for yourself."

Loren's nostrils flared, and his mouth smoothed to a thin line. Without another word, he bowed to the Princeps and turned to exit. The crowd parted quickly, sensing the fury bubbling from him.

As he disappeared, Damen and Giselle watched. The former silently calculated his own power on the Council, while the latter did not hide her tears. Whether they were of shame or sorrow, Azriel could not tell.

Nor did he care.

Markus turned to speak with the Gards while Azriel pivoted to Ariadne. She dragged her gaze from the guests still staring and looked up at him with silver-rimmed eyes. Her free hand twisted in her skirt, the other still clinging to his arm.

"Are you alright?" He brushed a curl back from her face, his fingers sliding across her cheek.

Ariadne swallowed hard, nodded, and said on a breath, "Yes."

She spoke the lie so easily, he almost believed her. But he knew the truth. Nothing about this—confronting the Gards nor Loren's outburst—was alright. He certainly couldn't claim to be, and he'd faced off with far worse. His only highlight remained Markus's praise.

"Although," she continued, glancing around them and lowering her voice even further, "I am far from ready to no longer be the center of attention."

Azriel nodded in agreement. He could use time away from the constant scrutiny as well. After catching Markus's eye and nodding in thanks, he led Ariadne away in search of Emillie, Camilla, Revelie, and Madan. A turn about the garden with friends was what they both needed most.

CHAPTER 22

Laeton Park stretched out before Emillie as she exited the carriage with her new guard, Sul's, assistance a week after the Teaglow's ball. The pale, thin redhead, a sullen and silent shadow in the wake of Azriel and Madan's departure, insisted on escorting her sister any time she wished to travel into town. Gracen, on the other hand, a stalky man with dark skin and a shaved head, accompanied Emillie more often than not, and for that, she was thankful.

When the more enjoyable guard appeared from behind the carriage, she breathed a sigh of relief. Let Sul observe from afar as he was wont to do.

"How are you this evening, Miss Harlow?" Gracen asked, his black eyes shimmering in the light of the small lanterns on the outside of the carriage.

Emillie smiled back at him. "I am quite well, thank you."

Behind her, Ariadne exited the carriage and thanked Sul quietly. Her long-sleeved cerulean dress blended in with the darkness around them, the subtle floral pattern shimmering in and out of sight. For the first time in many nights, her sister's eyes shone with excitement. She began searching the moment her feet touched the grass, not to avoid others as she once had, but to seek out.

"Miss Harlow," Gracen said with a bow to Ariadne. "How do you fair this evening?"

Ariadne smiled back. "Quite well, thank you."

"Are you excited for the coming nights?" He closed the carriage door and stepped around them both.

Emillie bit her lip. The wedding. After suffering through the loss of Darien and the humiliation of Loren, at last, her sister was bound for the altar. How she felt about it all, Emillie could only guess. She had yet to ask her sister herself for fear of dredging up unwanted anxieties.

"Yes."

The simple answer sent a jolt of anticipation through Emillie. Of anything Ariadne could have said, she did not expect that.

"Well, I'm pleased to hear it." Azriel appeared from the far side of the carriage with his sword strapped to his back. If it were not for the casual Caersan clothes he wore, he would look as he did prior to his ascension.

And never in all her life had Emillie seen her sister's face alight the way it did at the sight of him. Ariadne's lips split into a wide smile, and she hurried to her fiancé. Azriel's usual cold, hard expression softened as he bowed, scooping her hand up to his lips.

Emillie turned away to give them a moment of privacy to speak. She focused on the park sprawling before her and could not help the pit which opened in her stomach.

She and the woman from the Bistro, Kyra, had discussed meeting here before they had been forced apart. As much as she knew it to be for the best—she could never pursue her interest in women amongst the Society, and dragging Kyra down with her would be unacceptable—she still wished it to be possible.

Though there were ways. Revelie, after all, managed to straddle the line between the Society and freedom. Camilla, too, openly pursued her interests. Perhaps Emillie merely needed to find her path to achieve the same.

A gust of warm wind crept by, lazy and filled with the sweet scent of summer. The perfume of flowers, fresh-cut grass, and the hint of humidity leftover from the day's sun. It brushed against her bare arms like a gentle reminder of what life used to be like, and for a moment, Emillie saw Laeton Park as she once did at midday.

The emerald lawn rolled out before her. Several dirt and gravel paths cut through, winding in and out of sight behind hills and shrubbery. Trees, lush with new foliage, spread their branches wide to shade the Rusan, who primarily utilized the park while the Caersan slept.

All too soon, her night vision took hold of the memory and washed the space with dark hues. Though she could see as well as she once did in daylight, it did not change the tones of night.

A hand brushed against hers, jolting her from the thoughts. Emillie looked to her sister, who smiled and gestured forward.

So Ariadne's final promenade about Laeton Park as an unmarried Caersan woman began.

"I must admit," Emillie said as they started off and looked up at Azriel, "I am not happy with you."

Ariadne whipped her gaze around, and Azriel's face paled as he said, "Pardon me?"

She could not hide the curl of her lips. "You are taking from me the one person I rely on most to keep me from withering away from boredom."

Now Azriel smiled a slow, cat-like smile. "It appears you'll need to visit often, then."

Emillie groaned. "But Monsumbra is *so* far away."

"We will not be leaving right away," Ariadne reassured her and took her hand for a big squeeze. "After the wedding, there are Council meetings and, of course, Soltium."

Her heart leapt at the mention of her favorite holiday—Summer Solstice. The three days and nights of celebration took place at the home of several Caersan families with their closest friends. Camilla's parents had already expressed their intention to invite them all to their manor for the duration.

"But who will be taking care of Eastwood throughout all this?" Emillie looked up at Azriel expectantly.

The new Lord Governor did not miss a beat. "Madan and the Steward are more than capable of handling business while I am unavailable."

"No doubt."

They started down a gentle slope onto a wide gravel path that looped the perimeter of the park. A family of low-ranking Caersan vampires Emillie had not seen before played nearby with their young. The boy, no older than twenty, still sported his round face and small, gangly limbs. His sister, less than a handful of years old, rode along on her mother's hip, giggling merrily at her brother's silly games. Both parents watched their offspring with bright eyes, oblivious to the passerby.

Ariadne, however, took note of them, same as Emillie. She did not comment or even probe Azriel about his feelings on building a family together. Her gaze flickered from one vampire to the next before fixating on a distant point ahead of them.

No, she did not suppose Ariadne looked forward to those prospects. While she never explained what happened in those mountains, her sudden aversion to touch and affection painted a vivid image. One Emillie desperately wished she had not conjured—and one she hoped was as fictional as her sister's favorite books.

To his credit, Azriel glanced at Ariadne then and said nothing. He had always been observant of her sister's moods—her wants and needs and distastes—and this was no different. Nothing seemed to slip his notice.

"Have you seen your friend from the Bistro again?" Ariadne asked suddenly, turning to her with a pointed look.

Friend. Of course, she meant Kyra but could not say precisely what they had been together. If they had been anything but a passing kiss.

"No," Emillie said with a small smile. "Perhaps it is for the best."

"Pity." Ariadne frowned. "She seemed nice enough."

Emillie snorted back a laugh. "You could say that."

"Did you know," Ariadne said conspiratorially and leaning closer to drop her voice, "Madan also has a good friend back east. Perhaps you will meet him when you come to visit."

For a long moment, Emillie's mind went blank. Then all the dots connected, and she laughed, nodding. "Yes, I would like that."

Azriel, however, did not look amused. Nor did he appear angry with Ariadne's loose lips. Instead, he looked between them, jaw tight and brows furrowing with concern.

"Will we not be meeting him?" Ariadne turned her face up to him and tilted her head.

"Whelan doesn't come to town often." Azriel sighed. "It's very difficult, really. He travels a lot."

Emillie pursed her lips. "Madan is very patient."

"He's had to deal with me his entire life," Azriel said with a grin. "He's the most patient man I know."

"So the two of you grew up together?" Ariadne asked. "Were you not raised by your father?"

Azriel nodded once. "Yes. It's part of the reason why his pure Caersan blood's been ignored by the Society."

"What is the other part?"

"He was too young to make himself known before his mother died."

Ariadne frowned. "Were your mothers sisters?"

"Yes."

Emillie slowed her pace, letting the betrothed couple go on ahead of her. One night the pair of vampires may very well be her. With whom would she walk through Laeton Park? A Lord Governor? A merchant lord? A military officer?

No matter what route her mind journeyed down, she knew it would not end with her marrying someone like Kyra. In none of the scenarios would she be with a woman. Her father would never allow such a thing.

So better to imagine herself with the most likely outcome: a rich, Caersan man with political power. Perhaps she would find joy in it somewhere—somehow.

They rounded a corner, the trail leading them through a dense crop of trees. Her eyes adjusted to the lower light, and she sensed more than saw the tension in the guards behind her. Azriel shifted closer to Ariadne, his chest expanding with a deep inhale.

Once a guard, always a guard.

Picking up on the subtle change of mood as well, Ariadne glanced back at her. No one spoke for a long moment.

"Should we turn around?" Emillie looked back at Gracen.

Azriel slowed to a halt. "Perhaps it would be wise—"

The massive, horned shadow came out of nowhere. It barreled into Azriel, ripping him away from Ariadne in one fell swoop and sending him to the ground on his back. He rolled, heels over head, to his feet, where he wrenched the sword from the sheath on his back.

As if he knew he would need to use it on the stroll through the park.

A scream tore through the darkness as two more dhemons hurdled out from between the trees. Their midnight blue skin allowed them to blend in with the night—all but their vivid red eyes.

"Run!" Azriel glanced at Ariadne. "*Run!*"

She did no such thing. The sight of the monsters from her nightmares froze her to the spot, and as Emillie's heart hammered hard in her chest, she lurched forward to grab her sister's wrist. Behind her, both guards rushed in to engage the newcomers. Their swords flashed in the low light.

"Ariadne—"

A dhemon snarled something in his guttural language, a wicked grin spreading across his face. His vicious rows of sharp teeth—not as long as a vampire's but just as sharp and far more numerous—glinted in the moonlight. He crooked a finger at Ariadne as though taunting her.

"Ariadne, please!" Emillie yanked at her arm.

The tug pulled her sister out of her daze, and Ariadne stumbled back, mouth opening and closing like a beached fish.

Azriel's blade flashed against the dhemon's twin short swords, and though he held his own, even his strength did not hold up against such a huge adversary. Beside him, Sul's thinner frame buckled under the force of a blow while Gracen pushed back with everything he had. It would not be enough.

"Come," Emillie hissed and turned to find two more dhemons stalking down the path. No exit. "Fuck."

In a whirlwind, Azriel twisted one, then the other short sword from the dhemon's grips. He kicked the blades aside, one spinning dangerously close to Emillie's ankle, and shoved his sword through the monster's chest. Blood rained down, soaking his hands and arms.

To Emillie's shock, Ariadne stooped and picked up the short sword in a shaking hand. Her wide eyes turned from the dhemons in front to those behind as though calculating what to do next.

A dhemon behind them chuckled, then said with a thick accent in the common tongue, "What you do with that, *princess*?"

Her sister paled. "Do not call me that."

"Found your tongue, I see."

"Don't speak to her." Azriel leveled his sword at the dhemon who spoke. "Don't even look at her."

The dhemon tilted his head with a smirk and said something in his language. It grated on Emillie's ears. When he finished, Azriel's mouth twisted as though he understood exactly what was said. Maybe he did.

The next moment, Azriel charged forward. The dhemon laughed, but before he could pull the sword from his hip, the vampire was there. Emillie gaped. The dhemon dodged the sword and backhanded Azriel so hard, he nearly collapsed to the ground.

A small sound escaped Ariadne, and she lurched forward, then froze again as the other dhemon clicked his tongue at her and shook his head.

Why the dhemons did not attack her or Ariadne, Emillie had no idea. All she knew was that the moment Sul and Gracen unsheathed their weapons, they became targets, too. To their credit, neither had fallen to their foes.

The dhemon knocked the sword from Azriel's hand with a swift kick. He grabbed the vampire's hair and yanked him back to his feet, snarling something else in the foreign tongue. Azriel glared back and spit in his face.

The dhemon released him in disgust, and Azriel righted himself. Slamming into the dhemon, just as he had done in his duel with Loren, Emillie was unsurprised to find the dhemon did not go down as easily as the General. He shoved harder and pulled at the back of the dhemon's knees, but the monster would not budge. Rather, he leaned onto the smaller vampire's shoulders and shoved him to the ground.

Azriel scrambled away from the sudden turn out of his favor. He gripped the dhemon's ankle and yanked his foot out from under him, pinning it to his chest. Standing, he grabbed the dhemon's horn with his free hand and kicked the back of his ankle, taking him to the ground. Azriel landed on top of the dhemon and slammed his fist into the monster's jaw. Now the second dhemon rushed forward, making to grab Azriel, but he twisted out of reach. As he moved, he gripped the horns of the one on the ground and pulled the dhemon's face closer.

What Azriel did next reminded Emillie just how far removed he was from the Society. He bared his long fangs and ripped into the dhemon's throat like a hound.

Ariadne gasped and grabbed Emillie's arm in alarm. Emillie's stomach churned. The brutality numbed her mind.

Azriel released the horn, and the second dhemon wrapped an arm around his neck to haul him back. He hissed something in Azriel's ear, then looked up at her and Ariadne. A jolt of pure terror radiated through her body. Azriel's sudden frantic attempt to get free told her everything she needed to know.

He knew what the dhemon said, and it did not bode well for them.

"We have to run, Ariadne," Emillie spoke quietly and looked down the path the way they came. They would have to get around the throatless dhemon and past the one cutting off Azriel's airway.

Ariadne said on a breath, "I cannot leave him."

"You must!" Emillie pulled on her arm and blinked back tears. "You must!"

A hand landed on her shoulder, tearing a cry of panic from her lips. She wrenched away to find Gracen clutching his stomach, the dhemon he fought dead behind him. Blood gushed from between his fingers, and his wide eyes said it all—they needed to get out. Now.

In the next moment, Sul appeared. He limped up beside Gracen, sporting his own injuries where he had been stabbed multiple times in his thigh. A massive bruise swelled enough to close one eye, and the dhemon he left behind still breathed, though it was incapacitated. The worst part, however, was the broken and dangling arm at his side.

"Get them out," he rasped to Gracen. "Go!"

Gracen took two steps before his knees gave out just as Azriel wrenched himself free of the dhemon's vice-like grip. One vampire fell. The other sucked in a much-needed breath and charged back in.

In a single, swift movement, Azriel gripped the dhemon's arm and pivoted, tossing the massive figure to the ground. He stepped over the dhemon's chest, still holding the arm, and yanked hard.

A loud crack rang out, followed by the dhemon's scream of pain. Azriel knelt over the monster, pinning his unbroken arm under a heavy boot, and grabbed the horn again. For a moment, Emillie thought he would tear into his throat. Instead, he did something far more alarming.

He spoke in the dhemon language. Back and forth, the two went as she watched in shock. Emillie had never known of a vampire—Caersan or Rusan—who spoke the tongue.

Ariadne let out a shuddering breath as Azriel stood again, dragging the dhemon's own blade across his throat. When he turned to them, both sisters froze. Blood dripped from Azriel's mouth and hands and coated the front of his shirt. His eyes shone like twin flames radiating untempered rage.

"What did he say?" Ariadne asked, her voice small and cracked. She watched him with a wary gaze but did not back away as he moved closer.

"Nothing of import."

"But you know what he said?" Sul growled, lips lifted in a sneer. "You speak that foul tongue?"

Azriel glared at him. "A good soldier knows his enemies well. Don't worry about me—worry about your charges."

"Azriel," Ariadne breathed and dropped the short sword as she stepped toward him.

"I'll escort you to the carriage." Azriel reached for her, then dropped his hand before smearing blood on her unscathed skin. "Sul will get you home."

Emillie knelt beside Gracen and pressed her fingers to his neck. The slow pulse felt weak under her touch. "Will he live?"

Azriel turned to Sul. "Not if you don't go now."

Then the ex-guard slung the unconscious vampire over his bloody shoulder and started off.

Ariadne stood for a long moment, taking in the dead bodies around them. How she held herself together in the midst of that carnage, a reminder of the past she had suffered through and survived, Emillie could not fathom. The fight had shaken her, and she had not endured horrors as her sister had.

Perhaps Ariadne was numb to it. The way she froze and let the monsters approach demonstrated the extent to which they had poisoned her. Whether her fawn-like reaction had been due to fear of or discipline by the dhemons, Emillie could not tell. If there was one thing she recalled Ariadne repeating again and again, it was that she had tried so hard to get away. At first.

Now she froze.

Emillie slid her hand into her sister's and squeezed.

The weak response said enough.

Leave from duty as General did not bother Loren as much as he anticipated. He continued to utilize his office space at the Hub, Valenul's main base of military operations, but not for his usual paperwork and meetings. Those had been handed off to his second-in-command until the Council decided his fate.

As if they could keep him from leading his soldiers for long.

Loyal officers continued reporting to Loren as they would have prior to his temporary removal. He knew the ridiculous demands being asked of them and gave instructions on how to best question and refuse the duties assigned in a subtle strike against the Princeps' decision.

Between the visits, Loren poured over books and scrolls filled with the history of vampires. Dating back to their time as mages, nearly five thousand years prior, he chose the hand-written books describing the first vampires to enter Keonis Valley and create the vampiric kingdom of Valenul. The first were the Caldwells.

And their family line did not extend far, as Loren suspected.

The Caldwells who took up their place in Monsumbra never left, and when the extended family arrived, they were not accepted in the same manner. Many lines ended as daughters married into other families and sons died at the hands of dhemons. So many, in fact, the likelihood that the last Lord Governor Caldwell had many cousins left to carry on his lineage was slim.

However, Loren did find the woman Azriel claimed as his mother. No children were recorded in any text he found, though her unmarried status would only corroborate the idea that he was born of a fae male.

The only issue was the lack of fae knowledge amidst the vampiric histories. Loren's connection to the high fae General provided few documents.

And none of them mentioned a fae by the name of Azazel.

Loren sifted through his notes again. Names, birthdates, marriages, and offspring blurred before his eyes. Few vampire and fae marriages occurred, particularly in the Caldwell family. None of it added up to produce Azriel Tenebra, yet the way the Society was prone to hide unwanted pregnancies did not make for valid information.

He turned back to the most recent Caldwells. The original Lord Governor to settle in Monsumbra did so with his first wife and two sons—all of whom were slaughtered by dhemons. His second wife bore only one son and, according to the records, took in an Original daughter from another family—the Wynnes. That Caersan girl, Margot, ended up marrying their son, Garth, upon his maturity.

Margot and Garth had only one daughter, Mariana, who married once and bore two children. The names and dates of all her relations, however, were blacked out after their death at the hands of dhemons. An entire family, removed from the histories.

To his displeasure, this was also not uncommon. A number of family lines came to abrupt ends and were inked or burned from the books. No one wanted to remember such terrible times.

Loren leaned closer to the blots of ink beside Mariana, forcing his eyes to focus on the thin lines which protruded and disappeared beneath the mess. A curl at the top of her husband appeared as an N or M. The children's names, almost completely illegible, showed signs of common vowels with no clues as to what they were.

The door opened before he could wager any guesses, and a young messenger slipped into the room. He bowed quickly, placed a letter on the desk, and departed. As quick and efficient as ever despite Loren's demotion.

The nondescript white seal of the letter told Loren precisely who sent it before he even cracked the wax. He unfolded the paper with deft fingers and scanned the short missive.

General—

Attack at Laeton Park. Harlows are fine. Gracen killed in action. AT speaks dhemon tongue.

Sul

Loren's chest swelled. This was precisely the damning information he had waited so patiently for. With mere nights from the wedding, he did not have time to save Ariadne from the inevitable nuptials, but he could utilize the event to gather more evidence.

He stood and moved to the fire crackling low in the hearth along an adjacent wall. The letter crinkled in his fist, then he tossed it into the flames. For a long moment, Loren watched the edges catch, curl, and disintegrate to ash.

Then he returned to the notes on his desk, dipped his pen in the inkwell, and scrawled in the empty space above Azriel's name two words: *dhemon sire.*

CHAPTER 23

The night Azriel never in his wildest of dreams believed possible arrived. After everything he'd done, everything he'd endured, everything he'd put her through, she'd chosen him. Chosen him over the memory of her first love, the General of Valenul, and her father's hopes. Despite the constant battle of will within himself, his fae bond won out, and he'd achieved the one thing he needed to complete himself.

By morning, Ariadne would be his wife.

His *wife*.

The rational side of him screamed. He still had time to run—to disappear into the mountains and never be seen in Valenul again. It begged him to stop the madness, remember everything she'd suffered, and put her out of the misery before it began. For that was all he had to offer her once they exchanged those vows.

Yet Azriel didn't listen. He buttoned his black trousers and vest with shaking hands, straightened his deep red cravat, and slid his arms into the matching jacket. Everything would be perfect.

Even after the dhemon attack in Laeton Park, he'd make sure it went as planned.

Nimera, a young Rusan girl serving in his new household, knocked and entered with a quick curtsy. She pulled the collar of his vest into place before forcing him into a chair and combing his hair.

"I'm quite capable of tying my hair back," he said as she moved it from side to side. "I've done it myself for years."

Nimera snorted without looking at him in the mirror. "And you think that'll do for your wedding?"

"It's not that bad."

She yanked his hair enough to make him wince, then tilted his head to the side. "It's not enough."

Her nimble fingers gathered the hair at his temple and began braiding. He watched with curiosity as she pinned the end of the braid down, then tilted his head in the other direction and repeated the endeavor. She then straightened his head and smoothed the top of his hair down to meet the twin braids at the back of his head, where she wove it all together.

"There." She tied off the braid and gave it a quick tug. "Much better."

"Thank you, Nimera." He shoved his feet into tall leather boots and stood again. "Truly. It looks great."

"You're very welcome, my Lord," she said and flounced back to the door. "Your carriage is waiting for you."

Azriel grunted in affirmation. Carriages didn't suit him. Riding freely on Jasper was his preference. But bringing his new wife home required the comfort and safety of a coach.

"Don't ruin your hair by riding." Nimera gave him a warning look and disappeared, leaving the door open behind her.

Indeed, ruining her work would result in him paying dearly. Over the last few weeks, he'd learned the ins and outs of his staff just as much as they'd taught him the ways of the Society. While he knew who he could taunt or goad, he also knew the trouble he'd be in if he pushed too far—and an unseasoned dinner was as unappetizing as he remembered it being. Swift apologies smoothed over the issue of his loose tongue, but it'd been a learning curve for certain.

So when he departed from the manor not long after, it was in the carriage with Madan riding along outside.

Each minute on their way to the event space made Azriel's heart beat a little harder, a little faster, and a little more dys-regulated. At his destination, he'd enter the ceremony hall, where he'd see the woman of his dreams for the first time since the dhemon attack at Laeton Park.

The very memory made his stomach roil. He leaned his elbows on his knees and pushed his fists against his eyes.

All he'd felt the moment those dhemons arrived was sheer terror. For the first time since Vertium, they'd gotten close enough to kill Ariadne. To finish what had been started in those mountains a year ago.

But it was what the dhemon he'd questioned told him that made his blood run cold: "He knows where you are, what you're doing, and how to make you suffer for what you've done. Your death will never satisfy him."

Him. The dhemon of his waking terrors. Ehrun. Ehrun, who'd locked him away and tortured him in a way he never thought possible: forcing him to listen to Ariadne's screams. Her pleas for it all to end. Despite all that, the worst part had been the silence. The not-knowing if Ehrun had finally taken it too far and killed her.

A fae's bond was meant to be reciprocated by another fae. It connected them, whether they wanted it or not, and because of it, a typical fae bond meant knowing whether their mate lived... and knowing when they died.

Azriel didn't have the luxury of knowing since Ariadne had no fae blood. She didn't feel the connection to him as he did to her, and while part of him was grateful she needn't suffer in such a way, it played games with his mind. Too long without seeing her sent him into a spiral of darkness.

It'd been that spiral which had him slipping a noose about his own neck. If it hadn't been for Madan, he wouldn't have made it far enough to see this wedding.

Marriage, however, only tightened the hold his bond had on his mind and actions. Knowing that Ehrun was after him—after *her* to get to him—only tormented him more. He needed to get Ariadne back to Monsumbra, where he could protect her in the way he knew to be most effective.

He would not watch her die like so many others at the hands of monsters. His mother. His father. Even the guard, Gracen, took his final breaths in Azriel's arms. Another death because of his failures—*her* death—would ruin him.

The carriage rumbled to a halt, cutting off his morbid thoughts, and the door swung open. Light poured into the coach from the bright temple before him. Smooth, shiny obsidian stone walls stretched overhead with lanterns dangling from the overhang. Steps leading to a pair of open doors squat wide and shallow at his feet as he leapt from the carriage.

The Temple of Keon.

While apt to hold a wedding in the temple of their patron god, Keon's position as God of the Underworld made it feel strange.

Nonetheless, Azriel climbed the stairs and entered the temple with sure steps. Nothing would keep him from this wedding. No dhemons, no god... no one.

No windows lined the stone walls of the long hall and, instead, bore shelves stacked with candles all the way to the ceiling. Three massive, wrought iron chandeliers hung from the ceiling at equivalent intervals and lit the space brilliantly. Two rows of benches lined the outer edge of the hall, all facing the center altar rising from the floor on three steps.

No wedding decorations were present. They never were in the gods' temples. Instead, the traditional decor of Keon broke up the monotony of the candles and shelves. Skulls hung from the stone—bears and deer and cougars and—

Azriel paused to inspect the dhemon skull close to the door. On one hand, the dhemons were crafted by Keon himself to protect the god's mortal wife. On the other, for vampires to possess a skull to display in such a crude manner churned his stomach. Sure, he'd killed his fair share of dhemons, but he'd never imagined hanging one up like a trophy.

Rather than linger on it, Azriel refocused on the task at hand. Guests began to arrive, eager to witness the union of their newest member of the Society to their Golden Rose. He moved to the foot of the center dais and greeted the families upon their entrance. Given their comfort with the location, he gathered that the Temple of Keon was a regular place for weddings amongst Caersan.

He wouldn't have chosen it.

Madan joined him not long after, his short hair slicked back from his face and boots shining as always. He stood beside Azriel, hands clasped behind his back, and said, "A strange place for nuptials."

"According to their ease at being here," Azriel murmured back, nodding to the vampires claiming seats on the benches, "I'd wager this is normal."

"I don't recall this from the wedding we attended," Madan huffed. "It was outside."

Azriel glanced at him. "It was still a Priestess of Keon."

"Do these vampires even realize how similar their customs are to—"

"No," Azriel cut in, "they don't."

His brother said nothing else as the wave of arrivals slowed. Instead, Madan gave him a quick hug, then found himself a seat. His absence only made Azriel's mind race more.

Azriel looked around the room. The Fletchers and Tea-glows sat nearby. Lord Moone and Lord Governor Nightingale whispered between themselves. Every member of the Society in Laeton had come, filling the seats to capacity and requiring others to stand. Even Lord Governor Gard and his wife and son.

He didn't give Loren a second look.

Outside the temple, a final carriage trundled to a stop at the foot of the steps. Sul, his arm in a sling but otherwise spry, opened the door. First, Markus stepped out in his cobalt and brown suit, then Emillie, her curls piled high on her head and wearing a blue gown with tulle and silver stars. The younger Harlow stared up at the temple with wide eyes but waited patiently for the final addition to their party.

Breath didn't come easily as Azriel waited, rooted to the spot near the altar. This would be the last time he saw Ariadne arrive anywhere without his family name—without *him* if he could help it.

When they left here tonight, they'd finally be bound to one another.

Behind him, a door he hadn't noticed opened with a bang. Azriel's heart skipped a beat, and he glanced back to see the High Priestess striding into the hall. She wore long, grey robes cinched at the waist by a belt of leather with satchels dangling from it. Her deep, brown skin, weathered by age and wisdom, seemed to glow in the candlelight. Atop her head was a grey veil covering her hair and held in place by a crown of foliage dotted with antlers. Resting above it all was a crescent moon on its side, points facing up like wicked horns.

She moved with grace and agility uncommon for a vampire her age. If Azriel had to guess, she was old enough to rival the late Lord Governor Caldwell. Yet her spirit and body kept pace.

By the time he refocused on the doors, Ariadne had exited the carriage and stood, hidden, behind her father and sister. He could see only the white lace veil held in place on her head by a circlet of golden roses.

They entered the temple, and the din of voices lowered to a low hum. Gasps and excited chatter erupted when the Harlow family passed the onlookers, only heightening his own anticipation.

Ariadne. She'd arrived. Even though he'd told himself again and again that she would, that terrible voice in his head still whispered in his ear: she would never truly love him.

I'm doing you a favor, really.

The High Priestess spoke, her voice strong and filled with ethereal power that silenced the hall and slammed Ehrun's words from his mind. "Whose blood do you present?"

Azriel's heart skipped a beat. Thanks to Alek Nightingale the previous evening, he'd been warned how the ceremony would proceed. Much different than the few informal Rusan weddings he'd attended in recent years.

"The blood of Ariadne Harlow," Markus replied before stepping aside in unison with Emillie.

Azriel's chest swelled at the sight of Ariadne. Her ivory dress cut in at her waist with an intricate corset before flowing out at her hips. The silky fabric shone beneath a layer of tulle, stitched with delicate gold roses and inlaid with crystals, that stretched up to her shoulders and swept down her arms where it came together with small, golden buttons at her wrist. Her dark hair parted down the middle and twisted back from her face with strands of gold ribbon. Loose curls flowed down her back, half-hidden beneath the thin veil still obscuring her face.

So lost in his search for her eyes, Azriel almost missed when the High Priestess asked, "To whom is it given?"

His lips moved without words at first. He closed his eyes and shook his head before repeating, "Azriel Caldwell. I shall be its keeper."

"Rise," the High Priestess said, "and take your places before me."

Azriel held out his arm level to the ground, and Ariadne laid hers on top. He silently thanked Alek for his explicit instructions. Though it had seemed foolish at the time to practice with the Lord Governor, it helped tremendously. Without his guidance, he'd have made a fool of himself before the most prominent figures of the Society.

Together, Azriel and Ariadne made their way up the steps to stand before the High Priestess. Between them sat a column of obsidian with a bowl carved into the top. Another piece of the puzzle Alek had been kind enough to impart on him so he wouldn't be caught unawares.

"Since the construction of our world," the High Priestess began, "the union of two people has been the marking of new life."

Ariadne tensed, her fingers gripping his a little harder. He turned his hand over and squeezed hers once. She pulled in a steady breath, released it, and squeezed back again.

"As we stand within the Temple of Keon," the High Priestess continued and pulled from a satchel at her waist a short knife, "it is pertinent to remember the teachings of the God of the Underworld. Of all those who reside amongst the celestial, it is he who understands the importance of such unions, for it is he who intertwined with a mortal soul."

Keon's human wife, Anwen, had been born enslaved in the southern plains and drew the attention of the God of the Underworld through her beautiful songs begging for freedom. When at last he'd answered her call, he fell to his knees at her feet and promised her the world and a throne at his side in the darkest depths of the celestial realm.

Yet when Keon brought her to his kingdom after their marriage, she suffered. Mortals, after all, could not live where the dead roamed. So he constructed her a palace at the northernmost reaches of Myridia and created dhemons in his own image to be her protectors.

As the God of the Underworld, he could visit Anwen a mere once a year. He freed her family and friends and delivered them to her in her palace so she would want for naught. Gifts and feasts and prosperity rained upon Anwen, Mortal Queen of the Underworld, and she worshiped her husband with the same love and devotion he showed her.

Year after year, however, he failed to find the cure to her mortality. So year after year, her beauty gave in to age, and her voice chipped away. Her face took on lines, and her hair shone with silver, yet Keon's heart never wavered. He still fell to his knees at her feet, even when she struggled to stand for him.

Until one year, he arrived at an empty palace. Only a letter remained detailing Anwen's death and burial.

Keon hadn't known. He couldn't have. Anwen's pure soul rose to the heavens of Empyrean, where his sister, Sora, ruled. As the King of the Underworld, he'd long been barred from the golden gates.

Keon never saw Anwen again.

The god's agony caused a devastating earthquake. It rippled through the north, and from it sprung a semicircle mountain range and, at its heart, the Keonis Valley. The shape, curling like horns to point to the long-lost ruins of Anwen's palace, became the symbol of Keon. In recent depictions of this symbol, the crescent shape rested above three simple lines to mark Keon's descent into the third and deepest level of the Underworld so he might never be tempted to love a mortal again.

So when the High Priestess raised the knife, Azriel knew what came next. The union between Keon and Anwen centered around the sharing of blood—something vampires revered as much as the gods. It was, in part, why the Caersans coveted the blood of their women. With their roots as human mages from the plains, they believed themselves to be from the same line as Anwen.

"Devotion," the High Priestess said, dragging Azriel's attention back to the ceremony before him. He gave a start when he found her dark, milky eyes searing into him. "Love. Protection. These are the values passed from the Father to the Mother."

Keon and Anwen.

"Devotion. Love. Worship." She looked to Ariadne. "These are the values passed from the Mother to the Father. Each upholds their three pillars throughout their union and, with the blood shared, swears to do so beyond their final parting."

Indeed, for after Keon and Anwen shared their blood during their wedding ceremony, it kept them connected beyond the limits of death. So even when Keon hid away in his dark kingdom, he carried with him a drop of his love to cherish for eternity.

The bond in Azriel screamed for the same. It demanded to be satiated by ensuring he, too, held even a minute piece of Ariadne.

And the little control he held on the bond slipped further and further from his grasp the longer the High Priestess spoke. On and on, she droned about marriage and their positions within the union. One as the leader, the other as subservient. For someone meant to be wise, she certainly didn't grasp the concept of equality of a couple. He wouldn't stand for anything less between him and Ariadne.

"Your hand." It wasn't a request, and when Ariadne didn't react fast enough, the High Priestess snatched up her arm.

He bit back a low growl. All part of the ceremony. No need to be so protective. Yet.

Still, when the knife scored Ariadne's palm and she hissed from the pain, Azriel wanted nothing more than to rip the knife away and stab it through the High Priestess's eye. Then the scent of her blood reached his nostrils, and his brain switched from defensive to desperate. He *needed* it.

"Repeat after me." The High Priestess squeezed Ariadne's hand so a steady stream of crimson dripped into the obsidian basin. "With this blood..."

"With this blood..." Ariadne repeated in a quiet voice.

"I give unto thee..."

"I give unto thee..."

The High Priestess released her hand, switching the steady grip to her wrist. "My body, soul, and heart..."

"My body, soul, and heart..."

"Until my dying night and beyond."

Ariadne looked up at Azriel through the veil. "Until my dying night and beyond."

"Your hand." The High Priestess looked to Azriel now, and he extended his arm before she could grab him. And before he could consider what came next, the blade slid across his skin.

Sharp pain rippled up his arm, and when she demanded he, too, repeat the vows as his blood mingled with Ariadne's in the bowl, he did so without complaint. The words were easy enough to say. Living up to them would be just as simple. Not knowing if she understood to what depths he meant it all was the most difficult part.

"Intertwine your fingers." From another satchel, the High Priestess presented a long, thin white cloth. They did so, and she wound the cloth about their palms and continued, "These wounds, created and healed together, bind your body as one in the eyes of the gods and all those who bear witness this night. The blood you spilled now mingles together in harmony."

The High Priestess produced a thimble-sized crystal chalice, taken from yet another of her satchels, and dipped it into the shallow pool. She lifted it high for all to see, blood dripping from its rim and trickling down her hand.

Azriel stilled as Ariadne used her free hand to lift the veil obscuring her face. She draped it back over the circlet and looked up at him with those perfect, shining eyes of ocean blue. Her dark lashes were curled, and liner swept across their line, emphasizing the curve of her eyes. Rouge swept up her fair cheeks, and a deep red stain tinted her lips. At her throat lay the black velvet necklace, its ruby glinting brightly in the candlelight.

Her beauty was, as always, unmatched.

"This first taste of your life together," the High Priestess continued, though her voice now sounded distant, "shall bind your soul as one..."

She spoke, and Azriel stopped listening. The tiny chalice passed to Ariadne first. Her gaze never left him as she drank. When it came to him, he lifted it to his lips, and the rush of their combined blood across his tongue nearly sent him to his knees. Though none made it up the hollows of his fangs, it coated his mouth with its metallic tang.

"At last, we arrive at the end of our ceremony," the High Priestess said.

Finally. Azriel could skip the reception to follow. All he wanted was to bring Ariadne home and worship her however she pleased. The shot of her blood sent his mind into a frenzy of possibilities.

"We close with the witnessing of the first feed." The High Priestess pulled the cloth from their hands.

Ariadne pulled her hand away, the cut closed with naught but an angry red line remaining. Azriel's had hardly scabbed. Just another reminder of the inferiority of his birth.

Unperturbed, Ariadne unfastened the buttons at her wrist. He did the same.

"As you partake in one another for this first time," the High Priestess said, "remember this: you are now but one being, and to each vein, you shall be faithful."

All around them, the Caersan vampires repeated the final words as though to drive home the message of the ceremony: "And to each vein, you shall be faithful."

With that, Azriel brought Ariadne's wrist to his mouth. She did the same with his. He shut everyone out. Instead, he watched his new wife as she bared her fangs and sank them deep into his arm. The jolt of their entry rippled through him, and he followed suit.

The shock of his fangs, something he knew she'd never experienced before, brought her eyes flashing to him. Their gazes connected, and her alarm dimmed to a heady acceptance.

As her blood rushed along his tongue, undiluted by his own, Azriel understood why Caersan men kept their women's veins untouched until marriage. Even without his fae bond roaring triumphantly in his ears, the taste of her made his body shake. By the look on her face, she felt it, too. If they were alone, he'd have torn that gown right off her and gone about claiming every single inch of her body.

The High Priestess spoke again, a faint burble beyond the crashing happening in his mind to keep himself under control. He took the cue to release Ariadne as his wife—fuck him, his *wife*—retracted her fangs. Together they turned back to the woman leading the ceremony, still unhearing, as the High Priestess cut the long, white cloth in half with her knife and tied each portion around their wrists. The sting that accompanied it made Azriel jerk his arm back.

Ariadne laid a hand on his forearm and whispered, "Salt."

Of course. To ensure the puncture wounds healed with a scar. He hadn't noticed the mineral's presence when the cloth wrapped around the outside of his hand.

"Presenting," the High Priestess said as vocalized music echoed through the hall, driving away the maddening roar in his head, "Lord Governor Azriel Caldwell and his wife, the Lady Ariadne Caldwell."

CHAPTER 24

Ariadne left the ceremony breathless. She had envisioned how it would go many times with several Caersan men. Darien, Loren, and even Alek Nightingale when she was younger. She had not had the time to imagine how the proceedings would move with Azriel beside her on that dais. The weeks leading up to the night had been busy with more wonderings than not.

The top of that list included the dhemon attack at Laeton Park. Why had they come back? And if they had not been there for her...who had they been there for?

Twice now this Season, they had attacked her where she should have been safe. Outside her own home and in a public park. The purpose of both remained a mystery—one better left to investigate after the wedding.

The wedding with a far more powerful conclusion than she could have ever dreamed. One that pushed all thoughts of dhemons from her mind for the first time since watching Gracen succumb to his injuries at Laeton Park.

Yet when they exited the temple, guests calling their congratulations in their wake, Ariadne's heart thundered. She had never before accepted the hand of a man and entered a carriage alone with him. Though she heard of what occurred between newlyweds in the time it took to travel from temple to reception, Ariadne's stomach churned at the thought. It warred with the fire blossoming in her core, a simultaneous desire and revulsion as the door closed behind her and Azriel.

While the spacious carriage provided more than enough room for them both to sit across from one another, the close confines made Ariadne's head spin. She could still taste his blood on her lips, feel his fangs in her arm, and scent the musky spice which clung to his skin. All of it called to her, but each time she considered what came next, she recoiled from him.

The carriage jolted forward, jerking her toward Azriel. He held out a hand to steady her, still careful to not touch her more than necessary.

"Are you well?" Azriel's low, rocky voice pulled her attention to his face. He scanned her with knitted brows.

Ariadne sucked in a slow breath and nodded. "It is all so new."

A slow, tight smirk twisted at his lips. "What? Being alone with me?"

"I—I—yes."

"If I may," he said, sounding far too much like the Lord Governor he now was, "I do believe that is precisely what landed us here."

Despite herself, Ariadne huffed a laugh. The knot in her gut loosened a bit, and she shook her head. "You are quite right, I suppose."

"Then tell me," Azriel continued and leaned forward so his elbows rested on his knees, "why are you so distant?"

Ariadne gaped at him, and his eyes dropped to her mouth. The peridot darkened. In an instant, she understood precisely why the carriage ride provided adequate time for such devious activities.

And with the way he watched her, she wanted him to hold her as he had the night of his duel, the past be damned.

"Kiss me," she breathed, fingers twisting in the tulle of her skirt.

Azriel shifted closer, hands still to himself. His eyes slipped to her shaking hands and drifted up her body to rest at her throat. "I won't do anything unless you truly want me to."

She forced her palms flat on her legs to hide their quivering. "Azriel—"

"No." He took her hand, fingers sliding up her thighs to retrieve it. The light touch sent a shiver through her. Azriel ignored it and held her firm. "I'll never ask you to do anything you don't want to do."

Ariadne bit her lip and took another deep breath at the triggered memories. She shoved them away with equal force and, releasing the breath, she said, "Then kiss me. Please."

Whatever hold Azriel had on himself snapped. He launched forward and cupped a gentle hand on the back of her neck, drawing her in to him. In a blink, he went from calm and composed to hungry and eager.

The feel of his lips on hers was precisely what she needed in that moment. It distracted her mind and replaced her racing thoughts with him. Just Azriel and the way his mouth moved—the way his tongue stroked and his teeth nipped.

At first, she froze. The switch from total control to the sudden lack thereof shocked her. But as his familiar scent filled her nose and his tender touches brushed her skin, she melted into his grasp. Then his fingers curled into her hair, urging her closer.

She answered the call by sliding to her feet, where she pulled her long skirts above her knees to climb onto his lap. He moaned against her lips as she settled there, straddling his hips. It sent fire coursing through her veins, so when she shifted even closer, her heart thundered at the feeling of his hard length pressing against that sweet place at the crux of her thighs.

First to break away, Azriel let out a low growl and drew his fangs across her throat. A shiver ran down her spine as he murmured huskily, "Your blood sings to me."

Ariadne released a breathy sigh. She could not remove the taste of him from her mouth, nor did she want to. The very memory of his blood gushing across her tongue, then through the hollows of her fangs, sent a rush through her core.

He groaned again, fingers weaving through her hair beneath the veil to ease her head back, exposing her throat and drawing the tip of his tongue up her neck. "Do you like that?"

"Yes," she gasped.

A light chuckle rumbled from deep in his chest. "I can smell how much you like me touching you, and it drives me out of my mind."

When he released her hair, Ariadne tilted her head back down to look him in the eyes. His heady gaze seared back at her with amusement. She leaned forward to kiss him again, and he sat back and away.

"What—"

"We'll be at the reception any minute," Azriel explained. "If we continue this now...we'll never make it there."

"Then let us go home."

Azriel closed his eyes, a smile curling his lips, and laid his head back with a sigh. "You'll be the death of me."

"Is that a no?" She drew her fingers down his throat to hold his cravat and tugged just hard enough to make him look at her.

"Patience," he murmured and dropped his forehead on her shoulder, arms wrapping tight around her waist. "Patience."

Ariadne huffed. "I believe I have been quite patient."

"I'm not speaking to you." His hands roved from her body to her bare knees and slowly slid up her thighs. "I'm reminding myself."

She stilled at the firm weight of his palms on her bare skin. Everything had been good and well with the clothes still between them—with his lips reminding her precisely who she was with. Flesh on flesh in such an intimate place sent her mind reeling into the dark depths of her memory.

Azriel froze and jerked back, removing his hands in a flash. "What's wrong?"

"Nothing," she said a little too quickly and shook her head with a small smile. She shifted down his legs, slipping off his lap to sit back on her own seat. "You are right. Patience."

"Ariadne." He frowned at her and sat forward again. "Don't do that."

"Do what?"

"Hide from me." His voice cracked. "Please."

The carriage slowed and stopped, saving Ariadne from explaining what terrors haunted her. She had hoped that, with time, those particular fears would have alleviated. Evidently, she was terribly mistaken.

Getting through her own wedding day without confronting her past became less and less of a possibility.

Ariadne adjusted her skirts and hair. "Is my lipstick—?"

"You're perfect."

The door opened, and a Rusan man she did not yet know stepped aside. Azriel exited the carriage without a word, held out his hand, and waited. She dropped her veil back into place before following suit.

Applause broke out from the awaiting wedding guests as she settled on the lantern-lit gravel path before her. The sudden shift from privacy to, once again, having all eyes on her caught the air in her chest. She slid closer to Azriel, drawing strength from his solid presence at her side.

"You ready?" Azriel murmured, his deep voice rumbling in his chest and through her.

The vibrations soothed her tension, so when he held out an arm, Ariadne slid her hand through the crook and followed when he started forward. She leaned in close so her cheek brushed his arm, focusing straight ahead to ignore the whispers and sharp looks.

At the end of the long path stood her father. Azriel released her and stepped forward so they could clasp arms. The Caersan men spoke in low voices for a moment, then her father reached up, grabbed the back of Azriel's head, and they pressed their foreheads together.

The customary gesture of acceptance eased a knot in Ariadne's stomach, so when her new husband retreated and she stepped forward, it was with a lighter heart.

"Daughter."

"Father."

He lifted the golden rose circlet from her head, then pulled the veil off completely. "I will miss you."

Not the words she expected to hear, and the sudden rise of emotions was far from what she anticipated feeling after so much fear and so many threats. Still, as her only parent left, she could not help the love she had for him.

She blinked back tears, eyes burning. When she spoke, her voice rasped from the tightness in her throat, "This is not goodbye."

"No," he admitted, and she bit her lip at the silver shimmer in his eyes. "But you will not return the same. You never do."

The nod to her abduction and her change since pushed her over the edge. Ariadne sucked in a strained breath, a tear rolling down her cheek. "But maybe this time, it will be for the better."

"I hope so." He gripped her shoulders, and they, too, pressed their foreheads together.

Despite the gesture lasting a mere breath, it cut deep as the moment that would change her life forever. Everything he had done throughout her life had led to this. Each decision—stepping up from General to Princeps after her mother's death, pushing her into her first Season to meet Darien, and piecing her back together in his own way after the abduction—paved the way for her to stand before him, about to leave him of her own accord.

"I love you," she whispered as he pulled away.

Her father did not smile. He did not cry, though his throat bobbed. Instead, he pushed back a curl, tucking it behind her ear as he did when she was a child, and kissed her forehead. Then he placed the circlet back on her hair.

Without a word, he took her hand and placed it in Azriel's. He patted it twice, nodded to her husband, and stood aside.

Before them sprawled a garden of night-blooming flowers, lush fruit trees, and stately shrubs with winding paths and tables speckled amongst small clearings. At its center lay a stone dance floor with a string quartet playing soft melodies. Tall lamp posts flared with life along each path, and small oil lanterns hung from the trees and bushes, sparkling like faerie magic. Decor of dusty rose and deep green adorned the chairs, tables, and benches.

Azriel huffed, drawing her attention up, and his brows creased. "The color you chose—"

"I chose it before everything happened." She laughed airily and shook her head. "I loved that fabric, you know, back at Revelie's."

His lips parted at the memory. "Why'd you choose it for your wedding?"

Your wedding—not *our* wedding. A clear distinction between what would have been and what came to be. Ariadne shrugged it off. "I suppose it made me happy after that night. I needed something to make me happy again."

At the edge of the garden dance floor, Azriel paused and stroked his thumb across her cheek. How he made her forget about the crowd watching them, Ariadne had no idea. But the way he looked at her in that moment made the very night turn to day, such warmth flooded her veins.

Perhaps she would make it through the day with him after all.

The first song to play had not been chosen by Ariadne. She stilled, knowing full well it was to be their first dance as a married couple. Traditions from the days as mages were hard for long-living Caersans to relinquish. Nonetheless, her instructions for the dance had been clear.

"What song is this?" She looked to the quartet.

Azriel smiled and pulled her to the dance floor. "It's what played the first time I ever saw you."

She could not recall the music from Vertium. Everything blended together, from the breathing exercises to the irritation at being assigned a new guard to the attack of the dhemons. The entire event had become a blur in her memories.

"How did you remember?"

His arm curled around her waist, bringing her body closer than she had ever danced with anyone before. Not so long ago, she had pulled away from any man attempting to hold her the way Azriel did as they moved through the steps.

"For the sake of honesty," he said quietly as a handful of dancers joined them, "I must confess that I've loved you, Ariadne, since the moment I laid eyes on you."

Ariadne gaped at him, her mind racing as a flutter in her stomach gave way to that rush of warmth. All the romantic tales of the fae described a single, unyielding connection between true lovers—something she never imagined to be real. Fae bonds were said to be unbreakable, immediate, and soul-deep. For one to form, however, could take centuries of searching for the correct individual, who were not always of fae descent.

"Can half-fae bond?" she whispered, feeling almost conspiratorial.

He swallowed hard and, seeming at a loss for words, nodded.

She twirled out, her stomach knotting again at the thought. Did he love her—choose and fight for her—only because of some uncontrollable force within himself? If he had had the choice, would he still choose her?

As she twisted back in, Ariadne forced herself to inhale deeply and clear her thoughts. Even if the bond had started it all, fae could reject them, though usually to their detriment. While fae females could stand their ground and break a bond without much harm to themselves, males often went mad at an unreciprocated bond. Had that been what caused him to want to leave so suddenly?

"Be honest with me," she said, chest searing at the possibilities of his answer. "Do you love me, or are you merely bonded to me?"

Azriel's face twisted with pain. "I love you, Ariadne, more than the breath in my lungs."

Tension eased from her, and she moved her hand from his shoulder to his face. He leaned his cheek into her palm as she asked, "Until the very end?"

"Until the very end."

Those four simple words held more weight than any vow spoken by the High Priestess. They sang through Ariadne like a melody, lighting her up from inside.

Ariadne leaned her cheek on Azriel's chest for the remainder of the dance, listening to his heart. Each steady beat synced with her own as though they had become one without her knowledge. Perhaps they had the moment they met. She found she did not mind it as much as she first thought. After all, it had been almost as long since she had chosen him, and even that had occurred without her realizing.

When the song ended, they wandered off the dance floor, hand in hand, to greet their guests. Caersans from all across the provinces made an appearance to give their congratulations. To Ariadne, none of them mattered. For Azriel's sake, she pressed on. He needed as many of the lords on his side as possible, particularly those from Eastwood.

Every event turned into a political spectacle, no matter how hard she tried to avoid it.

The next dance began. On the stone floor, Madan twirled Camilla, their eyes bright and jovial. Emillie watched from the sidelines, her gaze following Hyacinth Hooke as the young beauty swayed with Lord Moone.

If Ariadne could stop time, it would be on this night. This night, when everyone she loved appeared so happy and carefree and together. She wanted nothing more for them all, for as soon as morning came, everything would change.

CHAPTER 25

While summer remained the prime season for weddings, short nights meant the reception did not last as long as Ariadne had hoped. For once, she enjoyed the party, the people, and the attention. Those who whispered as she passed spoke of the classic style of dress and beautiful circlet—not backhanded compliments and guesswork.

Before she knew it, she took Azriel's hand and returned to the carriage. She settled into her seat, stomach growling. After speaking with so many people, she had been left with no time to enjoy the food. She rested her head back on the seat and closed her eyes.

The door shut behind Azriel, cutting off his final goodbyes. Their knees brushed as he adjusted his long legs in the space built for a Caersan man much smaller than he.

Then the scent of roasted chicken, herbs, butter, and fresh bread filled her nostrils.

Ariadne sat up, eyes flying open again to find Azriel cradling a plate towered with food. Her mouth watered, and her stomach rumbled again.

"I thought you might be hungry," he said and held out the plate, two forks stuck beneath the stacks of meat and vegetables. "I'm ravenous."

"Thank you." She eased the fork closest to her out and gathered up a scrap of everything. After several bites, she paused. Azriel had not moved except to balance the plate. "Are you not eating, too?"

Azriel scanned her face. "When you're finished."

She frowned. The last time someone scrutinized her eating had been after returning thin and weak from the mountains. She had refused food at first. It became easier to avoid it altogether after the dhemons used it against her—a reward for doing as they demanded during those daylight hours. Though she still ate much less than prior to the abduction, those negative connections did not hold the same weight in her life.

"Eat with me." She pulled the second fork from beneath the pile and held it out to him. "I want us to have our first meal as husband and wife together."

A light sparked in his gaze, and he took the fork after readjusting the plate to balance on his knees. "As you wish."

He dug into the food with her then. The carriage ride grew silent as they ate. For once, Ariadne did not feel the need to fill the reticence. His contentment at sitting with her as she was with him was worth every uncomfortable decision leading to that moment.

When the carriage slowed outside the Caldwell family's Laeton manor, Ariadne pursed her lips at the plate. "Did you eat the chicken?"

Azriel raised a brow. "Some. I prefer the vegetables."

"Do you not eat meat?"

"I do." He set the plate aside, forks resting on its near-empty surface. "I just don't eat much of it, I suppose."

Odd for a man of his size, whether half-fae or not. Though many high fae that she had met were, in fact, vegetarians, most were not. The lycans and dhemons, on the other hand, subsisted almost entirely on raw meat. Though it made no sense in her mind how it worked, any cooked meats made those fae ill.

Before she could inquire any more—had his father been vegetarian? Did Madan eat less meat, too?—the carriage door opened, and Azriel leapt out. He turned on his heel and held out a hand. "Welcome home."

Ariadne stepped down from the carriage, eyes glued to the manor before her. Though it towered over her, the size did not compare to the Harlow Estate. Once upon a time, she would have been bothered by its lack of grandeur. Her materialism used to rival other Caersan women; now she swept a discerning eye over it. This would be her first home with Azriel—the estate in Monsumbra would be her last.

"My Lord and Lady," called a red haired Rusan man as he flung the front doors open, "we are delighted to see you both!"

"Thank you, Petre." Azriel held out his arm, then led her up the steps and into the foyer.

Petre—whom Ariadne assumed to be the butler—bowed to them both. "The curtains are drawn around the house, and your things, my Lady, have been unpacked into your closet. Shall I—"

"That'll be all, thank you." Azriel smiled at the Rusan, who bowed again and disappeared down a hall.

"He seems lively."

With a snort, Azriel grinned at her. "He was quite reserved when we first met. Much has changed."

"It would seem that way."

"Would you like tea?" He nodded to the sitting room with a small, popping fire. "Or anything else to eat?"

Ariadne shook her head. "I would like to wash up before bed."

His eyes dipped down her body, and in an instant, she felt naked before him. At once, it sent a heated thrill through her and chilled her blood. She craved his touch, just as she had when they had kissed in the Harlow drawing room, when they had exchanged blood at the Temple of Keon, and during their heated exchange on the way to the reception. Many nights had passed since the duel when she thought of what it would be like to run her hands down his bare chest. It warmed her core, and she even relieved the mounting pressure herself alone in bed at times.

This morning, however, was different. It no longer remained a story in her mind, playing through every moment with idyllic precision. Now reality approached, and she ran toward it while simultaneously screaming to have a little more time to prepare.

But nothing prepared her for what happened with the dhemons. The moment meant to be shared with her husband—with Darien and now Azriel—had been stolen from her.

"Take your time," Azriel said after a breath, her racing thoughts nearly drowning out his words. His brows furrowed slightly. "Bella!"

A moment later, a Rusan woman with striking dark eyes, thick black twists, and dark skin strode in from the hall Petre had disappeared down. She curtsied, surveying Ariadne with a mixture of interest and reservation. "Yes, my Lord?"

Azriel's hand brushed Ariadne's low back. "Will you show Ariadne where she can wash up?"

"Of course." Bella smiled and gestured to the stairs. "Right this way, my Lady."

"Thank you," Azriel said to Bella, then turned to Ariadne and continued, "I'll be up in a moment."

Ariadne followed Bella up the sweeping staircase in silence. She frowned at the portraits on the walls. Some bore the images of the former Lord Governor Caldwell, while most depicted the same two Caersan women, both with dark hair and brilliant, peridot eyes. The elder, she guessed, was the Dowager Lady Caldwell per the wedding portrait at the landing. The younger woman, however, looked strangely familiar. Their daughter, most likely—killed, if Ariadne recalled correctly, by dhemons.

"What is her name?" She stopped abruptly at a portrait of the young Caersan woman, this time with a round belly, holding the hand of a small boy, his face neutral and pale green eyes almost solemn.

Bella paused. "Mariana. The late Lord Governor's daughter."

With a nod, Ariadne stepped a little closer. "And her son?"

"Yes." Bella moved a little closer. "I never met them."

"Why not?"

"They died before I was born, my Lady." Bella smiled grimly. "Many of these portraits were completed post-mortem and hung in memory of her."

"The Lord Governor must have been heartbroken." Ariadne's stomach sank, and she brushed a gentle finger over where the woman clasped the boy's hand. "For them all to die like that."

Bella hummed her soft agreement. "Unfortunately, he was no stranger to such tragedies. They plagued the Caldwell line for quite some time."

The price of being the first family to settle in the Keonis Valley. Without them, Valenul would never have been established. It put a target on their backs, though, which none of them could outrun. Except the elder Lady Caldwell, it would seem. A five-thousand-year-old Original vampire. Most were fortunate to live half as long, and yet somehow, she had been the sole Caersan to oversee the development of an entire kingdom.

"My apologies," Ariadne said and gave herself a quick shake.

The Rusan woman smiled. "Not a problem, my Lady. Shall we continue?"

"Please." She gestured to Bella, and they continued down the corridor. The long emerald runners, speckled with six-petaled white and red flowers, stretched out ahead of them. She studied the flowers as they walked, grappling with why they looked so familiar. "What flowers are these on the rug?"

Bella glanced down and said without looking back, "Gladiolus tristis. They're the Caldwell's family flower."

"The moonlight flower." Ariadne's breath caught. The single flower sent the night after Vertium. She had assumed it had been delivered from Alek, and the entire time, it had been Azriel.

"Yes, that." Bella stopped before a set of double doors and opened them with a flourish. "Would you like us to draw you a full bath?"

Ariadne shook her head. "That will not be necessary. Just a washing basin, please."

Without another word, Bella led her into the grand room beyond. From the high ceiling, painted with a mural of the heavens, hung a crystal chandelier. Massive curtains lined the far wall where, Ariadne guessed, they covered a large bay of windows. A set of plush chairs and a chaise sat before a welcoming fireplace with a gilded mantle. On either side of the hearth were closed doors, and across the room was another pair, this time open, leading to what appeared to be a washroom on one side and a closet on the other. What impressed her most were the bookshelves covering almost every inch of spare wall.

"This is magnificent," Ariadne breathed, staring at the vase of moonlight flowers on the thin table behind the couch. So it *had* been Azriel who sent that single flower after the Vertium ball.

"You will find all you need just over there, my Lady." Bella pointed to the washroom. "A basin has been prepared for you already."

"Thank you, Bella."

The Rusan woman curtsied again, then left.

The doors closed with a snap behind her, leaving Ariadne alone in the foreign room. She ignored the closed doors beside the fireplace and instead began a slow walk of the room, running her fingers along the spines of books as she went. The closet was, as she suspected, just that—though twice the size she was accustomed to. On one side hung her dresses, the traveling trunks set aside. Along the other, trousers and shirts and vests and jackets hung in moderation. At the far end, a gold-framed full-length mirror reflected back her uncertain expression.

She retreated from the closet and swept into the washroom, where she poured a splash of water into a wide silver basin. Scooping some of the cool liquid into her cupped hands, Ariadne splashed it on her cheeks and ignored the thundering of her heart.

In a few brief moments, Azriel would arrive, and she needed to center herself. Although he did not appear to be a man who expected anything from her, it remained their wedding morning. Certain expectations came along with such unions, and she had, once upon a time, ached for this night.

Gods, up until now, she had looked forward to it.

With the time upon her, however, Ariadne did not know what to do. She should tell him what happened with the dhemons—be open and honest about everything they did to her, for not all the damage was written on her skin. No, it remained engraved on her heart and mind and in the most intimate of places.

He would know soon enough whether she wanted him to or not.

Ariadne patted her face dry and leaned heavily on the wash basin's table. She stared at her distorted reflection in the water and took a long, deep breath.

Ten...

On and on, she counted her inhales and exhales. She made it to three before the doors of the suite opened again to jolt her from the breathing exercise. Swallowing hard, she looked up and into the mirror hanging before her instead. There she saw her husband pause at the washroom door and lean a shoulder against the threshold.

"What's wrong?" Not an accusatory question, nor did his rumbling voice sound demanding. Rather, his mossy eyes appeared sad and searching. Was the bond he claimed to have with her capable of feeling her emotions?

She smiled and turned to him. "Nothing."

Azriel shook his head, standing straight again and taking a single step closer. "You are not being entirely truthful."

"All is well," she said and, before her mind could hold her back, she closed the distance between them to press her lips to his. His scent filled her nose, so even when she could not see him, she knew who she touched.

At first, he melted into the kiss. He drew a hand across her jaw to cradle her head and deepen it, their tongues exploring one another's mouths. Then, as though remembering himself, Azriel froze and drew back just enough to say, "Please tell me what bothers you."

Ariadne tried to kiss him again, to make him and herself forget about it all as though he would not see everything for himself before long. When he pulled back to search her face, she sighed and glanced away. "I am certain you know what bothers me. Please do not make me say it."

"Alright." Azriel tucked a curl behind her ear and brushed a thumb over her lower lip. "Nothing has to happen between us. Ever, if you don't want it."

"I do."

He raised a speculative brow.

"I truly do—tonight, even." She bit her lip and cupped his face. "In part, I fear how you might react, if I am honest."

Now he frowned. "I wouldn't ever be angry or upset with you about something you couldn't control."

Pushing her hair aside, Ariadne's shaking fingers found and unclasped the golden buttons at the nap of her neck, then switched to the corset ties at her lower back. Her heart thundered in her ears. He would be the first to see her body since the abduction.

After a moment of watching her struggle, Azriel asked, "May I?"

"Please." She turned and ignored her reflection as he dipped lower to release the complex bindings. His steady hands made quick work of the dress, and bit by bit, piece by piece, it fell away until she stood before him as naked as in her imaginings.

As she suspected, Azriel stood stalk still, his face draining of color. He stared, unblinking, at her back. She had spent the last year very carefully curating her wardrobe. Some might have believed her to develop a taste for modesty, perhaps in the hopes of finding another suitor. In truth, the high backs and gossamer additions hid what shamed her the most: a slew of scars made permanent by fistfuls of salt.

After a moment, Azriel's fingers traced the largest set of them all—the scars, carved out numerous times by the same dhemon, bore that wretched name in all capitals.

EHRUN

It marked her as his for all to see, and the longer it took for Azriel to say something, the more her stomach knotted. Tears stung her eyes. She tilted her chin to the ceiling to blink them back in.

"I should have told you before the wedding," she rasped, silently cursing the cracking of her voice. "You deserved to know before making your decision—about the scars and the... the ra—"

"Stop." Azriel took hold of her wrist as he kicked away the dress and knelt before her. For a long moment, he stared up at her, his own eyes rimmed with silver, before pressing his forehead to her bare stomach and wrapping his arms around her legs. "That monster's actions could never keep me from you. I love you, Ariadne, until the very end. Do you know what that means?"

She sucked in a burning breath. "Hmm?"

He looked up at her again and slowly stood, his hands running up her thighs and waist as he went. "It means I breathe for you—every single part of you—until this very universe ceases to exist, and even then, the void of eternity could not keep me from you."

Words failed her. After Darien's death, she assumed marriage would be a contractual obligation. Loren's interest in her—prior to the reveal of his true nature—had been more than she had hoped for. She believed she could love him as he had hinted he loved her.

With Azriel, everything happened naturally. After he put himself between her and the dhemons attacking on Vertium, she trusted him. He understood her, it seemed, better than she understood herself. When he avoided her after the lashings, it ate away at her. Now she knew the reason why: she loved him even then.

To have him see her—all of her—without questioning his love was incomprehensible.

"I love you, too," she whispered, the tears finally breaking free and sliding down her cheeks. She wiped them away with the heel of her hand.

Azriel released a long breath as though he had held it, awaiting her response. He wrapped his arms loosely around her again. "I meant what I said—nothing has to happen."

She shook her head against him and laughed quietly before leaning her chin on his chest to look up at him. "No, Azriel. I need you to rewrite it all with me. I need *you*."

Cursing under his breath, he stooped down and swept her up into his arms, planting his mouth on hers as he walked from the washroom. The cool air shifted across her bare skin, sending goosebumps up and down her body. His insistent exploration of her lips and tongue tightened her core and puckered her nipples.

They did not make it to the bedroom before Azriel laid her down. When he pulled away, she found herself on the chaise lounge before the fireplace, the flames' warmth licking up her toes and ankles. He shouldered out of the jacket and yanked the cravat from his neck, all the while eyeing her body laid out before him. Off went the vest, and by the time his hands reached the buttons of his shirt, he bent over to kiss her again. This time his lips trailed along her jaw and neck, drawing a small gasp from her as, once again, her entire body tightened with that heated sensation.

Ariadne drew her knees together, hips shifting so her thighs rubbed her sex. His shirt fell away, exposing the scarred chest and back she had already seen.

He laid a heavy hand on her stomach, lips brushing against her earlobe as he said huskily, "If you ever want to stop, say so. No questions asked—we'll stop."

She nodded her acknowledgment, his words of under-standing only heating her core more.

His hand slid down her body to her hips and held firm, slowing the grinding she had already begun and leaving her wanting more. Before she could express this, Azriel sank to his knees beside the chaise. He gripped her thigh, just above the knee closest to him, and urged it wide so the air—a sensational mix of temperatures—rushed against her exposed, slick sex.

Slow and steady, he drew his fingers up and rested the heel of his hand against her bud. Mouth moving from her neck to her collarbone, he said, "Now keep going."

When she moved her hips again, that wonderful, tight heat washed through her. So different was it from her own hand that she could not stop the light moan that escaped her. She felt more than saw—gods, her eyes could not focus on anything—Azriel grinning against her skin before pulling a taut nipple into his mouth and sucking.

He paused as she gasped, releasing the tip and drawing his tongue over it again languidly. "Do you like that?"

"Yes," she said, breathlessly grinding her clit against his hand. Each movement wound her up a little more, searching for the release she knew would come with time.

"Good." He kissed his way from one breast to the other and swirled his tongue around the other nipple. He drew it into his mouth and sucked again, that magnificent tongue flicking along its tip. When he let it slowly pull from his lips, he locked eyes with her and said, "I want to taste you. Is that okay?"

For a moment, Ariadne did not know what that meant. She blinked down at him, her sluggish brain scrambling to keep up with what it was he wanted next. It was not until he removed his palm from her mound, letting his fingers slip between her folds before bringing them to his mouth, did she understand.

A new fire burned in her at the very thought of that talented tongue against her sex. He licked the wetness from his fingertips, and she let her head fall back as she said, "Gods, yes."

He adjusted his seat to the end of the chaise and, holding her hips firm, dragged her to the edge. She squealed, her smile mirroring his. Azriel stretched her thighs wide, draping one leg over his broad shoulder, and drew his fangs down the soft, sensitive flesh of her inner leg. The anticipation built. His eyes almost glowed as he watched her every breath. The closer he moved, the more she twisted in his grasp, hips thrusting up to meet him.

The warmth of his mouth on her sex nearly sent her over the edge on its own. She gasped again, a hand flying to his hair. He pinned her hip to the chaise with one hand, eyes still boring into her. His tongue, gentle and firm all at once, slipped between her folds to lap her up. Azriel groaned against her, and the rumble vibrated against her clit.

As though eager for more, he pulled her even closer and dragged his tongue along her opening. Its soft prodding made her moan again.

Yet each taste, each lick, each slow, savoring movement of his tongue only built her up toward what he did next. His free hand drifted up and across her belly to grasp a breast firmly. Her back arched into his touch, begging for more. More. More of his hands on her—more of his mouth worshiping her.

And he did not disappoint. He licked again, the heat of his tongue drawing right across her clit before he shifted from stroking it to sucking it.

Ariadne cried out, unable to contain the burst of pleasure rocketing through her as she climaxed. Her core pulsed, and she ground her hips against his mouth, riding the wave. Still, he held her firm, so when her eyes opened again, she found him watching her writhe beneath his touch.

With a final, leisurely flick of his tongue, Azriel withdrew. "You taste magnificent."

Despite the still-dissipating orgasm, heat ricocheted through Ariadne again. All at once, she felt sated, and yet her sex ached for more—something she never imagined possible after all she had endured. Still, she reached between her legs to hold his face and urge him up to kiss his wet lips. A strange thrill rolled through her at the taste of herself lingering on him.

"I want more," she whispered against his neck and slid her hand down his chest to where his hard length strained against the trousers still buckled fast. Though not entirely certain what to do, she gripped what she could and drew her palm up and down over him.

Braced above her, Azriel groaned as he stretched his head to the side to expose his throat to her fangs. "Anything you desire—it's yours."

"You—all of you."

Ariadne sank her fangs into his neck, his blood rushing out and across her tongue in a tangy symphony. She closed her eyes, relishing the taste of him almost as much as he had savored her. Perhaps she could return the favor. The concept seemed simple enough. She merely needed to figure it out.

As she drank from him, her fingers fished for the buttons of his trousers. He remained steady as she found her way by touch. Without much trouble, she unfastened the waistband and pushed the trousers down from his hips.

When she released his neck, blood dribbled from the puncture wounds. For a beat, she worried his slower healing abilities would inhibit them from closing properly.

Azriel did not let her think on it. He dove his mouth to hers and pressed his hard, heavy cock into the palm of her waiting hand. She wrapped her fingers around the thick girth and stroked, the velvety soft skin shifting beneath her touch. His soft moan of pleasure filled her up.

He hummed against her lips. "Gods, Ariadne...is this what you want?"

"More than anything," she breathed and walked her shoulders back so he could kneel between her thighs. "I want *all* of you."

It was more true than she could have ever imagined. That Azriel would be the one to wash away the terrors she had lived with for so long made her entire body tight with anticipation. She needed it—needed him.

"Are you—"

"Shh," she cut him off and kissed him again, still stroking his incredible length. Up and down, slow and steady, up and down. "Do *not* stop."

She breathed in deep so his scent enveloped her. Her eyes remained open so she could watch him, haloed by the firelight. Anything to ensure her mind stayed present with Azriel.

Azriel.

Only Azriel.

With that, Ariadne angled the head of his cock to the entrance of her slick, throbbing sex. He eased forward, the blunt tip pushing into her. The pressure heightened the heat pulsing through her core, and she tilted her hips to provide a better angle.

At first, his sheer size and gentleness kept him at bay. She slid a hand down his back, against his backside, and pressed down, urging him forward. He followed her silent command and thrust with more vigor. Each pump of his hips pushed the length of him deeper and deeper.

Ariadne sucked in a sharp breath as he filled her. He paused at the small noise, but she shook her head. "Keep going."

It was all he needed to hear, and with each subsequent thrust, the foreign pressure and fullness turned to pleasure. Before long, Ariadne moaned. She finally understood what made this act so unbearably tempting for men and women alike. As she gave herself over to him, that hot tension built within her again.

Azriel kissed her hard, their bodies working in tandem. He gripped her breast, rolled the hard nipple between his fingers, and pulled it lightly. A gentle tease to coexist with him pounding into her wet sex. Each moan he drew from her only drove his hips harder until she knew every inch of his cock slid in and out of her.

It did not take long for her to find his rhythm. She bent a knee to better grind against his pelvis, and he folded onto his forearms to bring them closer. His hot, heavy body draped over her, providing a better angle.

She twisted her fingers into his hair and tilted her head back. Azriel did not need more of an invitation—he struck, fangs sinking into her neck. At first, a sharp pain jolted through her. She stilled long enough to adjust to the feeling of him penetrating not only her sex but now also her throat. The overwhelming claim he placed on her body—her soul—burned through her as each pull of her vein synchronized with the pounding of his cock.

And she understood then why couples only fed from the wrist at the wedding. The sensation of his mouth on her neck sent her spiraling into euphoria. He had appeared to enjoy it when she partook of his throat. Now she knew he had held back.

Her climax shattered her into a thousand pieces. She cried out, and her sex pulsed along his cock. He thrust hard, riding the wave of the orgasm until it rippled through him as well. Releasing her throat, he swallowed back a shout of ecstasy and buried his face beside the unpunctured side of her neck.

As she floated back to reality, her body slowly stitching together again, Ariadne breathed hard. She shifted beneath him, still relishing the feeling of his cock inside her. When he kissed her neck and pulled himself free, she was left with a strange sensation of emptiness. He had filled her so perfectly, she did not want it to end.

"You are perfect," he murmured and kissed her softly.

She hummed her satisfaction. "I love you."

Azriel laughed breathily, pushing back to kneel between her legs again. "I love you more than I can ever say."

Ariadne took in his impressive figure. Every curve of muscle and jarring line of scars. Each one of them, good and bad, made up the man she loved and chose over all others. Given the chance, she would do it all over again.

Marriage to Ariadne placed Azriel in a strange, personal hell. Everything from her adoration to the full trust she put in him with her body tormented the sane piece of himself. Yet somehow, it soothed his less controllable aspects and eased the pressure of the bond. Each time she reminded him of her love, that horrible monster inside purred with delight while his mind screamed for her to run.

For Ariadne Harlow didn't love Azriel Caldwell. She loved the version of himself that he carefully constructed to entice her. If she knew who he'd been before their first meeting, she'd never speak to him again.

And it shredded his soul as he kissed her sleeping brow later that day before pulling on loose trousers and slipping from the suite barefoot. After their time on the chaise, he'd carried her to their bedroom and entwined their bodies a second time. Between the exertion and excitement of the night, Ariadne fell asleep as he held her, cursing himself for every second of it all.

Azriel descended to the main floor of the house, the heat of the summer day seeping through the closed curtains. In the foyer, he followed the sound of low voices to the kitchen, where a handful of the Rusan staff sat around a small table, eating their dinner before bed. Sunlight poured into the room, and he paused in a ray to soak up its warmth. Sometimes being a half-breed bastard had its perks.

"My Lord?" Petre called from the table as the conversation rolled to a halt. Five pairs of eyes widened at his lack of clothing.

"I'm looking for my brother."

"Ah, yes." Petre stood and made to lead the way out of the kitchen.

Azriel held up a hand. "Just tell me where and I'll find him. Rest."

"The library." Petre bowed.

After a quick, thankful inclination of his head, Azriel turned and left them to their meal. Whispers followed him into the hall. Not accepted by the Caersans and no longer a member of the staff. An awkward place to be.

The library, while not as extensive as at the Harlow Estate, still stretched high enough to require a sliding ladder to reach the top shelves. Dark wood gleamed with polish, not a speck of dust in sight. Madan lounged near the center of the room, a safe distance from the draped windows, and read by candlelight. His full Caersan blood barred him from the same daylit pleasures as Azriel.

"Brother." Madan, draped across a deep blue couch, didn't look away from the small book balanced precariously between his fingers over his face. "Enjoying your morning?"

Azriel collapsed into a chair near his brother's feet. "Yes. No."

He leaned forward, elbows to knees, and pressed his fists against his eyes. The short walk through the manor had been enough to rattle his nerves. There was too much to say.

The shift of paper told Azriel that Madan turned a page. "Care to share or just here to cry about it?"

"You know what I'm thinking." He looked up, brows drawn tight.

"Yes." Madan's marbled eyes flickered to him, then back to the book at hand. "And you know there's nothing left to be done."

"Maybe I shouldn't have—"

"I swear to every god listening," Madan sighed and set the book on his chest to glare at him, "if you say you shouldn't have married her—again, mind you—I will fucking throttle you. You made your decision and now must live with the consequences."

"She's been ruined by me." Azriel shook his head. "If anyone found out the truth, she'd be shunned."

Madan rolled his eyes. "Everyone knows you're half-fae. What's done is done."

A long silence stretched between them. Madan picked up his book and began reading again while Azriel leaned his head back to stare at the ceiling. His stomach clenched and twisted into sickening knots.

He opened and closed his mouth several times, unable to voice the words until finally, he said, "They forced themselves on her."

Madan said nothing. Only silence closed in on him, drowned out only by the blood pounding in his ears.

"I heard it happen—I heard her begging them to stop," Azriel's throat tightened, and a fresh wave of rage heated him. "I'd hoped it wasn't true, but she confirmed it for me tonight."

He looked to his brother when there was no reply. Madan's face, paler than usual, spoke volumes. "I know."

Everything stilled. Azriel grit his teeth hard as Madan pushed himself to a sitting position on the far end of the couch. A wise choice with the way Azriel's hands twitched.

"What?" His voice didn't rise above a gravelly whisper.

"I know everything that happened to her." Madan surveyed him like he was an angry, cornered animal. "I heard Ehrun talk about it afterward."

"And you didn't tell me?"

Madan shook his head. "I gave her a tea on our way to Laeton to ensure—"

"What the *fuck*, Madan?" Azriel shot to his feet and drew his fingers through his hair, heart slamming against his ribs. Every fiber of his being demanded he return to the mountains and finish what he'd started. He itched to wrap his fingers around Ehrun's neck and watch the life drain from his eyes, then shred his corpse and force-feed it to the grunts who helped him torture her. "Why wouldn't you tell me something like this?"

"Would you rather her get pregnant by them?" Madan snapped back and stood, squaring off in front of him. His finger remained in the book to mark his page.

"That's not what I mean, and you know it." Azriel stared at him. That Madan had had the foresight to provide her with such a concoction was a blessing. The secrets he'd kept, however... "I'd have rather *known*."

"So you could do what?"

"I would've killed every single one of them."

"No!" Madan stepped forward and threw the book onto the couch. "No, Azriel, you would have *died*!"

Azriel bared his fangs at his brother. "Traitor."

"You saw what happened to your father against Ehrun!" Madan took another step closer, undeterred by Azriel's temper. "If *he* fell, you would've been annihilated at best—or kept as their fucking plaything."

None of it registered. The words were mere hot air making no sense. Madan had kept the truth from him and actively prevented him from exacting the vengeance owed to him.

"She is my *mate*, and you'll never understand—"

Madan laughed. Azriel's blood boiled at the sound. None of this was a joke. None of it was funny. None of it should be met with any amount of mirth.

"She is your *wife*." Madan jabbed his bare chest with a finger. "As you've reminded Whelan and me many times, *mates* are reserved for reciprocated bonds."

The edges of his vision blurred, and he sucked in a deep, calming breath. "Get out of my house."

Another laugh. "Oh, it's *your* house now? After all you've claimed about us working together?"

"Get the fuck out."

Madan's grin faded. "It's midday."

Azriel turned and stalked to the doors, flexing his fingers into fists again and again. "Then I better not see you when night falls, or I'll fucking kill you myself."

He ripped open the door as Madan called, "As you wish, *dhomin*."

Ice flooded Azriel's veins at the dhemon word. It'd been a great while since he'd heard it at all. It'd been even longer since it was directed at him. He paused, allowing the discomfort to run its course, then slammed the door and retreated to his rooms.

Chapter 26

Marrying Azriel felt right. Ariadne's entire life turned upside down the night they pledged themselves to one another—body and soul. Something lifted from her which had, for too long, kept her pinned in the dark, melancholy world of her grief and self-pity. Once more, she basked in the beauty of what life had to offer.

Perhaps that was what happened when someone listened and empathized.

Their first night together, Ariadne did not see much of the manor. She explored nothing beyond their luxurious suite, where the servants drew her a steaming bath of milk and honey, and she drank tea or wine and indulged in platters of food brought up to them. Her favorite activity soon became the hours spent tumbling through the sheets, learning every surface of Azriel's body.

The second and third nights, they ventured forth from their comfortable confines. He gave her a tour of the manor despite his minimal knowledge of the Caldwell family history. In comparison to the Harlow Estate, the smaller house and garden did not take long to get through. They asked questions of the servants, and both Petre and Bella were happy to oblige.

It was not until the following night, as they laid in bed together, arms and legs entangled and their bodies hot from exertion, that Ariadne finally asked, "Shall we go to town?"

Azriel stilled at the question, the back of his fingers stroking down her side—not her back, never her back—then kissed her shoulder and said, "Promise me something."

"Hmm?" She arched her body to get a better look at him.

In the dim light of the low fire, his eyes almost glowed red as they reflected the coals. "Never leave the grounds—neither here nor in Monsumbra—without me. Never."

Ariadne frowned and ran her fingers over the network of scars on his chest. "Why?"

"I won't make you travel with a guard," he said, searching her face, "because I don't trust anyone to keep you safe."

She snorted a laugh. "Except yourself?"

"Gods," he breathed and kissed her softly. "I don't even trust myself. But yes."

Pursing her lips, Ariadne squirmed back a bit. Her stomach sank at the seriousness on his face. "Why do I need a guard now that we are married?"

Azriel did not respond right away. His brows pinched up in the center, and he wound one of her dark curls around his finger. The reticence drew out as he decided on his words. His jaw flexed, and he sucked in a long breath before saying, "There's been reports of more dhemon sightings in Laeton."

"In town?" Her heart felt heavier with every beat. After the attack at Laeton Park, she had thought them to be more cautious. Those monsters were, as she well knew, persistent and unyielding.

"On occasion." He scanned her face again. "And they're after me."

Ice cold dread leaked into her gut. For a long moment, the air seized in her chest. Everything made sense. The bolt on Vertium had not been aimed at her but at her guard, standing right beside her. The dhemons in the park did not come after her—they focused on Azriel and anyone who stood in their way. Gracen died to keep her husband from their clutches. The question, then, became: *why* were they after him?

"Was this discussed by the Council?" She ran her finger over the brand on his chest—the twin to her own.

He dropped the twist of curl and rolled onto his back, closing his eyes. "No. No one else knows."

Ariadne gaped at him. She sat up, pulling the sheets up to her chest as she moved to stare at him. "Then how do you know?"

"The dhemon that attacked us in the park told me."

When he spoke their language. Ariadne had been so overwhelmed by the very appearance of the dhemons that she had forgotten. Almost as though their presence numbed her mind. After all, she knew what happened when someone tried to disobey a dhemon.

Their name got carved into your back night after night, and they sent others to visit your cell day after day as a constant reminder of who was in control.

Her blood chilled. "What does that have to do with me?"

Azriel's eyes snapped open and swiveled to where she sat. They almost glowed through the darkness. "Because they know what you mean to me."

And just like they tortured Darien, they would use her to get to him. "Why do they want you so badly?"

"They blame me for their leader's death." He draped an arm over his eyes as though blocking out the world would shield him from its evils.

Yet the evil of the dhemons always prevailed. She had attempted to keep them at bay in the same way many times. The true haunting lived in her mind and stalked her thoughts, just as they seemed to do to Azriel.

Then it dawned on her. That timeline did not match up. The Dhemon King, the Crowe, died the night Madan rescued her. She had seen him, in fact, as they escaped, with two more dhemons in his wake. They ran in the opposite direction—into the mountain keep where Ehrun fought with her kidnapper. The memory flashed through her mind, vivid as the night she had witnessed it. The one and only time she had laid eyes on the Crowe.

"You were there." She stared at her husband, breath caught in her lungs. "You were in the mountains with Madan."

Slowly—oh, so slowly—Azriel removed the arm from his face. Through the dim light, she watched the color drain from his cheeks. "Yes."

She had always wondered how Madan got in and out of the keep unscathed. No dhemons had seen them, except the Crowe and his cronies. He had slowed just enough to take in Madan and her before barrelling on. One of his companions stopped completely to gape at them yet never moved to stop them. While she knew her old guard's skills outranked most soldiers, Madan never drew his sword.

Someone else had to distract the dhemons to get her out.

"You could have died," she breathed, the words burning in her throat. Her fingers curled a little tighter around the sheets in her hands. "You got us both out."

No wonder he had dueled Loren like a dhemon. Such skills were needed to clear a path for their escape. Without it, he would have fallen. Without it, Madan would have been killed. Without it, she never would have been freed.

Azriel watched her like a caged animal, eyes wide and lips parted in fear. All he said in response was another simple, "Yes."

"Why did you keep it from me?" She frowned lightly, heart throbbing from the secrecy. "Why would you not say anything to anyone? You would have been praised the same as Madan this entire time."

"I told you," he said, gravelly voice quiet, "I bonded with you the moment I saw you."

"There was music playing when you first saw me."

He chuckled airily. "I'd visited Valenul and filled in as a guard the night you were taken. Outside. I saw you through the windows with Darien Gard."

How had it felt for him that night? To have a bond snap into place without notice, as it did with the fae, and endure watching her with another man? Her fiance, at that.

"When you were taken," he continued and returned the arm over his eyes with a shuddering breath, "I saw the soldier below your window die—saw you carried from the balcony—and pursued you relentlessly."

Had he been on the same route as Darien? That they never crossed paths was strange. It made sense, though, if Azriel went to find Madan to assist. Their home, so close to the dhemon keep in Eastwood Province, provided a central location to meet, plan, and prepare. All were pieces to a dangerous puzzle that Darien did not have.

"Despite all you did," she said, "you let Madan take all the credit. Why?"

"Your father knew I had a hand in it. Madan told him I'd provided shelter for you after."

She shook her head and clutched at her throat. They had downplayed his assistance even to her. "Why? Why lie at all? Why not tell him—tell *me*—the truth?"

"Like you said." Azriel exchanged the arm for both hands to rub his face. "I almost died."

How different her life would be in that moment had he not survived the dhemon keep. Mere nights ago, she would have married Loren, oblivious to his capacity for abuse. Would she have loved him still? The very thought of it all made her stomach roil. Azriel had become as important to her as the moon in the sky—a beacon of light amidst the darkness in her life.

"Yet you did not." Ariadne slid closer and gently peeled his hands from his face, the sheets dropping from her grip. She laid across his bare chest to hear the strength in his heart. "And you did not come back until Vertium."

Azriel drew his fingertips up her arm before brushing them across her cheek. "This—us, together—wasn't a possibility at the time. To be so close, to see you with someone else...I couldn't—"

His voice broke, and the words faded. Again, his hands went to his face, hiding him behind his palms. Ariadne stilled as his chest heaved beneath her. She did not know what to do. She had never seen a man succumb to his softer emotions in such a manner. Particularly not someone she loved.

"Azriel," she said quietly and touched his wrist. "Azriel, I did not mean to make you think on such things."

He shook his head, curled his fingers into fists, and pressed them against his eyes as he loosed a shuddering breath. A tear slipped down the side of his face. "It's not your fault. I'm not sad. I'm happy. Elated, even."

"Then why ever are you crying?"

"The gods have blessed me more than I deserve."

Ariadne's face softened and shifted to kiss the curve of his jaw. "You deserve the world for all you have done."

The fists lifted away from his eyes, and Azriel gave her a melancholy smile. Without another word, he pulled her up to kiss her softly. He pushed her hair back from her face, and she lost herself to him again.

Soltium arrived sooner than Azriel anticipated. Leaving the manor and giving up the precious time he had alone with his wife didn't sit high on his list of priorities. He'd freeze time if he could to prevent the outside world from interfering with his happiness.

For it poked and prodded its way into his life more often than not. Papers piled onto his study desk, a sign of his neglect as Governor. Letters and documents describing the ins and outs of Eastwood Province from Lord Knoll, requesting lands and tax extensions, required his signature and blessing.

Even as he sat at the desk to pour over the legal papers and contracts, he couldn't focus. Two drastically different thoughts stole into his mind.

The first, which he preferred over all else, was how he and Ariadne could make better use of the desk's surface. If she were to so much as poke her head around the door, he would sweep the pages away and replace them with her. He'd indulge in her body—a far more pleasant way to spend his evenings.

Yet no matter how much he tried to focus on the work laid out before him or even the fantasies of what he'd rather be doing, he couldn't stop the less-palatable intrusive thoughts. Those of his brother.

After sending Madan away almost a week ago, Azriel hadn't heard a word from him—nor had Razer, his one constant connection to the Caersan. Above all, that frightened him most.

With almost five centuries of life together, fights with his brother were nothing new, and Azriel had gone weeks without seeing or speaking to him. They'd threatened each other's lives before, yet most often, their disagreements ended in blows. Madan had given him many of the scars on his body, including a rather gruesome stab wound to his gut. While Azriel knew he'd given Madan just as many in return, his brother's full Caersan lineage hid the damage beneath the quick-healing properties in his blood.

Bastard.

Throughout it all, however, he always knew of Madan's whereabouts, thanks to their telepathic friends. Between his link to Razer and Madan's to Brutis, they'd never been able to stray far from one another.

It was the threat of dhemons closing in on Laeton that made Azriel wary of the silence. Perhaps Madan had quietly returned to Eastwood Province. It would've been the wise choice as he still owned a small house in Asterbury where he and Whelan often spent days together. The estate in Monsumbra was more likely, however.

Getting there safely, though? Impossible. Madan had as big a target on his back as Ariadne, and Brutis wouldn't be able to carry him there unseen. It'd be by horseback or carriage alone.

Azriel shook the image of his brother, dead on the side of the highway, from his mind. This is exactly what the dhemons wanted. The more he panicked, the more likely he was to slip up.

No news was good news, he told himself again and again. Madan was safe.

Madan had to be safe. Because if Madan wasn't safe, he'd rain hellfire down on every last monster who dared raise a hand against him. He'd done it before. He'd do it again.

A soft knock on the study door dragged him from the sudden rush of white-hot fury. He loosened his grip on the pen in his hand so it dropped to the desk, a crack running from the nib through the handle. His hands shook, and he pressed his palms onto the desk to keep them steady.

"Enter."

Ariadne slipped into the room, her dark hair braided into a crown around her head. "It is time."

He stared at her, mind blank for a long moment.

"To go to the Dodd's," she supplied with a small smile. "Are you ready?"

The Dodd's for Soltium. The summer solstice meant being locked away in a manor with close friends and family to celebrate the longest day of the year. By doing so in a closed home, curtains drawn and doors locked, Caersan vampires could make use of the entire manor without fear of the sun.

He'd seen what happened to pure-blood vampires when they contracted aegrisolis. The steady decay of a living vampire caused by the exposure to sunlight made his stomach churn. Mere minutes in daylight provided enough time to set the process in motion at a cellular level, and after many nights, the blight would finally claim the sorry soul.

Which was why he'd killed any vampire he met suffering from aegrisolis.

It's midday.

He'd tried to make his brother leave at the sun's highest point of the day. It could've been Madan he killed next—out of mercy.

"Azriel?" Ariadne took a step closer.

He shook his head to clear away the gruesome thought. Madan was due to be at Camilla's for the celebrations. They could make amends then.

"My love." He pressed heavily into his palms and stood to walk around the broad, wood desk. "I'm ready."

Color flushed her cheeks. "What did you call me?"

Warmth flooded his chest, and Azriel closed the distance between them in two long steps. His fingertips brushed over her collarbone before curling around the back of her neck, thumb stroking her cheek. She tilted her head back to look at him with wide eyes, and he pressed his lips to hers, gentle and restrained. When he pulled back, he said, "My love. Are you not?"

Ariadne pulled her lower lip in as though savoring the kiss, a smile curling at the corners of her mouth. "I am, yes."

Oh, if he hadn't already claimed to be ready to leave, he'd take her right then. Between the flush of her cheeks and the curve of her mouth, she appeared the same as when she wished for more than a kiss. Most nights, he'd happily indulge her—if she hadn't glanced at the door.

It'd been nights since she'd seen her sister and best friends. To keep her from them any longer than necessary would be cruel, particularly when she would soon go weeks or even months between visits.

"Hmm," he growled and pulled her close so their bodies pressed together. "I'd be satisfied locking that door and keeping you to myself all night, but I suppose I can share you this once."

The smile broke free, her fangs flashing. "How generous of you."

"I can be," he said huskily, bending to nudge his face into the crook of her neck. He inhaled her floral fragrance and released the breath with a groan. "Sometimes."

"It is strange, being married," she mused. He stilled, then pulled away again to look at her, waiting for her elaboration. "I feel like the same person—*you* feel like the same person to me—and yet we have both changed so much."

Azriel raised a brow. "How so?"

"I am more... peaceful. Like all my worries have somehow disappeared." Ariadne ran her hands up his chest, her nimble fingers pinching the lapel of his vest as she studied the brocade. "And you seem so much more at ease, even with your new responsibilities."

He twirled a loose curl around a finger before pushing it behind her ear, chest swelling. "I am. And I can't express how it makes me feel to hear you say all of that. If I can be honest...I've been so worried you've regretted your choice."

Her eyes lit up at his words, and she lifted onto her toes to peck his lips. "Never."

The single word should've made his heart soar. It should've caused pride to burst forth. It should've been all he needed to hear to feel even an ounce of that peace she spoke of.

Instead, his stomach soured, and a lump grew in his throat. The very air around him drew thin with each breath. She didn't mean it, even if she didn't know it yet.

But he smiled, kissed her back, and said almost imperceptibly against her lips, "Please always remember that."

To his utter despair, she whispered back, "Until the very end, my love."

CHAPTER 27

E millie paced the foyer of the Dodd Estate as the warm
night air settled in the latest arrival's wake. Captain Nikolai Jensen bowed and kissed her fingers with a sweep of his
cloak before excusing himself to the parlor filled with the
other guests waiting for the Soltium celebrations to begin.
Why in the world he had been invited, she had no idea, but
pleasantries were still required.

At least the shamed Loren Gard did not seem to be making
an appearance.

Neither, however, did her sister. Ariadne had promised to
prolong her stay in Laeton to attend the Dodds' festivities, yet
failed to make her arrival on time.

Newlyweds.

Each time the door opened, Emillie whirled around, heart
lurching, and each time the disappointment swallowed her
back up. Mere nights apart, and she already missed her sister's
presence in the manor. Quiet though Ariadne often was, it left
a gaping hole in her life.

No more breaking their fasts together or reading in silence,
side by side, in the library. Most nights, Emillie hardly left her

rooms. Why bother when all she would do was move about the house with her nose in a book? Sul's attention was superfluous with how little she did over the last week.

That would soon change. With the Golden Rose wed a mere halfway through the Season, the eyes of suitors turned to her. Soltium's opening night would be her first ball since she became the only unwed Harlow woman in the household, and her father's expectations had never been higher.

All the while, she finally felt more confident to explore her true self. Her father would receive a rude awakening soon when she entertained no suitors.

The door opened behind her, letting in a breeze of summer night air. Emillie sucked in a breath and turned to finally see Ariadne sweep across the threshold with Azriel in her wake. The former lit up with a smile at the sight of her while the other maintained his usual mask of neutrality, an arm loosely swept around his wife's back to rest his hand on her hip. His sharp, eagle-like gaze swept through the foyer before landing on her. He allowed a small smile.

"Ari!" Emillie shot forward to pull her sister from the Lord Governor. She squeezed Ariadne's hand once before being dragged into a tight embrace. Her heart skipped a beat. Hugs were far from the norm, so she took the opportunity to wrap her arms around her sister. "I missed you."

"And I, you." Ariadne stepped back and held her at arm's length. "I do not like being apart from you."

Emillie raised her brows. "Says the one on the brink of moving away."

Her sister glanced at Azriel, then grimaced. "Let us not speak of it now."

"Ah, Lord Governor!"

All three of them turned to the parlor where Lord Dodd exited, arms wide in greeting. His pale blond hair, a match to Camilla's, shone below the crystal chandelier. As he approached, brown eyes glittering and hazy from alcohol consumption, his grin widened. The apple did not fall far from the tree with this family and their openness.

"Welcome!" Lord Dodd held out his arm, which Azriel accepted with a nod. "Another hearty congratulations to you and your bride. You are welcome here any time, just as she has been all these years."

"You are most generous." Azriel's voice rumbled with his reply. "Thank you for the invitation for Soltium."

Lord Dodd chuckled. "We are honored you chose our halls to celebrate for the next few days and nights."

"The pleasure is mine."

"Come," the Lord said and gestured to the parlor. "Join me for a drink and to meet my associates. They are eager for an introduction."

With a nod, Azriel turned to Ariadne and took up her hand. He kissed her fingers, murmured something low, then followed Lord Dodd out of the foyer. What he said to her, Emillie could not fathom, for when her sister turned back around, her cheeks shone a rosy pink.

"Is everything alright?" Emillie asked with raised brows.

Ariadne smoothed the front of her skirts. "Quite."

"You look flustered."

The flush deepened. "Not at all. Where is Camilla?"

The sudden change of topic did not go unnoticed. Considering the subject matter, however, Emillie let it go. Whatever Azriel had said to her sister, it was meant for the two of them alone. "You know how she is—making an entrance draws more attention than being on time. Particularly when it is your own house."

Laughing, Ariadne tucked her arm through hers and pulled her toward the stairs. "Then let us go to her."

"Are you certain?" Emillie looked back to the parlor filled with Caersans paying no attention to them absconding away.

Her father held out his arm to Azriel, their greeting lost in the distance and din of conversation. Other Caersan men gathered around to speak, but before she could see much else, her feet hit the bottom stair, and she tripped forward.

Ariadne gave her an exasperated look. "When has Camilla ever given us the time to collect ourselves before barging into our rooms? It is our turn."

This was a side of her sister that Emillie had not seen in quite some time. Over the last year, Ariadne had been reserved, save for the occasional biting response. Quiet acquiescence to their father's whims had taken hold of her—until, of course, the duel between Loren and Azriel. That night changed everything.

The wedding only solidified the shift from the ghostly shadow to the woman Ariadne had once been. Outspoken, thrill-seeking, and mischievous. Whatever she found in Azriel healed much of the damage accrued in the mountains.

Up the stairs they went and along a wide, brightly lit corridor lined with many doors. Rusan servants moved in and out of the rooms beyond, suites prepared for the many guests lingering downstairs. The music for the ball would begin soon, and yet they moved farther and farther from the massive ballroom.

Much to Emillie's dismay, Ariadne did not stop to knock on Camilla's door before letting herself in. On the far side, the suite diverged into two rooms. Directly in front of them, a division wall hung with a large painting separated the two main rooms of the suite. To their left, Camilla's cerulean-painted bedroom shone with the flames from the fireplace. To their right, her matching sitting room opened like an invitation with comfortable chairs and sofas, a writing desk near the window, and a small table for tea.

They went right. Ariadne let go of her arm and called out for their friend as she swept through the sitting area before settling on one of the sofas farthest from the fireplace. Emillie followed at a distance, discomfort curling in her gut. It all seemed very intrusive.

Camilla poked her head out from a door to the space between the two main rooms, her hair half-piled, half-braided on her head. At first, those golden brows pinched together hard. At the sight of them, however, her face relaxed into a broad grin.

"Why, dolls, what are you doing up here?" She stepped out of the room wearing a sheer robe, her every curve on display.

Emillie swallowed hard and snapped her gaze to her hands, ignoring the sudden heat building in her core. This was not how she imagined the night beginning.

"Waiting for you," Ariadne said, standing to greet their friend.

Like Emillie, Camilla hesitated at the embrace before returning the gesture with uncertainty. "My, my, my. Things have changed, have they not?"

"More than you know." Ariadne smiled, then looked at Emillie with a raised brow. "Are you okay?"

Camilla chuckled and lowered herself into a chair. She crossed her legs and shifted the robe to obscure more of her features. "Do not be ashamed, doll. You are fine to look. After all, you came into my room unannounced. You are lucky I am clothed at all."

Heat rose to Emillie's face, and she glared at her sister. "I was dragged in here."

"Is that so?" Camilla raised an elegant brow at Ariadne. "It has been a while since you have wandered a manor like this."

Ariadne's small smile spread. "I no longer require a chaperone."

Another laugh from Camilla. "Indeed, you do not. How *has* marriage been?"

Emillie looked at her sister. After so many months claiming she would rather live out her life as an unmarried Caersan spinster, she seemed more than content now she finally shared blood with a man. Even if the man was half-fae.

Biting her lip, Ariadne's cheeks flushed again. "Delightful, actually."

"You seem far more at ease," Emillie noted, "than when you had been courted by the General."

Their friend scoffed and shook her head. "That putrid bag of flesh—"

"Camilla!" Emillie scolded and covered her smile with a hand. "You cannot speak of him that way."

"After what he did to her," Camilla scoffed and nodded to Ariadne, "he deserves far worse."

"He is still the General!"

"And he is on probation." The Caersan shook her head. "If he returns to his position after all he has done, I will be greatly surprised."

Ariadne raised her brows. "Do not forget the pull his father has with the Council. Even with Azriel as Lord Governor, he does not have the same influence as the Gards."

"Perhaps," Camilla admitted without sounding remotely as though she meant it. "*Your* father does, however, and he is the one who revoked his position. The *ex*-General will not be reinstated so long as he maintains his stance on the matter."

"Are the Gards in attendance?" Emillie asked with a glance at the door as though they could be standing just beyond, listening in on their conversation.

Camilla huffed. "No. They are throwing their own Soltium celebrations."

"Then it appears," Ariadne said with pursed lips, "there is a divide amongst the Society of Laeton."

"Indeed."

Camilla stood then and made her way back to the dressing room she had come from. Emillie could not help watching the way her hips swayed before shaking her head and looking away again. She could not allow herself to fantasize about a friend.

"Now tell me, doll," Camilla called from the room, "how was the wedding day?"

"As I said," Ariadne replied, "delightful."

The lack of details would not suffice. Camilla's curiosity would be sated whether either of them liked it or not. A long silence stretched out after her sister's reply, then their friend returned to the room in her shift. A maid followed her and yanked on the ties of a corset.

"Did you—"

"Yes, Camilla!" Ariadne laughed and waved her off. "Yes. We did."

"A maiden no longer!"

Emillie shook her head at the crassness of it all. While speaking of such things was not forbidden amongst Caersan women, it was also not encouraged. The men of the Society preferred such conversations to be kept at a minimum. Just another way to maintain their control through ambiguity. After so long of it, such conversations felt wrong.

"And how was it?" Camilla disappeared again to collect the next layer of her dress, the Rusan maid following close behind.

Ariadne glanced at Emillie and asked, "Is this alright?"

"I know what sex is." She looked pointedly at Camilla's dressing room. Their friend had never been shy about explaining the details of her adventures. "It has hardly been a secret amongst us for quite some time."

Her sister's laugh, like bells on the wind, made any tension left in Emillie's body evaporate. It was not often she heard the sound—to hear it now only solidified how perfect a match she finally made. Only someone who truly loved her, inside and out, could bring her sister back to life.

"It was fantastic," Ariadne admitted as Camilla poked her head back out, searching for an answer. "Better than I ever dreamed, actually."

Camilla's lips twisted into a smirk. "He went down on you, yes?"

"Excuse me?" Ariadne gaped at her, clearly surprised by the question. "This is something you never told me about!"

Their friend vanished yet again, and Emillie looked to her sister. Something did not add up in their conversation. "What is she talking about?"

Ariadne stared at her for a long moment. "Now that I am thinking of it...you would definitely need to know and—" she raised her voice "—no thanks to Camilla, we did not know of it."

"Why would I need to know?" Emillie looked from the now-silent dressing room to her sister.

"I imagine it will help you," Ariadne explained, "whenever you find yourself intimate with another woman."

Heat washed across Emillie's face again, and she sat back, creating distance between them. She searched her memories for anything which could help her understand that of which they spoke. Nothing came to mind.

"It is like a kiss between your legs." Ariadne bit her lip, color blooming on her cheeks as well. "And it is wonderful."

Emillie stilled. An image of Kyra scrolled through her mind. That pretty smile and the feel of her lips. The taste of her. The way her fingers slid to her most intimate place. If she had been able to, she would have loved to see more of the Rusan woman. With another way to satisfy the urge she felt building at her sex, she could now imagine how she would spread Kyra's legs and pleasure her with her mouth—a much better visual than using only her hand.

"And Azriel did that to you?" Emillie could not withhold the awe from her tone.

"He better have!" Camilla called from the dressing room before reappearing in a pale yellow gown with a pattern of white flowers. The curls of her hair bounced on top of her head as she flounced back through the room and landed on a chaise. "And I do hope it was good."

Ariadne's mouth twisted as she tried to hide a smile. "Indeed, it was."

"Fantastic." Camilla sat back, careful of her pinned hair. "A selfish man is the worst. If they are determined to keep us under their thumb, the least they could do is treat us like their queen."

With a raised brow, Emillie said, "The monarchy died when our ancestors were cursed."

"Your history knowledge is impeccable," Camilla said dryly, then winked. "But I am being metaphorical."

Emillie scoffed. "Figurative language should go where it belongs—in the gutter."

"But you are such a poet!" Ariadne teased and patted her hand. "Nevertheless, I agree with you, Camilla. I am quite content with my husband."

Husband. Married. Wife. Such a strange list of terms now associated with her sister. And to hear her so happy—at once, it made Emillie thankful for the man who finally made Ariadne come to life again and envious of his ability to succeed where she had failed for so long.

With Ariadne's departure to the Eastwood Province on the horizon, Emillie could not help but lament her lost opportunity to get to know her sister again.

Time amongst the Caersans of the Society didn't make the transition into aristocracy any easier. Although Azriel's youngest years were spent running the halls of manors with the vision of becoming one of vampires' finest, his most formative decades took place on the outskirts looking in after the grand reveal of his sire. He spent centuries hating everything about Valenul and searching for ways to make it crumble. Dancing beside the most pretentious Caersans in the entire Keonis Valley should've made his skin crawl.

But Azriel felt the muscle memory for the steps return with each song and, thanks to Petre's coaching, the speech pattern came more naturally. To his absolute horror, he was becoming the very vampire he once sought to remove from power.

All for her.

Ariadne laughed as he swept her into his arms, her feet running their own beat along the tiled dance floor. He kept her from tripping over herself with an arm loose about her waist. The light pressure on her hip provided enough support for her to remain steady and grounded, and by the way her eyes glittered when he spun her to him, he knew it to be enough.

Around the ballroom, three dozen of the Society either looked on or joined them. More lingered in the halls beyond or moved between their guest accommodations or gardens. More than fifty Caersan vampires were set to remain at the Dodd Estate, with others planning to travel between manors during the daylight hours by utilizing windowless carriages and underground driveways. Soltium brought even more of the aristocracy out of hiding than the Season or the wedding of the Golden Rose.

Like at the many balls he attended as the Harlows' shadow, Azriel didn't stop scanning the room. When Ariadne stepped aside with her sister or to whisper something to Camilla, he collected a glass of water and turned slowly. With dawn quickly approaching, he'd assumed Madan would have made an appearance, yet still no sign of his brother.

"You look lost."

The sudden male voice at his side made Azriel's muscles twitch, and his hands curl into fists. He turned to Nikolai Jenson with as neutral an expression as ever. "Says the lone pup. Where *is* your master tonight? Still hiding?"

Nikolai's mouth twitched into a scowl. "His family has their own celebrations."

"And you weren't invited?" Azriel raised a brow, suspicion clawing through him.

"If you must know," Nikoli said and sipped his wine, "my parents have been speaking with Miss Dodd's. Evidently, they want me married."

Azriel chuckled and turned to watch the dancers in their quadrille. "You're wasting your time with that, I can assure you. You can report back to your master not to worry about *Lady Caldwell*. She's quite satisfied."

"I am not here to spy." Nikolai glared up at him, then let a slow smile loose. "Tell me...does she taste as sweet as her lips felt on my skin?"

A sudden rage boiled in Azriel's veins at the mention of Nikolai's intimate moments with Ariadne as her Elit—something he continued to supply for Emillie. Did he always speak of his trusted time with them so freely? A rumble in his ears drowned out the din of the ballroom.

It took his many decades of practice not to let the anger take hold. Instead, Azriel shot back the rest of his water like liquor and stepped in front of Nikolai, forcing the Captain to tilt his head back to look at him. With a dangerously blank expression and even tone, he said, "Speak of my wife in such a manner again, and I'll have your skin as a rug."

"You dare to threaten me—"

"You and Loren have *lost*," Azriel cut in and lifted his lips in a snarl to bare his fangs. The roaring in his ears grew louder. "Even if, by some miracle, he returns as General, his name is forever tarnished, and your affiliation with him will haunt your every move. No Caersan woman of worth will have either of you as a husband."

Nikolai ground his teeth. "You have overstepped."

"No." He lowered his voice so it crackled like thunder. The edges of his vision darkened. "I'm the Governor of Eastwood, and the moment you threatened my wife's honor with your implications, *you* overstepped. Keep it up, and you'll see what happens when I do."

"Azriel?"

The ballroom snapped back into focus, the sound of the string quartet cutting through the growing cacophony in his mind, and he took a step back from the Captain. Ariadne laid a hand on his forearm, anchoring him back in the world. He nodded once to Nikolai in dismissal, then turned to his wife. After kissing her knuckles, he said, "Yes, my love?"

Ariadne watched Nikolai walk away with a light frown. "Is everything alright?"

"Perfectly." He gave her a small smile.

She eyed him, clearly suspicious, but said nonetheless, "I am tired and ready to retire for the day. Shall I wait for you?"

"No need." Azriel held out an arm. "I'm ready as well."

After bidding good day to the hosts and the rest of the Harlow family, they started up the stairs to the second floor. The manor, almost as grand as that of the Harlow Estate, had more than enough bed chambers to room those gathered for the solstice. All along the brightly lit, blue-painted corridor were doors with dainty signs on the handles, each scrawled with a guest's name.

When they arrived at their small guest suite, Azriel opened the door for his wife and locked it behind them. The tall windows of their cozy sitting room overlooked the pond in the lower gardens during the night hours, though the view couldn't be seen when they entered. Servants had already been through to tug the heavy velvet drapes shut to block out the inevitable sunrise. As Azriel double-checked each curtain's security, Ariadne sauntered into the windowless washroom, humming a melody from the quartet below.

Azriel couldn't keep his thoughts from wandering to Madan in the moments alone. His brother should've been present at the Dodds, whether he was still angry with Azriel or not. In fact, he'd seen Madan's name on a placard just two rooms down. They'd expected him to arrive as well.

It'd been wrong to send Madan away. The moment he'd opened his eyes the night following his threat, Azriel knew he'd made a mistake. He'd done everything to keep his brother safe all their lives, and in an instant, he'd lost control. By the time he'd gotten to Madan's suite, however, it was empty, and Rune was no longer in the stables.

He knew why he'd said what he did upon reflecting on his fury. None of it had to do with Madan at all. There'd been a part of him for over a year now which knew the dhemons had done more to Ariadne than he'd been told. He'd merely spent the last agonizing year and a half ignoring the truth—and all the signs laid out before him by Ariadne herself.

The aversion to touch. Her meekness before men. The quick shift of emotions at the mention of those monsters.

No, after so long pretending it hadn't happened, the moment she'd confirmed it, a piece of him broke. None of it was Madan's fault—not keeping it from him or what he did to protect her from possibly bearing their young. Rather, Azriel's anger stemmed from his own inadequacy.

He didn't protect her well enough. Not from any of the dhemons.

Azriel sat at the edge of the bed after checking the curtains and buried his face in his hands. Now he faced another issue entirely because of his selfishness: where was Madan? With the dhemons seeking their revenge, he became a walking beacon. They knew Azriel would do anything—*anything*—to protect his brother.

The wood floor creaked, and Azriel looked up, every thought dropping from his head like lead in an instant. Whatever troubles he had could wait for a solution just a little longer. No good in worrying about something he couldn't control.

After all, Ariadne stood before him in nothing but a black lace robe. Her long, dark hair, freshly released from their pinned confines, rolled over her shoulders in a wave of curls. A long, pale leg slipped from between the loosely tied lapels, exposing her hip and a sliver of the smooth expanse of her stomach. The dip between her perfect breasts slid in and out of view.

"Gods," he breathed, a sweet heat rushing through his veins.

Ariadne stepped closer, and the lace shifted. Her nipples flashed in and out of sight behind the floral pattern. Each elegant movement brought her closer, sending his heart leaping. The bonded part of him purred in contentment.

"You're beautiful." Azriel cupped her hips when she stopped before him and looked up at her in awe. How he'd gotten so lucky, he had no idea. "I love you."

She said nothing in return. Instead, Ariadne slipped her hands across his shoulders and pushed his jacket from his arms. He shifted out of the suddenly constricting piece of Caersan fashion, then waited to see what she chose next. Off with the cravat and vest and her fingers slid into the deep opening of his shirt to caress his chest with a hum. She gave the fabric a small tug, and it was enough of an invitation for him to yank it off over his head and toss it to the floor.

Then—gods help him—Ariadne knelt between his legs. Light as a phantom, she dragged her hands down the top of his thighs before pulling off one boot, then the other. Back up his inner legs went her fingers, every touch like fire he couldn't get enough of, until she reached the waist of his trousers and the last thing keeping his erection at bay.

Azriel leaned back onto his palms so her wandering fingers could more easily access the buttons. Her hands brushed along his stiff cock as she worked, and he swallowed hard. She knew precisely what she was doing. By the way her eyes sparkled, she enjoyed it.

She pushed the last buttons loose, and he sprang free right into her waiting hand. He sucked in a sharp breath. Her fingers wrapped around the thick length then began a steady stroke. Up and down she went, her eyes sliding from his face, down the contracting muscles of his abdomen, and to the cock in her hand.

Each slide up and down his shaft seemed to pulse through his entire being. To see her as enthralled by his body as he was by hers, Azriel almost couldn't handle it. Her mere touch on his bare skin was enough to send him over the edge—for her to not only initiate intimacy but to seek his pleasure as he'd sought hers? He was going to lose his mind.

A groan rolled from deep in his chest, and it only served to spur her on. Ariadne bit her lip as she watched him, moving a little faster and gripping a little harder. He couldn't help the jerk of his hips to drive himself against her palm.

Her gaze shifted back to her working hand, lips parting at the sight of the wet bead at his tip. She hesitated, her steady strokes missing a beat, then she locked eyes with him again as she licked the head of his cock.

He swore and let his head fall back to stare at the ceiling. The image of her there on her knees before him would forever be burned into his memory—and damn, what a beautiful picture it was. But he had to look away to collect himself, or he'd finish before knowing where any of this would lead.

"Do you like that?" Ariadne's voice, usually so light and sweet, was husky and breathless. She slid her hand up and down and up again.

"Fuck yes." He had no other words.

Azriel dragged his attention back to her, head fuzzy from the absolute pleasure pulsing through his body with each stroke of her hand. The moment he laid eyes on her, however, she stopped again as though to assess the truthfulness of his words. She studied him for a long moment. Her free hand slid up his leg to grip his inner thigh and pin it to the bed.

Then she slid his cock into her mouth.

He barked another curse and gripped the bedspread beneath him to steady himself. Her lips wrapped around his thick girth, and the length she couldn't take in, she continued to stroke with her hand. As she got used to the size of him, she adjusted. Her tongue found the rhythm of each suck, and in a matter of seconds, Azriel's mind went blank.

Ariadne found a steady pace, her head bobbing up and down. She looked up at him and he moaned loudly, pushing his fingers into her hair—not to drive himself deeper, but to touch her in any way he could.

Soon her fingers slipped up and down his length, slick and tiring from the constant movement. Though Azriel could watch her there forever, his pleasure wasn't enough for him. He shifted his grip from her hair to her face and eased his hips back until she slowed, then released him. His cock glistened, and her lips remained parted and plump.

"Was that okay?" She drew a finger across her mouth.

Azriel groaned, leaned forward, and kissed her hard. As she leaned into him, rising up a bit, he grabbed her by the back of her thighs and dragged her up to him. He laid back so she fell onto his chest, straddling his legs. The lace robe opened down the middle to expose more of her naked body.

"Everything you do is perfect," he said and kissed her neck before dragging a fang along her throat. She pushed closer, and he struck, digging his fangs into her. Her tangy blood rushed across his tongue before shooting up the hollows.

Ariadne sucked in a sharp breath and shifted so his cock pressed against his belly and slid between her slick folds. Again and again, she moved her hips so her clit rubbed against his length. The pressure and friction and each draw from her vein sent him spiraling once more.

Withdrawing his fangs, he licked the small holes on the side of her throat. He watched a trickle of blood run down her neck, soak into the black lace where the edge of the brand on her chest hid away—a twin to his own—and said in a gravelly whisper, "I'm yours. Do with me what you wish."

To his delight, Ariadne shifted back onto her knees and reached between her legs. She angled his cock up so when she eased back down, he slid into her sex. She continued the grinding, her clit rubbing against his pelvis with each movement, hands braced on his chest. Her low, primal moan of pleasure raced through him.

He ran his palms up her thighs, the lace spilling over his hands, to grip her hips. The slow, fluid rhythm she set at once teased him and fulfilled every need demanded of his bond. The incessant desire to feel her—all of her, inside and out—eased the knot in his chest with every smooth rock of her body. Somehow the lace obscuring his view of her breasts and curves only heightened the sensations.

So when Ariadne found her release, her core undulating with it, Azriel hissed a curse and closed his eyes to ride out the tight ripples which gripped him. Her euphoric cry swelled in his chest, knowing it was he—his body, his cock—who gave her such powerful orgasms. And as she slowed, he urged her weight forward so he could begin thrusting.

While he rolled his hips, driving himself into her warm, wet sex, she splayed her hands across his chest. Her fingertips roved over his scars as her lips traveled up his sternum and from one pec to the other. Each soft kiss streaked across his skin like lightning, shocking him through his middle and down the length of his shaft.

With a gentle touch, Ariadne tilted his chin back to expose his throat. She drew her tongue along what he knew to be one of the vivid blue veins, not unlike the way she'd licked the tip of his cock. The very thought made his breath catch in his lungs. When he released it in a groan, she sank her fangs into his flesh, smooth as a knife.

She hummed her delight while she drank from him, her hips surging at the rush of vitality. Azriel couldn't hold back the low cry of pleasure and gripped her a little harder, fingers digging into her to hold her steady. A sudden thrust from her made his entire body alight. Too much, and he'd finish too quickly. He wanted to savor her just as she did him.

Too soon, she retracted her fangs and, after a quick lick, pressed a palm to the wounds which wouldn't close as quickly as hers. She tilted her head to the other side to kiss his neck and tease his ear with gentle nipping and sucking. In return, he pounded his cock up into her in a steady rhythm. He slipped one hand out from under her robe to hold her by the back of the neck and kiss her hard.

Ariadne pulled back to scan his face. "I love you so much, Azriel."

"You are my sun," he breathed, never ceasing his thrusting, "my moon, and my stars. You are the air I breathe."

She slammed her mouth down on his with a moan and, balancing herself on one hand, she tugged open the ties of her robe. The lapels fell open, exposing that which had tantalized him since her appearance in the doorway. In one smooth movement, Azriel rolled Ariadne onto her back, cupping a breast while still steadying her hips. Now at a better angle, he thrust into her and drew her tight nipple into his mouth. He flicked the tip with his tongue and sucked until she moaned again and drew her fingers through his hair. Then he repeated on the other.

Ariadne writhed beneath him, panting and moaning as he rubbed and pinched the taut pink buds and worked his cock in and out. He reveled in the pleasure he gave her and in the euphoria he drifted through with each stroke. Deeper and harder, he went into her slick sex as she lay steady beneath him. She tilted her hips and gasped as she took every thick inch of him.

Then she cried out his name, stilling beneath him as another orgasm cascaded through her. This time Azriel pumped his hips hard, drawing out her pleasure and shattering as he, too, found his release. He buried his face in her neck and inhaled her intoxicating scent, riding the waves of the climax.

In the wake of their throws, Azriel held her as he always did. She tucked her forehead against his chest, and he stroked her side with the back of his fingers.

"Hold me," she whispered without looking up at him.

He frowned into the dim light of the room. "I am holding you."

"No." She guided his hand beneath the lace robe to the skin of her back. "*Hold* me."

His stomach lurched into his throat. He'd never touched her back—not like this. Not after watching her twist out of hugs or bat away drifting hands.

Not after seeing what had been done to her.

Nonetheless, his hand slid across her skin, starting on her lower back, dotted with small, knotted scars. Each one sent a dagger into his heart. Then he drifted higher. There the scars grew longer and wider, and she inhaled sharply.

"Are you certain?" He brushed his lips on the top of her head. "I can hold you in other ways."

"Please." Her quiet voice hardly reached his ears. "I want to remember the feeling of hands who didn't hurt me."

Azriel swallowed hard. Didn't hurt her. He hadn't. Not really. It'd been Ehrun. That monster tore open her flesh and engraved himself on her.

Fire ripped through him at the thought. He should've killed the monster for all he'd done. Now that he had power as a Governor, he could use resources to find the dhemon and make him pay for all the damage he'd done.

He splayed his hand across her back and pulled her close. With another firm kiss to her head, he whispered back, "I'll never hurt you."

Not again.

CHAPTER 28

The fading soreness between Ariadne's legs provided a reminder of her time entangled with Azriel as she sat at the long table for breakfast the following evening. After dancing until her feet hurt and surprising him with the black lace robe Revelie insisted she take upon their engagement, she felt herself coming back to life. What surprised her most was how much she enjoyed watching him as she sucked his cock. If what he had done to her brought as much pleasure to him as the previous day's activities had for her, she understood precisely why he did it.

It certainly made her want to do it for him more often.

"Ariadne?"

Emillie's voice cut through the image of Azriel looming above her, his hand in her hair, and dragged her abruptly back to reality. She blinked hard, shook her head once, and looked to her sister. "I apologize. What were you saying?"

Across the table, Azriel's nostrils flared, and he shot her a heated look of warning before returning to his conversation with Lord Dodd. She would never get accustomed to his fae senses smelling her arousal—though it always benefited her when she wanted him between her legs. Her core throbbed.

"When are you leaving for Monsumbra?" Revelie cut in, peering around Emillie, a spoonful of yogurt and fruit in hand. She had arrived not long after Ariadne and joined them in Camilla's suite to relax before the festivities.

Ariadne glanced again at Azriel, who pretended he hadn't heard the question. "The end of the week, I believe. After the final Council meeting."

Her stomach knotted as she spoke the words. Eastwood Province lay almost two nights away, and Monsumbra, at its heart, another night's travel. With the threat against Azriel, the journey could be treacherous. Though he had reassured her they would have a guard of soldiers to protect them, the last time she had gone east, it had not been for entertainment.

Not much of the towns, and certainly not the capital city, stood out in her memory. Only a mixture of snow, a couple of small huts, and the twinkling lights of homes in the distance. That the dhemon who had abducted her even thought to provide her a place of refuge from the sun only underscored his determination to get her to the final destination: the dhemon keep.

The first morning after she had been taken from her bedroom, rays of sunlight trickled through the white-flecked evergreens. It had been the only time she shrank in close to the dhemon riding behind her on the horse. The strong mage rope securing her wrists held her firmly to the saddle, and for a beat, she believed he would let her fall victim to aegrisolis.

After all, she had no idea what he had in store for her.

To her surprise, the dhemon had shrugged off his cloak and draped it over her before guiding the horse into a darker copse of trees. They arrived at the first small hut on their journey not long after. He untied her from the saddle and carried her into the building, where he drew the curtains and lit a fire in a hearth hardly large enough for a log of wood.

Her sleep those few days leading up to the dhemon keep had been the last peaceful rest she had for months. Though her time under Ehrun's torment had not been long, he continued to haunt her for weeks to come. He still haunted her.

So the prospect of moving closer to the keep made Ariadne's skin crawl. Though this time she would be on the main highway between provinces, the journey would be similar enough—longer, even, given the slow pace of a carriage.

"You will leave before the end of the Season?" Emillie asked, looking crestfallen. "I had hoped you would remain until Noctium."

The autumn equinox and final ball of the Season were always an abundance of revelries—proposals from suitors and the passing of congratulations to everyone who married within those six exciting months. Ariadne, the Golden Rose and first wedding amongst the Caersan, had already had enough of the outpour from well-wishers. Half were backhanded blessings or accompanied by pitying glances. She wanted no more.

"Azriel must return to take his place as Governor," Ariadne explained, noting the slow tension building in her husband's shoulders. "He has been eager to get back."

Camilla chewed thoughtfully and, after swallowing, said, "You will return when he comes for Council, yes?"

With a small smile, she nodded. "Most likely."

The return trip to Laeton from Monsumbra did not appeal to Ariadne, either. Despite it not being filled with the same level of terror as when she headed east, it had been overshadowed by the constant threat looming behind her and Madan.

"Fantastic!" Camilla nudged Emillie with a gentle elbow. "We will need to visit them as well, I believe."

Emillie's eyes brightened at that. "May we?"

"I do not know what I would do without your company," Ariadne admitted. "You are all welcome in Monsumbra."

Revelie raised a brow. "Will you not need an escort?"

Of course they would. To travel so far unaccompanied would encourage rumors bound to ruin Emillie or Camilla. As a business owner and proud Caersan woman who has long since written off the Society's burdensome rules, Revelie would be free to do as she wished. With the dhemon threat, however, none of them would be safe without family or a set of guards.

"I am certain an escort could be arranged." Ariadne glanced at her father, still deep in conversation with Lord Dodd. Between his influence both financially and politically, finding a company of guards would be no issue. "Perhaps Madan would be able to assist as well."

Azriel stiffened beside her but said nothing. Something had happened between them, and he had yet to speak of it. Madan's prolonged absence was odd, though Azriel had explained he'd wanted to give them space after their wedding.

"Perhaps I can join you for Brutium," Emillie said and leaned forward with a hopeful glint in her eye.

"Does your family not hold a ball for the winter solstice?" Revelie tilted her head with a pout. "I know I will be too busy to travel at that time of year anyway."

Camilla smiled. "Perhaps we could host this year so you could visit Monsumbra."

The planning continued, though Ariadne knew it all to be mere air passed between hopeful Caersan women. Without the approval of the men in their lives, none of it would come to fruition. Between Council business and the incessant desire to marry off both his daughters to acceptable men in the Society, her father would find any deviation from his plans to be second-rate.

Too bad he did not yet know Emillie would not be marrying a man at all if given any choice in the matter.

As their conversation found its natural conclusion, the four friends turned their attention back to their food. They ate in silence for a moment before Emillie reached between them and took her hand, squeezing once.

"I will miss you," she said softly without looking over. Ariadne knew without seeing that her eyes would be filled with tears. "A lot."

She squeezed back. "I will miss you as well."

Camilla and Revelie picked up a conversation on other matters to give them privacy. Leave it to their friends to be more intuitive than anyone else at the table.

"Will I see you again before you leave?" Emillie stared into her teacup before taking a sip.

"Come for dinner," Ariadne said, still holding firm on her sister's hand. "The night before we leave."

When Emillie finally looked to her, eyes rimmed silver, she smiled sadly and nodded once. After a century and a half together, they had never been separated long. Only once prior to this were they apart, and that had been a time of fear for them both.

This time would be different.

The highway through Laeton bustled with Caersans moving from manor to manor each night. After the first ball held at his parents' home, Loren joined his soldiers along the road to oversee the travel and ensure safe passage to the vampires. While his provisional leave continued, the dhemons remained close to the capital of Valenul and therefore created an unseen threat to any vampire too reckless. The Rusan soldiers with enough mortal blood to allow them into the sun would take over the watch upon the rise of the morning sun.

Although most soldiers continued to look to him as their General, others maintained their distance. He did not blame them for it. The face-off with that half-breed bastard had tainted his image to the public. Perhaps their parents wished for them to remain neutral. Still, the longer it took for the Council to decide on his position, the more soldiers returned to him.

With enough support from his men, Loren could regain his position by force rather than through the muddy channels of politics if needed.

The one friend he could count on from the very beginning of it all, however, was Captain Nikolai Jensen. The Caersan stood by him and provided the intel from officer debriefs to continue his work.

Carriages passed Loren on his stallion at a decent enough clip going in either direction of the highway. Lord Moone nodded to him through the window as he passed, and Councilman Locke saluted on his way to the next ball. Meanwhile, Councilman Theobald merely glared before averting his attention back to the road. The delineation between Provinces had never been more clear. The north versus the east with their Lord Governors at odds.

When the evening turned to midnight, Loren finally saw her. His heart hammered against his ribs as Ariadne passed in her carriage, moving at an amble.

Her dark curls swept over her far shoulder, exposing the two small healing spots on her throat—the mark of another man's fangs taking from her neck. She smiled at the person across from her. No, not person. The bastard-born thief who poisoned her mind against him and then sullied her by taking her to his bed.

As they drew nearer, her gaze flickered out the window and connected with Loren's. Those beautiful ocean eyes widened slightly, and her lips parted. Damn him, he would still have her, no matter what. He would save her from the filthy half-breed and raise her back to the pedestal where she belonged.

Loren inclined his head to her, a hand laid over his heart.

She looked away, color rising to her cheeks, and he smirked as they trundled past. The view shifted from Ariadne to Azriel. The false Lord Governor did not smile. He merely stared back, expressionless. No cocky quirk of his lips or threatening glint in his eye. The bastard only stared.

Before the year was out, Loren vowed to put an end to that man's rule.

The past weeks without his usual duties as General provided him the time to continue digging into anything to use against the bastard. Of what he could find, the most damning had been the purer lineage of his cousin, Madan. The vampire had been born a true Caersan and should have, by all accounts, taken the title of Lord Governor long before Azriel had been considered.

Proving this before the Council would be pertinent. Though he knew his father, Lord Governor Damen Gard of Notten Province, would back his findings, he had yet to share anything with his family. After his drunken outburst at the ball, they had also been treated with less respect. His actions had put shame on himself and his parents.

The meager response to their invites for Soltium underscored their ostracism.

Now Loren would do everything in his power to set things right. The first step would be to provide evidence of his accusations, so they needed to be foolproof.

Not long after the Caldwell carriage passed, Nikolai rode down the highway and came to a halt beside Loren. They waited for any listening ears to pass before so much as nodding in greeting.

"What did you learn?" Loren kept his voice low. Though he had not intended on sending Nikolai to the Dodd Estate for Soltium, their invitation as a way to encourage a suitable relationship between the Captain and Camilla Dodd had been too good to pass up. Eyes and ears behind enemy lines always proved useful.

Nikolai watched a young, low-ranking Caersan man gallop by. "They depart Laeton in a week's time."

Loren's stomach knotted. No. If they left, he could not free Ariadne from the bastard's hold. "We must find a way to keep them here."

The Captain shook his head with a frown. "I do not understand, General. Why is she so important to you? She is married—unchaste now—and yet you still wish to find a way to wed her. Why not her sister?"

"Believe you me," Loren growled at the intrusive thoughts of Ariadne opening her legs to that half-breed, "if all else fails, I will have Miss Harlow instead."

The creases between Nikolai's eyebrows deepened. "What is it about the Princeps' daughters which entices you so?"

A low, humorless chuckle left Loren in a rush. "Have you not seen them?"

"Is that all?" Nikolai shook his head. "They are, indeed, beautiful, but so are many other Caersan women. You could have anyone, yet you pine after them?"

"*Pine* is a strong word." He glanced at his Captain. "*Require* is more suitable."

"I thought you loved her."

Ariadne. Had Loren truly loved her at all? Possibly. She had been wild and untamable before her kidnapping, though his brother had attempted to do so by proposing. Whatever happened with the dhemons had done the trick. Ariadne's spirit broke, and it was he who built it back up. He whom she turned to for comfort. Due to that, Loren had been certain it would be he she chose again and again.

Whatever dark fae magic Azriel wielded clouded her mind and sullied her judgment. That was what kept him hopeful. If he could prove the bastard had tricked them all and break the spell, he would then have her back.

If not, Emillie would do just fine. The younger Harlow daughter had always been more reserved and impressionable anyway. Just as beautiful and far less troublesome. She had always been a backup plan.

Her father, however, remained the wild card in it all. After the duel and then his outburst at the Teaglow's ball, Loren had done everything but grovel to return to the Princeps' graces. Their private meetings and his repeated apologies were the only reason Markus no longer spoke out against him in Council meetings. It was down to the other Councilmen to return his title.

"I loved the idea of her." Loren glared down the highway where the Caldwell carriage had disappeared. "I loved what she would do for my name and my power. As the elder sister, she is the key to that."

"And Miss Harlow cannot provide that for you?"

"Perhaps." He nodded to another passerby. "Either way, I will need to be rid of the false Governor."

Nikolai raised his brows. "You have a plan, then?"

Mind whirling, Loren nodded. Much had happened over the last few nights, and he was certain that his latest discoveries would only propel his plan into motion soon. Only one piece of the puzzle continued to evade him.

"Well, then, General," Nikolai said, "whatever it is, it needs to happen fast."

"Indeed." Loren's mouth twitched at the thought. Soon, everyone would understand his hate for the half-breed bastard who stole his woman.

Loren, dressed in military uniform, overseeing highway traffic, made Azriel's blood boil. That he continued to dress as General undermined the Princeps' decision and the Council's stalemate. With the Princeps refusing to vote on Loren's position and Alek's Lower Council split, he and Damen had yet to come to an agreement.

Ariadne's reticence after passing the disgraced officer only added insult to injury. She withdrew into her seat and bit her lip, fingers curling in the skirt of her gown. He should have killed him in that duel and been done with it.

"Did he do something?" Azriel asked, tone rumbling deep in his chest.

Ariadne winced a smile. "Not really."

He tilted his head and leaned forward to rest his elbows on his knees and take her twisting hands in his. "He'll never touch you again. I promise."

"You cannot shield me from everything," she whispered and sat up a little straighter. "But you can teach me to be more confident when around people like him."

Azriel froze and searched her blazing gaze. "What?"

Color spread across her cheeks again. "You taught me to hold a dagger when I was engaged to him. Teach me more."

He gaped at her for a long moment. The very thought of her being in such peril to require that knowledge churned his stomach. That's why he was there—to keep her safe. Not to teach her to fight.

She shouldn't *need* to fight.

Then again, he wouldn't always be around. He'd leave her at the Caldwell Estate at some point to take care of Council business or to see to the districts of his province. And if Madan didn't come home, she'd be alone. Alone and vulnerable in a time of war.

"Alright," he acquiesced softly. "I can do that."

She nodded without another word, and the tension eased from her shoulders and hands. He kissed her fingers as she sank back into the cushions of the seat.

The silence pressed in on Azriel after that, allowing his mind to wander back to his missing brother. Madan never made his scheduled appearance at the Dodd Estate, and it wasn't only he who noticed his absence. Caersan after Caersan asked after him.

"Where is Lord Caldwell tonight?" asked one with a curious glint in their eye as soon as he'd entered the Dodd's parlor.

A woman had leaned in not long after and said, "I had hoped to find your handsome cousin here."

Still more had cornered him later in the evening as others danced to ask after him. Worst of them all was a man who followed up his question with, "I do hope he is safe. Too many dhemons about to be certain."

"I can assure you," he'd told each loose-tongued vampire, "he is perfectly safe. If he arrives, it'll be because he's finished the duties I've given to him."

Between the questions, comments about the threat of dhemons, and his own lies, he'd nearly left to begin a hunt. If Ehrun had gotten ahold of Madan, his brother was as good as dead. The dhemon would string him up for the sun and then present his poisoned and rotting body in the most horrific way possible.

But Azriel had kept a straight face through it all. He kept his thoughts and concerns to himself as he spun Ariadne across the dance floor. Already he'd told her too much about the dhemons. The last thing he needed was for her to worry about Madan, too.

Closing his eyes for a long moment, he felt out with his mind. If Razer were close enough, he could ask his friend to search for Madan. He clawed through the void, grasping at the thin, telepathic lines connecting them, and came up short. Razer kept to the mountains, as instructed. Too far from Laeton to be noticed or contacted.

"Gods," Ariadne breathed.

Azriel's eyes snapped open to find her leaning to look out the carriage window. Her face drained of color. He sat forward. "What is it?"

"A dhemon."

As though his own worries had summoned them.

He slammed a fist into the ceiling of the carriage twice, and the driver slowed to a stop. Azriel took up his sword from the seat beside him.

"Wait!" Ariadne grabbed his wrist, eyes wide. "No! Do not go out there."

"Stay here."

"Azriel, please—"

He couldn't hear her anymore. If the dhemons lingered on the street to his own house, then they knew where he lived. They'd continue being a threat so long as he didn't take care of them first.

"Please, no!"

The cry followed him as he leapt from the carriage and closed the door. He looked up at the driver. "If more arrive, take her to Laeton—not home. Don't go home."

"Yes, sir."

Azriel stalked back down the road, scanning the darkness for the telltale signs of a dhemon. Their dark blue skin allowed them to blend into the shadows between trees despite their massive forms, but their glowing red eyes gave them away if they weren't careful.

He didn't need to search long. A dozen paces beyond the carriage, the dhemon stepped out to greet him, a wide grin on his face displaying the rows of sharp teeth. He held his arms out as though offering Azriel a hug.

"*Dhomin!*"

"Where is he?" Azriel demanded in the dhemon language, ignoring the jab. The rough syllables rolled off his tongue like gravel. "Where the *fuck* is my brother?"

The dhemon laughed. "You worry about *him*? What about *her*?"

Azriel didn't look back at the carriage. The dhemon was trying to distract him—to tear his attention between the two people who mattered most to him. He wouldn't let them. Not again.

"Tell me where he is, and I will make your death quick."

The dhemon's smirk only grew, and he pulled a pair of long, wickedly curved knives from his belt. "If you think I will tell you anything, you are more foolish than your father."

"My father was ten times the man you'll ever hope to be." Azriel dropped the sword, and it clattered on the stone road. If the dhemon wanted to fight close-contact, he'd make that happen. In one fluid step, he pulled a long dagger from his boot.

The dhemon cracked his neck and stepped closer. "Ehrun will be pleased to have you back, *dhomin*. In pieces, of course."

Azriel charged forward and hurled the dagger, hilt over tip, at the dhemon's head. The beast laughed and side-stepped—right where he wanted him. Before the dhemon knew what he planned, Azriel gripped the dhemon's closest arm, yanked him off balance, and back-kicked his foot out from under him.

The breath left the dhemon in a rush as his back hit the ground, punching the air from his lungs. Before he could recover, Azriel kicked his wrist hard to knock one blade from the monster's grip. It flew toward the dagger while the second knife sliced at his leg.

Searing hot pain lanced through his thigh. Blood splattered across the stones as he cursed in the dhemon tongue. He shifted his weight off his injured leg and kicked again, forcing the dhemon to curl in to protect his face. His foot connected with the massive, curling horn closest to him with a resounding crack. Though nothing broke, slivers splintered down the bony annuli.

The dhemon swung his feet around to force distance between them. Azriel charged forward, took hold of the beast's boot, and shoved it to the side. He took advantage of the split second he had to pass and slammed his weight to the dhemon's body. To keep him from wriggling out from under him, Azriel pushed the dhemon's hip down with one hand and held firm to the knife-wielding hand with the other.

"Fucking traitor!" The dhemon snarled, yanking his arm away with his incredible strength. "You will choke on the blood from your deceptions."

Azriel roared right back as the hilt of the dagger slammed into his temple. He slid a knee onto the dhemon's diaphragm and leaned onto it. Again, air coughed out from the monster, and his attention turned to pushing Azriel's knee away. It was all he needed to control the dhemon's wrist and twist hard enough to force the knife to drop.

Before the dhemon could recover, Azriel jerked the arm to his chest and adjusted the placement of his weight to pin the massive horns to the ground. Grabbing his own wrist to create a lock on the arm, he sat up straight and yanked the dhemon's arm behind his back.

Another loud snap, followed shortly by the dhemon's scream, told Azriel he'd broken the shoulder as intended.

"I will raze Keon's mountains to the deepest levels of hell before you hurt her again," Azriel hissed into the dhemon's ear. He snatched up the fallen knife, dug his knee into the dhemon's chest again, and held the blade to his throat. "Now tell me where my brother is."

"Fuck you."

Azriel slammed his fist into the dhemon's face and said louder, "Where is my brother?"

The dhemon laughed, blood pouring from his broken nose. "May you suffer for the rest of—"

Another punch. Blood splattered. Now he yelled, "Where is my brother?"

"Kill me like you did your comrades."

Memories flashed through Azriel's mind, burning into his vision. He screamed in rage. "Where the *fuck* is he?"

"*Dhomin*," the dhemon taunted him by drawing out the word. "*Dhomin* then, *dhomin* forever."

Azriel brought the blade down next, stabbing through the dhemon's face again and again. Blood splashed across his face, the heat of it mixing with his tears.

They had him. They had Madan and would do anything to torment him with that knowledge. If he wasn't dead already, he would be soon.

And it was all his fault.

He sat back onto the stone road, feet flat before him. The knife clattered to the ground beside him, and he crossed his arms over his knees to rest his forehead on them. His head pounded, his vision darkened, and the steady drip of the blood leaking from the dhemon's destroyed face echoed in his ears.

Dhomin. Dhomin. Dhomin.

"Azriel." Ariadne's voice was quiet and cautious behind him. "Azriel, are you hurt?"

Sucking in a breath, he turned to her, and, for a moment, horror flitted across her face. The dark, oily feeling of shame twisted through his gut. He knew what he looked like. He'd seen his reflection after a fight like that.

"Not bad," he croaked and stood, thigh screaming in protest. Warmth streamed down his leg.

Ariadne's eyes snapped to the wound. "Not bad?"

"I'll live."

A long moment passed. He stepped closer, and—thank the gods—she did not recoil from him. In fact, she held out a hand to his face, and when he paused just within her reach, she brushed his cheek with her thumb. A stream of blood ran down her wrist before dropping to the ground.

"Why did you do it?" She searched him for an answer he didn't want to admit even to himself.

But his face crumpled anyway. His throat burned, and though he tried to hold them back, fresh tears escaped. "They have him."

Ariadne's eyes widened. "Madan?"

Azriel nodded. "I don't even know if he's alive."

"They would not—"

"They would." He wiped his face on his sleeve, smearing the crimson everywhere. Then he leveled his gaze at her. "And they will come after you next."

CHAPTER 29

E millie thanked Sul as he helped her down from her horse at the front of the Caldwells' Laeton manor. The guard nodded in silent acknowledgment and, not for the first time, she lamented Gracen's death. He had been far more pleasant company on such ventures out of the house.

The butler opened the door wide upon her approach and swept a deep bow as she entered. "Welcome, Miss Harlow."

"Thank you." She pulled the long green cloak from her shoulders and handed it to him. "My sister?"

"In the drawing room, miss." He smiled and gestured toward the stairs. "Tea has just been brought up."

Up the steps and down the corridor to the deep blue drawing room with its gold trim, a fireplace at either end, and several arrangements for sitting. Plush couches and chairs sat before the hearths, and a pianoforte rested beside a tall window filled with moonlight. At the table near the center of the room was her sister.

Ariadne looked up from the book pinned open between her fingers and smiled before standing. "Good evening."

Emillie's heart throbbed. She rushed forward and tucked herself into her sister's open arms. With the Caldwells' departure date approaching, these quick visits would soon become a thing of the past.

"How have you been?" Ariadne pulled back and held her at arm's length, cheeks flushed and eyes shimmering.

"I had a handful of suitors over the last few nights." She made a face at the prospect of entertaining any Caersan man. All she could think of while sitting across from the peacocking vampires were the women she flirted with at the Dodd Estate during Soltium, the Rusan maid, Sephone, included.

Laughing, Ariadne sat again, pushed her book aside, and poured them both a cup of tea. "Who were the lucky Caersans who made it past Father?"

In an instant, Emillie sobered. She took her place across from her sister and accepted the tea. "General Gard was one."

Ariadne choked on her drink. "Excuse me?"

"Father believes it is only a matter of time before he returns to his position." Emillie's stomach sank. "The General has been meeting with him privately over the last fortnight, and they have made amends."

"Amends." Ariadne scoffed and placed pieces of lemon cake on a plate for them both. "Did Father forget what he said—what he did?"

With a shake of her head, Emillie accepted her serving and bit her lip. "It would seem all is forgiven. Father claims he lost his temper and made a brash decision that he was then forced to stand by due to its publicity."

"Stay away from him." Her sister sipped the tea again, this time successfully. "Do not trust him."

"Do not trust who?" Azriel stepped through the door and bowed to Emillie. Dark circles lined his eyes. If she did not know better, she would have assumed him ill. "Welcome."

The huge Lord Governor strode around the table, laid a heavy hand on his wife's shoulder, and pressed his lips to the top of her head. Like when he was a guard, he moved with as much grace as a Caersan man—save for the limp to his step, more exaggerated than usual. Emillie eyed his leg and noted the way he shifted his weight to lower himself into the chair beside Ariadne.

"Apparently, Loren Gard has taken an interest in Emillie." Ariadne poured her husband a cup of tea and sliced him a piece of lemon cake as well. "He called on her earlier this week."

Whatever exhaustion plagued the half-vampire vanished in an instant. He sat a little straighter, eyebrows pinching. "Excuse me?"

"He has made amends with our father," Ariadne explained. "Now he is attempting to court her."

Azriel shook his head, vibrant green eyes cooling from his long-standing vendetta. "I'll speak with your father."

Emillie nodded in thanks, though she was not certain he would have much impact on her father's decisions. The political aspect of a Caersan marriage outweighed anything else. What needed to happen was the one conversation she dreaded the most. Only then, perhaps, would he understand her reservations.

Understand, but not acknowledge. As was customary within the Society, she would still be married off to whichever suitor her father preferred. She could only pray to any god listening that it ended up being a Caersan she could tolerate.

Loren Gard did not make it onto that short list.

They ate their cake after that, discussing the merits of the other suitors and which Caersan ladies Emillie had spoken to. With Azriel's recent insight into the vampires of the Society due to his new position, his input became invaluable. Some of the lords, he claimed, would not mind a wife who preferred women as he was almost certain that they preferred men. A marriage of convenience would be the best choice for two like individuals.

"Perhaps Madan would be willing," Emillie said thoughtfully after a moment. "I know he has a fae lover, but just in the eyes of the Society?"

Azriel inhaled his tea and sputtered. "No. Absolutely not."

Emillie frowned at him. "But then I could come to live in Eastwood, too."

Ariadne glanced at her husband and bit her lip. She rested a hand on his, then turned a smile to Emillie. "That would be wonderful! Perhaps we can get into touch with the lords of Eastwood to determine other potential suitors."

Warmth flushed across Emillie's cheeks at how quickly they both pushed her idea aside. Madan was a handsome Caersan who her father would likely approve. Their dismissal made her sit back in silent shock.

"Excuse me." Azriel stood suddenly and gave her a weak smile that did not meet his eyes. "I need some air."

He left before she could respond, leaving the room in silence. Ariadne bit her lip and stared at the door as it swung closed. Her hand, now empty on the table, twisted into her serviette.

Emillie followed her sister's line of sight and asked in a quiet voice, "Is everything okay?"

For a long moment, Ariadne said nothing. She slowly turned her gaze back to the table and her half-eaten plate of cake. "Yes."

Lies.

"Talk to me." Emillie reached between them and squeezed her sister's hand hard. The touch seemed to drag her back into the room. "What happened?"

"Madan is missing."

The room seemed eons away in an instant. Emillie's lips parted, and her stomach dropped. The very idea of the vampire who had spent the last year and a half protecting her going missing made her skin crawl. Something horrible would have had to happen for it to occur.

"What do you mean?" They were the only words she could muster.

"Neither of us has seen him since the wedding." Ariadne held her hand but did not squeeze back. "No word, either."

Emillie looked at Azriel's abandoned plate. He had hardly touched the food. "Could he have returned to Monsumbra?"

Ariadne shook her head. "Azriel sent a message to ask, and no one has seen him."

Uncertain of what else to say, Emillie apologized for bringing him up and changed the subject again. No matter what they discussed, however, the shadow of Madan's disappearance loomed over them.

Before long, Emillie stood before the front doors again and hugged her sister. "You will be at the ball tomorrow, yes?"

Ariadne gave her a tight smile. "Maybe."

Emillie pouted. "A last hurrah for us both this Season? Please?"

"It is at the Gards."

"All the more reason to not abandon me." She raised her brows hopefully. "Help keep Loren away."

Ariadne laughed. "Alright. We will make an appearance."

Squealing in delight, Emillie threw her arms around her sister and held tight. Even if it would be the last time she saw her for weeks—possibly months—she would find it in her to be happy. She could not keep her sister forever, but she could certainly try her hardest.

The doors closed behind Emillie and Sul, leaving Ariadne alone in the foyer as Petre walked away. She twisted her fingers together and turned back to the stairs. For a long moment, she considered retreating to the library where she could continue reading the romance novel she had been indulging in prior to her sister's arrival. But even as she rested her hand on the banister, her stomach clenched and twisted. She would not be able to focus so long as she knew Azriel was alone.

So she swept down the hall to the study he so often locked himself in to avoid the world. She did not knock before turning the handle and letting herself in.

The study, all deep green walls and dark wood, cast a somber feeling when paired with the man sitting behind the desk. Azriel's elbows rested on the surface, and he covered his face. Shoulders hunched and quaking, he may not have heard her enter the room.

"Azriel?" She slipped around the chairs sitting before the glowing coals in the fireplace, each step a careful calculation. In the months she knew him, she had never seen him so withdrawn.

He grunted in response, something he had not done for many weeks.

"Look at me," she said, making her way around the desk to lay a hand on his shoulder. He twitched away. "Please."

After a long moment, Azriel lifted his face and turned to her. His eyes, red from tears, shone bright. "I can't do this."

A heavy feeling sank through her. "What do you mean?"

"All of this." He gestured at the room and papers on the desk. "I'm living a lie—a lie he made me commit to."

The air felt thin around her. Ariadne took a half step back to look at him more clearly. Yes, it was all new to him. None of it had been meant for him to endure. The fate of the Caldwells landed in his lap just as surely as her own as the Golden Rose. The difference between the titles, however, were stark; while hers lasted a Season, his now remained his responsibility for life.

"He?" Ariadne searched him as he pushed back from the desk and stood, putting distance between them. "The Lord Governor?"

"Madan." The name left Azriel in a quiet, raspy rush. He turned away from her, and a soft pounding told her he hit his chest several times. "Madan made it all happen. For me. So I could have hope. But I don't deserve it. It's a mess. I'm a liar. A fraud. He was supposed to be here—to help me."

Ariadne shook her head, unable to keep up with what he said. Again she reached for him. "No, you have done so much to earn this position. My love—"

"Don't." He pulled away again, swinging his wide-eyed gaze around to stare at her. "You should hate me."

Now she froze. Nothing connected. His thought patterns, his words, his reasoning for feeling as he did. None of it made sense. After all he had done for her, she could never hate him. "Why?"

"Because I am a *monster*." He pounded his chest again, a little harder this time, as tears spilled down his face.

Ariadne shook her head. Yes, what she witnessed leaving the Dodd Estate had been shocking, but he had done what was required to keep them safe. Before he could move away, she closed the distance between them and caught his fist. She kissed the bruises fading from his knuckles. "No, you are not. You did what you must to protect me—protect *us*."

Still, Azriel cried, and he looked to the ceiling as though imploring the gods for their help. He gasped for breath. "But I didn't protect you."

She took his face in her hands, forcing his gaze back to her. "You did everything you could. The dhemons—they are the true monsters."

He gaped at her, a pained silence stretching out between them. "You're right."

"I know I am." She kissed his lips softly. "I know I am. You saved me, and you will save Madan, too."

To her surprise, he did not return the kiss. Only more tears slipped down his cheeks. When he spoke, his voice was a soft, crackling whisper. "I can't lose either of you again."

A crease formed between Ariadne's brows. Her heart thundered in her chest, and she pulled back, dark thoughts pushing their way to the forefront of her mind. None of it added up. Fraud. Liar. Monster. "What do you mean *again?*"

"Ariadne..."

"What does that mean, Azriel?" She searched his face. "You never lost me before. I *chose* you."

Panic flashed in his eyes, and he opened and closed his mouth several times as though having just realized what he said. What it meant. What questions she would ask next. "No...I—"

"I need to know what you mean."

"I can't."

She covered her mouth and shook her head, hoping the movement would shake the horrible possibilities from her mind. The direction this conversation went had not been what she expected. Her lungs burned with each inhale. "Why not?"

"It will ruin everything."

"How?" Her voice cracked on the word.

He had been there the night she had been kidnapped. Did he not prevent it from happening for some reason? Did he let the dhemon into the manor?

"Please," he said softly. He stepped forward, and she bumped into the desk as she backed away. "Please, forget I said anything."

"Tell me the truth."

"The truth is I hate myself." He scrubbed his face with his hands. "And if you hated me like that, I wouldn't be able to live with it."

Ariadne clutched at her burning throat. "You are not making me feel better."

"You have to understand," he said after another long moment, "how much my life has been fueled by hate. Centuries of it. It's too much."

"Stop speaking in riddles!" The sudden shout made her clamp her mouth shut. Anger would not help her.

"I should've left that night." He watched her like a scorned animal. "I should've let Loren kill me."

"Do not ever say that."

"You don't understand."

"Then *make* me."

But what happened next underscored his words. At first, she moved toward him when he doubled over, clutching his middle as he groaned in pain. He held out a hand to force the distance between them. Several loud, sickening cracks echoed in the room, and he clamped his mouth shut to muffle a scream. He grabbed his head and writhed in place before his knees gave out, landing him in a heap on the floor.

"Azriel!" She touched his shoulder gently, and he choked back a cry, whipping his head around to look at her.

Her mind went blank. The air stuck in her lungs and, after struggling with it for several deafening heartbeats, she released a mortified breath. Azriel did not look up at her. Those perfect, peridot eyes had vanished.

Instead, a pair of eyes as bright as rubies stared back. His mouth opened for another scream, baring two rows of sharp teeth, and a navy hue crept across his tan skin. From his hairline, two black horns spiraled out like a ram's.

Before she could find her voice, a dhemon swayed to a standing position where her husband had been a moment before. The Caersan clothing stretched to its limits across the larger form. His chest heaved, and the expression twisting his face as he leveled his gaze on her was one of shame.

"It was you," she breathed, mind numb. "It was *you*."

"Listen to me." It was not Azriel's voice—it was a voice she had prayed to never hear again. A voice that haunted her each time she recalled those moments of struggle in her bedroom—the voice which told her to stop screaming before clamping a hand over her mouth as she called for Darien. "Please listen."

"*You*."

"I didn't have a choice—"

"There is *always* a choice!" She slammed her hip into the corner of the desk as she backed away. "You said it yourself."

The dhemon—Azriel—stepped forward, and her heart launched into her throat. "Ehrun had Madan—was going to kill him and—"

"So you ruined *my* life instead?" She could not wrap her mind around it all. The dhemon who stole her from the safety of her own home stood before her. Her abductor. The one who delivered her into that hell. She had *kissed* him mere moments earlier.

"I never intended on any of it."

"You *gave* me to him," she gasped, backing into a chair and nearly tripping. "You let him do...everything to me."

"No," he gasped and took a deep breath.

He screwed up his face in pain again and, faster than the transition into the form of a monster, that of her husband returned. As he stumbled, gaze unfocused, she started for the exit. The room spun around her.

"Wait!" Azriel fell against the door, blocking her way. "Listen to me, *please*."

Ariadne shook her head, eyes stinging. "You have spent months lying to me. You let me fall in love with you when, the entire time, you were the one who destroyed everything."

"Let me explain."

"No."

"He's your half-brother!"

That made her stop. She stared at him, incredulous. "What?"

Azriel's face glistened with sweat, and he blinked several times, eyes still unable to focus on her face. "Your father was married to my mother, and he *hated* me because he knew I wasn't his, but Madan...he was."

"My father's first family died." She gaped at him. "Dhemons killed them."

"No," he breathed. "Markus killed my mother, and then he tried to kill me—my father, the Crowe, saved Madan and me and raised us."

She held her head and squeezed her eyes shut. None of it made sense. "Stop lying."

"I swear to you—"

"You told me you loved me," she said, shoving him aside to reach the handle. She ripped the door open and hurried down the hall away from him. Away from the pain which throbbed through her soul.

He did not try to stop her, but he followed. "I *do*. I love you so much, Ariadne."

She reached the foyer where several servants stood, called by the rise of voices. They looked on as Azriel grappled for her wrist, and she yanked away. He let her go as though her skin were alight with flames. "Do not touch me."

"Please listen to me," he begged. "Let me explain."

"Petre." She turned to the butler, ignoring her husband—if she could even call him that. "The carriage. Immediately."

"Of course, my Lady." Petre bowed, glanced uncertainly at Azriel, then left.

The others shifted nervously before slinking away down the halls. A lover's quarrel was all they saw. They could not know or understand the depths of the deception laid upon her life.

She needed to get away. To get away from the man she thought she loved and could not even look at.

"You can't go." Azriel's voice broke behind her.

Ariadne turned to find him on his knees in the middle of the foyer. His green eyes—damn her, those eyes which still made her breath catch—shone silver. "And why not? It is only you who can do what you will with someone's life?"

"No," he gasped. "If you leave, I can't protect you. They'll come after you, just like Madan."

She stepped back to the front door and felt for the handle. "I'll be protected."

His eyes widened with understanding, tears sliding down the damp paths on his cheeks. He shook his head again and again. "Don't."

"The General will keep me safe."

Because now she understood Loren's reservations. He had been right the entire time, and she should have listened. Of the two of them, the General had always been the better choice. At least he had never lied.

"Ariadne, please—"

She turned from him, opened the door, and paused. "You were wrong, by the way."

"What?"

Without looking back, she said, "I hate you more than you hate yourself," and slammed the door behind her.

CHAPTER 30

The world crashed around him. It burned. It swallowed Azriel into depths darker than he could've ever imagined possible. The very foundation of his existence walked out the door and left him in ruins of his own making.

And that only made it worse—he'd done it to himself.

So he curled in on himself, arms wrapped tight about his body. He rocked back and forth, unable to contain the sheer agony ripping through him. His entire soul shattered.

Without Ariadne, he was nothing.

I hate you more than you hate yourself.

The words played in his mind again and again. Whether spoken from fear or anger, it didn't matter. She had every right to think the worst of him. He'd done nothing to retain her trust, and marrying her despite their history only proved her right.

I hate you...

Every memory leading to the door slamming behind his wife only made him want to crawl farther inside himself. They blinked in and out of his mind, solidifying each terrible choice he made—all beginning with listening to Ehrun.

After Madan's partner, Whelan, had been reported captured to be sold into the fighting Pits of Algorath, Ehrun claimed Azriel to be too invested to think clearly on a rescue mission. In response to Madan's frantic desperation, Azriel's father, the Crowe and long-standing Dhemon King, promised to free him. Azriel remained behind with his brother.

No one believed Ehrun would go directly against the Crowe's decree: do not attack Valenul unless provoked.

But Ehrun had a vendetta after the vampires slaughtered his family. Holding a dying mate and infant daughter changed a man forever. He'd do anything to get his revenge on the one who ordered the massacre: General Markus Harlow.

So the Crowe left, and Ehrun, his trusted general, had taken Madan to manipulate the only dhemon capable of hiding amongst the vampires—Azriel.

"Bring me the eldest daughter of Markus Harlow," Ehrun instructed as Madan struggled against his bonds, feet slipping out from under him as they neared the dungeon steps.

"Don't do it, Azriel, or—" The only words Madan had said before Ehrun's cronies knocked him out.

Ehrun smirked. "I'll teach that fanged bastard the true meaning of pain."

I hate you more than you hate yourself.

Azriel opened his eyes and stared at the floor of the foyer, the tile swimming beyond the sea of tears. After all he'd sacrificed, endured, and wrought, he still lost everything.

He pushed to his feet. His legs wobbled beneath him as he staggered forward. The front door seemed so far away, but he had to reach it. Had to focus long enough to get through.

Ariadne wasn't safe. So long as the dhemons hunted him, she would be a target.

I hate you—I hate you—I hate you...

The night they met hadn't been Vertium, as Ariadne had once believed. It'd been a late-winter celebration. He'd waited patiently outside the Harlow Estate in his vampire form, watching the greedy Caersans dance. Hate rolled through him.

Hate for the way he'd been treated. Hate for how much he longed to be a part of it. Hate for himself at what he had to do.

At first, he'd seen Emillie. The knowledge-loving younger sister, laughing and eyeing the women in their ball gowns. Though he'd spent the journey to Laeton steeling himself against the horrible deed laid at his feet, his strength wavered. She didn't deserve Ehrun's wrath. Her sister didn't, either.

Emillie had swept through the crowd, and as she disappeared from view, Azriel desperately pieced together a plan to ensure neither sister would be harmed by the deranged dhemon. Once he had Madan safe, he'd break the elder sister free.

Then he had found Ariadne in the arms of another man—Darien Gard. The bond snapped into place, and everything changed.

I hate you more...

He ripped open the front door of the manor he didn't deserve and almost vomited at the sight of the carriage pulling away. The hole in his heart—gods, the wounds cracking through his soul—would be more than he could endure. Something he knew would happen the moment he agreed to join Madan in Laeton.

Mistake after mistake. How had he been so thick to believe he'd make it out unscathed?

He nearly had, though. For those few beautiful nights, he had everything he wanted. Everything he needed.

Despite Ariadne's altered views of him, his feelings would never change. He belonged to her, body, mind, and soul. So he would do anything possible to keep her safe—whether she wanted him to or not.

To die for her was all he had left.

I hate you...

Changing into his dhemon form had never been painless, but there'd been a time he could endure it in silence. He'd done so in the shadows of the Harlow Estate before vomiting into the bushes at what he'd been about to do. Then he scaled the walls to her balcony and waited for her appearance after the ball.

Her screams when he had dragged her from the room almost destroyed him. He'd let her go several times. Then the memory of Madan's limp body steeled his resolve, and he convinced himself he could make it work. Somehow, he'd free his brother and save Ariadne before she had to endure anything.

He'd hated himself then.

...more than you hate yourself.

He still hated himself.

Azriel backtracked into the manor and ran back to the study. The desk was askew, and the foot of the chair Ariadne had tripped into had gouged a line into the wood floor. None of it mattered, though the displaced objects reminded him of their struggle through her bedroom.

He collected his sword from behind the desk and slipped a dagger into his boot holster. Though she believed the General would keep her safe—his stomach roiled at the thought—she'd be dead within a day. That useless sack of flesh was more concerned about his own neck than the woman he once claimed to want to marry.

Before he almost broke her arm, of course.

... hate... hate... hate you...

The dawn of the first day, he'd shielded her from the sun in a small hut in the forest. Again, he almost left her there and let her go. But he'd built that hut years prior for Madan. His brother used it to stave off the sunlight when traveling, and if he left Ariadne there, he'd forfeit Madan's life.

By the time he'd reached the dhemon keep built into the mountainside, Ariadne stopped begging to be released. He presented her to Ehrun with as straight a face as he could muster.

"Miss Harlow," the dhemon had purred and stroked her cheek.

Azriel's body jerked in response, an automatic need to break the bastard's fingers for touching her. He held back, but it'd been too late.

Ehrun's eyes snapped to him, and a slow grin spread across his face. He switched to the dhemon tongue and said, "Oh, this will be fun."

Then those same dhemons who'd dragged his brother away marched forward. Ten of them. They grabbed Azriel, kicked out the back of his knees, and dragged him back. His frenzy to escape increased when the doors opened again.

Darien Gard stepped in, sword at the ready.

Then he screamed, knowing precisely what would happen. The Caersan didn't stand a chance against the horde of dhemons. In the confusion, Ariadne spat in Ehrun's face and tried to run to her fiancé.

The last thing he'd seen of her before the door closed between them was Ehrun backhanding her so hard she collapsed to the ground before advancing on Darien.

I hate you more than you hate yourself.

Azriel raced back to the front door and took off into the night on foot. Saddling Jasper would take too long. He needed to be ready for a fight at any moment, and sitting atop a horse made him a target.

He made it a dozen paces outside the manor gates before he saw the red eyes. The dhemon's sharp teeth flashed in the moonlight as he smirked at Azriel. Until that moment, anyone watching the house would've assumed he and Ariadne were together in that carriage.

Now they knew the truth.

Fuck. *Fuck*.

The dhemon disappeared into the shadows, his dark blue skin and black clothes fading from sight. He moved like a wraith. No snapping of branches or shuffling of the underbrush. No sign of which way he moved except, maybe, the direction of the carriage.

I hate... I hate you...

The flogging Azriel endured at the hands of Ehrun's cronies had been nothing compared to being forced to listen to Ariadne's screams. Pain and suffering he'd caused for a brother he wasn't even certain still lived. Worse than that, however, had been the endless silence. He didn't know whether she slept or had perished at Ehrun's hands.

Yet somehow, Madan had freed himself with a deal of his own, concocted a plan, and prepared to do what Azriel failed to accomplish. As Azriel clawed at the handleless door and rained empty threats upon anyone who passed close enough to hear, his brother did what needed to be done.

"We have to leave," Madan had hissed when he opened the cell door and started down the hall toward the back exit. "Now."

"No." Azriel grabbed his arm, stopping his brother mid-stride. "Get her out. I'll keep him distracted."

Madan's face had paled in the low light. "He'll kill you."

"So be it."

With that, he had taken the stairs from the dungeon three at a time. He'd wanted so badly to make Ehrun pay for what he did—for what he'd made him do. But Azriel didn't yet understand the thoughtless rage of a bonded dhemon. Separated by death from his mate made Ehrun far more powerful than Azriel could dream of being.

Hate—hate—hate—

Now he knew. Now Azriel had glimpsed the suffering Ehrun endured for decades before seeking vengeance. It broke even the strongest man.

Though he'd suspected the dhemons to be watching his home after killing one a few nights before, Azriel hadn't expected them to act so swiftly. They knew something was amiss between them, and this was their chance to act. Even if they didn't plan to go after her, they'd need to gather their numbers to come after him again.

Because now that she hated him, he had nothing left to lose and everything to gain by killing them all.

CHAPTER 31

By the time Ariadne reached the Harlow Estate—no, *home*—her tears had dried. She had spent the carriage ride bent over double and praying for the waking terror in which she now found herself to end. Again and again, memories of fear and pain pelted her. Each one began and ended with the face of the dhemon who started it all.

Azriel's face.

How had she not seen it before? The similarities were undeniable. The shape of his eyes, the quirk of his mouth, and the way he pinched his brows when asked a question he didn't want to answer.

The navy complexion, ebony horns, and crimson irises of her memories distracted her from seeing what was right in front of her in the guise of a vampire.

A monster.

When the carriage halted at the foot of the manor's front steps, Ariadne sat up straight and dragged her palms across her face. Though she doubted she looked remotely presentable, she smoothed out the skirt of her dress nonetheless.

The door opened, and she looked up at the familiar, towering manor.

Ariadne's hands shook as she made her way up the front steps. It had not been long since Emillie departed from the Caldwell manor. What would her sister think of her showing up unannounced? Would her father send her back?

She could not go back. Not now. Not ever.

"Lady Caldwell," the butler said upon opening the door. The name grated on her ears. He bowed her into the foyer and shut her inside. "The Princeps is not expecting you."

"Has my sister returned?"

He inclined his head. "Of course."

"Tell my father I am visiting." Ariadne started for the stairs, unable to keep eye contact with the Rusan. "I do not know for how long."

The butler frowned. "Shall I prepare a room?"

A room—not *her* room. She did not belong here anymore. Whether she liked it or not, she had been married off to a man she despised. A man whose face loomed in the shadows and leered at her from over Ehrun's shoulder in her sleeping terrors.

And to think, she had once thought it to be General Loren Gard.

"Yes, please," she rasped, ignoring the burning in her throat.

"Will the Lord Governor be joining you this evening?"

Ariadne swallowed hard, and her grip on the banister tightened. "No. No, he will not."

The better question was whether Azriel would ever join her again. Despite her loathing, she could not find the courage or words to expose him. Explaining to her father who, or what, Azriel Caldwell truly was made her blood run cold. The thought of him in chains again, this time headed for the gallows...

At the top of the stairs, she paused again, a jolt of pain ricocheting through her heart. She clutched her middle and stared straight ahead with wide eyes. No, she would not cry again. Not here where questions would be asked.

"Ari?" Emillie's voice floated down the corridor from the direction of her suite. "Did I forget something?"

She dragged in a shuddering breath and stood a little straighter. Forcing a small smile on her face, she turned to her sister. "No. I realized how much I missed home."

"Home is with your husband now." Her father's voice echoed from the foyer. Her whole body tensed again. "Why have you come?"

Emillie's brows creased. Her sharp eyes never missed anything. No matter how hard Ariadne tried to hide her true emotions, her sister discovered the truth. Without a word, Emillie slipped a hand into hers and squeezed once.

"He is busy," Ariadne said as she turned toward her father. He paused at the landing and lifted a quizzical brow. She continued, "I am hoping to stay until the ball—to spend one last day with you both before the move."

Something softened in his features. His eyes went distant for a breath before refocusing as though shaking off a memory long-forgotten. "Azriel will be attending, yes?"

She bit her lip, stomach churning. There would be no escaping the prison she had locked herself in. Oh, if she could go back and fix it all, she would have let him leave. She would have stepped aside before he could discover the bruise, before she could make the terrible mistake of kissing him. All of it would have been avoided.

"Of course," she breathed with the shadow of a smile. "Of course."

"Very good." Her father nodded once. "I need to speak with him before your departure."

She should tell him. Every fiber of her being screamed to speak the truth: Azriel Caldwell was a liar, a sheep in wolf's clothing, a *dhemon*. Worse, he was the son of the Dhemon King, the Crowe. The one who had spent centuries waging war against Valenul. Her own husband had likely been a part of it, in fact.

Dhomin.

The dhemon from the road used that word. Again and again, and each time, Azriel grew more and more enraged.

"What does *dhomin* mean?" She blurted the question before weighing the consequences.

Her father stilled. "Where did you hear that word?"

Emillie looked between them, recognizing the harsh language and calculating the risks of such knowledge. She bit her lip and shifted her weight from foot to foot.

"I remembered it recently," Ariadne lied and hoped her expression did not give her away. "From... before."

Enough of a truth neither of them would question. To get her to say anything about her time in the mountains was a miracle.

Still, her father tilted his head and searched her face. "It means *little prince.*"

So Azriel had been a fae prince in disguise, as Camilla had once joked. The problem with his title, of course, remained which fae lineage he hailed from. At the time they had assumed him to be high fae from L'Oden Forest—not a dhemon. Not an enemy of Valenul.

"Never speak that tongue in my house again," he added.

"Yes, Father." Ariadne's heart hammered in her chest, and she dipped her chin to refocus elsewhere. In her periphery, Emillie looked between them, gaze lingering on her face. Whatever she saw there, Ariadne knew she could not hide it forever.

Not when she needed to think of a way to convince them to let her stay. To convince Azriel to leave her alone. Perhaps he would do so in exchange for her silence. He could return to Eastwood on his own, and she would only suffer his presence when he visited Laeton.

"Excuse me," Ariadne said after the silence stretched out too long. "I should wash up."

"Ari, may I join—"

"No." She did not look at her sister as she turned toward the next set of stairs. "I need a moment alone."

Emillie remained silent after that, and Ariadne hurried up to the third floor. As much as she wanted to speak with her sister, tell her everything, and glean whatever advice she might have to make it through the crumbles of her life, she could not. She could not condemn Azriel because, gods damn her, she still loved him. The thought of him in handcuffs again—or, worse, killed—made her want to scream.

Penelope, in charge of preparing her room, opened the door from the inside at the same time Ariadne reached for the handle. The Rusan maid curtsied and said, "Fresh linens on your bed, my Lady. Would you like tea?"

"No, thank you." Ariadne slipped by and locked the door behind her.

She had not made it even a fortnight since she last set foot in the room sprawled out before her. In those few short nights, she discovered both nirvana and the true meaning of despair. All of it stemmed from the one man she swore to hate yet could not stop loving.

Unable to draw in a full breath, Ariadne crossed the room and, for the first time since her return from the dhemon keep, flung open the doors to the veranda. Warm, summer air curled around her.

Ten...

It filled her lungs as it passed down her burning throat. Her chest expanded, and she held it, desperate for any relief from the pain. Her knuckles turned white as she curled her fingers around the rail.

Azriel had been dragged away not long after delivering her to the keep. He roared—no, screamed—as Darien appeared, ready to fight Ehrun. He struggled against the hands, forcing him back. She had seen only rage in his face, but now she knew the man behind the horns. Knew his heart.

It had been fear. Not rage.

Nine...

She exhaled hard. The air left her in a long, low wail. Her elbows bent, and she let the tears fall again.

The first night had been long and silent in her dark cell. All that interrupted the reticence were shouts at the far end of the cell block. Shouts and something slamming hard against a wall or door. Had it been Darien? She had not seen what Ehrun did with him at first.

Or had it been Azriel, locked away and branded as she had been?

Eight...

Inhale. Everything would be easier if she could hate him as she claimed—if she could harden her heart to forget all they had done together. To forget all he had done for her.

When Ehrun had first come for her, he told her the tale of a massacre. In the beginning, she had thought it to be a dhemon attack on a vampire village. Then he described his wife. His newborn daughter. He carved each detail into her back, then smeared it with salt to make his story permanent in her skin.

Seven...

She covered her mouth to dampen the next shaking sob. Her body quaked with the force of it as her mind wrestled with the juxtaposition of the two vastly different people she now knew Azriel to be.

Her own husband had not only ensured her torture but her late fiance's death. Darien's fangs were removed—a death sentence unto itself for vampires—and as he fought against Ehrun, she witnessed the end of his life. Ehrun had crushed Darien's skull right in front of her, extinguishing every hope she had of freedom.

Six...

In a single breath, she could hear Azriel's laugh and see those ruby-red eyes looming through the darkness of her bedroom. Each memory warred with the other. The feeling of his lips, so gentle and loving, against her skin careened headlong into the sensation of falling as he hauled her over the veranda railing.

The tales Ehrun had told after that were lost to her. She had stopped begging for his mercy; it would never come.

All because of Azriel.

Five...

Beyond her whimper, she could hear someone knocking on the door of her room. Likely Emillie.

The night Madan pulled her from her cell, she had been convinced she had died, and Ern, the God of Wind, had come to collect her soul and carry her to Empyrean. The dash from the keep had been nothing but a blur of back halls and hidden doors, shouts of alarm and dhemons fighting one another.

Four...

The air rushed into her lungs, and she tilted her head back. The stars above her winked, not a care in the world. Some-where amidst their shimmer lay the heavens where the gods sat on their thrones. Did they mock her?

Prayer had not helped in the mountain dungeons. She had given up on them for some time after that.

Three...

"Please," she rasped, kneeling. Her hands slid from the rail to the balusters beneath. She let her head fall between her arms, and she squeezed her eyes closed. "Make it stop. Make it all go away."

She needed to forget it all. Forget the pain and, most importantly, the love.

Two...

Ariadne opened her eyes again and sucked in a sharp breath. A shadow at the edge of the garden. A pair of grounds guards moved in to investigate.

Not again... not again...

Had Azriel come to collect her once more?

One...

"Gods." She covered her mouth again, this time to force back the scream rising up her throat as the first guard stumbled back, a bolt lodged in his chest. He fell in a heap. The second could not so much as call for help before having his throat slashed open and joining his companion.

Three dhemons, all unfamiliar faces, breached the treeline. The one in the middle lifted a long knife and pointed it up at her. He said something she could not hear, and they stalked forward, keeping to the shadows. With their dark complexion, they slid in and out of sight with ease.

She shot to her feet and reeled back. Not again.

If you leave, I can't protect you. They'll come after you—

Azriel's words replayed again and again. She had claimed Loren would keep her safe. The words had left her before she considered their truth. They had merely been what she knew would hurt him most.

What if he had been right? Three of the monsters from her past were back and closing in.

And even though she claimed to hate him, Ariadne knew in her gut that Azriel did not reciprocate the feeling. He may have been the one who dragged her from this very manor, but what if he had been telling the truth? Were he here, they would not have killed those guards. Were he here, they would not be trying to get to her.

After all, it was him they wanted. Not her.

A shout rang out, and the three dhemons froze, the only sign of them the glint of their weapons. No guards moved in to block their path. In fact, as Ariadne looked around, she could see no one else. Had they all been killed?

She reached behind her for the door to shut herself inside. There would be no staying in that room. Not with the threat outside and no idea whether more dhemons lurked beyond her keen vision.

That's when she saw the fourth dhemon at the edge of the woods. Her heart stumbled as she took in the Caersan clothes and sword strapped to his back. He held out a hand and from his grip—her stomach churned—dropped a severed dhemon head.

Another shout, this time more clearly in their gravelly language, and he pulled the sword from its sheath. When the three dhemons just beyond the garden walls did not move, he kicked the head, sending it tumbling closer to them. He yelled a third time, pounded a fist on his chest, and brandished the blade.

Whatever he said, the three dhemons could no longer ignore it. They turned and started back toward him at a run.

Before Ariadne closed herself in the room, Azriel looked up at her with those vibrant red eyes, inclined his head, and disappeared into the woods with the dhemons on his heels.

A bolt struck Azriel's shoulder before he made it a dozen paces into the forest. He snarled in pain and leaned behind a tree to break off the fletched end. The tip stuck through his shirt, beside the brand on his chest.

The twin scar to Ariadne's.

Stooping low, he pulled the dagger from his boot and, pivoting around the tree, let it fly. The wet crunch and heavy thud told him he'd hit his mark and one of his adversaries was dead. With the sentry he'd stalked now decapitated as well, Ehrun's numbers dwindled.

Unless the traitorous bastard indoctrinated more dhemons to his genocidal cause, his command was slipping. The moment Ehrun's blade went through the Crowe's belly, by accident or on purpose, it didn't matter. He lost dozens, if not hundreds, of warriors' and clans' support. Regicide had that effect—even if the Crowe had been King by name alone.

Which only made the taunts from the final two dhemons that much more infuriating.

"*Dhomin*," one called with a low chuckle. He continued in the dhemon tongue, "Come out, little prince. We just want to talk."

Little prince. How long had he put up with the insult? He worked harder than any other under his father's rule at the mountain keep—called *Auhla*, or Palace, by the dhemon clans—to gain the respect he desired.

What hadn't helped was his inability to change form from vampire to dhemon until his transition when he turned sixty-one. He lost track of how many times his siring had been questioned by his thirtieth birthday.

"Look at him," they'd sneer when he passed, lanky and pale and unimpressive. No matter what they said, he couldn't retaliate due to his title and size. "His mother was a lying, fanged whore and tricked the Crowe into keeping him."

Azriel adjusted his grip on the sword in his hand. Thinking of the past wouldn't help him face the dhemons Ehrun sent after him. Though he couldn't name them if he tried, they knew full well who he was—what he was—and precisely what to say to get his blood boiling.

The dhemon who taunted him made his way to the left of Azriel. He moved with big, clunky steps that caused more noise than his comrade. The second shifted through the underbrush with such little sound, Azriel couldn't pinpoint their location.

Neither bode well for him. While one could sneak up on him, the other was likely much larger and stronger.

The first to make an appearance was, as Azriel suspected, the massive, lumbering brute holding a long hunting knife. His horns swept back from his face and came to a vicious tip just behind his pointed blue ears. The short length meant only one thing: the dhemon had yet to reach his first century. Young. Too young.

As a race of god-born fae, they could live for thousands of years—almost as long as a healthy, warless Caersan vampire.

The youth pivoted as Azriel lifted the sword. He lunged forward with his wicked knife, and Azriel parried. Even as a dhemon, which gained him almost a foot of height compared to his vampire form, the younger dhemon stood almost a head taller.

"Is this why they call you *little* prince?" The dhemon snickered and lunged forward with the knife.

Azriel twisted his injured shoulder back to avoid the jab, stepped between the youth's feet, and, using his hip as leverage, yanked the outstretched arm down to throw the dhemon to the ground. He raised the sword to stab down when a bolt lodged into his exposed side. The momentum lurched him away from the prone dhemon with another roar of pain.

The youth lashed out with the knife, and Azriel stumbled further back. He tugged the bolt free, hissing through his teeth, and heat leaked down his side.

If it hadn't been for drinking Ariadne's blood mere hours before, he'd bleed out in minutes. With her pure Caersan blood, however, he'd heal faster than either dhemon before him. There were some perks to being a half-breed bastard.

It didn't save him from the pain, though.

The smaller, more agile dhemon slid out from behind a tree. Azriel froze at the slim, elegant horns and sharp, vicious face. It wasn't often a woman was allowed in the ranks—at least not when he lived at *Auhla*. Ehrun ridiculed those granted a position by the Crowe, and that only meant one thing: he was desperate.

The woman steadied the crossbow on her hip and loaded another bolt, never once taking her eyes off him. She knew what she was doing, and this wasn't her first fight. Unlike the youth now clambering to his feet.

Azriel tucked his left arm down tight over the wound between his ribs, grateful both bolts hit the same side. He groaned but lifted his sword again. "Run back to your general and tell him you lost."

The youth chuckled again. "General? Ehrun?"

"That ill-tempered bastard, yes."

"Ill-tempered?" The woman clicked her tongue. "You sound like those fanged cunts."

Azriel snorted. "Did he forget to tell you that I *am* one of them?"

She lifted the crossbow and took aim. "Not at all."

He leapt closer to the youth to avoid the bolt and blocked a swing of the long knife. The huge dhemon's fist came out of nowhere, slamming into Azriel's face hard enough to shatter a human's cheekbone. He stumbled, then fell to a knee.

His head spun. Spots clouded his vision. The night rang with a shrill sound that hadn't been there before.

The dhemon swung again. Azriel, just present enough to see the flash of steel, rolled back over his shoulder and staggered to his feet. Another ungainly slash of the knife—had no one taught him how to use it before sending him into the field? Or had they anticipated using his brute strength to haul off a Caersan vampire?

They'd come for Ariadne.

No. Not again. The thought snapped Azriel back into focus. He did this for her. He'd kill anyone who tried to hurt her.

The youth moved forward again. With a lunge, twist, and jerk of his wrist, Azriel sent the knife tumbling to the ground. Another quick slash, and he removed the youth's outstretched hand.

The resulting scream echoed off the trees.

Slapping a hand over the dhemon's mouth, Azriel leaned in close and whispered, "You're too young for this fight. I can help you."

"Get away from him." The woman pulled the next bolt into place and stepped closer. "Keep your fang-loving poison to yourself."

"Please," Azriel hissed. "Let me help."

The youth clutched his bleeding stump of an arm to his chest and lifted his mouth away from Azriel's hand to grind out, "Liar."

Azriel moved at the sound of the next bolt's release. He ducked behind the youth, shoving him onto the arbalist's path and letting the huge dhemon take the bolt in the neck. Blood sprayed everywhere and drowned the dhemon's cry of shock.

The woman yelled in dismay and stepped forward as though to help, then thought better of it. She set her jaw and dropped the crossbow. "I will bring your head to the king."

Something ugly twisted in Azriel's gut. "King."

"Did he forget to tell you?" she mocked, and a wicked smirk spread across her face as she unsheathed two short swords. "Ehrun is king now."

Azriel choked on a hollow laugh, straightening and squaring up with the woman. "My father hated that title anyway. All hail King Ehrun the Inept. King Ehrun the Traitor. King Ehrun the Murderer of Peace."

"Peace," she spat and circled closer. "Peace with these cursed rats?"

"Peace," Azriel repeated. "Something Ehrun would never understand."

Something his father had been speaking to Lord Governor Garth Caldwell about for months. The reason, Azriel suspected, for Ehrun's coup. And the reason for Garth's sudden death. Old age didn't take Caersan vampires hundreds of years younger than their wives.

What caused his quick decline, however, remained an enigma.

"If you think peace will ever be an option," she hissed and closed the distance between them in a flurry of movement. He barely had time to block the attack. "Then you've ignored the destruction they've caused."

In an instant, Azriel was back to the night outside the Caldwell Estate as his mother had bled out before him. She'd turned her shimmering green eyes to him and whispered one final word: "Run."

He hadn't run fast enough.

Azriel lifted his sword to block the next attack. He grit his teeth against the jarring pain, unable to use both hands to leverage the blade.

"No," he bit out and swung back at the woman. "You're too blind to see the possibilities, and kidnapping an innocent woman has nothing to do with any of it."

The dhemon laughed, parried, and lunged, missing his stomach by a breath. "You're one to talk."

Heat bubbled through his veins. Azriel smacked her swords to the side with all his strength, sending her reeling, and stabbed fast and hard. One moment she laughed. The next, blood splattered from her mouth.

As she collapsed to the ground, she glared up at him, unable to speak. He kicked the sword away and stepped over her. She didn't deserve any more words from him.

From the estate grounds came the frantic shouts of guards gathering near the woods. Azriel stalked away from the dead and dying dhemons, keeping the lights from the manor in sight between the trees.

A handful of guards slowed as they reached the treeline. One shouted something about the dismembered head. Another about the dhemon sprawled a few paces farther back, Azriel's dagger buried in the chest.

Well, fuck. That'd been a good blade, too.

"Report back to the Princeps," ordered a guard, "that Lady Caldwell had been correct. Dhemons in the garden."

Lady Caldwell. So Ariadne had sent the guards out there. Had she hoped they'd help him? Or kill him?

Though he hoped for the former, the latter was more likely true.

I hate you more than you hate yourself.

Try as she might, it'd take more than a half-dozen Caersan guards to kill him. Not when he had an entire list of things to accomplish now.

First and foremost, he had to keep her safe. If that meant sitting outside her rooms and killing anything that breathed wrong, he'd do it.

Next, find his brother. Madan had been gone for too long, and the dhemons were as tight-lipped about where they were keeping him as he'd been about his true identity.

Finally, and possibly the solution to the first two tasks, he needed to kill Ehrun.

Azriel slipped farther from the guards before easing closer to the manor. He kept within the trees as he gazed up at the massive house, scanning each window. She had to be there somewhere.

When he found her, his heart dropped.

Ariadne stood on the veranda of her old bedroom. The very same one he'd climbed the walls to breach. A single candle glowed from a table inside, lighting her from behind. She wore a simple nightgown and robe, not unlike what she'd been in when he took her away.

And she stared right at him.

While the commotion of the guards took place to his right, she shifted in his direction, wrapped her arms around herself, and gazed out at him.

Ice-cold guilt leeched through him. He swallowed hard but didn't move. What she thought of him surviving, he didn't want to know. All he could do was wait and see. Tomorrow night, they'd talk. He'd make sure of it.

After all, he couldn't watch her attend a ball at the Gards' manor without him.

CHAPTER 32

How Ariadne fit into one of Emillie's ball gowns, she may never understand. It had been a dress from the previous Season made of a soft cream fabric and lavender lace. The back scooped lower than she liked, so she layered a diaphanous shawl beneath to hide her scars. As she did so, she refused to linger on the cause of the horrible name now etched into her flesh.

Because now, each stroke of that knife connected the pain to Azriel.

What would she do when she saw him again? Would she choose to forgive and forget? No. There would never be a chance to forget what he had put her through.

Still, when he led those three dhemons away from her that morning, she could not help the relief she felt. She had run from her room calling for Sul—the personal guard she did not care for but who had proven he could hold his own against a dhemon. He had come racing from a servant's hall, and when she explained what she had seen—three dhemons in the woods beyond the garden—he had launched into action. Every floor-level door to the manor was locked, curtains drawn. Guards took off for the woods.

Three, she had told him. Only three dhemons.

The moment Sul disappeared, Ariadne had hurried back upstairs and went to the room she avoided for so long. The room she once begged to leave.

And that room had not been touched since her mad rush to abandon it. The books she had coveted on the bookshelves remained in their places. The one she had been reading that terrible night still sat on the chair where she had left it to investigate the sound on the veranda.

On her way to that same door, Ariadne had brushed her fingers along the leather cover of the novel. They caressed the gold-stamped letters like a long-forgotten lover. Then she continued on, a single candle in hand, and opened the door. Warm summer air swirled in around her.

Guards descended on the woods as she set the candle on a table and slipped outside. No one would expect her to be there. No one would check this room to ensure her safety.

No one except Azriel.

He kept to the shadows of the trees, but she knew then what to look for. His midnight blue skin and black horns blended in with the darkness, so it was his eyes which gave him away. Always his eyes. Whether green or red, they watched her with the same melancholy intensity.

She had wrapped her arms around her then as the flood of emotions hit. He held his side as though injured, and one eye swelled. But still, he stood. He fought, and he won. For her.

She wanted to go to him then. Even as a dhemon, she wanted to touch his face and ask where he was hurt. To feel the weight of his cheek pressing into her palm.

Then a guard shouted up at her to go inside, breaking through her thoughts and shattering the memory of her husband's face shifting from the one she hated back into the one she loved. She retreated into the manor and left that room behind.

Now she stood before a mirror, hair braided like a coronet around her head. She shifted to ensure every scar remained hidden, the heat of anger sluicing through her again. He did this to her. Frightened her. Ruined her. To think she could continue to love such a twisted man who lied and betrayed her—

A knock on the door jolted her just as the guard's shout had. "My Lady, Lord Caldwell has arrived."

Her stomach twisted, and her breath caught. No, no, no. She needed more time. More time to compose herself. More time to decide what to do.

She could still tell her father and demand he be arrested. She could expose Azriel for the snake he was, watch with satisfaction as the man who destroyed everything she loved was taken away—not to be lashed, but to be killed. She could apologize to Loren and tell him everything she knew about Azriel and the dhemons.

He would take her back. He would keep her safe.

Yet somehow, the memories of the General made her just as sick. She rubbed at her wrist as she turned to the door. If he had been so quick to harm her the first time, he would do it again.

"I will be down in a moment," she said and pulled in a long, shaking breath.

After a beat, Ariadne crossed the room and opened the door. No one stood in the hall. Hardly a voice could be heard except, by her keen Caersan ears, the low voices of those in the foyer. One, a gravelly rumble, made her heart kick into high gear.

How could she face him again?

She drew her shoulders back and stood a little straighter. Once, she had stared into the eyes of a dhemon with the refusal to back down. It had been the first time Ehrun struck her.

Right after Azriel had been dragged away, yelling something in the dhemon language, to the same dungeons she lived in all those nights. Dragged away. Fighting. Though she had not known the words he said, she had recognized the tone. At the time, she had assumed he had been angry about not getting the credit for her retrieval. Now she understood.

He had been scared. Frightened, even, to be taken away.

I didn't have a choice—I never intended on any of it.

Had he been telling the truth?

Ariadne started for the stairs, heart slamming against her ribs like a hammer and anvil. If only it gave her the strength of steel to face him. To listen—or expose.

Down the first flight of stairs. She paused at the landing overlooking the foyer and gripped the banister hard, knuckles white, as Azriel turned his face up to her. No horns. No sharp teeth save for his fangs. Only peridot irises and dark brows drawn together in concern. A bruise arched around his right eye and his sword, a contradiction to his fine Caersan clothes, was strapped to his back.

Azriel parted his lips as though to greet her, then he closed them and hung his head. He could not even look at her.

Good.

She descended the stairs and stopped an arm's length away. "Husband."

He swallowed hard before bowing with a wince. She let him take her hand and kiss her fingers, lips lingering just long enough for any prying eyes to not suspect anything negative between them. Despite her resolve to hate him, her heart fluttered as it always did in his presence.

"Wife?" The single, whispered word lifted into a question as he raised his gaze and straightened his back with another grimace. Whatever injury he acquired the night before still hurt him.

She did not answer but accepted his arm nonetheless. Her stomach churned, and she shoved away the memory of his rough hands covering her mouth as she screamed for Darien.

Sensing her discomfort, Azriel released her to open the door and followed her down the front steps to the carriage waiting outside. He waved off the coachman to help her in before closing the door behind them both and sitting across from her.

Ariadne watched him with a wary gaze, uncertain what to say or do next. Likewise, he did not look up from his hands.

"You didn't tell them." His voice cracked. Had he expected to be arrested upon his arrival?

"Has Madan returned?" she asked quietly, ignoring his words and twisting her fingers into the skirt of her gown.

Azriel shook his head. "No."

At once, the news did not surprise nor comfort her. Madan continued to be a victim in all of this, same as her.

"You called him my half-brother," she said after a moment, shuffling through all he had said the night before. It had all been such a blur, and she could not recall most of it after the transformation. "Explain."

He looked up, then, with wide eyes. "You want to talk about it?"

She lifted her chin. "I ask the questions. You answer honestly."

"As you wish." Azriel surveyed her for a long moment, then blew out a long breath. "Your father's first wife was Mariana Caldwell. The only daughter of Lord Governor Garth Caldwell."

Ariadne raised a hand to stop him. "Why does no one seem to remember his first family?"

He let out a bitter laugh. "Because he hid us away—never brought us to Laeton and spoke of us to no one."

"Why?" She paused, studied his choice of words again, and said, "Wait... *us?*"

"Shame. Embarrassment. I don't know." Azriel glared out the window for a long moment, then continued, "Mariana was my mother. Madan's mother."

Ariadne mapped out the family tree in her mind, complete with two separate wives for her father and the children he sired. But Azriel did not belong on it. Not really.

"Your father is the Crowe?"

"Was," he corrected. "My father died protecting me from Ehrun. My father died to ensure your escape."

For a moment, her mind went blank. She blinked a couple times before shaking her head. "We will come back to that. Tell me about your family. How does my father not recognize you?"

"I was born Isaiah Harlow." Azriel grimaced. "Madan was Mattias Harlow."

"So you changed your names." She frowned at him. "Still, I would not think your faces are so unrecognizable."

Azriel tilted his head. "It's been almost five centuries since he's seen us and, if I'm not mistaken, he burned every family portrait he had of us. He assumed us dead."

"Why?"

"Because he assumes all dhemons are monsters." Azriel looked at his hands again with another bitter laugh. "Perhaps he's right."

She almost grabbed his hand then to reassure him he was wrong. The twitch in his direction did not go unnoticed. His gaze latched onto her hands before closing his eyes hard.

"He always knew I wasn't his child." Azriel looked up again and gestured to his face. "I may look enough like my mother to pass as a Caldwell, but I hold none of his features. My mother's family married her off to him when they discovered her pregnancy. They kept it a secret and played it off that I was a Harlow."

Ariadne gaped at him. "Your mother was pregnant before her wedding?"

"She loved my father, and he doted on her." A shadow of a smile flitted across his face. Whatever memory he conjured had been a good one. Then his brows creased, and the light disappeared from his eyes. "The Crowe bonded to her, and when Markus left her in Eastwood, she visited him often."

"But Madan is not a dhemon?"

He shook his head. "No. When Madan was born, my oddities stood out even more."

"But my father," she said slowly, "still did not accept him?"

"He had his reservations." The corner of his mouth quirked up. "For good reason, I suppose."

Ariadne rubbed her forehead. It was all so much to take in. An entire family's history forgotten. All except for by the Caldwells, of course. The painting of a woman with two young Caersan boys floated to the forefront of her mind. The Caldwells never forgot any of them. What would her father say if he had seen the painting?

"What happened to your mother?" She shifted on the carriage seat. "You once told me she had been murdered."

"By an officer." Azriel nodded. "Your father discovered her running away. She'd finally gotten the courage to leave Valenul with the Crowe."

Something oily squirmed through her gut at the implication. Her father had been the General before taking his position as the Princeps. "My father killed her?"

"Yes." This time he did not look away. His eyes burned into her with a fierce intensity. "He put a sword through her, then turned it on me."

"How old—"

"I was fifteen."

A child. With the slow growth of Caersan children, he would not have been any larger than an eight-year-old human. Madan, then, would have been even smaller. A mere toddler.

Azriel continued, "My father arrived just before the blow landed. He saved my life and protected Madan. When we left, we thought Markus was dead."

"How did he survive?" She did not want to know. Not really.

"My father went back later to retrieve my mother's body." Azriel glared out the window again. "She was gone. I believe he drank her blood to heal himself."

The thought of her father drinking from his dead wife's body made her sick to her stomach. What kind of man did such things?

A monster.

A long silence passed between them after that. The carriage trundled down the highway as she grappled with the new knowledge of her family's history. It extended farther than she previously thought and entangled more lives than she cared to admit.

"Why did you follow me last night?" she finally asked, unable to keep herself from thinking back to those moments on the verandas.

Azriel sighed and raised his eyes to her from his hands. "They were watching our home."

Our home. She opened and closed her mouth twice before choosing to say nothing. What could she say?

"I'd rather die protecting you," he said, voice a quiet rumble, "than live another night without you."

Her heart sank, and her eyes stung. "Then why did you take me to Ehrun?"

Azriel's throat bobbed, and he pressed the heels of his hands against his eyes for a long moment. He released a shuddering breath. "Because he would've killed Madan, and I swore on my mother's ashes I'd keep him safe."

Her brother, too. "What did Madan think of it?"

"He told me not to." Azriel dropped his hands to his lap and stared at the ceiling of the carriage. "He told me to let him go. For you."

So Madan had been ready to die to keep her safe. Of course. He knew she was his sister the entire time.

"But he's an optimist." Azriel smiled grimly. "I knew Ehrun wouldn't stop hunting you even if I refused. So I agreed and devised a plan to save you both from him."

She had not expected that. The carriage slowed to a crawl, and suddenly, she did not want it to. She wanted to know more. So she remained silent.

Taking the cue, he continued, "I'm not very good at planning, as you now well know. And bonding with you hadn't been part of it, either."

"So that was the truth?" She had assumed it to be just another one of his lies. The lies he now exposed willingly.

"Until the very end," he rasped and shook his head, unable to keep the corners of his mouth from turning down. "Ehrun figured it out and locked me away. I don't know how Madan got out. I've been too ashamed to ask. Now I may never know."

This time, Ariadne did take his hand. He jerked back, almost pulling away and eyes widening with fear. She gave him a single, firm squeeze. "You will find him."

The carriage stopped. Azriel's eyes shimmered with silver, and he pulled a dagger and small holster from under his seat. He glanced at the door. "Put this on. Please."

She frowned at the weapon. "What?"

"Those dhemons last night..." He held out the dagger. "They were only the beginning."

"I do not know how to put it on."

He hesitated. "On your thigh."

Ariadne pulled up her dress as the carriage moved forward again. They were in a queue. "Help me."

Again, Azriel hesitated. He reached out, stopped, and looked up at her with uncertainty.

Her heart thrashed. Was she really doing this? Had she forgiven him? No. But the truth had been a start. It gave her hope and enough trust that he would, in fact, fight for her.

"You can touch me," she reassured him and stuck out her bare leg.

"Ariadne..."

She closed her eyes for a long moment at the sound of her name on his lips. Oh, she still loved him, and she hated it so much. When she opened them again, he searched her face. She nodded once and said, "You are my husband, are you not?"

He sucked in a sharp breath and pulled the straps around her thigh, adjusting them to the perfect tightness.

"Do not confuse this with forgiveness," she said quietly as he worked.

He glanced up at her, and she noted how his fingers barely touched her skin. When he finished, he sat back, and she pulled the dress into place.

After a long moment, as the carriage stopped again, he nodded and said, "I know."

The carriage door opened, and Azriel stepped out, turned, and held out his hand to her. The relief on his face when she accepted him made a knot twist in her gut. No, the road to true forgiveness would be a long one. But the first steps had been taken.

Despite his insistence against it, Loren's father invited the Caldwells. While he hoped the half-breed bastard would not attend, he still looked forward to seeing his future bride. Ariadne—or Emillie, if he must—would be his before the winter solstice, and with his recent discoveries, the timeline may be shortened.

Carriage after carriage rolled past the front doors of the grand Gard manor. He greeted the guests as they exited and thanked them for attending the ball. Most returned the welcome with warm responses. Others, mostly those still in Laeton from Eastwood Province or close friends to the Harlows, remained less charming.

Soon enough, they would all regret placing such faith in a lying bastard.

When the Caldwells came to a halt at the front of the procession, Loren took a step back. Azriel stepped from the carriage as Ariadne smoothed her skirts on her lap. The implication of the motion made Loren's blood boil. That should be him mussing up her skirts.

As she took her husband's hand and gave him a small, secretive smile, Loren cursed under his breath and moved to the carriage behind theirs. The Harlows.

Markus stepped out first. Loren gripped the Princeps' arm in greeting before offering a hand to Emillie. No harm in making ground with the younger sister in case he could not free the elder.

"Good evening, Miss Harlow," Loren said and kissed Emillie's fingers. She gave him a polite, reserved smile and curtsied. "May I escort you inside?"

Emillie looked to her father, who nodded his approval, then back to him. Her smile did not falter, though neither did it grow. "Yes, thank you."

He did not need her to like him—only the Princeps and, given the recent discussions they had had, Loren remained hopeful. Ruining Azriel's reputation came second to lifting his own standing with Markus.

They made their way up the steps to the manor several paces away from Azriel and Ariadne. The former gave him a cold, curt nod. The latter offered a smile.

Perhaps he could hope after all. If the new Lady Caldwell proved dissatisfied with her husband, Loren would be more than happy to reclaim her. While some Caersan men may consider her impure or, worse, tainted, he would not allow her to feel that way.

Until she gave him that opportunity, however, he needed to remain focused on the younger sister.

"You look beautiful this evening, Miss Harlow." He smiled down at her.

Emillie continued looking straight ahead as they entered the manor. "You flatter me, sir."

The pointed drop of his title struck a nerve. His mouth twisted, but the smile did not falter. "Would you do me the honor of a dance this evening?"

This time she looked up. Her eyes, a twin to her sisters' oceanic pools, sparkled in the light of the chandelier as she said, "The honor would be mine."

Loren picked up a dance card from the nearby table and signed his name to the top of the list before sliding it onto her wrist. His fingers brushed her inner arm as he took her hand to kiss her again. "I shall see you soon, then."

With that, he turned and slid into the crowd. Too many eyes watched his interaction with Emillie. The gossip he was certain would arise from his abrupt switch from one sister to another would be suboptimal. He needed to control the narrative.

Ariadne had yet to confirm anything publicly about the incident which caused the duel. Any discussion of the matter must be put to rest. To do so, he had to locate the loyal officers still in the ranks. They would steer any gossip toward his positive attributes while denying any ill claims.

Before he could do that, however, more pressing matters weighed on him. After the near-attack on the Harlow Estate the previous night, security was stretched thin. Maintaining vigilance and securing specific areas of the manor was top priority.

No one would get on or off the grounds without him knowing of it.

Dancing with Loren Gard made Emillie's skin crawl. He swept her into his arms at the first note of the waltz and held her uncomfortably close. While she could understand why some Caersan women, her sister included, had been enamored by him—the military rank and handsome face—she felt nothing but disgust.

And it had nothing to do with her preference for women.

No. Even if she had not been aware of his mistreatment of her sister or even turned a blind eye to the enjoyment he received from harming others, Emillie could see the cruel glint hiding behind his public mask. When he spun her out, the corner of his mouth twitched up as his cold eyes slid down her body like ice. Upon her return, he inhaled deeply as though memorizing the scent of her hair.

"You are an excellent dancer," he said, hand sliding to her lower back. "You move quite well."

Was that meant to be an innuendo? Emillie furrowed her brows. "I am a quick study, my Lord."

He chuckled lightly. "Indeed, you are. Not all Caersan women are so adept."

"I must ask," she said as she twirled with him, ignoring the jab to her sister, "do you attempt to flatter every woman you dance with?"

Loren's smirk grew. "Only those I am truly interested in."

"Do you not find it strange how quickly you shifted your interest from my sister to me?" She lifted her chin and met his gaze full-on. "You had been ready to marry her."

The grin vanished, and he sucked on his teeth a moment, breaking eye contact to glare over her head. There was the side of him he did not want anyone to see. Just as quickly as he let the mask slip, he put it back on and said, "Your sister did the same from my brother to me, then from me to...Lord Caldwell. Is she the only one allowed to change her mind?"

"No." Emillie's mouth tightened. The loss of thought for Azriel's name said enough. The slanderous remarks he threw at the Teaglow Estate had not been the only time he used such foul words. "Though keep in mind, *sir*, the Society is not forgiving of those who blame others for their shortcomings."

The song ended and, foregoing the customary curtsy, Emillie marched off the dance floor. She would not hear another word from a man so shortsighted. Her blood pumped hard through her veins, so when another Caersan man approached to ask for a dance, she ignored him and continued on.

With the Golden Rose of Valenul married, too many suitors' sights had turned to her. She desired none of them and wanted even less attention from the rest of the aristocracy. Her sister's previous hope of becoming an unwed spinster suddenly appeared enticing.

As if her father would ever allow such a thing.

Emillie pushed through the crowd of guests to the table of refreshments across the ballroom. The pale yellow walls and bright chandeliers lit up the room with enough dazzling light to blind a mole. It made her head hurt.

Snatching up a glass of sparkling wine, she meandered around the edge of the room. Gaggles of debutantes moved from place to place, whispering behind fans or over the rims of their glasses. She wanted to simultaneously be one of them—single-mindedly focused on the one thing Caersan women had, marriage—and loathed their very existence.

So she shifted her attention to finding the only people left in the Society who agreed with her. Camilla would be just arriving, late as always. Likewise, Revelie would be somewhere on the outskirts.

She slid between the guests, smiling politely or greeting lords as necessary on her way through the throng to the foyer. The corridors, though quieter, still hummed with noise. Between the din of gossip and the ensemble's music, there was no escaping the incessant cacophony.

Most conversations did not draw Emillie's attention as she passed. Not until she overheard the tail end of one with a familiar voice. She stopped dead, leaning closer to the corner around which they spoke.

"—that bastard's cousin keeps quiet all night."

Loren.

"Of course, General."

Nikolai.

"Check the rotations while you are out there."

A pause, and then Nikolai asked, "If I may, what is the purpose of keeping him? It has been almost a fortnight."

"Questions like that," Loren hissed, "will get you killed. Now go."

Emillie sucked in a sharp breath and hurried back the way she had come as the footsteps neared. She slowed her pace and peered over her shoulder. Nikolai marched away, through the front doors. Loren appeared moments later, and she turned back to the crowd, sipping her wine.

When neither vampire approached her, Emillie released the breath. What was he planning now? Though she had missed crucial details of the conversation, she could draw enough evidence to understand what she had heard.

There was only one *bastard* whose cousin was missing.

Setting her glass on a nearby table, she set off in search of Ariadne.

CHAPTER 33

Two sides of Ariadne warred within her. One demanded justice for what Azriel did. For the pain he caused. For the incessant stream of dark memories. The other wanted him to look at her as he once did. Not with fear or sorrow but an intensity that thrilled her and made her breath catch.

At the start of the first waltz, she kept her distance from him. She lingered along the outskirts of the dance floor to watch as Emillie took Loren's hand and moved through the same steps she once did with the General. The look he gave her sister appeared suddenly familiar. His mouth quirked up at the corner, and his icy blue eyes glittered in the candlelight. Where once she saw him as a handsome, warm-hearted suitor, she now saw the truth.

Loren Gard cared for nothing and no one—except himself.

Emillie, to Ariadne's relief, had none of it. She danced politely, making small talk as necessary, then left abruptly at the end. As the other dancers bowed and curtsied to one another, she walked away without so much as a goodbye.

She could not hide the smile it brought to her face to see her sister's spirit had not been extinguished. That could change, however, if what she had just done was seen by the wrong people. Namely, their father.

Ariadne scanned the ballroom for any sign of him and found him deep in conversation with another lord, his back turned to the dance floor. He had not witnessed what had occurred. Perhaps he would not care if Emillie gave the General the cold shoulder. After what happened between her and Loren, she hoped her father would be wise enough to keep them apart.

Then again, if he had indeed written off Loren's abuse as an anomaly and held to his belief that he had overreacted, her sister may be in trouble.

She scooped up a glass of red wine from a passing servant and took a sip. The tannins bounced across her tongue pleasantly, a welcome distraction from the constant twisting of her stomach.

Glancing up at the cause of her distress, she found Azriel watching her from across the room. He spoke with a Lower Councilman and nodded or smiled as necessary, but his gaze always wandered back to her. His face remained neutral as he had done when overseeing balls as her guard. His ability to put on such a mask unnerved her. Like Loren, it was something she had not recognized as negative until it was too late. In this case, it was inescapable.

Unless, of course, she revealed the truth about him.

Would she, though? She sipped her wine again and wove her way back through the crowd. He tracked each step. Those pale green eyes always snapped to where she was, no matter how many Caersans passed between their line of sight. When she turned in his direction and began making her way toward him, his eyebrows twitched together.

She eased closer, and he cut his conversation short. Grasping the lord's arm, he inclined his head with a quiet word of farewell, then turned to her.

For a breath, she saw it. The heat flared in his gaze as he took her in. His lips parted, and the start of a smile flickered across his face. Then it disappeared behind the worry. The concern. The uncertainty.

Ariadne sipped her wine and slid in beside him. Close enough to not draw attention to their discomfort while still not touching him. She glanced up and smiled a smile that, had Emillie seen her, would have given her away in an instant.

"Will you dance with me?" Azriel asked quietly, his voice rumbling from his chest.

She closed her eyes and drew in a long, deep breath to relish the surge of butterflies in her stomach. That was the feeling she had searched for since she stepped into his study the night before. A lightness washed over her. She felt as though she could fly. The mere sound of his voice—this voice, as a vampire—made her feel whole again.

Because all she could hear in her mind, no matter how she pictured him, was the voice of a dhemon. The dhemon who had told her to sit still as they rode to the east. The dhemon who had scolded her for screaming for help. The dhemon who had pulled his cloak around her and said to keep low as the sun rose above the horizon.

And when she opened her eyes again, she found him. The man she had fallen in love with. The one who stood up for her and took a brutal lashing for her honor. The one who was there whenever she searched for him. The one who dueled the man who hurt her. With his hair pulled back into the half-knot and that perfect peridot gaze, he looked down at her with what she could only describe to herself as hope.

Hope that maybe, just maybe, she did not hate him as much as she had claimed.

"Yes," she breathed and brushed her fingers over the bruise on his cheek.

Azriel stilled and slowly, oh so slowly, tilted his face into her touch. He closed his eyes. Breathed in. Exhaled. Opened them and gave her a small, optimistic smile.

She dropped her hand into his, and he led her without another word onto the dance floor as the string ensemble adjusted for the next song. They took their place together. She placed a hand in his and the other on his shoulder. He brushed his hand along her side, then let it hover over her lower back.

Despite her previous request for him to hold her—to really hold her—he knew better than to touch her again. Not without her permission.

The music began, a jovial tune that had them moving at a more brisk pace than Emillie and Loren's dance. At first, she did not look at him. She focused on her feet, which stumbled and tripped more than usual. Her heart beat faster and faster. Her head felt light.

"Breathe," Azriel whispered. "Breathe."

She sucked in a breath and looked up at him with wide eyes. Somehow, he remained just as calm and composed as she always knew him to be. Until recently.

"I admit," he continued at his conspiratorial volume, "I was surprised to not be greeted by a prison wagon when I arrived this evening."

Ariadne frowned, then winced as she stumbled again. "Why would you be?"

His hand on her back gripped harder, keeping her from falling. He glanced up at the watching Caersan as though daring anyone to laugh. When he looked back down at her, his face softened again. "You said you—"

"I know what I said." She blocked out the feeling of his hands on her—not the soft, gentle guiding of the present moment, but the rough ghost of the past. "I know."

He searched her face. "What do you plan to do now?"

"I do not know." She shook her head, heart heavy. "But I cannot let them..."

The way the chains clinked when he had been led away in front of the Court House echoed in her mind. They mimicked the sound ingrained in her from the mountains. The steady clink as her wrists lifted above her head. The rhythmic jangle as Azriel stepped onto the platform before the lashes.

"Ariadne." Azriel's voice cut through the image of him removing his shirt, revealing all those scars for the first time—through the memory of her gown being cut open down the length of her spine. "My love, come back to me."

She drew in a strangled breath and grasped his hand harder. He returned the firm grip. The room spun around her in broad arcs. "Azriel."

"Look at me." His eyes bore into her as she turned her gaze up. "You're safe."

"No, I am not."

In an instant, his calm intensity shifted. Azriel looked up and around. For what? An adversary he could defeat in her name?

"No." Her hand drifted from his shoulder, down his arm around her waist and back. "*You* put me in danger."

"I never meant for any of it." A sickly pallor took hold of him, and he closed his eyes for a long moment. "Please believe me. None of it."

"How can I?" She swallowed hard. "I have spent so long cursing you for what you did."

Azriel sighed, focusing on the distance between their bodies. No such space existed the last time they danced. When he spoke, it was almost too difficult to hear his words. "Then hate me, my love."

"What?" She gaped at him. He would not fight for her, then.

"Scream at me," he continued and raised his gaze again to hers. "Hit me. Never speak to me. Find a lover who makes you happy again. But please...please, Ariadne...don't leave me. Don't go to *him*."

Him. Loren. The General she had threatened to run to for safety. The one man she knew would hurt him the most to hear of her finding comfort in. She should have weighed her words more carefully, for she would never go back to such a despicable vampire.

The song began to fade. Azriel spun her away from him and, upon her return, dipped her low, never once taking his eyes off her. When he righted her, he kissed her cheek and whispered, "Until the very end, my love."

With that, he pulled away to give her space, then inclined his head and turned toward a small group of lords. She wanted to call him back. To hold him and inhale his perfect scent. To reassure him that she did, in fact, still love him. At least she continued to love the part of him she believed to be real.

Ariadne swept away, heart aching anew. Gods, it felt as though the pain would never end. The hurt ran deeper than any blade or loss. If she were to choose between this betrayal and Ehrun's dungeon, she would gladly take the latter, for this was true torture. A true hell in the face of immortality.

So when she caught sight of her sister, Ariadne leapt at the opportunity to bury her grief in whatever news Emillie had in store this time. No sign of Camilla or Revelie meant she had yet to divulge what had occurred on the dance floor. The perfect distraction.

"Ari!" Emillie grabbed her wrist and dragged her to a solitary alcove. Guests passed without glancing their way. No one lingered close enough to overhear whatever gossip was about to be spilled.

"What happened with the General?" Ariadne asked, sliding an interested smirk of mischief into place. "You did not look pleased by the dance."

"Worry not about the dance." Emillie shifted the hold from wrist to hand and squeezed tight. Too tight. "Have you seen Madan yet?"

Her heart stumbled, and her stomach knotted. She straightened to look around. "No. Where is he?"

With a shake of her head, Emillie yanked at her arm. Ariadne turned back with a frown and stopped short at the look of panic on her sister's face.

The rush of excitement soured into dread. "What happened?"

"After the dance," Emillie whispered, drawing her in close with the quiet tone, "I overheard the General speaking with Captain Jensen."

Nothing new, though Ariadne's pulse began to quicken. She looked around the room for a second time. Loren had taken to the dance floor again, but she could not see Nikolai anywhere. "What does this have to do with Madan?"

"I think they have him."

She was going to be sick. For two weeks, he had been missing. Two weeks in which she had watched Azriel slowly spiral out of control until he finally broke. His brother—the last of his family—had been taken, and for what? What did they have planned?

"What did they say, Em?" Ariadne croaked, gaze landing on Azriel, who once again seemed to sense her and look up. She wiped her face of any expression and turned back to her sister. "Why do you think this?"

Emillie shook her head, face paling more. "The General told the Captain to make sure...to make sure that *that bastard's cousin keeps quiet*. I have never heard him speak of anyone else but Azriel in such a manner."

"Gods."

"He told the Captain to check the rotations," Emillie continued, and now her eyes shimmered with tears. "And that asking questions about it will get him killed."

Ariadne could hardly think straight. Keep him quiet. Check the rotations. Get him killed. None of it made sense except for exactly what Emillie suggested: Loren had abducted Madan for his own purposes. What they could be was bad enough to not even tell his most trusted officer.

"Where do you think he is?" Emillie's voice sounded so far away.

Rotations. The guard rotations. Ariadne remembered the night she had waited by the pond at the Harlow Estate for Azriel to pass. He had been checking on the guard rotations.

"Stay here." Ariadne squeezed her sister's hand and scanned the room again, careful not to catch Azriel's eye. "Tell no one else what you heard."

Emillie nodded, then froze as Ariadne pulled away. "No—wait. Wait...Ari, what are you doing?"

"Please, Em." Ariadne gave her what she hoped was a convincing smile. "I will be right back."

Before her sister could argue further, she slipped away to join the tail end of a small group of debutantes and pulled an earring from her lobe. Emillie could not come with her. Not this time. A single vampire would be more than enough for a bit of reconnaissance. She could not approach Loren or anyone else without foolproof evidence of his misdeeds.

Ariadne abandoned the young Caersan women when they passed by the foyer. She smiled at the butler, claimed to have lost an earring in her carriage, and ignored his protests to find it for her as she exited the front door on her own.

No one walked the front lawns but the coachmen and servants looking for a bit of fresh air. Looking over her shoulder, no one followed. A relief that neither Emillie nor Azriel demanded to know what she was doing. If she was going to get any confession out of Loren, she needed to see for herself what he had done.

Each step farther from the manor made Ariadne's hands shake a little more. The long drive, lit by hanging lanterns, seemed to stretch on forever into the darkness. Bushes lined the narrow gravel roadway. If she focused too long on one, her mind played tricks on her.

Red eyes glowed out from the shadows.

But at the perimeter of the grounds, the guards still roamed in pairs, talking and laughing as though there was no threat to any of them. Fools.

The guard house near the front gates lit up like a beacon. Though guards were stationed at the top, their focus remained outward, and their chatter just as jovial as the others. No need to keep eyes inside the place they were protecting. Again, a mistake.

Ariadne kept to the shadows and crept toward the guard house door, pausing at a window to look inside. No one. Not yet, anyway.

It was not long before an inner door opened, and Nikolai Jensen stepped through. She sucked in a sharp breath of alarm before hiding around a corner. The Captain closed the outer door with a bang.

"This is not a game, gents," he called to the guards at the top of the gate towers. "Vigilance requires concentration."

"Yes, Captain," another called back, and the laughter evaporated.

Nikolai's footsteps faded. Ariadne counted back from ten in her head in a desperate, futile attempt to calm her nerves. Had the method ever truly worked? She could not think of a time it centered her completely.

It would have to be enough.

Checking around the corner again for any lingering guards, Ariadne took another deep breath and eased her way to the guard house door. It opened and shut without a sound. Praying to the gods her luck kept up, she slunk past the winding stairs that went up to the rooms and roof and to the door Nikolai had come out of.

Locked.

"Oh, fuck," she whispered and looked around the room. Of course they would not keep a key lying around the room. Nikolai had taken it with him. If Madan's state was as gruesome as she imagined it to be, she doubted many people had access to whatever cells lay beneath her.

After a minute of turning in circles, Ariadne stopped to examine the lock. It had been ages since she picked one. So long, in fact, she had done it in broad daylight after Emillie had locked herself in a cupboard while playing a game of hide-and-seek. A useful bit of knowledge Alek Nightingale had passed on to her.

She pulled a long pin from her hair and crouched in front of the door. Sticking the pin into her mouth, she bit and bent the end into a pick. Once satisfied, she pulled out a second pin and bent it in half.

Ariadne paused to check over her shoulder, then inserted her pins, one down across the barrel of the lock and the other she wiggled in until she found the first pin. She turned it, slow and steady, listening for the tell-tale click. When it finally happened, she silently thanked Alek for his tutorage in such destructive tactics.

Down the barrel, she moved the makeshift key until each lock pin clicked into place. She held her breath and turned the handle. The door opened, she pulled the pins free, and she slipped into the dark stairwell beyond. She tested the inner doorknob, and when it threatened to lock her inside, she left the door ajar just enough for her to get back out.

The narrow stairs took her down into an unlit cellar with a single, thin window at the top of one wall. Enough light trickled in to reveal a room straight from her most haunting dreams.

Chains lined the stone walls. A set dangled in the center of the room beside a large table with four thick metal straps and wood covered in stains. Beside it sat a smaller surface covered in knives of all kinds. A single vial sat amidst them, giving off an eerie, golden light. Along the nearest wall, highlighted by the glow, a fae shifter male sat slumped, one mutilated and hairy arm chained above his head. His vacant eyes stared at the floor.

Ariadne made her way farther into the room, stomach churning and a silent scream ricocheting through her mind. This place looked and felt so familiar. So horribly the same as the dungeon she had been kept in. All it missed was the forge and its collection of brands.

At the far end, something—someone—moved. Ariadne froze, again checked over her shoulder, then hurried forward. She almost vomited at what she found.

Madan slumped against the wall, arms chained above his head that lolled against his chest, not unlike the dead shifter. His face, almost unrecognizable from the bruises and swelling, lay half-hidden by shadows. Beneath his chin lay prominent ribs behind a smattering of wounds. None healed. One leg lay at an odd angle, and the other dripped blood.

Yet of all his injuries, his left arm caused her the most distress. While the other seemed healthy, aside from the systematic cuts and malnourishment, the other appeared dead. Two fingers had rotted away from a foul and decomposed hand. The black skin peeled away, exposing bones and sinew, and continued up his forearm. The gruesome decay ended just below his elbow, though the farther it reached from the hand, the less it seemed affected.

Ariadne turned back to the table and picked up the small, gold-filled bottle from its place beside a pair of leather gloves.

The liquid inside sloshed, and she carefully pried the cork loose to sniff it.

"Don't." Madan's croak of a voice almost made her drop the vial. She slammed the cork back into place and whipped around to find him unable to lift his head as he continued in a rasp, "Liquid sun...shine."

"You are still alive," she breathed and abandoned the bottle back on its table to hurry to his side. The stench of his hand made her stomach roil. "Gods, Madan..."

His eyes fluttered shut again, and he wheezed in a breath. "Leave."

"No!" She cupped his face and held his head up to look at him. "I will get you out of here."

His rattling exhale tore through her soul, and he peeled his eyes open again. Marbled green and gold. Green like the Caldwells. Gold like the Harlows. "Please. Go."

Uncertain what else to do, Ariadne tore her fangs through her wrist and held it to his mouth. Half-siblings be damned. Even if its strength would not be as potent for him, something would be better than nothing. Without it, he would certainly die.

But he did not drink.

"Madan, please," she whispered. "Please drink."

He let his lips part enough for her to push her wrist closer. At first, he did not draw any from her. He merely closed his eyes and let the blood drip into his mouth.

"I know who you are," she said, throat burning from the emotions and stench. "I know who you are to me."

Again Madan blinked his eyes open to look at her, dazed.

"Drink, Brother."

He released a small breath and eased his teeth into her flesh. The feeble draws of her blood slowly refocused his gaze. After a moment, he made a small, pitiful wail of a sound as though the mental clarity brought with it the pain of his body.

"Shh." She looked to the stairs again.

After a few more pulls from her vein, Madan jerked away with a groan and let his head fall back against the stones. He stared at her for a long moment before turning his attention to the decaying hand at the end of his arm.

Ariadne followed his gaze and stood, pulling the pins back out from her pocket and freeing one shackle, then the next. His dead hand slapped the floor like a piece of meat. He sucked back a cry of pain and instead let out a string of curses under his breath.

"Why are you down here?" she asked as she stooped down to wrap an arm under his good side.

Madan hopped slowly to his feet, gritting his teeth as he adjusted his weight off of his broken leg. He breathed hard, unable to keep himself from shaking. "Loren...is suspicious."

She frowned, and they took a slow step forward. "Of what?"

"Me." His voice crackled. She knew that feeling well. The soreness, which came not from words but from screams. "Azriel."

When he said nothing further, Ariadne swallowed hard and said, "I know about him, too. He showed me."

He stopped moving forward and turned his head so fast he had to close his eyes as he swayed. When he recovered from the vertigo, he blinked a couple of times before saying, "It isn't what you think."

"It is exactly what I think." Ariadne tugged at him gently to keep him moving. "He ruined my life."

"No," Madan ground out as he lifted one foot for the lowest step of the stairs, then the next. "Ehrun ruined... all of our lives."

Now Ariadne almost stopped in her tracks. She had not thought of it that way. Though she had been the most innocent in his games, she had been far from the only one affected by Ehrun. If what Azriel—and now Madan—claimed was true, they had been just as manipulated by the dhemon as she.

She did not respond. Instead, she set her focus on getting him up the stairs. Reconnaissance be damned, she would not leave her brother to continue being tortured—killed, even, if his hand and that vial were any testament. She would bring him right into the manor and demand a public explanation from Loren. Then she would happily watch him hang for his horrific deeds.

At the top of the stairs, a sliver of light shone from the crack in the door. She thanked the gods for looking after her and pushed it open.

Sitting at a table on the far side of the room, two guards launched to their feet. They looked between them with bewildered expressions, then marched forward. One drew a sword, and the other lifted a lip in a sneer.

"The General ain't gonna be happy with you, wench," the latter said and grabbed her arm, yanking her away from Madan.

Her brother swayed at the sudden loss of his crutch and tried to yell something, but his voice caught in his throat. He coughed and fell against the wall.

"Time to go, missy." The guard dragged her toward the door, his fingers digging into her arm. She gasped and squeezed her eyes shut against the rush of panic.

They were not Ehrun. Her breaths came and went in short, quick bursts. She writhed against the hold until she fell to the floor, but still, the guard pulled. One moment she was in the guard house. The next, the forge's fire blazed beside her face. Chains rattled from the ceiling. Cold shackles held her arms aloft. Huge, strong hands pinned her to the floor.

Past and present mingled, and Ariadne shook her head again and again. The guard yanked at her arm, demanding she stand. Demanding she walk back to the manor.

What manor?

The mountain breeze blew in from the front door of the dhemon keep as her kidnapper—no, Azriel—pushed her into her latest prison. She stared up at the guard with his mousy brown hair and saw instead curling black horns and cruel, red eyes.

And she learned quickly not to run.

Never run from Ehrun.

It only caused pain.

"Ariadne!" Madan's rough voice cut through her, dragging her back to where she was and what she was doing.

She looked behind her for what felt like the thousandth time. Madan ducked away from the swing of the guard's sword. He was too slow. Too weak. He would never win in a fight. Not now.

Ariadne pulled her arm back away from the guard with all her strength. He laughed and stopped to click his tongue at her. She felt through her skirt and unclipped the dagger on her thigh. The guard turned back, snatched her arm with a growl, and tugged again. Heart hammering in her chest at what she was about to do, she yanked up her skirt, unsheathed the dagger, and stuck the blade in his neck.

Blood sprayed everywhere.

Before she could think too long about the dull thump of the guard hitting the ground, she scrambled to her feet and sprinted back to Madan. The guard frowned just before she barreled into him as she had seen Azriel do. He flailed, off-balance, and swung the sword wildly to the side before dropping it on the floor with a clatter.

Ariadne drew up short at the cry of pain. She pivoted back to find Madan clutching his stomach with his good hand, blood gushing from the fresh wound across his belly.

"No," she breathed. This could not be happening. Not after everything. She had finally found him—rescued him as he had once done for her—and now she had failed.

Turning back to the guard, he held up both hands as she closed the distance between them and shoved the dagger into his chest once, twice, three times before leaving it between his ribs as he collapsed beside his sword.

"Ari..." Madan choked, a dribble of blood spilling from the corner of his mouth. "I'm sorry."

"Stop it," she said, voice steadier than she expected. "You will be fine."

She wrapped her arm under him again, and they started toward the door, slower than when they had begun in the cellar. Madan's feet shuffled. His broken leg buckled under his weight, and it took all of her strength to keep him upright through the guard house door.

Outside, Ariadne reeled to a halt. A half-dozen guards ran toward them. Why? Did they see what she had done?

"Forgive my stupid brother," Madan croaked, his body slumping toward the ground. "Let me go."

She turned wide eyes to him, struggling to hold on. "No."

The guards closed in the distance. Some held swords aloft. Others yelled commands for them to kneel down. One shouted for the guards at the top of the towers, and they, too, turned their sights on them.

Madan's knees buckled and, unable to continue supporting his weight, Ariadne cursed as he fell to the ground. He closed his eyes and grit his teeth, the blood still leaking from his gut and mouth.

She was going to lose him. After just learning who he was to her—the brother she had always believed him to be—she would lose him. And his death had not even been caused by Loren but by her pitiful excuse for a rescue. If she had only asked for help, perhaps he would not be in such a position.

He would die, and it was all her fault.

"Madan!"

Ariadne whipped her head up at the sound of Azriel's voice echoing across the grounds. He sprinted down the drive, picking up speed at the sight of them. Even from a distance, she could see the mixture of relief and panic on his face. Left in his wake, Emillie, Camilla, and Revelie followed with their skirts in their hands.

Azriel pulled his sword from his back in mid-stride, swinging the blade at the first of the guards between them. The vampire's head tumbled from his shoulders. The next turned to face the newest adversary and lost an arm before Azriel's sword stuck through his chest. Then a third fell. Then the fourth.

One after another, each guard fell. Those on the towers made their way out, and he dispatched each of them with uncanny ease. The singular focus turned the man she knew, the man she loved and married from the one who defeated a General one-on-one to the half-dhemon who razed a squad of Caersans without batting an eye.

But it was who he became at the sight of his broken and dying brother which frightened her most. Once certain no one else threatened them, Azriel dropped his sword and fell to his knees beside his brother. Ariadne stood beside him, too stunned to move, and felt her heart break. Truly break.

Azriel let out a keening cry she had never heard before and gathered Madan into his arms. When Madan did not open his eyes, Azriel let out another wail. "No, no, no…"

Ariadne stepped closer. She opened her mouth to speak. To say something, but nothing came.

"Please, Madan," Azriel sobbed, "please…don't leave me. Come on, baby brother, wake up. Please wake up."

Behind him, Emillie and their friends picked their way through the dead bodies with wide eyes. Her sister turned her attention to Ariadne, mouth agape with surprise. The others edged closer to the men on the ground.

"What happened?" Emillie breathed.

Ariadne opened her mouth again and, as the words spilled out, so did her tears. "I found him like this. They locked him up. When I tried to get him out, they...they..."

"Why did you not ask for help?" Camilla asked, covering her mouth.

"No time." Ariadne stared at the dying vampire in shock. "His hand."

Emillie knelt beside Azriel and carefully lifted Madan's arm. The elder brother flinched back as though to keep her from touching Madan but stopped when she turned a frightened face to him. He settled, like a caged animal, and she leaned in closer. "It looks like aegrisolis."

Azriel let out another sob and clutched Madan closer. He looked up to Ariadne, his green eyes wide and pleading. "Help him. Please. Find someone—anyone."

"No one can survive aegrisolis," she choked out and clutched at her throat.

"This is not normal," Emillie said and sat back. "It seems contained to his arm. For now."

"I tried to give him blood," Ariadne said and held out her healing wrist. This could not be happening. "I tried, but it...it did not work well enough."

Emillie frowned. "Why not?"

But before anyone could explain, Revelie stepped closer. "Let me try."

"He won't wake up," Azriel rasped, looking at each of them like a lost child. "He's breathing but...but he won't—"

"Open his mouth." Revelie ripped into her wrist with her fangs. "This is all we have left."

She knelt beside Emillie and pressed her wrist to Madan's mouth, held open with tender care by Azriel. Ariadne covered her mouth as, once again, Madan responded. He drew the blood offered, and slowly, oh so slowly, the gash in his gut began to seal.

CHAPTER 34

Azriel looked away for one minute. *One minute* and Ariadne disappeared. At first, he figured she had absconded with Emillie and Camilla to find Revelie, perhaps in a sitting room as she so often did at these events. Nothing new.

Until he saw her sister tucked in a corner with her two friends. Ariadne's notable absence and their tense expressions told him enough. His heart sank like a rock. Lord Moone's voice faded into the background as a high-pitched ringing took up in his head.

"Excuse me," he said to the Councilman and pushed through the crowd to the Caersan women. They turned round eyes up to him at his approach. He couldn't breathe. "Where is she?"

"I do not know," Emillie admitted. She bit her lip, glanced at her friends, then said, "She went to find Madan."

As if he could feel any worse. Azriel demanded she explain everything, and Emillie divulged all she knew. She barely finished speaking before he moved, mind whirling at what he needed to do: find her—find them both—and protect them at all costs. At the Gards'? They would be in trouble. "Stay here."

But none of them listened. As he took off out the front door, they followed close behind. Then he smelled the blood. Ariadne's blood. Madan's blood—so, so much blood from his brother. Too much.

His mind went blank at the sight of them. Ariadne soaked in crimson and Madan unable to stand alone. She had found him, found their brother, and—based on the sheer volume of another vampire's blood coating her—she'd fought her way out. The pride which swelled in him vanished as fast as it grew when the guards converged on them, and his brother fell.

"Madan!" He ripped the sword from its sheath on his back, and everything went dark.

It wasn't the first time he'd hacked his way through vampires to help his brother. The way his mind shut out what he did, what he saw, had saved him from centuries of torment. No matter how much he tried to forget it, though, it always came back to remind him at the worst of times.

But the state of his brother at the end of it all tore through him like an explosion. He never would've been in such a position if Azriel hadn't made him leave. None of it would be happening.

Only Revelie's quick thinking stemmed the flow of blood and dragged Madan's pure Caersan immortality back from the brink. But only for some of the wounds.

As he took another, more urgent pull from her arm, the state of Madan's hand didn't change. The decaying flesh remained. His bones continued to protrude from the blackened skin.

"Enough." Azriel pulled Revelie's arm away. "He'll drain you if you aren't careful."

"I can help." Camilla's voice, quieter than he'd ever heard it before, drifted down to him.

But he shook his head. "We need to leave."

He clutched Madan to his chest and rose to his feet, mindful of the injuries still very much present across his brother's body. The leg, which he had not noticed before, hung at a bad angle. It'd need to be rebroken and reset now the healing had begun.

"Go back to the manor," he said to the Caersan women. "Say nothing about any of this. No one can know."

Emillie gaped at him. "But the General—"

"The General will pay for this," he assured her, a fire stoking in his chest at the thought. "I'll make sure of it. For now, you need to return to the ball and clean yourselves up. Let no one know you were here."

After a beat, she nodded and took Revelie's hand. The Caersan seamstress held her wrist to her chest and stared at Madan for a long moment. "Will he survive?"

Azriel's brows pinched, and his heart throbbed. "I don't know."

"Ari." Emillie held out her other hand.

But Ariadne didn't move. She merely stared at Madan, then lifted her eyes to him and shook her head as she answered her sister, "If anyone asks, we went home early."

Relief flooded through him. He hadn't realized how much he needed to know she'd remain by his side. If not for him, then for Madan.

Camilla took the outstretched hand, and they hurried away. He turned to look at the mess across the lawn. Guards lay in pieces around them, their life source fodder for the grass. Hiding such a disaster forever would be impossible. Come daylight, when the Rusan guards took their positions, there'd be no hiding the red stains.

"I have an idea." Ariadne grabbed the nearest guard by the hands and dragged him to the guard house. Azriel followed to watch her push the body down the steps to a cellar. "It will take them a while for anyone to figure out what happened."

Azriel grunted in agreement and set Madan on a chair. His brother groaned, eyes flickering open for a moment before he rested his head on the wall beside him. A good sign, even if he wasn't out of the woods yet.

Then he hurried back outside, and side-by-side with his wife, he carried the bodies of vampires and threw them down the cellar stairs. Neither of them said anything as they worked. They merely hauled corpses off the lawn in silence, smearing blood across the guard house floor, and when they finished, Ariadne closed the cellar door with a snap. She jiggled the handle to ensure it locked, then nodded to him.

How she kept so calm throughout it all was a mystery.

He picked up his sword, wiped the blood on his trousers, and slid it back into the sheath. Then he gathered Madan into his arms again, and they departed from the guard house, Ariadne closing the door behind them in silence. They hurried back up the drive. As they reached the manor, they slowed their pace until they reached their carriage at a near-crawling pace. No one looked out the windows. No one saw them, covered from head to foot in blood, as they hauled Madan into the carriage and ordered the coachman to drive—fast.

With his brother laid out across one bench seat, Azriel sat beside Ariadne. They trundled down the driveway, past the empty gate towers, and onto the highway. For a handful of minutes, they still didn't speak. He didn't know what to say. All at once he wanted to scream at her for putting herself in such danger while simultaneously throwing himself at her feet to thank her.

Ariadne broke the reticence with a quiet question, "What is liquid sunshine?"

He stared at the rotted hand for a long moment, understanding dawning. "Mages created it. It holds the same properties as the sun and is used to kill vampires."

"Why?" she whispered. "Why would they make such a thing?"

"Because Caersans have been using their blood to null mage magic for centuries."

Ariadne looked up at him with wide eyes. "Excuse me?"

"It's not something the Council wants everyone to know." He grit his teeth. Once again, their greed had come back around to destroy his family with his brother, the most kind-hearted vampire he knew, the latest victim.

"Why do they do it at all?"

"Prisoners," Azriel said and rubbed his face, the drying blood crumbling beneath his fingers. "And anyone who demands equal treatment in Valenul."

Her jaw dropped in disbelief. "What about the fae?"

"Caersan blood doesn't do any permanent damage to them." He pushed loose hair back from his face and sighed. "But it can dampen their powers temporarily."

"Gods..." She shook her head. The same reaction he had when he uncovered the extent of the Council's hidden atrocities. "And my father?"

Azriel grimaced. "He discovered it."

Ariadne covered her mouth with a hand and stared at Madan. Her father—*their* father—had begun a silent war against not just the dhemons but the mages of Algorath. Some of the most dangerous mortals across the continent of Myridia.

"I almost touched it," she said after a long moment of silence. "There was a vial of it in the cellar with Madan."

He buried his face in his hands again, elbows on knees. He couldn't handle it anymore. With the way the night began, anticipating an entourage of soldiers to haul him away, facing the very real possibility of his wife leaving him, and then everything with Madan. No. It was all too much. If she'd touched the liquid sunshine, she'd be in the same boat as his brother. Possibly worse.

"Azriel," she whispered and laid a gentle hand on his forearm. "I am not hurt."

"But you could've been." Hot tears rolled down his face from behind his hands. "Everything is my fault. All of it. From the very beginning. I'm so sorry, Ariadne. I'm so...so sorry."

She pulled his hands away from his face and replaced them with her own on his cheeks. Her blue gaze swept across the blood-flaked skin before landing on his eyes. "I know."

"I don't expect you to forgive me," he rasped and leaned forward slowly until their foreheads touched. She didn't move away. He closed his eyes and inhaled deeply. "But I'll spend every breath left in my lungs proving myself to you."

Ariadne's thumbs stroked his face, slow and soft. "I do not hate you, Azriel."

His eyes snapped open again. "What?"

"I cannot say—"

"I don't mind," he cut in, breathless. The dark, consuming shadows that had encroached on him over the last few hours eased. The knot in his stomach loosened. "Just...I want to make things right for you."

A sad smile curved her perfect lips, and she sat back a bit to look at him fully. Her hands dropped from his face. "No."

He frowned. "No?"

"Make it right for *you*." She took his hand and kissed his calloused knuckles. "Fix that, and this—us—will find a way back together."

Hope blossomed in his chest like the dawn breaking across the horizon. Light shattered the endless stretch of night, and he nodded again and again. He could do that. He could do anything for her.

Perhaps everything would be alright after all. If he and Ariadne could find a way, then anything was possible. He would find a mage healer for his brother. They would all return to Eastwood together, and he would do everything in his power to right every wrong in his life.

Azriel sat back in the seat, a weight lifting from his shoulders as he did so. Beside him, Ariadne did the same, edging closer so she could lay her head on his arm. He closed his eyes again with a contented sigh.

The coachman pounded on the carriage twice. Then twice again as they slowed to a sudden halt.

No.

No.

Ariadne sat up with a frown. "What is it?"

Every fiber of his being lit up with adrenaline. Azriel looked at his wife with wide eyes. She stared back with a slow understanding of what that knock meant.

Then the screams started.

"Stay in here." He locked one carriage door, pulled a knife from his boot, and pressed it into her hand. "Kill anyone who comes through that door."

"Azriel—what—"

Foregoing everything else he'd just promised, he kissed her hard. "I love you."

Then he launched through the unlocked door, slamming it closed behind him. The two coachmen lay on the road in twin pools of blood, with their innards spilling onto the gravel. Five dhemons stalked out from the darkness, one licking his blade with a wicked grin.

He scrambled for the telepathic link between him and Razer. They needed help. Anything. Anyone, be it Kall or Whelan or any number of their friends still connected through the links. He couldn't fight them all alone.

No one answered.

Azriel pulled his sword out for the second time that night, steeling himself against Ariadne's cries behind him, and leveled the blade at the handful of dhemons. He recognized two from his time in *Auhrl*—Lhev and Mikhal. The rest were new recruits and therefore not likely trained.

"Run back to your master," Azriel growled in the dhemon tongue. "Or I'll send you back in pieces."

Lhev and Mikhal chuckled. They had been part of the group to lock him away. Mikhal had wielded the whip used to remind him of his helplessness. Likely, they'd been a part of Ariadne's torture as well.

They deserved to be ripped apart.

So when Lhev moved forward with a great swing of his ax, Azriel slid below the arc and slammed his elbow up into the dhemon's diaphragm. He choked on the air and stumbled back, leaving Azriel open for another dhemon he didn't know to move in with a sword. Azriel blocked the downward strike and twisted away. Though his strength didn't compare to the larger males, his smaller form made it easier to evade them.

Azriel doubled back before Lhev could catch his breath. He side-stepped a jab from a third dhemon and turned his sword to point behind him. As he cracked his fist against the attacking dhemon's jaw, he thrust the blade backward and into Lhev's chest.

Ripping the sword back out, he caught the second dhemon's wrist in his hand and, yanking him to the side, swept a foot back to hook his leg. The dhemon landed on his back hard, and Azriel kicked him in the head before shoving his sword through his neck.

Two down.

He hopped back in time for the tip of the third dhemon's blade to slide across his cheekbone, just under his eye. With a hiss of pain, Azriel jerked his head back.

Then a too-familiar scream ripped through the air from the carriage. He whipped around, taking a blow to the side—right where the bolt hit him the night before—and his knees buckled beneath him.

Ehrun stood at the open door of the carriage, the picture of perfect calm as Ariadne writhed in his grasp. His fingers wrapped around the back of her neck, and he hissed something in her ear. She stilled in an instant, face paling.

"What a good girl," Ehrun said in the dhemon tongue, stroking his fingers down her face. "So obedient. I've missed her."

"Don't fucking touch her," Azriel snarled and lurched forward. The sharp edge of a sword dug into his neck, and he froze, glaring up at the third unnamed dhemon, then Ehrun.

The last time Azriel had seen the bastard, he'd put a sword through the Crowe's chest. The blow had been meant for him. His father's death, like everything else, lived forever on the list of his failures.

"You brought this on yourself," Ehrun said in the common tongue so Ariadne could understand.

Azriel leaned away from the blade at this throat, but it followed. "I did nothing."

A wicked grin stretched across the bastard's face. "You killed our King."

Numb understanding crept through Azriel. That was what he'd used to convince all the dhemons to continue following him—how he'd gained the title the Crowe once held. Ehrun blamed the death of their leader on Azriel, the Crowe's own son, as though he'd ever vie for the position.

"Liar."

"I wonder," Ehrun mused, ignoring his accusation, "what decision will you make this time?"

He reached into the carriage and, to Azriel's horror, dragged Madan out by his mangled arm. His brother shrieked and tried to pull away. The abrupt movement only peeled off more of his ruined flesh.

Ehrun laughed. "Now, doesn't this look familiar? Your brother or your *mate*?"

Ariadne's lips parted in horror. She twisted to look at Madan, but Ehrun's grip tightened, and she whimpered, eyes squeezing closed.

Choosing between his brother and his wife had never been an option. It hadn't been in Auhla, and it remained so even in the face of the dhemon who frightened him the most.

Fire lit through his veins, and Azriel closed his eyes against the pain as it ripped through his body. Bones cracked, lengthened, and settled into place. His skull split, making room for the two horns to form. He grit his sharp teeth and growled as he blinked his eyes open again.

"No," Azriel snarled. "Not again."

The sword disappeared from his neck as the dhemon holding it barked a curse. Ehrun's eyes widened. The last of the unnamed cronies, a pace away, yanked a long, serrated knife from his belt.

At first, Azriel didn't understand. They'd all seen him transform before. The latest additions to Ehrun's ranks, perhaps not, but they'd have been told the truth about their old dhomin, just like the two in the Harlows' garden the previous morning. Why, then, were they surprised?

The dhemon who held the sword to his throat fell face down onto the road before him, a massive ax buried in his back.

Before Azriel could turn to see the latest adversary, a scarred, midnight-blue hand gripped the ax handle and yanked it from the dhemon's back. Azriel looked up and almost cried in relief.

Kall's twisted face was at once utterly terrifying and beautiful. Three broad, jagged scars stretched from the horn base across one foggy red eye to mar his nose and lift his lip in a permanent snarl. With his hair shorn close to his head, the black tattoos of dhemon runes stood stark against his blue skin. The one, seeing deep ruby eye, narrowed in on Ehrun, and he pointed the head of the ax at the dhemon. "Release them."

Of course. Madan had told him Whelan and Kall would be nearby for the wedding. Though there'd been silence along his connection to Razer, his plea for aid was still heard. Kall answered, not with words, but action—as the horned fae was wont to do.

Before the others could regain their composure, Azriel launched forward, aiming for Ehrun's legs. The massive dhemon dropped his hold on both Ariadne and Madan to step out of reach.

"Run," Azriel snapped to Ariadne, and to his relief, she did not freeze. She gaped, then took off in the direction they'd come.

When Mikhal started after her, Kall grunted in annoyance and charged. The dhemon fell, a hair's breadth from grabbing Ariadne again, as his friend tackled him to the ground. They grappled there for a moment before Kall snapped the bastard's neck.

Ehrun's fist collided with Azriel's face. He staggered back, head spinning. His vision flickered, and Madan pushed to his feet with a grimace. The movement reopened several cuts, including his stomach, but Azriel couldn't find his voice to tell him to stand down.

The last dhemon stepped in behind Azriel and wrapped an arm around his chest, holding him steady as Ehrun pulled out a knife with a smirk. He stepped forward and flipped the blade once. "This is going to be so fun."

To his horror, three more dhemons stepped out of the shadows between the trees and stalked forward. This was it.

At least Ariadne ran.

Madan lurched forward and grabbed Ehrun's wrist. He snarled and jerked the dhemon down with enough surprise force he could sink his fangs into the bastard's neck.

"No!" Azriel wheezed as one of the latest dhemons punched him in the stomach. He curled in on himself.

It didn't take much for Ehrun to shake Madan off. A firm push and the vampire fell to the ground again, where Ehrun kicked him hard in the ribs. "Maybe I should make you watch him die first."

Azriel writhed in the dhemon's grip and, planting his feet wide, picked him up on his back and twisted his shoulders to drop him to the ground. The dhemon landed on his back. This time Azriel didn't kick his head; he stomped his foot straight down on his face. The hard skull cracked beneath his force the first time. The second time, it caved in.

Then he grabbed both of Ehrun's knees and slammed him backward onto the gravel. The knife flew from the dhemon's grip. They scrambled, Azriel on top in a desperate attempt to keep the bastard on the ground. With the size difference, he didn't manage it for long.

Ehrun's grappling had always been the best in *Auhla*.

As the final two dhemons converged, Kall hurdled back. He engaged the two, ax in hand, pressing them further and further away.

Azriel felt his world tip upside down as Ehrun bridged his entire body to one side, landing on top. In a desperate attempt to keep the dhemon from hitting him again, Azriel shoved a knee into Ehrun's chest and let his body lift up onto his shoulders. Twisting under him, he grabbed the dhemon's ankle and yanked as he pushed with his leg.

Ehrun hopped back on one foot, arms pinwheeling to keep his balance. He snarled and brought his lifted foot back down onto Azriel's outstretched arm.

Pain lanced up the limb, but nothing broke—not like his femur the last time they'd fought. But it pinned Azriel long enough for Ehrun to kneel on his chest with all his weight and slam a hand around his throat. Azriel coughed, then pressed a hand to the knee keeping him on the ground. His vision flickered.

One moment everything went black. The next, Ehrun reeled back off him, snarling a string of curses. A knife stuck out from between his ribs, just beside his heart. Azriel's head swam, but the full picture slid into view bit by bit.

Ehrun whipped around to face Ariadne. She held Azriel's sword aloft between them and bared her long fangs.

"You little bitch," Ehrun growled and stepped forward.

One of the cronies disengaged from Kall, who gripped his bleeding gut with one hand and charged toward them. Azriel shoved back to his feet, still unfocused, and leapt onto his back. He wrapped his legs around the dhemon and ripped into his throat with his fangs.

Ariadne backed away from Ehrun and swung the sword, much to the dhemon's amusement. Ehrun yanked the knife from his side with a hiss and held it tip down, ready to stab.

Kall landed heavily on his knees as the final dhemon crony slammed an elbow into his face. The next blow made Kall's eyes roll into the back of his head. He toppled to the ground and didn't move again.

The dhemon, satisfied with Kall's unconsciousness, turned to Azriel with a snarl. Azriel tried to circle around, but the dhemon saw through the maneuver and held his ground. "You've failed, little prince."

"No." Azriel glanced beyond the dhemon, adrenaline spiking. "Not tonight."

Madan dragged himself to his feet and, clutching the dagger from the carriage, stumbled to Ehrun. He shoved the steel between the dhemon's shoulder blades once, twice—

In a whirl, Ehrun turned and slammed his horns into Madan's chest, sending him spinning. Then the bastard's knees gave out.

The false Dhemon King heaved a breath and looked to his last-standing warrior. "Go."

As Ehrun struggled to stand, the final dhemon pulled him over his shoulders and took off into the woods. In just a few paces, the pair disappeared into the darkness.

Azriel surged forward to follow but stopped short when a small hand wrapped around his wrist. He looked back at Ariadne. "I can end this now."

"If you go after them," she said, "then you condemn your brother—and your friend."

He looked beyond his wife to where Kall, then Madan, lay unconscious. Fresh blood leaked from the wounds, old and new.

She was right. Though he knew Kall would survive, if they didn't get to a mage fast, Madan would die. Revelie's blood may have helped, but it wouldn't keep him from succumbing to his injuries—or the aegrisolis—forever. Ehrun would have to wait.

Loren could not believe what he saw. So outrageous was the scene in the distance that he doubted anyone else would believe him, either.

But after finding a dozen guards in various states of deceased strewn down the guard house cellar steps, he knew exactly who had been behind it. They left the ball early, Emillie had claimed when the other Caersans asked. But the hem of her dress had been torn, Revelie kept hiding her wrist, and Camilla would look no one in the eye.

No one else noticed the blood on their shoes.

So Loren headed down the highway at full speed atop his stallion in time to see a pair of dhemons racing into the woods, leaving Ariadne alone, wielding a sword as another dhemon approached her. She did not flinch away. She did not react other than to lay a gentle hand on the monster's face.

Loren's stomach twisted, and heat flared through his blood. This entire time, she had been plotting with the very beasts who had abducted her. Had this been her plan the entire time?

Behind them, another dhemon staggered to his feet, and after exchanging a few words with his comrade, hobbled away. Then Ariadne and the remaining dhemon turned to a form on the ground. In the three steps it took for the dhemon to reach the body, he changed. The horns seemed to reverse into his skull, his body shrank, and every piece of evidence Loren had been searching for revealed itself.

Azriel *fucking* Caldwell was a dhemon.

The *Lord Governor* stooped down and cradled the body—Madan—to his chest. Ariadne opened the carriage door so Azriel could lay the vampire inside, then closed it after she, too, sat on one of the inside seats.

The monstrous half-breed bastard climbed up to the bench at the front of the carriage and called to the horses. They started forward, leaving behind a wreckage of bodies and blood.

Loren watched them go, his sneer twisting into a grin. Finally. Finally, he had the bastard.

With this knowledge, he would finally have everything he deserved. Azriel would be arrested. He would have Ariadne as his wife. Markus, so impressed by Loren's investigative work and how he saved the Golden Rose of Valenul from complete ruin, would name *him* successor as the next Princeps.

He chuckled to himself and turned the stallion back down the highway. A dozen guards died to protect his secrets. Now he would ensure their lives had not been in vain.

CHAPTER 35

Ariadne flew through the front door of the Caldwell manor with Azriel on her heels and Madan in his arms. Petre reeled to a halt at their sudden appearance, eyes widening at the state of the younger Caldwell brother and the blood covering them all. Behind him, Bella clapped a hand over her mouth, tracking Azriel as he took the stairs two at a time.

"The coachmen are dead," Ariadne told Petre before he could ask. "Send the fastest servant into Laeton to find a mage healer."

The butler floundered and stared at the trail of blood on his foyer floor. "Y-yes, my Lady, I—"

She grabbed his arm and squeezed tight. "Immediately."

He nodded once and hurried down the hall, calling for a servant named Roque. Bella stepped aside to let him through as though numb to everything around her. She stared at where Azriel had disappeared.

"What can we do?" Bella asked in a small voice after a moment to recover from the shock. Her dark eyes swept over the shaking hands and blood-crusted face before her.

Ariadne gaped at her for a long, silent minute. Her heart had not stopped racing since Azriel left the carriage back on the Old Highway. It felt as though she would never recover from the onslaught of events. One breath after another, there was no moment to slow down.

"Bandages. Water. Any salve you have and..." Ariadne swallowed hard, twisting her hands into the blood-stained skirt, "and a saw."

Bella's face paled. "Excuse me?"

"I do not know," Ariadne admitted and looked up the stairs. "But I do not think a mage can fix..."

All at once, the pain and fear and sorrow slammed into Ariadne. The dam broke like a punch to the chest, and she folded in on herself, unable to hide it all behind the mask she had worn the entire night. She heaved a quiet wail and closed her eyes to block it all out.

But seeing Ehrun again almost destroyed what scraps of stability she had left. Hearing his voice sent her straight back to that cell. Feeling his hands on her in a familiar mix of rough and gentle as he gripped her neck and stroked her cheek—it had been too much.

"I'm so glad you're here," he had whispered to her as she watched Azriel restrained by one of the dhemons who had visited her cell. "My men have missed their entertainment."

That had been the moment she knew with absolute certainty she would rather die than go back. If she had to put the sword through her own heart, she would.

But she did not have to. She got away. Again. Because of Azriel. Because of Madan. Because of a dhemon she did not even know who almost died to protect her.

Now her brother—gods, her brother—was dying in his room upstairs, and her husband would never recover if he did. Not after everything Azriel had gone through to keep him safe.

"My Lady," Bella said and laid a gentle hand on her shoulder. "I will fetch the supplies. Go to them."

Ariadne nodded, drew in a long breath, and straightened. Now was not the time to break. Not when she needed to help Madan—not when she needed to keep her husband from shattering.

Up the staircase she went, ruined dress fisted in one hand. She swept past the portrait of the Caldwell woman and her two sons—the two sons now in charge of the household. Mariana. The Caersan woman who loved a dhemon.

If only Ariadne could speak with her. How had she found herself with the Crowe? How had she seen past the histories and loved him despite the war? The hate? The betrayals? The pain he had brought to her family and to Valenul through his raids.

She shook the questions from her mind. Focus. She needed to focus.

Madan's door stood ajar. The only light in the suite streamed in from the moon, highlighting the emptiness of the sitting room. Beyond the extinguished fireplace and lounging furniture, the bedroom lay in darkness. Ariadne slipped around the couches and chairs before pausing to peer past the threshold. Inside, the Caersan lay atop the bed, unmoving. Azriel knelt on the floor beside him and pressed his hands to his brother's stomach. The blood flow had slowed but still leaked between his fingers.

Head bowed and eyes closed, Azriel whispered in a language Ariadne did not understand. The dhemon tongue. She had always heard it to be harsh and unpleasant—a rumble of consonants and jarring vowels.

As he spoke so softly to his brother, however, it took on a different sensation. It rolled off his tongue like a mournful song. A plea to the gods, or perhaps to Madan himself. Though she did not grasp the precise meaning, Ariadne understood.

They had spent nearly five centuries speaking the language in a place they considered home. It served as a sanctuary from the man they once called Father—her own father—who turned his back on them and even attempted to kill one. Had Azriel loved him like a father at the time? Madan surely had, being of his own flesh and blood.

Rather than continue her voyeurism to the sacred moment, Ariadne stepped back and waited for Bella. She hovered in the bathing room, where she washed her hands and face in a stale bowl of water. Dust floated on its surface, which she ignored, and she used a small towel to peel the blood from her skin.

As she did, she could not stop thinking of those final moments with Azriel in the carriage. The look on his face, the shaking of his voice, the force of his mouth on hers...

He expected to die.

"I love you" would have been his final words to her. No request for forgiveness or explanation of his past actions. No demand for her except one thing: stay safe and know he loved her.

Two simple requests.

And the urgent feeling of his lips had only solidified how she truly felt: she loved him. She would not stop loving him. Not for something outside his control.

From the moment Ehrun had held her and Madan and presented his ultimatum, she knew Azriel had never lied as she once suspected. He protected his brother at all costs, even if the price was his own life.

And yet, when he took on his dhemon form, Ariadne could not help the spike of fear and loathing.

"My Lady," Bella said, arriving only moments later. "I have what you requested."

Ariadne nodded, dried her face, and joined Bella as she made her way to the bedroom. They entered together, drawing Azriel's attention, and closed in.

"Bandages, my Lord." Bella laid out the supplies. "Clean water and an Algorathian salve."

Azriel grunted in response, snatching up a pile of clean bandages to press to Madan's stomach.

"Thank you, Bella." Ariadne nodded to the door. "Please make sure the mage is directed here as soon as possible."

"Of course." The Rusan woman curtsied. "Let me know however else I can help."

The maid disappeared through the door, and Ariadne stepped closer. She took a towel and dipped it into the warm water before circling around Azriel and dabbing at Madan's face. Her husband took another towel and began cleaning his brother's uninjured hand.

They worked in a silent tandem. She moved down, clearing up the mess from Madan's cheeks and neck and chest. Azriel moved up his arm, then began again at his bare feet. He pushed the torn trousers out of the way, and when he touched the twisted leg, Madan groaned.

The response, even in pain, was better than nothing.

"How are you faring?" Ariadne asked quietly, glancing up at him. She knew the answer.

Azriel did not say anything for a long moment. His brows furrowed, and he continued revealing the bruises and scars beneath the grime. With time and rich Caersan blood, they would heal and fade.

"He told me to leave him," he said after a time. "Again. He told me to leave him when Ehrun used him to make me..."

"Make you get me," Ariadne finished for him.

He nodded, still not looking at her. "He's my only family left."

Her heart sank. "He will live."

"And I'll continue putting you both in danger." He shook his head and turned away to hide his face. "I never meant for any of this to happen."

Ariadne stared at a particularly large bruise on Madan's sternum. Then she turned her gaze to Azriel, reached across the distance between them, and took his hand.

Azriel froze. He stared at their hands and dragged his eyes to her. His brows pinched together.

"I believe you."

His lips parted as he searched her face. "You do?"

She nodded, a grim smile forming. "I would do the same for Emillie."

"I wouldn't have left her there, either," he said quickly, the panic returning to his gaze. He searched her face for something—anything—that told him she would believe him. Her heart cracked at the sincerity. "If Ehrun had told me to take her instead, I mean."

"I know."

The door swung wide. A young Rusan girl, gasping for breath, reeled to a halt. She bent over her knees and let her head hang. "My Lord—my Lady—"

"Catch your breath, Roque," Azriel said and stood to steady the girl as she swayed. "Easy."

Roque looked through her golden bangs with wide, hazel eyes. "The mage is almost here."

Tension seeped from Azriel. He took hold of the girl's shoulders and guided her back into the sitting room. A few low words were exchanged before Roque sat on the wing-back chair and rested her head.

The door opened to the suite, and Petre, Bella, and a human swept in. Before any greetings were exchanged, Petre turned to Bella and gestured to the cold fireplace with an urgent whisper. She nodded once and pulled wood from the nearby rack to stack neatly in the grate.

Then the flurry of movement began.

The mage, introduced as Izara, straightened her charcoal gray head covering and, gliding like a regal swan across water, passed Ariadne without a word. Her sharp, dark brown eyes assessed Madan in a single broad sweep. She passed a hand over his chest, and the bruise there almost entirely disappeared, but it was his ruined hand where she pulled up short.

"Aegrisolis." She spoke to no one in particular in a lilting, accented voice and placed both hands on his arm, just above the tattered flesh. Her brows knitted together.

Azriel stepped forward. "Can you fix it?"

With a soft scoff, Izara shook her head, hands staying in place just below the elbow. "The hand is dead. I'm no necromancer."

Ariadne shifted closer. "Can you stop the spread?"

"The poison moves slowly." Izara closed her eyes to focus on the arm. "I can't feel it above the elbow."

"Take it off." Azriel's stared at his brother's too-pale face with wide eyes. "Take off the arm."

Izara's dark eyes flew open. "He'll die without feeding first."

Ariadne pivoted and grabbed Petre's arm. She pulled him from the room. "Find me a willing vampire with the purest blood. Anyone."

Petre gaped at her as he thought, then nodded and left without a word.

In his wake, Bella approached, the fire now crackling behind her. "My father is Caersan."

Ariadne blinked once, her sluggish mind not quite understanding what the woman had said. As the words clicked into place, she sucked in a breath. "I had no idea."

Bella shrugged it off. "I prefer for not many to know. How can I help?"

"Madan is…" Ariadne glanced over her shoulder at the too-still body on the bed. "He might not survive without feeding. He drank some blood earlier, but then…"

Ehrun's face in the carriage window flashed through her mind. His wicked grin as he had torn the door nearly off its hinges only grew when she screamed and dropped the dagger Azriel had given her. His had been the last face she had anticipated seeing.

She wheezed in a breath and refocused on Bella's face. "He got hurt again."

"I'll feed him," Bella called as she stepped past Ariadne.

Izara beckoned her closer and spoke in a low voice as Bella rolled up her sleeve. Then the mage looked at the supplies on the bed. "I need a strap of leather and as much liquor as possible."

The credenza on the far side of the sitting room supported one need while Azriel rooted through Madan's drawers for a clean leather belt. They placed both items on the bed as Petre returned with one of the stablehands, Oli.

"You are his brother?" Izara asked Azriel, her expression professionally neutral.

"Yes."

She pointed to the door. "Then get out."

He froze, hands balling into fists at his side. "Excuse me?"

Ariadne took hold of one of his hands. Harming the mage preparing to save Madan's life would not be a wise decision.

"You're too close to him." Izara turned away as though the matter had been settled. She did not see the blaze in Azriel's eyes. "He is too lucid now with the blood, and he *will* feel this."

"No."

"Azriel." Ariadne put herself between him and the mage. "Listen to her."

Whether he ignored her or just could not comprehend her words, she did not know. He stepped forward. "He's my brother. I won't leave him."

"You are a liability." Izara did not look up as she worked, first assessing the broken leg, then the arm. "Get out, or I'll remove you."

"No," he repeated.

"Then I'll leave, and he'll die."

Azriel grit his teeth and, after a moment of calculating, jabbed a finger at her. "If he dies because of you—"

"If he dies," Izara snapped, finally glaring at him, "it is because his injuries were too severe, and you kept me from helping him. Out. Now."

Ariadne pushed at Azriel's chest. He glanced down at her, mouth a thin line, then turned to the door. At first, his feet did not move. He stared at the sitting room beyond with wide, silver-rimmed eyes.

When at last he stalked out, Ariadne followed and shut the door behind her. With Petre, Bella, and Oli, inside to help Izara, she had to place her faith entirely in the small group. No sooner had Azriel sat on a couch and buried his face in his hands than the screaming began.

Azriel couldn't do this. Not again. The helplessness to stop the pain of someone he loved. It was like being in the *Auhla* again, locked in the cell, to hear the endless torment of the woman he loved.

Torture unto itself. Ehrun knew what he'd done when he ordered it. He'd reveled in it just as much as he enjoyed inflicting the physical agony on Ariadne.

And if it hadn't been for Ariadne blocking the entrance to the room, Azriel would've ripped the door from the frame and gone after Izara—just as the mage knew he would.

"You have to trust her," Ariadne said, but he could barely hear her. All that echoed in his ears were the screams.

Her screams. Madan's screams. They mingled together like a cocktail of misery. Harmonizing just right so he could identify them both. Even the bond, usually so keen on adhering to Ariadne's demands, wavered as though that horrible, uncontrollable part of him couldn't differentiate the cries of pain.

"He's going to die!" Azriel reached for the handle.

Ariadne blocked his path. "He will live. You will speak with him again soon."

The room beyond her went quiet. He leaned a little closer, though the proximity was useless. Those inside spoke and drowned each other out. None of them were Madan's voice.

"We should sit," she said and urged him back toward the couch. Roque had left at the first sign of trouble, so they were alone. "Talk to me instead."

Azriel nodded slowly and stepped away. He sank into the cushions again. Beside him, she sat too—though not as close as she once had. That she even deigned to be with him was a miracle. She could have left and returned to the Harlow Estate.

Gods, she could've left Madan in that cell.

"Tell me about your childhood." Ariadne turned to look up at him.

He frowned. There had been so much of it that had been beautiful and good. The years before his mother's death were filled with laughter and her love. Secret visits with his father in the woods where they laughed and wrestled, his father always letting him win. Chasing Madan through the house, listening to his mother sing, and reading in the garden would forever remain some of his fondest memories.

But they were a mere blink in comparison to the rest of his youth. His father had tried so hard to pick up where his mother left off. He took in Madan and never treated him any differently than Azriel. The laughter had disappeared, though, and no one sang lullabies. Dhemons had few books—most had been burned by the vampires when they arrived in the Keonis Valley.

"Aside from my mother's death," he finally said, "it was good. She loved us dearly, and my father always did his best for us."

She remained neutral, though he saw the flicker of calculation at his words. *My father.* Not Madan's father or the one he had once been cautioned to call that no matter what. Not *her* father.

"What was your mother like?" Ariadne cringed as another scream lit up the room.

Azriel's heart cracked, and he braced himself against the sound. "She was kind to everyone, but I think she was scared."

"Of what?"

"Markus." He let out a breath when silence descended again. "My father. Everyone."

At first, Ariadne didn't respond. She twisted her fingers in the stained skirt and stared at the fire. "I think I know how she felt."

And if that didn't feel like a punch in the gut. Of course she was scared of him. Why wouldn't she be? He'd been the first face to give her cause to be frightened. Ehrun only solidified it.

"My father frightens me, too," she continued and looked up at him again. "Now more than ever."

Now, he hadn't expected that. "Why?"

She snorted with dry humor. "Who would not be afraid of a man willing to murder his entire family?"

Azriel reached out, paused, and returned his hand to his lap. "He loves you and Emillie. He loved your mother."

"How do you know?"

"Well," he said with his own humorless chuckle, "he lives with you, for one."

Another scream—louder this time. It shot through him like fire. He lurched to his feet, and Ariadne, quick as ever, seized his wrist to yank him back to the couch. He sat with a groan, eyes locked on the door.

Ariadne's next question dragged his attention back. "Do you love me *because* of the bond, or do you love me *despite* it?"

The air in his lungs stuck. He turned to her slowly, and for the first time, the scream from the bedroom faded into the background. He searched her face—every perfect curve. The way her eyes lifted at the outer corners. Her straight nose with the slight bump at the end. The angle of her cheekbones and noted how the hollows beneath them appeared a bit less defined since the wedding.

Beautiful, yes, and while that'd attracted him to her, it'd merely been the tip of the sword for him. Her sharp mind and fondness for books spoke to him. She could sense the truth in others' words without trying and always knew when to play the game of life in the Caersan Society. The strength it took for her to not only endure what she'd been put through but continue to thrive despite the scars—literal and figurative. He envied her mental fortitude in the face of every terrible thing that passed her way.

To him, she was perfect. How could she ever ask such a question?

Then again, his own brother had asked him the same thing not too long ago. Bonds didn't automatically mean love. They meant obsession. They meant protection at all costs. They meant taking without thought. They meant never being able to think about anything else.

Some fae bonded and resented their mates. Perhaps they'd loved another and still desired that other individual but couldn't bring themselves to be with them anymore. Fae struggled under such bonds. With no escape from them other than death, they sought fights or, in moments of complete mental collapse, took their own life.

"At first," he said slowly, "it was merely the bond."

"Oh." She looked into the fire again.

This time, Azriel reached out and, with a gentle hand, turned her face back to him. "But I fell in love with you—everything about you—and that would've happened whether the bond was present or not."

She searched his face. The fire's reflection danced in her oceanic eyes like waves of light. "When did it happen for you?"

"The first time I heard you laugh." He smiled to himself. It'd been right before the dhemons' attack on Vertium when she sat outside with him, rubbing her feet. "I knew I was in trouble."

She nodded and leaned her face into his hand.

Azriel swallowed the lump in his throat, his chest swelling with hope again. His heart slammed into his ribs, and all he wanted to do was kiss her. To wrap his arms around her and remind her how much he really, truly loved her.

The bedroom door opened, and Izara swept out, wiping her hands on a towel. Azriel dropped his hand and stood to watch the mage with a wary eye. The bond demanded he stay with Ariadne. His mind screamed to see Madan.

"Your brother will live." Izara leaned a hip against a chair and picked at her nails as though everything she'd just done was a normal evening for her. Perhaps it was. "He's awake."

Azriel gaped at her. "I owe you a life debt."

Izara clicked her tongue. "No. All I require is payment—in coin. I'll come by tomorrow evening to collect."

The mage laid the towel over the chair and left without another word. It didn't matter what she said. He'd be at her beck and call for what she'd done for Madan. Anything and everything.

And yet, as the household servants who'd helped keep his brother alive left as well, Azriel couldn't find his feet to enter the room. A part of him had been preparing to say goodbye. After seeing all that Loren had put him through, Madan shouldn't have survived.

"Go," Ariadne said quietly and pushed at his back. "Go see him."

So he took the first step.

Ariadne looked on as Azriel took the first step to see his brother. It was hesitant, as though he could not believe Madan had survived. She followed, watching him cautiously for any sign of despair.

"Madan." Azriel's face twisted with a deluge of emotions. He took another slow step forward, then hurried to the bedside and fell to his knees.

Her throat tightened at the sight. The silent big brother who had spent so many nights glaring at the world and scorning his younger sibling. His heart was bigger than he let anyone see—even her.

"I'm so sorry," Azriel rasped and took his brother's remaining hand in his. He pressed his forehead to it and shook his head. "I'm so, so sorry."

Madan glanced at Ariadne through the dark, then looked back at his brother. The corner of his mouth ticked up, and a mischievous sparkle lit in his eyes. He winked at her as a slow smirk formed on his swollen face. It'd gone down considerably since partaking in Bella's vein.

"This never should have happened," Azriel continued and looked up. He froze. His brows furrowed as he dropped the hand and pulled back. "What the fuck, Madan? This is *funny* to you?"

Ariadne covered her mouth with her hand to hide her own amusement. At least her old guard's sense of humor remained despite it all.

Madan's grin only grew. "It's about time you realize you've been a complete ass."

Azriel stood and crossed his arms. "I should've let you die."

"But then I wouldn't get to hear all your apologies as you wept upon my grave." Madan laughed. The sound cut short. He turned in on himself and groaned. "I much prefer this."

Azriel smiled. "You'd hear them. You're too petty to not haunt me for the rest of my life."

"Right you are." Madan lifted his stump of an arm, the new flesh at the end pink and soft thanks to the mage's work. "Now I just get to lord this over you forever."

Azriel laughed, and the sound washed through Ariadne as warm as sunshine. He had laughed with her, of course, but she had never heard it quite so carefree before. Had the two always bickered like this? Ariadne and Emillie had certainly had their own similar tête-á-têtes, but none quite as morbid as theirs.

"But in all seriousness," Madan said and eyed Ariadne again. He dropped his voice and leaned closer to his brother as though it would hide his words from her keen-hearing Caersan ears. "When did you tell her the truth?"

Ariadne stiffened but said nothing. The memories of the previous morning tripped and stumbled through her mind. The concern at his sorrow surrounding Madan's disappearance slammed into the fear of his revealing transformation. She bit her lip as her own parting words echoed through the memories: I hate you more than you hate yourself.

Oh, if she could take back those words...

Azriel's smile faded as he glanced at her. "It's been...a process."

"He lost his mind without you," Ariadne interrupted, watching her husband warily. "He let it slip more than confided in me."

A tense silence fell in the room. Madan looked between them, his face twisting with unspoken words. He took his brother's hand and gave it a single squeeze. Ariadne tracked the motion. When had they begun doing that?

"Azriel," Madan said after staring at his brother in a way that made Ariadne feel as though they could somehow communicate without spoken words—something more than just a sibling connection. "Give me a moment alone with my sister."

No niceties, then. She edged into the room, and Azriel watched her with that familiar expression she had seen so many times over the last few months—as though he had been cornered and knew the fatal blow would land at any moment.

But Azriel did not argue or say anything at all. Instead, he listened and left, closing the door behind him.

With just the light of the candelabra on the bedside table remaining, Madan surveyed Ariadne fully for the first time since she had learned of her connection to him. He grunted and shifted up in the bed.

In a flash, Ariadne moved to his side. She pulled pillows from the far side of the bed and propped them behind his back to provide more support. She could not do much to help him but this? This she could do.

"Thank you," he said and settled back into the mountain of cushions around him. "Sit, please."

She looked behind her and, upon discovering no chair nearby, slowly sank onto the bed beside him. Despite her haste to help him, she didn't look at him. Instead, she studied her hands and her fingers rolling the fabric of her skirt. What could he possibly want to say to her without Azriel around? That he even remembered she knew of their relation was a miracle.

"What do you know about us?" His head fell to the side on the pillows, and he studied her carefully.

Ariadne bit her lip. Us. Her and him, not him and Azriel. The very notion made her heart skip a beat. Sucking in a deep breath, she turned her full attention to him. "You are my half-brother. We share our father. You are also Azriel's half-brother. You share a mother. Our father was unkind, left you all often, and killed your mother when he discovered her going to the Crowe—Azriel's father."

He hummed and rolled his head to stare at the ceiling. "So he told you about our childhood."

"And that he did not have a choice when he took me—that your life was on the line, and he had done it to save you." She kept her voice low. Though it had been Azriel who told her everything, it felt strange to be speaking of him in such a manner. She glanced at the door.

"He's not eavesdropping."

She froze and studied him. "How do you know?"

"It's not what he does." Madan shrugged and winced at the movement. "It's never been in his nature."

Interesting. So many people of the Society were prone to listening in on conversations they had no business in. Collecting half-truths and gossip provided an individual power to be used at their leisure. That Azriel did no such thing only highlighted how separated he was from it all.

"Keep going," he said and went to gesture with his left hand before pausing at the sight of his amputated arm. He let it drop with a sigh.

Ariadne looked away again, cheeks flushing with heat. "I do not remember much else. I was so upset when he tried to explain, I left. It has been a blur ever since."

"Let me tell you something about my brother." Madan adjusted his seat again. "He's notoriously hard-headed and difficult to convince of anything. I spent all last winter begging him to join me in Laeton as a personal guard for your family for one reason: I trusted him to protect you and Emillie more than anyone else in this world."

Her heart stumbled, and she raised her eyebrows. "I know why now."

Madan shook his head. "You aren't hearing me. He told me *no*. He told me no a thousand times."

"Why?" Ariadne's eyes stung at the implication. She knew why—at least her heart did—but she did not want to admit it to herself.

"You." He smiled grimly. "He and I were sent to Valenul almost a hundred years ago and ordered to become guards to get close to your father. It'd been a mission from the Crowe at first."

She stilled but said nothing. So Madan had been a part of the terrors on Valenul, too. He, the brother and guard she trusted more than anyone, had sought to harm her in other ways—by taking her father from her.

"The Crowe called it off long before Ehrun ordered your abduction." Madan swallowed hard. "He'd been speaking with Lord Governor Caldwell and making a plan for peace. Azriel and I were stationed at the Caldwell Estate to help facilitate the meetings. Garth Caldwell knew who we were the entire time."

"Peace." Now Ariadne gaped at him, scraping her memories for anything that would corroborate his story. "I have never heard of a potential peace treaty."

"I believe Garth Caldwell, our grandfather, was poisoned with liquid sunshine before he could bring anything to the Council."

She stilled, her heart picking up its pace. Who would have killed Garth to prevent the end of a war? She could only think of one individual who depended on the continuation of the raids and deaths, and he had once put an engagement necklace across her throat.

"Does Azriel know?" Ariadne looked to the door again.

"No." Madan took her hand, drawing her attention back to him. "And you shouldn't tell him, either. Not yet."

She hesitated, then nodded. She had now witnessed what happened when Azriel got something into his head. He would not rest until he had razed everything in his path to discovering the cause. Even their marriage.

"As I was saying," Madan continued, "neither Azriel nor his father wanted to hurt you, and it's haunted him ever since."

"He has hardly seemed haunted." Ariadne gave him an exasperated look that shifted into grim understanding at the memory of him kneeling on the foyer floor, begging her to stay. "Until I left him, anyway."

Madan let out a humorless chuckle. "He tried to hang himself not a month after freeing you."

The world dropped out from under her—not as it had when she first saw her husband's red eyes and fear had taken over, but as though a chasm of hopelessness opened up around her, swallowing her whole. Not for the first time, she could not help wondering what the world would be like without Azriel in it.

She sat back and stared into the darkness for a long moment, her mouth opening and closing several times. "But he had just saved you, too."

"If you have not noticed," he said, raising his brows, "a fae bond can be rather violent. Do you think that duel with Loren had been a mere matter of your honor?"

Ariadne bit her lip and said nothing. She had thought it to be precisely that and nothing more.

"It took everything in him not to kill the General outright." Madan smiled sadly. "That anger and violence and hate aren't reserved for others alone. He's felt it for himself since the moment he went through with taking you."

"I hate you more than you hate yourself," she whispered and covered her mouth, that chasm growing with every new detail.

"Oh?"

"I told him that last night."

Madan winced. "I'm certain that went over well."

"I do not know," she admitted. "I left right after I said it."

"And you had every right to do so." Madan smirked at the horror on her face. How could he say that after everything he had seen and gone through with his own brother? "Your thoughts and feelings are every bit as valid as that gods for-saken bond of his. He made his decision when he did Ehrun's bidding, and now he has to live with the consequences."

"But—"

"No." He sat forward, face twisting with pain, and took her hand again. "No. You owe him *nothing*. I only tell you all of this because he's an absolute dolt who can't explain himself well in any situation. You deserve to know all the details and to make whatever decision you wish based on the facts presented to you."

Ariadne blinked hard, throat tightening, and squeezed his hand. "Thank you."

"He *does* love you, though." Madan fell back against his pillows. "He'd put a knife in his heart if you asked it of him. Gods, he'd lay his sword at Ehrun's feet and accept his fate if he knew it'd make you happy."

She recoiled at the thought, though she still held on to him. "I would never."

Madan shrugged. "That's only for you to decide. All I ask, if you *do* choose to leave, is...make it a clean break. Don't give him any hope. I can only help him recover if you're done for certain."

Another quiet moment passed as Ariadne wrestled with her thoughts. Two distinct paths lay ahead of her. What she needed to decide was which path to choose. Neither would be easy. She squeezed his hand and stood. She laid a soft kiss on his forehead. "Thank you."

As she made her way back to the door, Madan said, "And Ariadne."

She paused, hand poised on the doorknob, and looked back at him.

"You're my sister as much as he's my brother." He gave her a smirk. "You're stuck with me, so don't expect me to disappear anytime soon, no matter your decision."

To her own surprise, Ariadne laughed. "I would not dream of it."

CHAPTER 36

H ow had it been only a week since Azriel's world collapsed around him? The time and distance between him and Ariadne felt like an eternity. Though he'd kept himself from her for more than a year, their marriage—and subsequent days filled with sex—had only strengthened the bond.

He was, in fact, *fucked*.

Ariadne slept in a guest suite down the hall and often left a room anytime he appeared. She wasn't cruel or haughty. In fact, she spoke very little to him and spent much more time with Madan instead.

His brother, back on his feet and adjusting to life without an arm, appeared almost normal again. Between feeding from Bella and Oli, he'd recovered quickly. When Izara had returned to collect her payment, she checked on Madan's arm and confirmed no poison lingered in his body. The news had eased Azriel's worries.

But the house remained quiet. The servants moved like wraiths from room to room, and meals, while communal, were almost silent.

"I don't know what to do," Azriel confided in Madan one evening as they sat together in the parlor. He clutched a glass of liquor and stared into the golden ripples.

Madan used a spare, empty glass to practice balancing it on the end of his arm, below the crook of his elbow. His eyes never left the precarious wobbling as he said, "Give her time."

"It's been a week."

"So give her two." He glanced up, and the glass tipped. He caught it in his hand, set it aside, and drank from his full cup. "Give her as much time as she needs to sort everything out. She's just as hurt and confused as you."

Azriel sighed and sat back, his head tilting so he looked to the ceiling. "I know. I know."

"She hasn't left," Madan pointed out. "And she's kept your secret—from even her sister and friends that I know of."

He sat forward. "How would you know?"

His brother smirked and sipped his drink. "They visited last night."

"When?"

"You were at the Council Chambers." Madan set down his cup and picked up the empty glass again. "Hard to miss anything they say—they're quite loud when they're together."

With a snort of wry amusement, Azriel nodded and took a sip, the liquor burning his throat. He shook his head, remembering the cackling laughter he'd overheard the times he'd chaperoned them to and from the Dodd Estate. Their loudest moments, however, were typically over the superficial gossip of the Society—not the serious events like those of the last week.

"What did they have to say about your arm?" Azriel nodded to the amputated side.

Madan smirked, the empty glass balancing precariously. "You've never been as pampered as I was when they saw me. I should get injured more often."

"And how does Whelan feel about that?"

"Getting injured or getting pampered?" He winked.

"Both."

Madan shook his head. "You know how he'd feel about either of them."

"Have you sent word to him about what happened?" Azriel tilted his head. "I'm sure he was ready to burn Laeton to the ground when Kall got back to him."

"I told him I'm safe." He grimaced, and the glass dropped into his lap where he left it. "And that we have a lot to talk about."

"You didn't mention your arm?"

"I don't need him coming here to coddle me." Madan glared at the fire, his marbled eyes colder and filled with more dark memories than Azriel had ever seen in them before. "It's too dangerous."

And that had been the end of the conversation, with neither of their love lives resolved. If Azriel could even consider himself to have a love life. What he had was a wife too terrified and wary to look him in the eye.

Because in her own house, she didn't have to pretend. She didn't need to put on a front that everything was fine in her life. She could continue to mull over her past and choose her future—whatever it may be.

Azriel wouldn't stand in her way.

He couldn't and wouldn't stop her if she decided to leave. He only wished she'd tell him what she was thinking. The silence weighed more than the hate.

So Azriel spent the rest of the evening avoiding Ariadne as much as she avoided him. If she planned to leave him, he needed to distance himself. Peeling back the attachments of a bond, though not impossible, would be a difficult feat. He needed to loosen it enough to get away and continue working towards a bondless life.

If it were even possible.

The dhemons he knew who had pulled away from the bond succeeded for a while. They seemed to thrive. Then they spiraled hard into a darkness they couldn't escape.

Ehrun had been one of them, and Azriel could still recall a time when the dhemon laughed. He'd never touched a sword or even lifted a finger in anger. The Ehrun he'd been introduced to as a child, with his wife and newborn daughter, had been entirely different. Then they were murdered.

The Crowe stumbled down a similar path when Azriel's mother died. His only saving grace had been him and Madan—his sons. They'd held together the shredded pieces of his bond by the very blood in their veins. Her blood.

Azriel had no such way to keep it intact, so his only choice remained to hope a slow separation would help. If all else failed, he'd leave the Caldwell Estate to Madan and go somewhere he couldn't hurt anyone.

Especially Ariadne.

It had taken a week of deep thinking, soul-searching, and even praying to the gods for Ariadne to make her decision. She spoke to no one of Azriel's true lineage after her one-on-one conversation with Madan. It would not be fair to him to reveal something he could not help to those who would ostracize him for being born.

To be born as a half-breed was not his fault, and for that alone, he should not be punished.

It was everything else—the abduction, the lies, the pain he caused—which placed the final nail in his coffin. There were some things that were unforgivable, and she had tried so, so hard to find that in her heart.

But it was not there.

So she packed up the meager items she had in the guest suite. She set her books in baskets and the clothes in the trunk she had dragged over to the room. They sat, waiting for their next destination.

Ariadne's heart picked up its pace as she put on the wool traveling cloak, fastening it at her throat. She glanced out the window to the summer rain pattering against the glass pane like a solemn melody. She would miss the distant view of Lake Cypher.

Inhaling deeply, she pivoted on her heel and marched to the door. The sooner she confronted Azriel, the better for them both.

The way he had looked at her over the last week had been difficult to bear. His uncertainty grew with each night while the hope waned. She never lingered long. She could not give him anything to look forward to—not when she had been so unsure herself.

Now she knew. Now she understood what had to happen, for better or worse.

She made her way down the hall, pausing to look, for what felt like the thousandth time, at the portrait of Mariana Cald-well-Harlow and her two sons. Isaiah and Mattias.

All three had been murdered in a way. She by the man who vowed to keep her safe. Them by the man who failed.

Down the stairs to the foyer and out the front door. She pulled her hood into place and paused to take in the front drive. It was not as large or as regal as the Harlow Estate, but it was beautiful nonetheless. With the gravel loop curving before the front steps, a statue and greenery at its center, it remained a simple and lovely entrance. Something else she would miss.

Stepping into the rain, Ariadne curled her shoulders against the cold. After so many nights without it, she had become too accustomed to the warmth of summer.

The stables where she had seen Azriel go earlier were tucked out of sight from the front doors. She had planned to wait for him to return indoors but decided against it. He deserved to know as soon as possible.

Following the path cut through the gardens, Ariadne took in the flowers and hedges. She quite liked the way the gardener took care of them and how they had been arranged over the years. Even the dahlias had been carefully curated throughout to not only match colors but maintain their annual growth. Such care could not be found everywhere.

By the time she reached the stables, the rain had eased from a deafening roar to a light pattering. The roof of the stables created a wonderful harmony to the windowpane earlier, and inside, the acoustics of the space only heightened the musical drumming.

Azriel stood toward the back, where he brushed his stallion. The moment she entered, he stiffened despite his back being turned, and he set the curry comb down before turning to her. He wore all black, as usual, though the style of clothing would not have suited a Caersan man. Mud dirtied his trousers, and his boots were dull from use. His sleeves rolled up to his elbows, hung a little looser than the tailored shirts she had grown accustomed to him wearing. His hair, pulled back as always, had fallen into his face, and when he swept a hand across his brow to clear it from his eyes, a smudge streaked across his skin.

She stared at him for a long moment. It had been some time since she had seen him appear so disheveled. It took her back to those memories of them together in the library at the Harlow Estate, in Laeton after pulling her from the Bistro, and every lingering glance which ever passed between them.

"What're you doing out here?" His voice was soft, and he picked up a grimy towel to wipe off his hands. He took a few steps closer. "It's pouring."

"I packed my things."

In an instant, his face paled, and he swallowed hard. "Okay."

She gripped her skirt with shaking hands beneath the cloak and took a deep, centering breath. "I am sorry it took so long to make my decision."

"I understand." He frowned at his hands as he pulled the dirt from them. His throat bobbed.

"I need you to understand," she continued, her voice breaking, "that I cannot forgive you for what you did."

At that, he said nothing. Instead, he nodded in silence. The muscles in his jaw flexed.

"It has taken me a long time to begin moving past what happened to me." She stepped closer, the sound of the rain fading behind the thundering of her blood in her ears. "You were a big part of that."

Azriel lifted his shimmering eyes to her and swallowed hard. He cleared his throat and rumbled, "I'm glad I was able to help while I could."

"That is the thing," she said, her voice almost gone entirely. "I still need help."

He stilled and watched her warily. Again, he said nothing. His lips parted, and he searched her face.

"I still need *you*, Azriel." The words broke, and the burning in her throat grew. "I do not want to leave you. I need you because I...I love you."

Azriel fell to his knees. He hung his head and sucked in a gasp of air. His shoulders shook, and he covered his face with his hands, hiding the twisted expression of disbelief.

Ariadne's heart cracked. She had not realized how close to breaking he had been. The last thing she wanted was to cause him more distress—her choice of words, while purposeful, may have been misleading.

"Azriel, I am so sorry." She closed the distance between them and knelt before him on the stable floor. "I never meant to—"

"I love you so much," he rasped as he bent at the waist and laid his head in her lap. There he cried, clutching her dress as though she were the last line to this life.

In a way, she was. The life he desired was one with her in it—one in which she stayed and loved him. She would—she did.

"I packed my things to return to our bedroom," she explained, laying a tender hand on his back. "I do not like being apart from you."

He inhaled deeply and shook his head, face still hidden in her skirt. When he spoke, the words were muffled and thick with emotion, "I don't deserve this. I don't deserve you."

"But you do," she said and took his face in her hands to guide him back up.

His brows knitted together, and he closed his eyes, hanging his head again. "After everything—"

"You have spent the last year and a half making up for what you did." She shifted so she could look up at him still, her hands moving to his chest. "I cannot forgive you for what you did because there is nothing left to forgive. You have proven yourself to me again and again."

"I would do anything for you."

"I know." She pressed her forehead to his. "I know."

Ariadne had lost count of how many times he had put himself between her and an adversary. He had even tried at the mountain keep, and though he failed, he ensured her escape. She remembered seeing him and Ehrun as Madan snuck her out, circling one another and ready to strike. She remembered him looking up as they passed and saying nothing—it had been odd then.

Now she understood.

She pulled back from him and stood. He watched with blatant confusion as she closed the stable doors and said, "I need one last thing from you."

"Anything."

"Change." She turned back to him, and her heart kicked up the pace again. Again and again, she had thought about what she would do the next time she saw him in his other form.

"What?"

"I want to see you as a dhemon." Ariadne swallowed hard and bit her lip. "I need to."

Azriel did not move for a long moment. He merely watched her as though waiting for her to tell him it was a joke. Then he nodded and closed his eyes.

It did not take long—not like when he had changed in the study. That had been painful to watch, though not as painful as it sounded. This time, he did not scream. He did not flinch. He merely melted from one form into the other.

Her stomach twisted, and her heart crashed against her ribs. She stepped closer, held out a hand, and said, "Now hold me."

Azriel's red eyes widened. His face was just as handsome as a dhemon, she realized. Different complexion and broader bones, but at the core, he remained the same. At his heart, he had not changed.

"Ariadne..." His voice, deeper than she was accustomed to, still said her name in the same tone and with the same yearning.

"Please."

He took her hand and stood. Still, he did not move closer.

So she closed the gap and laid a hand on his chest. "Hold me like you wanted to the night we met."

His face fell. His shoulders slumped, and he let out a long breath. Without another word, he wrapped his arms around her—gentle and loving—and pressed his lips to her forehead.

Slowly, she breathed in. He smelled the same, though with more sweat and dirt mixed in with his clothes in such a state. She wrapped her arms around his bigger body and curled her fingers into the back of his shirt.

This. This was how they were supposed to meet. This was how he had intended it to happen if not for the horrific circumstances. This was how they were meant to be.

"I love you," she whispered.

The last bit of tension left his body. Muscles beneath her hands loosened, and he stroked her side with the back of his fingers. When she pulled back to look up at him, his face remained relaxed.

"I love you, too." He bent a bit, those red eyes sweeping over her mouth, then stopped.

She hesitated. Searched his face. He pulled back, but before he could go far, she pushed up onto her toes to plant her lips on his.

He froze, eyes wide, as she sank back. Then he leaned forward and returned her kiss, soft and sweet.

Warmth bloomed in her core—not at all what she expected. She reached up and drew her fingers up his neck, then across the lower twist of one of his black horns. He remained still as she moved, touching and exploring him.

When she kissed him again, it was with more enthusiasm. She parted her lips so she could slip her tongue into his mouth. He responded with slow, calculated movements.

To her surprise and delight, he even tasted the same.

But Ariadne, not ready to take it any further than a kiss with him in that form, said against his mouth, "Change back. I need you."

Azriel grunted in response, and as she continued to hold him and kiss his jaw and neck, his body shifted back. The muscles returned to the size she was accustomed to, and his hands, roving her body now, used less pressure. His lips returned to her skin, drifting down her neck to the crook of her shoulder.

"Are you sure?" he whispered, fingers entwining in her curls to ease her head to the side so he could draw his fangs across her throat.

"Yes," she breathed and pressed her body against his.

With a low growl of satisfaction, he sank his fangs into her neck as he cupped the back of her thighs, lifting her from the ground to place her on a tall, standing table. The possessive pull of her blood only stoked the fire in her sex. She pulled up the skirts of her dress to her hips, and his deft fingers unbuttoned his trousers with ease. Then he yanked down her panties, baring her to him, and eased her to the edge of the table.

Then Azriel sank his cock deep into her. She cried out as he thrust, each slow, steady stroke the full length of him. He filled her so completely that, for a long moment, her mind went blank with pleasure.

Azriel released her neck and tilted his head back with a loud moan. A small drip of blood ran from the corner of his mouth. Gods damn her. The sight of it—her blood sustaining someone as powerful as he—rolled through her like a shock wave.

Ariadne lifted his shirt up and off him to feel his skin beneath her hands. His abdominal muscles contracted in rhythm to each rock of his hips. She angled herself back to better take him, moaning as he increased his intensity.

Bracing herself on her hands, Ariadne slid away bit by bit as he pounded into her. He grabbed her hip and dragged her back to the edge, then hooked an arm under her leg so her thigh rested in the crook to hold her steady.

"Harder." She wanted to feel his strength as he slid in and out of her. So many times now, she had seen him use his strength and endurance—and each time had been for her. Now she wanted to take it herself.

He barked a curse, and before she knew what was happening, she fell back on the table. His cock pumped into her with more force than she had ever felt before, and gods, it felt glorious. With her leg still lifted, he draped it over his shoulder and leaned forward so his pelvis rubbed against her clit with every stroke.

Azriel ran his free hand up her side and grasped a breast hard. Pulling the neck of her dress down, he freed it from the fabric and rolled the tight, pink bud between his fingers. She cried out again, her whole body tensing. With a groan, he did it again before sucking it into his mouth and teasing her with his teeth and tongue.

Ariadne closed her eyes and moaned. She dug her fingers into his hair, her hips working in tandem with his to stimulate herself with every part of him. Between Azriel's cock thrusting into her and his tongue on her nipple, she did not care that they were in a stable where anyone could walk in on them. In fact, the very idea of a voyeur at that moment only heightened the sensations.

He caught her mouth with his, fingers twisting in her hair again, and he groaned, "I am yours."

Between each fervent kiss, she said, "Until the very end."

Pleasure exploded through her. Her sex gripped him hard, and he rode out her orgasm until he, too, finished.

They remained there, draped over the tall table, for a long moment. Her breaths came and went in hard bursts, and he buried his face between her breasts.

When at last, he pulled himself from her, Azriel let out a low groan before carefully pulling up his trousers again. She sat up, relishing the soreness between her legs, and kissed him. He responded in kind, gentler this time, and fixed her skirts.

"We should get cleaned up," he said as he helped her down.

Ariadne could not hide her delighted smile. "We should spend the rest of the night in our rooms."

A grin spread across his face, and he kissed her again with more fervor. "As you wish."

None of it could possibly be real. It felt like a dream. After all the time she'd spent avoiding him, Azriel had been convinced she'd leave. When she'd come to him in the barn, he heard those same words again and again.

I hate you more than you hate yourself.

The uncertainty had been written all over her face. She didn't know how he'd react, and that tore at his heart. He'd never be angry with her, no matter her decision.

So when she said she *needed* him—that she *loved* him...it ripped through him like a storm. He'd been so scared. He'd been preparing for the worst. The relief was overwhelming.

Waking up next to her the following night felt the same. She curled in close to him, face soft with sleep, and the emotions overwhelmed him again. He draped an arm over his eyes and let them out so that when she woke up, he could smile and embrace the next steps of their relationship.

Which included, he realized, sitting down to tea with her sister, friends, and Madan—their shared brother. It was there he saw just how certain she had been about her decision. She shifted closer to him, held his hand beneath the table, and laughed.

Oh, that laugh could sustain him for all his days. The light dancing in her eyes and the sweet sound filled him with contentment. He'd missed her laugh, her smile, her joy.

"Tell me," Emillie said after taking a sip of tea and eyeing them and Madan with a discerning look, "why you claimed my blood would not be enough to heal Madan."

His brother's eyebrows shot high, and he turned his focus to his cake. He said nothing, just as Azriel kept his mouth shut. That was a discussion between sisters for now.

Ariadne cast him a withering stare and sighed before saying, "Madan is our half-brother."

The sound which erupted from the visiting Caersan women was akin to a stadium's roar. Ariadne laughed as their questions—only half-formed—overlapped one another. How did they know? Which parent did they share? Are they certain? Could it not be a trick? Why were they not told?

On and on they went until Ariadne held up a hand and shook her head. "You cannot tell a *soul*...Camilla."

Their friend's jaw dropped in feigned indignation. "How could you think so lowly of me?"

"I think," Ariadne went on, "you have more of a mind for gossip than secrecy. I am trusting you."

Laying a hand over her heart, Camilla smirked. "You have my word."

Azriel leaned forward. "He is also *my* half-brother."

In an instant, Emillie's face twisted in disgust and looked between him and Ariadne. "Excuse me?"

"They share a mother." Ariadne pointed between him and Madan. Then she pointed between Madan and them and continued, "We share a father."

Revelie gasped, her eyes widening. "You two are the first Harlow family!"

Beside her, Emillie gaped. "I thought they were murdered."

"That," Ariadne cut in with a stern voice, "is a long story to be saved for another time."

"You cannot leave us dangling on the precipice of understanding your father's past," Camilla said in an outraged tone. "We need to know!"

Ariadne's smile grew. "But then what would be enticing you to visit us in Monsumbra?"

To visit *us*. The words were music to his ears, despite the fresh wave of loud questions.

Azriel leaned back in his chair and smirked at his brother. Madan shook his head in silent reply. With his wife holding his hand and his brother safe by his side, Azriel could accomplish anything—even governing a province and convincing the Council to choose peace.

ACKNOWLEDGEMENTS

There came a time not too long ago that I ceased to believe I'd ever write an acknowledgement page. I went through so many ups and downs that I was certain I was on a rollercoaster. But finally, after drafting and editing this story too many times to admit...I'm here.

To begin, I must thank my husband, Nick, for his patience and understanding. It's not an easy feat to put up with me while I second-guess myself for years. You not only stood by me through all the late-night writing sessions and seemingly endless tears as I was bombarded with rejection after rejection, but you encouraged me to keep going because you believed in me (oftentimes more than I believed in myself). You did more for me than I could ever list here. I love you more than I can say.

A huge thank you to Sam, my cover artist and one of my best friends, for working alongside me to create a stunning piece of artwork *as well as* the gods' symbols and tidying up my map. You never once made me feel ridiculous for the questions I asked and were always so kind and funny, no matter what. When I felt overwhelmed, you stepped in with suggestions, mock-ups, and reassurances. You held me together in some of my most anxiety-ridden times, for which I can never express my full gratitude. But most of all, thank you for delivering art to me at quite literally the eleventh hour for the ebook preorder.

To my editor, Charlie Knight, I give my deepest gratitude for polishing my writing, providing much-needed insight and feedback, and working with me on what seemed like an almost impossible time crunch. I have looked up to you as an author, editor, and just a great person in general for many years now and I am honored to have had you work with me on this self-publishing journey. Your diligence and tutelage truly made this book the best it could be in so many ways.

And to my best friend since childhood, cheerleader throughout the decades, and best alpha reader an author could ask for, I give my greatest, heartfelt thanks to Nicole Nightshade. Without you first introducing me to the Lands of Flame where all of this began, none of it would be possible. My love for writing, my darling Azriel, and therefore this entire book would've never been born. I cannot express how grateful I am to have had you to help me troubleshoot storylines, fill in plot holes, and stay up past midnight eating bonitza, watching Vampire Diaries, and moving sticky notes around with me. You have never shied away from your honest opinion on things and always set me straight when I needed it. I look forward to many more nights of you poking holes in my ideas to make me even better.

There are so many more I'd like to thank than I can list here. My family for their unyielding support, my friends for putting up with my incessant rants, and my children for understanding when I wanted to stay home so I could write "just one more chapter." Without all of you, none of this would be possible. Thank you. I love you. Until the very end.

Reader's Group: www.facebook.com/groups/ennahawthorn/

ABOUT THE AUTHOR

Enna Hawthorn lives in the stunning evergreen Pacific Northwest with her beautiful family. Nestled between two snow-crested mountain ranges and surrounded by salty ocean water, she finds inspiration in everyday life as a mother and wife, teacher, and Jiujiteira. Whether high or urban fantasy, Enna's love for romance with dark twists began long ago and continues to influence that which she reads and writes.

www.ennahawthorn.com
enna.hawthorn@gmail.com

Made in the USA
Columbia, SC
14 July 2024

38607712R00328